"Don't try to [illegible] you know, I don't want you in my life any more than I do Lester."

"You're lying again," he said, "and we both know that. While you might not want me in your life, you damn sure want me in your *bed*."

"Damn you," she whispered, her eyes filling with tears. "You're playing dirty, and we both know that, too."

He leaned close to her, and she could smell his cologne; it made her light-headed.

"Fair or not," he said in a low, husky tone, "that's the way it is."

"Please leave," she said, swallowing.

"This is the second time you've kicked me out." Then totally without warning, he clutched her chin and gave her a quick but solid kiss on the lips, which took her breath away. "There won't be a third."

"With realistic dialogue and plenty of the dark side of human nature, Ms. Baxter vividly paints a picture of jealousy and greed."
—*Romantic Times* on *Hard Candy*

MARY LYNN
BAXTER

ONE SUMMER
EVENING

MIRA®

MIRA

ISBN 1-55166-523-9

ONE SUMMER EVENING

Copyright © 1999 by Mary Lynn Baxter.

All rights reserved. Except for use in any review, the reproduction or
utilization of this work in whole or in part in any form by any electronic,
mechanical or other means, now known or hereafter invented, including
xerography, photocopying and recording, or in any information storage or
retrieval system, is forbidden without the written permission of the publisher,
MIRA Books, 225 Duncan Mill Road, Don Mills, Ontario, Canada M3B 3K9.

All characters in this book have no existence outside the imagination of the
author and have no relation whatsoever to anyone bearing the same name
or names. They are not even distantly inspired by any individual known or
unknown to the author, and all incidents are pure invention.

MIRA and the Star Colophon are trademarks used under license and registered
in Australia, New Zealand, Philippines, United States Patent and Trademark
Office and in other countries.

Visit us at www.mirabooks.com

Printed in U.S.A.

ONE SUMMER
EVENING

One

Summer, 1990

"Know what?"

Cassie Wortham removed her attention from the low-flying seagull and turned to face her latest boyfriend. "What?" she asked.

"I think we ought to get married."

Cassie's mouth gaped in shock. "Now I know you've lost it. Your mind, that is."

Lester Sullivan frowned, deeply grooving an otherwise smooth forehead. "I'm a long way from losing my mind. In fact," he stressed in a conceited tone, "I'm probably the smartest person you know."

This time Cassie rolled her expressive green eyes. "Well then, you must have a fever."

"Ah, come on, Cassie, give me a break."

Cassie lifted her head and focused once again on the same bird, which continued to breeze through the sky as if it hadn't a care in the world. She should be experiencing that same freedom. After all, today was her eighteenth birthday.

She and her parents had come here a few days ago, to their summer home on the Louisiana coast, not far from Jasmine, where they lived. Yesterday her friends had driven down, and they had partied all day, swimming, eating and laughing.

This evening her parents and their friends planned to celebrate in grand style.

Wealth could do mighty things, and Cassie considered this luxurious beach compound to be mighty. Her mother's parents had owned it, and with their passing, her mother and aunt had inherited it. Cassie couldn't imagine her life without this wonderful place made up of hot sand and secret coves.

She had already celebrated her coming of age in *her* style, alone. Before her friends' arrival, she had slept for hours on end, and played in the ocean and the pool until her heart was content.

"Cassie."

The curt frustration in Lester's tone broke into her thoughts and angered her. She almost wished she hadn't invited him. He had arrived yesterday and had been in one of his moods since. Apparently popping the question to her had been preying on his mind.

Marriage.

Heaven forbid. That was the last thing she wanted, at least at this time in her life. And even if she did have the hots to get married right out of high school, like so many of her friends, Lester wouldn't have been her choice.

"So, what's your answer?"

Cassie looked back at him, swallowing the giggle that was dying to come out. But then that giggle died on its own. When she watched Lester's scowl deepen, she actually believed he was serious. No, she corrected herself mentally. He couldn't be; he had to be toying with her. Though for what reason, she had no idea.

Something didn't ring true, or maybe she didn't

know Lester as well as she thought. The Lester she knew was too focused, too driven, too unbending in his desire to reach his goal, which was a career in the military, to let anything interfere. And marriage would certainly do that.

Even so, she would go along and let him down gently. "You're sweet to ask, and I'm flattered, believe me. But the answer is thanks, but no thanks."

"You think I'm full of shit, don't you?"

Cassie thrust a hand through her cropped brown hair, then sighed. She wished her best friend, Jo Nell, were there. She would know how to handle this unexpected crisis. But Jo Nell had a bad case of strep throat and couldn't come. Her friend's timing sucked, Cassie thought, her gaze returning to Lester.

"No, I don't think that," Cassie said carefully, "but something obviously snapped inside your brain. You don't want to get married any more than I do."

"You don't know what I want."

Lester's tone had turned sullen now, which meant he was gearing up for an all-out argument. But she wasn't about to let him get away with that. Today was *her* day, and he wasn't going to ruin it.

"Look, Lester, why on earth would you want to get married now, when you're just a sophomore in college? I thought getting your degree and joining the service was what you lived for?" Cassie paused and squinted at him.

"My plans haven't changed, but that doesn't mean we can't get married."

"You think marriage wouldn't throw a kink in those plans?"

He didn't so much as blink. "Nope."

"Dammit, Lester, what's really up with you?" Cassie's tone was incredulous.

"I think I love you."

"Think?" This time Cassie's laughter did erupt.

He flushed. "Okay, so I *do* love you."

"And what's that love based on?" Without waiting for him to answer, she went on. "Our having had sex twice?"

"That's part of it."

Cassie shook her head. "This conversation is getting too weird. And we both know sex is not love. Besides, it's been almost three months since we've even done anything."

Hopefully that would remain the case, she thought silently. She hadn't enjoyed sex with him. Maybe it was because he had taken her virginity and hadn't known how. Right now, she didn't care to analyze the reason behind her feelings or his. It didn't matter.

"That's not my fault." Lester's tone was as hard as his blue eyes.

"What's not your fault?" Cassie asked absently.

"Us not having had sex more often."

Cassie did not respond, but she didn't back down from the look in his cold eyes, either. She liked Lester and would concede that he was good-looking, though a bit on the short side. Besides, he more than made up for his lack of height by lifting weights. Actually, he had too many muscles for her taste, but then, that was his business.

He was different, too. That was part of his attraction. He seemed more mature than the other guys she'd gone out with, more mysterious, too, like he was hiding something. What that something was, she had no idea.

Still, Lester was not the man she wanted to spend

her life with, so somehow she had to pour cold water on his unexpected desire to marry her, especially since, come the fall, she would be attending the same university.

If she couldn't stop this now, a nightmare was in the making.

"How do you feel about me?" he asked into the growing silence.

"You're a good friend, and we have a good time together." She paused, not knowing quite how to finish.

He cursed. "I don't like the thought of anyone else touching you."

"Holy cow, Lester. Is jealousy what this is all about?"

"That's part of it. I want you to myself. Marrying you is the only way I can be sure of that."

"God, you make me sound like some kind of trophy you want to flaunt in front of your friends."

Lester's flush deepened, which made her think she'd nailed him.

"Well, it would be great to have everyone know that we were a couple."

"We are *not* a couple, Lester. Granted, we've gone out together a lot. But make no mistake, when I go to school, I want no strings attached. I want to be free to date anyone I choose."

"I don't like that," he muttered darkly. "If your daddy knew we'd had sex, he'd expect us to get married."

"You're saying that just because he's a preacher."

"So what? I'm right."

Cassie laughed again, but with no mirth. "You may be right, but Daddy's not going to know about us, nor is he going to pick the man I marry."

"I'm not taking no for an answer."

"You're nuts." Cassie flounced over to the railing, putting as much distance between them as possible. "Say we were madly in love and were to get married, what would we live on?"

"My parents would help, and so would yours, I'm sure."

"Well, I'm not."

"You have some money, don't you?"

Cassie's full lower lip stretched into a thin line. "I have a small trust from my grandmother, but I can't touch that yet."

"We'd manage. I'd get a job."

Cassie held up her hand. "Look, I don't want to talk about this anymore. Our getting married is not going to happen. If that means you don't want to see me anymore, then so be it." She peered at her watch. "It's getting late, almost time to get ready for dinner."

As if on cue, her mother, Wilma, opened the French doors onto the deck and smiled her cool smile. "Hope you two don't mind some company."

Cassie examined her mother, who she thought was beautiful and always would be, even if she lived to be a hundred. At thirty-six, the same age as her husband, James, Wilma Hillcrest Wortham was tall and rather robust. Because her skin was like porcelain and her prematurely gray hair immaculately styled, one overlooked the fact that she could easily become overweight. With Wilma, that would never happen, Cassie knew. Her mother had too much willpower and self-discipline to be anything other than the best she could be, which was perfect.

At the moment, Cassie wanted to hug her, considering her timely interruption. Hugs, however, weren't her mother's thing. More often than not, Wilma held herself aloof. Cassie sometimes wondered if she really loved her or merely tolerated her.

"Where's Daddy?" Cassie asked in a bright tone.

"He's coming. And Alicia's already here," Wilma added.

"Good," Cassie said with less enthusiasm. Alicia was her mother's only sibling. Although she was only two years younger than Wilma, she had never married. Cassie suspected it was because she had chosen a career over a home and children.

Cassie couldn't figure out what made her dislike her only aunt, but she did; the woman flat got on her nerves. Too sweet. That was one reason, too cloyingly sweet. No one could be that nice all the time.

"Happy birthday, Cassie," Alicia said, breezing through the door, interrupting Cassie's thoughts. "And Lester, how are you?"

"Fine," Lester murmured, looking away.

What a rude bore, Cassie thought, tensing her mouth, then jerking her gaze off Lester and back onto her aunt, who favored Wilma in looks, though Alicia was smaller boned and had dark hair instead of gray. Cassie had always considered her mother standoffish, but Alicia, despite her surface sweetness, was even more so. Cassie thought she was a cold fish.

With Alicia watching her, Cassie forced a smile, then turned away so that her face wouldn't show. She feared Alicia could read her thoughts. Alicia was sharp that way, so sharp that she had put the family hotels on the map.

The chain was made up of three upscale, independent hotels whose concept was small and intimate, but that offered high-class service, minus the formality.

Her mother ran the one in Jasmine, enabling her to
perform her duties as a minister's wife whose husband
pastored the town's largest church. Alicia spent her
time between the other two—one in Baton Rouge and
one in Shreveport.

"More mint julep, anyone?"

Cassie's features brightened even more as her eyes
landed on her daddy, who stood in the door. Smiling,
she held up her empty glass. "Your timing's perfect.
I'm running on empty."

James Wortham chuckled. "You, my favorite daughter, on empty?"

"Your only daughter, Daddy dear."

His chuckle deepened, and he bowed. "I stand corrected. Still, I've never seen you empty. You're always
filled with high octane."

"Funny," Cassie responded drolly.

"I thought so myself," James said, walking over and
filling her glass, then turning to Lester, holding the
crystal pitcher out to him. "How 'bout you?"

"No, thank you," Lester responded in a clipped tone.

Cassie wanted to yank a handful of his short hair out
of his head, only she wasn't sure he had enough for
that. He wore it in the severest of military cuts, another
aspect that didn't suit her taste.

But then, nothing about Lester suited her taste today.
He had pissed her off, and she was not in a forgiving
mood, especially when it came to being rude to her
daddy.

"By the way, Daddy," she said, ending the sudden
silence. "Thanks for praying for the sun to shine today."

A sigh escaped Wilma's lips. "Mind your mouth,
child. That sounded almost flippant."

"Not so, my dear." James faced his wife with a smile. "Actually, I did pray for perfect weather. After all, it's our girl's special day. And she herself is perfect."

"Have it your way, James," Wilma said in a testy tone, which said loud and clear that, in her opinion, their daughter was *not* perfect.

Watching her parents and hearing that exchange made Cassie wonder again how they had ever gotten together. James was certainly not handsome. Though not short, he was shorter than her mother. His slightly stooped shoulders might have something to do with that. Added to that defect was a nose much too large for already mediocre features.

But his green eyes were sensational. Those, along with his well-modulated voice, could mesmerize anyone, especially his congregation. He was both a minister on the rise and a father she adored.

"By the way, where's Austin?" Alicia asked, breaking another silence.

James made a face. "Don't know. That scoundrel should've been here long before now."

"He's probably showing a house," Alicia said, flouncing across the deck, where she plopped down on one side of a flowered love seat.

Something was clearly not to her liking, Cassie thought snidely. Austin was too good in more ways than one for her aunt. Why couldn't he see that?

"He'll be here in time for dinner, I'm sure," Wilma said. "He's never let us down before."

"Who's never let you down?"

All eyes turned in the direction of the landscaped lawn and watched as Austin McGuire strolled toward them, a grin spread across his face.

"You, my friend," James was saying, meeting Austin halfway and slapping him on the shoulder.

Cassie couldn't understand what had drawn those two men together. But she'd heard the story many times about how James, a senior at the university, had met Austin, a freshman, and had taken him under his wing.

Something had obviously clicked, and they had been best friends ever since. In fact, Austin was almost as much a part of her life as her parents, though she never considered him a parent. A brother, perhaps, but *never* another father.

At thirty-two, fourteen years her senior, his six-foot-two, hundred-and-eighty-pound body was all muscle and brawn. But it was his dark hair that brushed his collar and his dark lashed eyes that were the kickers. Both gave him a sultry look that was a total turn on.

If he was aware of his sex appeal, he gave no indication. He seemed to take everything in stride, a trait she admired in him and something she couldn't do. She didn't have a laid-back bone in her body.

"Hiya, brat," Austin said, coming straight to her and kissing her on the cheek.

Cassie pushed him away and placed both hands on her hips. "From now on, that word is off-limits."

That brought a round of laughter.

"I'm eighteen today, in case you've forgotten."

"Who could forget?" His eyes glinted devilishly. "You've been rubbing our noses in it for weeks now."

"You're awful."

Again, everyone laughed, and for a while, they chatted about everything and nothing. Even Lester seemed to warm up a bit. Warm, however, was not the word for Alicia; hot was more appropriate. When she wasn't by Austin's side, she was looking at him like a lovesick cow.

Cassie was fighting the urge to puke when her mother took charge.

"I suggest we all go to our rooms and rest," Wilma said in a tone that brooked no argument. "It's not long till we meet again for cocktails, then dinner." She paused and smiled her cool aristocratic smile. "A few other friends will be joining us."

Within seconds, it seemed the deck had cleared and Cassie was alone. But that was always the way it had been. When her mother spoke, people obeyed, except her. She had as strong a will as Wilma; that was why they often clashed.

Cassie peered at her watch and saw that she had ample time to take a stroll on the beach, to feel the wind tumble through her short hair one more time. Tomorrow she would return home and begin to get ready for school, which was both exciting and sad.

She bounded down the steps, only to stop in her tracks when she heard his voice. "Where you headed, brat?"

Two

Cassie flung her head around, her eyes flashing. "I told you to stop calling me that."

"Old habits are hard to break." Austin's tone teased. "Besides, that's what you are."

"What I am is eighteen."

"So?" Again the teasing note.

"So I'm an adult, and it's time you treated me like one."

Austin grinned. "Ah, now is that a fact?"

"Yes, that's a fact." Cassie tipped her chin, but even though her eyes continued to flash, she couldn't quite control the smile that hovered over her lips.

Austin's grin widened. "Sorry, it's going to be tough to think of you as a 'grown-up.'"

"When you want to, you can be a real jerk."

Austin laughed out loud, then sobered. "Let's face it, most of the time I *am* a jerk."

"Not to me. To me, you've always been—"

He cut her an intense look, his grin only partially intact. "What?"

She wished she hadn't said anything. She had opened a can of worms that was better left unopened. Actually, she wasn't sure she could answer that question even to her own satisfaction. She just realized that her heart always seemed to do funny things when Austin invaded her space.

Maybe the truth was that she'd always had a itsy-bitsy secret crush on him and was just now recognizing it, which was absolutely ludicrous, of course.

"I'm waiting, brat," he prodded.

Cassie gave him a look that in turn spread another grin generously across his lips.

What was the matter with her? She'd never been uncomfortable or tongue-tied around him before. They had always enjoyed an easy camaraderie, able to laugh and tease and even insult one another.

Maybe it was her aunt's presence that bugged her. Austin had been seeing her for some time now, or so her daddy had said. Of course, her parents were overjoyed, since they seemed to think Austin could walk on the water. More to the point, they considered him family, and so did she.

"Forget it," she finally said in a sharper tone than she'd intended. "I was just babbling."

Austin shot out a hand and mussed her hair. "That's another thing you do well. You put your mouth in motion before shifting your mind in gear."

"Jerk," she muttered, slicing her eyes to him, more aware than ever of what a hunk he was without being pretty-boy handsome. It was his body that made him stand apart from other men his age, including her own father.

There was no comparison between the two men. James more than looked his thirty-six years of age, while Austin, only four years younger, did not. It was that hard-toned body, the body of an athlete. She wondered suddenly what it would feel like to touch... Ouch!

"You never answered my question," Austin said, breaking into her forbidden thoughts.

Cassie rebounded and gave him a sassy grin. "That's because I don't remember what it was."

"I asked where you were headed."

"Oh, right. I'm going for a walk on the beach."

His dark eyebrows shot up. "You serious?"

"Yep. What's wrong with that?"

"Nothing. I just figured you'd go to your room and start getting dolled up for tonight."

"Dolled up?" Sarcasm lowered her voice.

"Well, whatever."

"I still have time for the 'whatever,' as you put it. Besides, I don't have that much to do to myself."

"I agree." His gaze seemed to burn into her. "You're pretty damn perfect the way you are, brat."

Even though she wanted to hit him for his continued use of that word, she didn't. She was too busy battling another emotion. Her heart was betraying her again, doing those funny things that left her feeling somewhat breathless and confused. And frightened.

"Uh, thanks," she said, not looking at him.

"You want some company?"

"That'd be nice."

But he didn't move. His gaze continued to burn into hers. She couldn't read a damn thing in those eyes, and time was a wasting.

At this rate, she wouldn't have any time to spend kicking through the sand. Her mother would have a hissy fit if she was late to her own dinner party.

"If you're going with me, you'd best get the lead out."

Cassie wasn't certain he had followed her until he appeared at her side.

They walked for a while in complete silence. Cassie breathed in the tangy smell of the ocean and watched as the waves, though gentle, whitecapped as they came ashore. She lifted her eyes and noticed there wasn't a cloud in the sky. She couldn't have asked for a lovelier day to turn eighteen years old. What a trip, she thought, hugging herself.

"What are you thinking about?"

"Just stuff."

"Do you know yet what you're going to major in?"

"General business, probably. I sure don't want to teach."

Austin massaged the back of her neck, then peered at her from under thick lashes. "I still can't believe you're eighteen and on your way to college."

"Why not?"

Austin shrugged his lean shoulders. "Don't rightly know. It's just that you've always been James's little girl who wasn't supposed to grow up."

Cassie snorted.

"Hey, what brought that on?"

"Well, Daddies' little girls do grow up, you know."

"Hey, brat, cut the sarcasm. You know what I mean."

"No, I don't. Suppose you tell me."

"In some ways, you could almost be my—"

In spite of herself, Cassie felt her face flame. "Oh puhleeze, don't say what I think you're about to say. Trust me, I've never thought of *you* in that way."

Austin seemed to think on that for a moment before asking in a tight voice, "What about you and that boy?"

"That boy has a name. It's Lester."

"Okay. So where is Lester?"

Cassie shook her head. "Probably in his room, sacked out. Beer makes him sleepy."

"Shouldn't drink if he can't handle it."

For some reason, his veiled criticism of Lester annoyed her. "That's Lester's call, not mine."

Austin's brows shot farther up. "Did I by chance hit a raw nerve?"

Cassie gave an evasive shrug.

"So how serious is it between you two?"

Cassie cut her eyes at him, her voice taunting when she asked, "What you really want to know is if I'm sleeping with him, right?"

Austin pulled up short, his eyes narrowing. "Okay, are you?"

"What do you think?"

"Shit, Cassie, you ought to—" He broke off, scowling.

"Why does that upset you?"

"Because that's not something you take lightly."

"Now you *do* sound like my Daddy."

Austin's face drained of color. "What I'd like to do is turn you over my knees and wallop your bottom."

"Lester asked me to marry him."

Austin cursed. "Why, that's the craziest thing I've ever heard. You're just starting college, for God's sake."

"I told him the same thing."

"You don't love him, do you?"

"I'm not sure I know what love is, actually."

"Believe me, you'll know it when it hits."

"So are you in love with Alicia?"

Bingo. This time *she'd* hit the raw nerve. His eyes narrowed even more, until she could barely distinguish their color. "What makes you ask that?"

"Because she's in love with you." Cassie paused. "Or maybe she's just in lust."

Austin made a choking sound. "Kid, your mouth needs a good sudsing."

Cassie wrinkled her nose. "Turnabout's fair play. So, are you sleeping with her?"

Austin gave her a fierce look. "That's none of your business. Besides, our situations are different."

"Oh, really?"

"Yes, really. I know what I'm doing."

"It may surprise you, but so do I."

"Good, then I can assume y'all used birth control."

"You're not my parents," she snapped. "So stop acting like them."

"I don't like that guy."

"You'll get over it."

He smiled, but she sensed it was forced. "You're getting brattier by the second."

"What if I said I didn't like Alicia?"

"Of course you like her. She's your aunt."

Cassie shrugged, suddenly feeling depressed, unsettled, as if demons were having a field day inside her. She didn't want to feel that way—not today, anyway.

She wanted to be carefree, to laugh, to celebrate. After all, she had Austin with her, and they were alone.

Not liking where that thought might lead, she suddenly picked up a handful of moist sand and tossed it at him. It splattered across his chest, then stuck to the front of his T-shirt.

Austin peered down, then back up, giving her an incredulous look. "Why you little—"

Laughing, Cassie didn't give him time to finish the sentence. She took off running down the beach, certain he was on her heels. Before she realized her own intention, she headed up a hill toward the wooded area where she'd spent hours daydreaming about boys.

"What was that for?" he called out.

"For being so damn nosy," she hollered back without turning around.

Her breath was coming in gasps now, and she was having difficulty keeping her footing. The sand was dry and deep, and she didn't seem to be making any progress.

"Whoa, brat."

His voice she expected, but not his hand on her arm. Because of that unexpected gesture and what it did to her equilibrium, Cassie lost her balance and hit the sand hard, belly first.

"Hey, are you hurt?" Austin demanded, a breathlessness in his tone, as well.

Cassie didn't say anything for the longest time, though she heard the anxious note in his voice. Let him wonder if she was hurt. It would serve him right. After all, he had caused her to fall.

"Dammit, Cassie, answer me!"

Suddenly she twisted onto her back. He was kneeling beside her, leaning over her, close enough that she could see the paper-thin lines etched around his eyes and smell the mint on his breath.

It was in that moment that their eyes met. And held. It was also in that moment that Cassie did something so totally brazen and forbidden that even she couldn't believe it.

Grasping the back of his neck, she pulled his head down, stopping his lips just shy of hers. For that brief second, they were alone in a world all their own.

Waves lapped, seagulls squawked, wind blew. They

were unaware of nature, only of each other. Cassie's lips parted as she eased him closer.

"What the hell—"

Austin might as well not have opened his mouth. He knew he didn't have a chance of finishing his sentence, even if he'd wanted to, which he didn't. Still, he almost choked when she made a little mewing sound, then forced his lips onto hers.

At first he was too stunned to respond, a myriad of emotions stampeding through him, trampling every rational thought, every facet of his conscience. His mind was the worst; it seemed to short-circuit from disbelief.

And shock.

That had to be what made him take this madness to an even higher level. But when he tasted her soft, quivering lips at the same time that her tongue flicked his, he was a goner.

His mouth ground into hers, wet and hot and more demanding by the second. Instead of his boldness frightening her into ending this insanity, she gave him back as good as he gave.

She caught his bottom lip between her teeth and sucked on it. The top of his head nearly came off, not to mention what was happening below his belt. He was certain he was about to explode.

Yet somehow he found the courage and the fortitude to try to right the wrong that was happening between them. God, had he lost what mind he had left, letting her get the best of him like this?

No!

He jerked his head back, though not far. She had a grip on him that wouldn't quit. "Cassie, Cassie," he rasped. "This is—"

"What I've been wanting," she whispered in a

heated tone before fastening her lips onto his once again, as if determined to devour him.

If someone had put a gun to his head and told him that if he didn't stop, his brains would be splattered all over the sand, he would have said go ahead and pull the trigger. That was what her hot, wet, all-consuming lips were doing to him.

Crazed and making sounds that even he didn't recognize, Austin managed to expose her breasts, so he could suck one tender nipple, then the other.

Her animalistic sounds answered his as he yanked her flimsy shorts and panties down over her hips. With her help, they puddled around her ankles.

Before he could make another move, she shoved her hand down and unzipped his cutoffs, immediately latching onto his penis, positioning it between her thighs.

"Cassie!"

He might as well not have said anything. She seemed to have her mind and body set on one thing, and that was having him inside her. When she spread her legs and her stiff curls teased his erection, his groan pierced the air.

"Now, please," she pleaded, her eyes wide and glazed as they peered up at him. Begging eyes, he thought later.

He knew she was in the throes of an orgasm.

Groaning louder, he thrust into her, feeling her small cavity expand to take all of him. Even so, he didn't move, still praying for the strength to abort this insanity.

As if she sensed that his mind was a war zone, she positioned her legs around his thighs, locking him inside.

"Please!" she cried.

His entire body throbbing from the pain of holding back, he cursed caution and began riding her as if she were one of his frisky Thoroughbreds—hard, fast and explosive.

As quickly as it began, it was over.

Spent and sated, he collapsed on top of her, but only for a second. Then the realization of what he had just done slammed into his gut like a sharp knife.

He buried his hands in the sand on either side of her and raised himself far enough to glare into her still-wide eyes. "Dammit, Cassie, do you realize what the hell we just did?"

"We made love."

Austin's face darkened. "Love? I don't think so. Love had nothing to do with it. What *I* did was fuck my best friend's daughter."

"How dare you!" she whispered. "You...you make it sound so ugly, so dirty." Her chin was quivering, and tears darkened her eyes.

"That's because it is."

"Get off me," she cried suddenly.

"Dammit, Cassie, we have to talk."

"No! I said get off me."

Using words he hadn't used in a long time, Austin struggled to his feet. But before he could reach down and help her up, she bounded upright, yanked her clothes into place and took off running.

"Shit," he said, his mind racing at the same speed as his heart. "Cassie, stop!"

She kept right on going, and he didn't have the courage to run after her. Instead, he simply stood there, wondering what the hell he was going to do.

Cassie stared at herself in the mirror.
Even though she looked smashing in a short, black

silk designer dress that hugged her body just enough to do justice to her curves but not enough to look suggestive, she couldn't stand the sight of herself.

She grabbed her stomach and turned away, fighting off the nausea that threatened to send her to the toilet. What had she done? *And why?* She hadn't been able to answer that then, nor could she now. All she could think about was that she'd forced him to take her.

When his lips had finally claimed hers, a heady excitement had made her so dizzy that she had lost all perspective. And when he had jerked off her top, exposed her breasts, then sucked her nipples, there was no way she could have pulled back, not with heat spearing between her thighs.

Would he tell her daddy? That thought was what made her stomach heave again. Still, if she had to do it all over again, would there be a repeat performance? Yes.

She was sick, but not sorry.

With that unsettling thought in mind, Cassie hurried out of her room and headed down the stairs. She entered the dining room tentatively, as though she had a scarlet letter branded across her breasts.

"It's about time, my dear," Wilma said through gritted teeth.

Cassie knew her mother was in the midst of having that hissy fit, though she wasn't about to let anyone else see that. But Cassie knew; she could see the cold displeasure in Wilma's eyes. She wondered if Austin had been late, as well. No matter. She couldn't have looked at him or Lester if her life had depended on it.

However, she did force herself to speak to and smile at the other couples who had joined them—her parents' attorney and his wife, and the associate pastor and his wife.

James suddenly gave her an indulgent smile, which made Cassie feel worse. "Have a seat, sweetheart, here, on my right. After all, you're the guest of honor."

Once she was seated, James remained standing, a glass in his hand. "Now that the birthday girl is here, I'm ready to make my toast."

Somehow Cassie managed to lift the glass of champagne without it sloshing all over her and the table.

"We have two things to celebrate this evening, actually. First, my daughter's eighteenth birthday, which of course is no surprise. Stand, my dear, and take your bow."

Somehow Cassie managed to get to her feet, then sit right back down, without mishap.

Everyone laughed, then clapped.

"However, my next announcement *is* a surprise, but a delightful one, I have to say. Austin, you and Alicia stand please."

Cassie kept her eyes glued on her daddy, while her stomach bottomed out. It was all she could do not to grab it.

James's smile encompassed the entire table. "My old and dear friend Austin, and Alicia, my favorite and only sister-in-law, are engaged to be married as of now." His smile spread as he gestured for them to rise. "Please join me in toasting that union."

Cassie froze.

Austin engaged? To her aunt? Impossible, especially after what had just happened between them. But it was true, she told herself, horrified.

And there was not one thing she could do about it except keep quiet and plaster a smile on her face.

Three

Summer, 1999

Jasmine.

Had it been five years since she'd been home? Even if nothing else in this Louisiana town of thirty thousand had been familiar, the smell would have identified it. The sight and scent of cape jasmine was forever present and forever strong.

The bushes, filled with the white velvet-petaled flowers, were all around. Cassie cracked the window and inhaled deeply. The intoxicating fragrance never failed to buoy her spirits.

But there were other familiar landmarks that she drank in as she steered the car through the quaint, charming town, one of the South's unspoiled treasures, or so she had always thought.

Above her was the bluest of heavens, and around her were gardens of flowers.

But there was more. She couldn't forget the oaks that dripped with moss, creating umbrellas over the streets, or roads that were lined with fashionable boutiques and galleries.

And hidden away from visitors' eyes were murky and

mysterious bayous that wound their way sluggishly through the meadows.

"Mom, do you think this looks good?"

Cassie took her eyes off the road and glanced over at her son, Tyler, who was busy coloring a picture of a horse and barn.

"It's a masterpiece."

He giggled.

Even though this precious eight-year-old sat beside her in the flesh, his dark blond hair shinning like gold in the sunlight, she couldn't believe he was hers. But he was. She could attest to that fact, having gone through hell to bring him into this world, then to keep him.

Cassie swallowed an anguished sigh, not wanting to let on that her insides were in turmoil. Tyler's life had already been torn apart too many times to count. Because of that, he was much more in tune to her moods than he should have been at his age.

Thank God their tumultuous past was behind them and they were about to start afresh. However, she wasn't celebrating yet. She had one more large hurdle to jump—confronting her parents.

Still, whatever happened with them, her life had suddenly taken an unexpected twist, and she was so grateful and filled with relief that she wanted to shout her glee. Out of hearing range of her son, she had done just that.

But if her plans didn't work out, she and Tyler would simply move on and make other plans. Still, Cassie couldn't seem to control her pounding heart or her sweaty palms now gripping the steering wheel.

How could she have forgotten how hot it was in Louisiana in the summer? The heat, combined with the humidity, made for a sticky mix. Even with the air conditioner's blasting, she felt as if she were in a sauna, which was another clear indication that she was home.

Home.

What if her parents weren't glad to see her? What if they slammed the door in her face? No, the latter wouldn't happen; of that she was confident. However, embracing her with open arms might be another thing altogether. Tyler, on the other hand, was in the clear. They would be jubilant to see him.

"Mom."

"Huh?"

"When are we gonna get there?"

"Soon."

Out of the corner of her eye, she sneaked another look at him. Her heart melted. Jeez, he was beautiful, with his green eyes, duplicates of hers, which reflected his curiosity and his energy. But it was his mischievous smile that was the grabber, that made one want to hold him and squeeze him.

He wasn't perfect, though, not by a long shot. He was stubborn and tenacious, traits she was sure he'd inherited from his father. At that thought, Cassie's heart lurched, and another deep-felt sigh threatened to escape.

"How soon?" Tyler pressed.

Cassie shook her head as if to clear it. "Soon as in now." She forced a smile as she maneuvered the car between the gates of her parents' estate. "We're here."

She would have loved to drive by the church and the hotel to see how they had fared through the years. But that would have been indulging herself and prolonging the inevitable. Too, Tyler wouldn't have appreciated the auld lang syne.

Feeling his eyes on her, she glanced back at him.

A slight frown lined Tyler's forehead. "Aren't you glad?"

"Of course I am," she assured him, forgetting for a moment his uncanny ability to read her moods. She reached over and took his hand and lifted it to her lips. "It's been far too long since you've seen your grandparents."

He didn't respond right off, and Cassie was certain he could hear her pounding heart. He sensed something was wrong, but he couldn't figure it out, nor was she willing to explain. Her own emotions were so highly charged and mixed that even she couldn't sort through them.

"Do you think they'll still like me?"

Sudden tears burned her eyes; she blinked them back. "Of course they'll still like you, honey. Why, they love you."

Tyler closed his coloring book and placed it on the seat between them, then looked back at her, his small face full of trust.

Once she had mastered the long driveway, Cassie braked the car in front of the Tara-like mansion, with its tall, graceful columns that shielded balconies, verandas and courtyards, the ultimate in Southern charm and sophistication.

Surrounding the house were more beautifully manicured gardens filled with full trees and lush flowers. It was truly a breathtaking sight, even lovelier than she remembered.

She gave Tyler's hand another squeeze, then winked at him. "Come on, let's make their day."

He giggled again, then scrambled out of the car.

Moments later, after she rang the doorbell, Cassie wasn't sure her legs were going to hold her up. Under her long skirt, her knees were literally knocking together.

"Ouch, Mom. You're hurting my hand."

"Oops, sorry." She dropped his hand, unaware that she'd even grabbed it.

The door opened suddenly, and Joy, her parents' housekeeper, filled the space. She blinked as if her eyes were playing tricks on her, then a grin covered her face.

"Lord amercy, child, is that you?"

"Hello, Joy," Cassie answered with a wide grin at the same time that she walked straight into Joy's outstretched arms.

Once they broke apart, Joy stared down at Tyler. "Hello, young man."

"Hi," he said, edging closer to Cassie.

Cassie placed an arm on his shoulder and introduced them. "Joy took care of me when I was a child."

"Lord amercy," Joy said again, rolling her black eyes. "And some child you were, too."

Tyler smiled.

"What's going on out here?"

The sound of her daddy's voice was almost Cassie's undoing. She felt light-headed from both excitement and fear. What if they...? No, she wouldn't punish herself any longer with those thoughts. Besides, it was too late. She was here, and whatever happened, she would handle it.

"Why, Reverend James, it's Cassie and Tyler," Joy said in a jubilant tone.

"Thank heaven," he said, darting deeper into a foyer that smelled of cut flowers and beeswax.

"Hi, Daddy." Cassie's voice was unsteady, and tears once again burned her eyes, tears she didn't even try to control. Unsure of herself, she said the first thing that came to mind. "You're looking well."

And he was, though his shoulders seemed more stooped and his hair grayer and thinner. However, she was thankful to see that his incredible green eyes and mesmerizing voice remained intact.

"Come here." James reached for her and hugged her tightly. Then he dropped to one knee and smiled at Tyler, his mouth working. "Hello, young man. Long time no see."

"Hi, Papa."

James touched Tyler's cheek ever so lightly. "Mind if I give you a hug, too?"

Tyler shook his head, holding his arms out. Cassie averted her gaze, while more tears streamed down her cheeks and a huge lump closed her throat.

"I'll be in the kitchen, if you need me," Joy said, her voice sounding wobbly. "And welcome home, you two."

Cassie nodded in the housekeeper's direction before her eyes moved back to her daddy.

"So how's Mother?"

James's features changed. "Come on, I'll let you see for yourself."

"Oh Daddy, you have no idea how good it is to be home," Cassie declared, clinging to his arm, confident now that she'd made the right decision to just show up on their doorstep unannounced, though she had tried to call and hadn't gotten an answer.

Of course, she still had to face her mother. And when it came down to it, she didn't know her daddy's true feelings. No doubt they would bombard her with questions, many of which she couldn't answer.

Five years was a long time not to see one's family. A shiver went through Cassie.

"Are you all right?" James asked, pausing just outside the French doors that led into a large but cozy den, rich in furnishings, plants and expensive accessories.

"Oh Daddy, now that I'm home, I'm just fine."

"Well, you don't look it. You're white as a sheet and much too thin."

"I think my Mom's pretty," Tyler said, a hostile note creeping into his voice.

Before Cassie could intercede, James tousled Tyler's hair. "Me, too, but she was prettier when she had more meat on her bones."

Tyler giggled, which diffused the building tension. But Cassie didn't think for one minute that she would come through this homecoming unscathed, that she was home free.

"Your mother's resting on the sofa," James said as he opened the French doors and they entered the room.

The back of the long, flowered sofa faced the door. With Tyler's hand clasped in hers, Cassie made her way around to the front of it. Wilma was lying flat, with her eyes closed.

Cassie sucked in her breath and held it while her shocked gaze found her daddy. A pained expression dulled his features, and he shook his head.

Before Cassie could say anything, her mother's eyes opened, closed, then reopened. "Cassie," she said in a weak voice, struggling into a sitting position, though it was obvious just how difficult that movement was. "Is that you?"

Unable to respond right off, Cassie eased down beside her mother. Through the years, she had kept in touch by pay phone with her family and her best friend,

Jo Nell Benson, so she knew her mother was ill. But nothing short of seeing her decline in front of her eyes could have prepared Cassie for this shock.

Where Wilma had once been strong and hardy, she was now frail and thin. Yet her prematurely gray hair remained thick and salon-fixed. Her skin hadn't borne the brunt of her illness, either; it remained relatively unlined and rosy. On closer observation, though it could have been a fever that put the flush there.

"Mother," Cassie whispered, then hugged her, a rare gesture. Wilma had never encouraged physical contact, and Cassie had always obeyed that unspoken rule. Today she was making her own rules, and she wanted to touch her mother.

"So this is Tyler?" Wilma said, reaching around Cassie for her grandson. "My, but you've grown. Give Grandmother a hug."

Reluctantly, Tyler placed his thin arms around Wilma's shoulders, then pulled away.

"Mother," Cassie said gently, "are you all right? I mean, you seem much sicker than I thought."

"It's hard to talk about something so personal over the phone," Wilma said, a sting in her voice.

Relief washed through Cassie. Wilma's sharp-tongued jab and feisty spirit were living proof that her mother wasn't nearly as ill as she'd first thought.

"Your mother's right," James interjected, his tone also scolding.

Before Cassie could reply, Joy appeared in the doorway. "Excuse me, Ms. Cassie, but I'm baking some of your favorite cookies." Her eyes twinkled. "Would you be interested?"

Cassie laughed. "You know better than to ask that."

"What about me, Mom? Don't I get any?"

"Only if you mind your manners, young man."

"Shush, let the boy alone," James said, smiling at his grandson.

"Actually," Joy added, "I thought maybe Tyler might want to be on hand to sample the first ones."

"Can I, Mom?"

"Of course you may, silly." Cassie forced a light note in her tone. "But don't you dare eat them all."

When he had followed Joy out of the room, a silence ensued. Cassie sat stiffly with her hands clasped, feeling both sets of eyes on her. Questioning eyes.

James pushed his glasses higher up his nose. "You want to tell us what's going on?"

Cassie's gaze clung to them both. "I—we're home."

"To stay?" James asked.

"That depends on if you want us to." Cassie hated it, but she felt uneasy with her own parents. So much pain and many misunderstandings had preceded this trip home that she didn't know if their hearts could truly mend.

"Of course we want you to." James's gaze pinned hers. "But having said that, you owe us answers to a lot of questions. Five years without knowing your whereabouts is a long time."

"You're right, it is. But there's a lot of what happened that I can't share with you. It's against the rules of the women's shelter."

"I know they helped you, but still—"

"I hate those words," Wilma chimed in, her voice gaining in strength.

"How can you say that, Mother? The service they provide for abused spouses is wonderful. It saved Tyler's and my lives."

Wilma frowned, something she had rarely done in

the past for fear it would cause wrinkles. "I believe you, of course, but—"

"You don't understand," Cassie said in a small voice.

"Nor do I," James said.

"That's because neither of you lived with Lester," she explained with as much patience as she could muster. She was trying to see their side and trying to overlook the acute pangs of disappointment shooting through her, but it was hard.

"For the life of me, I still can't understand why you married him. But at the time, wild horses couldn't have kept you from doing so," Wilma said in exasperation.

"Look, Mother, do we have to open old wounds that are better left closed? I admit I made a big mistake, that I should never have married Lester."

"Which we tried to tell you," Wilma hammered on. "Not because he wasn't a good boy. We thought he was and still do. But you were both too young and irresponsible."

"Cassie's right, Wilma." James stood and walked to the fireplace, where he propped an arm on the mantel. "Now's not the time to dredge up the past."

When Wilma didn't respond, Cassie looked from one to the other and said, "It's important that I have your support and your forgiveness."

"I forgave you a long time ago," James said, "but it's hard to believe that Lester was the man you painted him to be, or that he was involved in the things you said he was."

"I know," Cassie said, unable to temper her bitterness.

"If only you had come to us," James pointed out.

"Oh please, Daddy," Cassie countered. "I reached

out to you, but you never heard me. Your only advice was for Lester and me to see a marriage counselor.''

"And I still believe that was the thing to do."

Cassie lunged to her feet. "Daddy, Lester was a gun fanatic and a member of a militia group. Tyler's life and mine were in danger every second we were around him. Why won't you accept that?"

"Because I still have room in *my* heart for forgiveness."

"Dammit, Daddy!"

James gave her a hard look. "I suggest you get hold of yourself and watch your language, young lady."

She was only twenty-seven years old, but Cassie had already learned a valuable lesson in the school of hard knocks. Some things in life never changed—her parents, for one. They were steeped in traditional Southern values that would never waver, regardless of the circumstances.

But then, she hadn't really expected them to. That was not what her return was all about. They would remain forever closeted in their safe world, where violence and fear played no part. Where bad things happened only to people who did something to deserve them.

Well, she and Tyler had done nothing to deserve their fate. Nonetheless, it had happened to them. They had experienced hell on earth during the years of her marriage to Lester, followed by the years of hiding from him.

If it hadn't been for her son, she could not have endured.

James rubbed the back of his neck, looked at his wife, then at Cassie. "You're home, and nothing else matters."

Oh, but it does matter, Daddy, Cassie cried silently. It matters more than you can imagine. She wanted their unconditional love and their support.

But she had known then, just as she knew now, that her daddy's job as a minister and her mother's family tree were more important than she or the truth. Clearly, they had been and still were embarrassed, and wanted to distance themselves from their daughter's dark past.

"Cassie."

Cassie blew out her breath and looked at her mother. "Ma'am?"

Wilma struggled to her feet and walked to stand beside her husband. "Where is Lester now? Is he dead?"

Cassie swallowed hard. "No."

"So why, out of the blue, have you decided to surface, to come home now?"

Cassie's unflinching gaze included both Wilma and James. "Lester's in prison."

Four

Cassie still glowed in the fact that she was home. In fact, she had pinched herself when she first awakened to make sure she hadn't been dreaming.

But the sound of the birds and the sweet smell of the jasmine outside her French doors banished the dream, and she hugged herself.

Now, as she left her room and walked the short distance down the hall to Tyler's room, there was a definite spring to her steps.

Easing the door open, she peeked in and saw that her son was sound asleep. That was another blessing. Many a night, while on the run, Tyler had refused to sleep by himself. She had taken him to counselors, and the last one had helped him. Once again he was sleeping alone.

Cassie tiptoed to the bed, smiled down at him, then leaned over and kissed his cheek. He didn't so much as move. He was no longer a baby in years, but he would always be *her* baby. She loved him so much it hurt; he was the glue that had held her life together, the only glue she needed to survive. She would die before she would let Lester or anyone else harm him.

Shuddering at the thought of her ex-husband, Cassie left the room and made her way downstairs to the cheery breakfast room. She pulled up short when she saw her parents already at the table, china cups in hand.

Not only was the aroma of coffee strong in the air, but the smell of bacon frying was there, as well.

Joy was already up and at it, she thought with a smile. About that time, her stomach growled, and it dawned on her that she was hungry and how much she'd missed Joy's cooking.

However, it wasn't Joy's culinary skills that were her primary concern now but the silence her entrance had brought. It was deafening—the worst kind. Cassie forced herself not to take offense. After all, when she had arrived yesterday, her parents' structured life had been turned topsy-turvy.

They would all have adjustments to make, despite the fact that she hoped to find a place of her own and a job, though not necessarily in Jasmine.

"Good morning, hon," James said, recovering first, then getting up and pulling out the chair that faced the garden.

"Thanks, Daddy." Once she was seated, Cassie feasted her eyes on the beauty of the plants and flowers on the other side of the huge expanse of glass. The sight was breathtaking. "I'd forgotten just how lovely this place was."

"It's your mother's doing." James's tone was proud.

"I can't take the credit," Wilma said. "I just tell Albert to do what has to be done."

Cassie didn't believe that for a second. Her mother was a control freak who oversaw everything concerning the estate, especially since it was her family's money that had built and maintained it.

Still, Cassie smiled, relieved to see that her mother seemed better and that for the moment the awkwardness had passed. "So Albert's still doing his thing right along with Joy. I'm glad."

"I don't know what we'll do when they retire," Wilma said after taking a sip of coffee at the same time that James filled Cassie's cup from the silver pot that graced the center of the table.

"Don't you worry, my dear," James said. "They're not going anywhere for a long time."

Cassie sensed that her parents were just making idle conversation until they were ready to hammer her with the next round of questions. It was too bad that Tyler's timing had been so poor. Right after she had told them Lester was in prison, her son had returned from the kitchen with a mouth full of cookies.

She wished she could have been a fly on the wall in their room that evening and heard what they said about her.

Switching her gaze to her daddy, she wondered what was going through his mind now.

Was he holding on to his optimism concerning her and Lester? If only he knew just how stacked the odds were against that, he would give it up. But then, she knew that the flow of eternal optimism was what kept James behind the pulpit.

Cassie took a gulp of her coffee, then said, "Mmm, that's the way coffee ought to taste." Nothing could take the place of Louisiana chicory. Stronger than a bear's breath, as the old-timers in her daddy's church used to tell her.

"So when and how did you learn Lester had gone to prison?" Wilma asked.

Cassie sighed, wishing this discussion could be postponed, hating to ruin this lovely morning, but she might as well get it over with, though there would be a lot of holes in her past that she couldn't fill.

"Two days before I returned home," she said with

care, "my contact from the shelter called and told me I was free at last."

"So they've kept up with Lester and his where-abouts?"

Cassie nodded. "That's part of the service they provide."

"I see," Wilma said, placing her cup back in its saucer.

Of course, she didn't see and never would. Cassie saw Wilma's hands were unsteady, and while that grieved her, there wasn't anything she could do about it. This entire scenario was painful. But old wounds apparently had to be cleansed before they could become a real family again. If ever.

"Mother, there are so many things I want to say." Cassie paused, praying for the right words. "For starters, I'm so very sorry about Aunt Alicia."

"It's something I'll never get over," Wilma responded, sadness creeping into her voice and eyes.

It had been during one of their phone conversations that Cassie had learned of her aunt's untimely death shortly after it had happened. Alicia had been married for five years to Austin and was pregnant with his child when a teenager ran a stop sign and smashed into her car. Both mother and unborn child had been killed instantly.

The news had been a devastating blow for Cassie. Although she and Alicia had never been close, the tragedy was still heartbreaking. It had saddened her even more that she'd been unable to attend the funeral.

She voiced her thoughts. "I wanted to come back, but I was afraid to take the chance."

Wilma pursed her lips. "I still find it hard to believe

that Lester was such a monster that you couldn't at least have returned for the service.''

"I happen to agree with your mother," James said.

Cassie wanted to vent her anger on them for judging her so unfairly. But it wouldn't do any good. It would only make things worse.

The only thing that concerned them was the bottom line, which was the breakup of a family. She had committed an unpardonable sin; she had gotten a divorce. Their piety sickened her.

"But first things first," Wilma was saying. "Why was Lester incarcerated?"

"On a weapons charge," Cassie responded. "He and some of his buddies in that right-wing militia group got caught buying and selling illegal weapons. But it was Lester who was nailed. He won't be seeing the outside for a long time."

"Oh my goodness," James said, shaking his head. "I hate that for Tyler. And for you, too, of course."

Right, Cassie thought bitterly, knowing that her parents hated it for themselves even more. The news about Lester was another kick in the teeth, especially as it would have a definite effect on their social standing in the community.

"We never saw that side of Lester." Wilma faced the garden. "He seemed like such a devoted husband and father. He never missed work. He—"

"Mother, please," Cassie interrupted, her suppressed anger rising to the surface. "Just trust me that Lester was a monster—in disguise, I'll admit, but a monster nonetheless."

"Did he ever strike you or the boy?" James asked.

"No, Daddy, but he was absolutely obsessed with guns. He was also a control freak, even though he never spent quality time with either of us. Lester worked all day and played with his extremist friends all night.''

"What a mess."

"I'd say it was more than that, Mother, but..." Cassie's voice faded into nothing. She knew she was fighting a losing battle by continuing to plead her case.

"We're not suggesting that the mess is all your fault, honey," James said. "It's just that we hate to see a family broken apart, especially since you were so determined to marry him."

Holding back the tears, Cassie rose and walked to the window, where she swung back around. "I know that, but believe me, I've been sorry ever since. The past, however, is a done deal, and right now I only want to build a new life for Tyler and me."

"That's what we want, too," James said on a bright note.

"For the first time in nine years, I feel free. It's like *I've* been in prison. Now it's Lester's turn, and I hope he rots there."

"My, my, but you're bitter," Wilma said, shaking her head.

Cassie stiffened. "And that won't change. I'll never forgive Lester for what he put us through."

"Never is a long time," James said. "Hopefully time and the Lord will change your mind."

"Yes, Daddy," Cassie murmured, knowing that was not going to happen but that she would just be wasting her breath telling him that. Obviously, James would never give up hope for a reconciliation between her and Lester. If only he knew the dark, painful secrets that lay buried deep inside her.

"So what are your plans?" Wilma asked, smoothly switching the subject.

"Like I said last night, I plan to hang out here for a while."

"I have a better idea," Wilma said forcefully.

"Oh?"

"Why don't you stay permanently and run the hotel in my place?"

Cassie's mouth gaped. "Surely you're not serious?"

"I've never been more serious in my life," Wilma said. "You've been working in various offices and even in some hotels, or so you told us."

"That's true," Cassie said again, her mind reeling, so much so that she sat back down.

"Someday my shares in the Hillcrest Hotels will be yours and Tyler's. You might as well take over now, since I'm somewhat under the weather."

When Cassie failed to answer, Wilma went on. "Besides, we've been robbed of our grandson long enough. We want to get reacquainted with him and have him become a part of our lives."

"And I want that, too, of course. Still, what you've asked is so sudden that I—"

The doorbell pealed, stopping Cassie's words and splintering her thoughts even more. She frowned. "Who on earth is that at seven o'clock in the morning?" Actually, she was glad of the interruption; she needed time to digest what her mother had proposed.

"I suspect it's Austin," James said, smiling and craning his head toward the hall.

Austin!

Cassie's breath left her lungs in a swish, and she almost grabbed her chest as though she were having a heart attack. Dear Lord, it couldn't be. He was the last person she'd expected or wanted to see.

What to do? If their visitor was indeed Austin, then

one, if not her worst, nightmare had come to pass. Her heart raced, and she broke out in a cold sweat. But she couldn't let her torn emotions show. She had to keep her cool.

"What's going on this morning?" Austin asked, sauntering into the room, a grin on his lips.

Cool be damned. Cassie's first inclination was to flee ,the room, to jump up and run like hell. She couldn't; she was trapped.

But so was he.

When Austin saw her, he stopped abruptly, and she watched the color fade from his face and his eyes narrow to slits.

"Good God, is that you, Cassie?" His voice sounded hoarse, as if he had a dilly of a sore throat.

"It sure is," James said, his face and voice glowing. "She surprised us yesterday."

Cassie didn't utter a word. All she could do was sit there like an idiot and stare, that funny feeling of old invading her system, bringing with it a churning nausea.

Admittedly, the intervening years had been more than kind to him, at least physically. Emotionally and mentally, she couldn't be sure. Having lost a wife and unborn child was bound to have left deep scars.

Cassie ached to look away, but she couldn't do that, either. His hair was still dark, though she could see streaks of silver threaded throughout. His tanned face had gained some deep grooves and lines, as well, but rather than detracting from his sultry looks, they enhanced them.

In fact, this more mature Austin exuded an in-your-face, don't-give-a-shit sex appeal that hadn't been there before.

Now that she was face-to-face with him again, she

couldn't believe it had been nine years since she'd seen him. Once they had returned to the table after their tryst in the sand and then his engagement to Alicia had been announced, Austin had walked out of her life and stayed put.

But then, that lengthy separation hadn't been by accident. She had worked long and hard to make sure their paths did not cross. In hindsight, that feat had not been difficult to pull off.

Distance had been on her side; she had lived in Lafayette and Austin in Baton Rouge. Their jobs had been another factor in her favor; both were extremely busy. And the few times she had visited her parents, she'd made sure in a discreet way that Austin was otherwise committed and wouldn't show up.

Austin himself, she suspected, had also played a role in keeping them apart. She was convinced that he'd been as eager to avoid her as she had him.

But their luck had finally run out.

"Before you arrived," Wilma said into the growing silence, "I was trying to entice her not to leave us again."

Austin grab a cup off the sideboard and poured himself some coffee—without being invited, Cassie noticed, which meant he felt at home there.

"By the way," James said, facing Cassie, "speaking of the hotels, Austin is now your mother's partner, having inherited Alicia's half, of course."

Terrific, Cassie thought, feeling faint.

"Excuse me for interrupting, Ms. Cassie," Joy said unexpectedly from the doorway, "but Tyler's up and asking for you."

Tyler!

Terror now rendered Cassie completely immobile.

Finally she was able to get to her feet, though she was shaking both inside and out. "Uh, tell him I'll be right there."

"Cassie, bring him back down," James said. "Breakfast is about ready, and I want Austin to meet him."

No! God, no. She couldn't let that happen, but how could she prevent it? She couldn't. Fate had dealt her another underhanded blow.

When Austin saw Tyler, would he guess the truth?

Five

"Mom?"

"What, hon?"

"Papa wants to take me to work with him."

Cassie smiled down at her son, who was in her bedroom. They had both been up a while, but she had just gotten dressed, opting not to go downstairs for coffee. She hated to admit it, but she feared a repeat of yesterday, for more reasons than one.

The delving questions aside, it was the thought of seeing Austin again that made her skin break out in a cold sweat. Thrusting thoughts of him aside, she forced herself to concentrate on her son. "Do you want to go?" she asked Tyler, who was sitting on the edge of her bed, bouncing up and down like a rubber ball. "Stop that," she added in a calm tone.

He stilled his body, then asked, "Will you come with us?"

"No, but you may go. I'll stay with Grandmother."

Apparently satisfied with that, Tyler jumped up and ran toward the door. "See ya later."

"Whoa, young man, aren't you forgetting something?"

"Aw, Mom," he whined, though he raced back across the room and planted a moist kiss on her cheek.

"Thanks, buddy." She hit him playfully on the arm. "Your kiss is my morning pusholine."

Tyler rolled his eyes before turning and racing out the door. Afterward, Cassie remained seated on her dressing table stool, smiling. What a great kid, she told herself, patting herself on the back, something she rarely did.

She was delighted, too, at the rapport that seemed to have redeveloped between her daddy and her son. Before they had gone underground, Tyler had thought James was a cool granddaddy, despite the fact that he was a preacher.

At that time Tyler had been only three, and James's occupation hadn't been important. Even though she and Lester had lived in Lafayette, a couple of hours' drive away, she had made sure that Tyler got to know his grandparents. And while Wilma certainly loved him, it had been James who doted on him and vice versa.

She hadn't excluded Lester's parents, either. Dewitt and Charlotte Sullivan had spent time with Tyler, though not as much as her parents.

Suddenly Cassie grabbed her stomach, feeling an acute stab of pain. Too bad extenuating circumstances were going to force all that to change yet again. To counteract the burgeoning pain, Cassie lurched to her feet and walked to the window of the bedroom that had been hers since the day she was brought home from the hospital, the first and only child of James and Wilma Wortham.

The grounds, as she looked across them, were once again glorious. Money. Old money. That was what it took to maintain an estate such as this. And that was what her mother had inherited from her parents.

Without question, the Worthams lived the life of the

Southern rich. To the outside world, everything was ginger-peachy. Wilma saw to that. Her mother coveted her privacy and, despite being a preacher's wife, could be vicious when it came to protecting it. If any problems arose, Wilma demanded they be kept behind the closed doors of this house. She would have it no other way.

That was why her own scandalous divorce and subsequent disappearance had been a blow to her parents from which they hadn't recovered and never would.

But neither would she. Cassie sighed, trying to concentrate on the beauty filling her gaze. Tall oaks, pecans and a multitude of other trees covered the rolling grounds. Nestled under and around them were beds filled with flowers so colorful they were blinding.

Cassie didn't want to cry, but she felt the tears well up behind her eyes as that old feeling of panicked fear clawed at her insides, the kind of fear she had hoped never to feel again, especially now that Lester no longer posed a threat.

What a joke on her. When Austin had waltzed into that room, fate had stabbed another knife into her heart.

Releasing a pent-up sigh, Cassie turned away from the window, yet she didn't move. Her limbs seemed frozen, while her mind was a melting pot of thoughts and images. She closed her eyes and rubbed her temples. Nothing helped.

Austin's face and the shock she had seen mirrored there would not go away.

Keeping her eyes closed, Cassie leaned against the wall for support as the past, in the form of a million fire ants, stung her mind, forcing her to recall the events that had unfolded at the dinner party after her fling on the beach.

When her daddy had stood and toasted her birthday in the same sentence with Austin's engagement to her aunt, her life had plunged from light into darkness.

No one had known. Cassie had made sure of that. In fact, she had become the life of the party, refusing to give Austin so much as another look. That hadn't been hard, since he'd seemed as glad to avoid her as she had him.

Somehow she had gotten through the remainder of the evening and returned to Jasmine, where she had buried that reckless encounter by pretending it hadn't happened and going on with her plans to enter college.

A few weeks later, the reality of that evening had reached out and brutally slapped her in the face.

"You're pregnant, Miss Wortham."

Cassie had stared at the on-campus doctor in total disbelief. "That's wrong." She had clamped down on her bottom lip to hold it steady. "*You're* wrong. That can't be."

Stupefied as she was, she had watched his lips twitch at that last statement. "Oh, but it can. It is. And there's no mistake."

She hadn't argued anymore, not after she had barely made it to the rest room before losing the contents of her stomach.

Later, dazed and loaded down with literature and vitamins of all kinds, sizes and shapes, Cassie had walked out of the infirmary straight into Lester.

Fate.

At the time, she had deemed their meeting as just that. But instead of feeling relief at seeing a smiling, familiar face, she had burst into tears.

Over Cokes, on a nearby park bench, Lester had forced the truth out of her.

"So you're pregnant," he said. "I don't see a problem with that."

"Are you crazy?" Cassie's voice rose to the hysterical level.

"No. What I am is still wanting to marry you."

"You *are* crazy," she muttered, lowering her head to her chest.

Lester grabbed her by the shoulders and forced her to look at him. "Listen to me. It'll work. I swear it will. We'll get married as soon as we can get a license. Our parents will think you got pregnant the first time we did it."

Cassie's eyes widened. "You mean you'd marry me knowing I'm pregnant with another man's child?"

"Yes."

"Why? What's in it for you?"

"I told you before. I love you."

Cassie covered her ears with her hands. "Stop saying that! You still don't know what that word means, and neither do I."

"You have a better idea?" Lester demanded sullenly.

"No, not at the moment."

"And you won't. Being a preacher's kid, your daddy's going to shit a brick, and your mother—well, with her rich-bitch attitude—"

"How dare you talk about my mother like that?"

Lester shrugged. "It's the truth. You just won't admit it."

"Look, I appreciate your offer, but—"

"But what?" he interrupted. "An abortion?"

She threw him a look. "God, no."

That would be the last thing she would do. For starters, she thought that was a sin. Furthermore, she was too frightened of the physical part, not to mention the emotional consequences.

"Okay, will the kid's father marry you?"

"No!"

"You want to tell me who he is?" There was a bitter edge to Lester's voice that didn't go unnoticed.

"It wouldn't change anything," she said dully.

"I could shoot him."

Her head jerked up. "That's not funny."

"I didn't mean it to be."

"Dammit, Lester, don't play games with me."

"Okay. Then I don't see that you have a choice, unless you tell your parents you're going to have a baby out of wedlock."

Her breath caught. "I could never do that."

"So let's get hitched."

"Oh Lester, I don't know. I'm so sick and confused."

"More reason to trust me. I can sure as hell make the confusion go away."

He'd worn her down, and three days later she had become Cassie Sullivan in a secret and private ceremony.

Telling her parents that she was getting married had been another nightmare, one she wouldn't care ever to repeat. All hell had broken loose. Wilma had grabbed her chest as if having a heart attack. James had dug his fingers into the arm of the chair—to keep his knees from buckling, Cassie had suspected.

"But why?" James had asked, white around the mouth. "It doesn't make any sense."

"We're in love, sir."

This time Cassie hadn't challenged Lester's lie, asking instead, "How can you get mad at us?" With that question the desperation gnawing at her had quadrupled. But she refused to let it show. "After all, you two ran off and got married when you were only eighteen."

And they had. They had been childhood sweethearts, and the night following their graduation from high school, they had eloped, much to their parents' chagrin.

Countering with that indisputable fact seemed to have wilted her parents on the spot, taking the punch out of their argument. While they did not offer their blessings, they promised to honor the marriage as long as she and Lester promised to complete their educations.

When she had announced her pregnancy, after what she considered to be a safe amount of time, they were not happy about that, either. Still, they'd had no choice but to accept that fact, as well, then deal with it in their on way. Thank goodness they hadn't disowned her.

If they had known the truth, they would have; Cassie had been sure of that. But she'd never been sorry she hadn't told them that Lester was not Tyler's biological father.

The truth would have done irreparable damage to too many lives, including of her own. Her parents could not have withstood the blow or the scandal, not to mention the betrayal of trust that her daddy would have felt toward Austin.

The truth would have destroyed that friendship forever.

No, Cassie had never regretted her decision to keep the secret concerning her child. What she *had* regretted was marrying Lester.

Living with him had been synonymous with living in a chamber of horrors. However, her scars, along with her secret, would share her coffin.

Her cell phone rang, disrupting her train of thought. Having put the gadget on charge last night, Cassie snatched it off its base. The caller was Jo Nell.

"Gosh, girl, it's good to hear your voice."

"I can't believe you haven't called me," Jo Nell responded in a huffy tone.

"Well, I've only been here twenty-four hours."

"That's no excuse. You could've called me from your car phone."

"So I screwed up. Cut me some slack, okay?"

Jo Nell chuckled. "Only if you'll come over soon and let me fix you dinner."

"It's a deal. So how did you know I was home?"

"Are you kidding? Have you forgotten I own a beauty salon?"

Cassie's laugh was genuine. "Sorry, guess I did."

There was a long pause. "So how are things?"

"Good and terrible."

"Ah, I get it." Another pause. "You've seen Austin?"

Just hearing his name spoken aloud almost stopped her heart. "Yes. Which reminds me that I could cheerfully strangle you."

"Me? What did I do?"

"It's what you didn't do that has me upset."

"I can't imagine."

"You didn't tell me Austin had quit his job with the real estate company and was overseeing the hotels."

"Jeez, Cass, I just assumed you knew, or that you would put two and two together. After all, he inherited Alicia's stock, so why not?"

"Because he already has a lucrative job," Cassie said.

Alicia shrugged. "That's all I know, kiddo. Sorry.

Besides, we never had time to discuss hardly anything, much less Austin and what he was doing.''

"You're right. In the precious amount of time I had on the phone, he was the last person I wanted to talk about.''

"Look, we'll talk more when I see you. But everything's going to be fine. You'll see.''

"I pray you're right,'' Cassie said, her voice brightening somewhat.

But after she shut off the cell phone, her world darkened again. Cassie hugged herself and let the tears flow, regardless of her makeup. It could be repaired. Her heart couldn't.

Unfortunately, Jo Nell was wrong. Nothing would be all right. She knew what she had to do. Not only couldn't she take her mother's place at the hotel, she couldn't even stay in town.

Once again, Austin had nixed that.

Six

Give him the wide-open spaces anytime.

Austin almost smiled at the trite expression that came to mind as he made his way toward the barn. He stopped for a moment and let his eyes wander over his most prized possession—his horse farm. Several corrals were filled with Thoroughbreds who seemed to be enjoying the gorgeous afternoon. There wasn't a cloud in the sky, which meant it was hotter than hell.

While he stood still, Austin lifted his hat and raked the back of his hand across his forehead. The hand came off wet with sweat just as a mosquito buzzed around him. He slapped at it, but with no success. It kept buzzing. Unless he could trap that little bloodsucker on a hard surface and squash the shit out of it, he might as well save his time and energy.

A horse whinnying drew his attention. Nothing was more beautiful and unpredictable than a stable of horses, he thought. That was what made this such an exciting venture. And a profitable one, too; he couldn't forget that.

He had slaved like a field hand to obtain this acreage and hold on to it. One day he hoped to make it into a real money-maker, the same as he'd done with the Hillcrest chain of hotels. Already he had some prize horseflesh that would eventually bring him a shipload of money, or so he hoped.

Turning, Austin squinted against the sunlight and focused on the house that he had hoped to move into. But Alicia had refused to spend one night in it, much less live there.

It wouldn't have mattered if it had been as palatial as any suite in the hotel either. She wasn't into "roughing it," as she'd phrased it. She had thought horses were for cowboys and had no place in their lives. But then, that had been just one of the many bones of contention between them.

Pain, laced with a feeling of failure, was so intertwined with his marriage and the tragedy that followed, he still couldn't separate the two.

Austin frowned and shook his head, determined not to let his mind veer down that road. Anyway, he couldn't afford to lollygag any longer. A filly was waiting for him to saddle and break in. He upped his pace toward the barn.

"Yo, boss."

Austin stopped midstride again, having recognized Robb Hancock's voice. Robb was his trainer and foreman, a man for whom he had the utmost respect and who he depended on without fail. He could not have maintained this place without Hancock, since he himself was out of town so much.

Austin swung back around. Robb was hurrying toward him. He smothered a curse, expecting bad news. If something had happened at the hotel that needed his attention, he would be fit to be tied. He had earned at least one afternoon off, for chrissake, having left his cell phone behind on purpose.

"What's up?" he asked when Robb halted in front

of him. Though his trainer's physical condition was as good as his own, Robb's breathing seemed a notch faster.

Before Robb could respond, however, Austin added, "It had better be something I want to hear."

"Otherwise get lost, right?" Robb said, his full lips breaking into a smile.

Austin didn't answer that smile. "That's about the size of it."

"Hey, you are in a pissy mood."

Not many people could get by with talking to him that way. But Robb was that good a friend. He had stood by him when he'd lost Alicia and their baby, had taken care of everything. Austin could never repay him, although he tried in every way he could.

Loyalty was important to him, and he made it a practice to reward that attribute instead of abuse it.

"I wasn't until I saw you." This time Austin did smile.

"Go to hell."

Austin tipped his hat. "Same to you."

That momentary bantering unkinked Austin's stomach, and he decided that Robb's appearance had nothing to do with the hotel in Jasmine after all. But it wasn't hotel problems that had him in such a huff, though he hated to admit that. Something much more personal figured into his mood. Cassie's unplanned and unexpected return was at the bottom of his ill humor and discontent.

Refusing to veer down that forbidden path, Austin said, "I'm about to take another round at breaking in Wonder Woman."

Robb's ruddy, sun-kissed skin crinkled into a full-faced frown. "That's the most god-awful name I ever heard. I wish you'd change it."

"Not on your life. I think it fits her to a tee."

"We'll see," Robb muttered, rubbing the belly that protruded over his belt.

Austin knew that paunch resulted from his trainer's love of beer. As long as he didn't drink on the job, Austin didn't care; he enjoyed a few beers himself on occasion.

"When Wonder Woman brings home the Triple Crown, you'll eat those words."

"I'd eat shit if that happened."

Austin's grin was sincere but short-lived. "Well, you'd better get your knife and fork ready."

Robb harrumphed, then said, "The reason I'm here is to tell you that Mannard called, and the two colts that were due to arrive tomorrow aren't gonna."

"Why?"

"One of 'em's sick."

"Sick?" Austin could feel his blood pressure rising again. "Sick how?" He'd paid a helluva lot of money for those horses, and he damn sure expected them to arrive in good health.

Robb removed his hat and ran a hand over his sweat-covered bald head. "Dunno. Couldn't get much out of him." Herman Mannard was a horse trader who wheeled and dealed in the big leagues. Until now, Austin hadn't bought from him, never having had the money to afford his prices. But the man had the best horseflesh around; because of that, Austin had saved and sacrificed in order to make the purchases. He wasn't about to be screwed around.

"Well, go back and get something out of that bastard. I've already paid for those colts. And if he doesn't want me to come over and rip his head off, he'll make good on this deal."

Robb's auburn eyebrows lifted. "He isn't going to like that."

"Do you think I give a damn?"

"Nope."

"So call 'im."

"Consider it done," Robb said, ambling off.

A short time later Austin had ridden the filly until she had learned to respond to the basics and he was beat. Feeling the need to relax, he mounted Bluebonnet and rode for pleasure through a portion of his cleared property. The hot wind felt good slapping him in the face as he gently kicked the horse into a gallop.

Soon he stopped at the edge of a small creek, where he dismounted. While the animal lapped up the cool, clear water, Austin leaned against an oak, its limbs dripping with moss, typical of bayou country.

It was in that peaceful moment that the past sneaked up and karate-chopped him from behind. Cassie again. Anger filled every corner of his mind as he tried to keep her image from intruding.

Suddenly Bluebonnet lifted her head and shook it. Water spewed over him, which sent another expletive flying.

Even though he didn't expect Cassie to hang around for long, her presence was disconcerting, to say the least. He'd recognized right off how the years had matured her, making her more beautiful and enticing than ever.

And just as forbidden.

He hadn't wanted to take his eyes off her, that evening racing to the forefront of his mind in vivid detail, as if it had happened nine days ago instead of nine years.

He would have given anything at that moment to

know what was going through *her* mind. If her facial expression had been anything to judge by, she hadn't felt anything. Oh, she'd looked at him through wide eyes, but they had registered no emotion. It was almost as though she had never laid eyes on him, much less rolled in the sand with him embedded tightly inside her.

Shit.

Thoughts like that could land him in big trouble. He'd dreaded that day, had gone to great lengths to prevent it. But it had happened, out of the blue—wham, like a two-by-four slammed upside his head.

Yet there were times when he couldn't believe in the existence of that one-night binge, that he'd gone insane and ravished her body, having betrayed himself, his friend and his fiancée. For the longest time after he'd married Alicia, it had been Cassie he'd made love to in his mind.

Still, he had tried hard to make his marriage work and to make Alicia happy, even though she had never turned him on sexually the way Cassie had. Where Alicia had been a cool, calm and methodical lover, Cassie had been hot, wild and tempestuous.

It had been two years since the car accident had taken his wife and unborn child. Given those tragic circumstances, he was proud of the way he had pulled himself back together and made a new life.

James had remained by his side throughout that ordeal and was still there. That personal tie, combined with his business connection to Wilma, put him in daily contact with the Worthams, which meant he would see Cassie often, as well. That thought made his blood curdle.

Avoiding her was more what he had in mind. Her presence had resurrected his guilt and given it new life.

Somehow, though, he had to bury it again. He couldn't afford to let Cassie undermine his newfound sense of peace or the coveted respect of the Worthams.

Although Austin had grown up without any of life's amenities, one would never know it. He'd been determined to overcome that handicap, vowing never to be poor again.

His daddy had worked long and hard in the oil fields. His mother had died while trying to give birth to another child. His daddy had been a cold man who'd had little time or patience for his son.

With the help of his sharp mind and wit, Austin had made and saved enough money to go to college, where he'd met up with James Wortham. That meeting had been the turning point in his life. Though he was a freshman and James a senior, they became firm and trusted friends.

That friendship was strengthened after Austin married Wilma's younger sister, Alicia. Following Alicia's death, Austin inherited her stock in the hotel chain. But it was only when Wilma badgered him into leaving the real estate business and assuming Alicia's responsibilities at the Jasmine Hillcrest that his life changed radically yet again.

Austin loved hotel work, something he hadn't expected. Wilma loved having him there, as well. His trusted presence gave her time off to help her husband. Austin also benefitted from the partnership. He had time to pursue his real passion, which was his horse farm, an endeavor both James and Wilma had encouraged and still did.

Not only was he lucky on that score, he had another project pending that Wilma approved of. He was in the process of finalizing a deal that involved buying a piece of prime land in New Orleans. Austin's plans were eventually to tear down the building that was already there and replace it with a new one.

Suddenly Bluebonnet shook her mane again, jarring him back to the moment at hand. Back to Cassie, dammit.

Why had she come home without warning? What had she been doing all those years while on the run from that bastard she'd married? James wouldn't—or couldn't—talk about the subject. Austin suspected it was too painful or too embarrassing, or both. And he'd never felt comfortable pressing James for that information.

Austin didn't realize he was no longer alone until he heard Robb's gruff voice, seeming to come out of nowhere.

"You're gonna be pissed," his trainer said from atop his horse."

"It's the hotel," Austin said flatly.

"You got it."

"Tell my secretary to call Wilma."

"She already did, and Mrs. Wortham's not feeling well."

Concern for Wilma took precedence over his own selfishness. "I'm on my way."

By the time Austin showered, changed clothes and headed his car toward town, the cobwebs had cleared and he was back on track. Cassie and her son wouldn't stay long. His gut instinct told him that. He had simply made a mountain out of a molehill. In a few more days she would be gone, and he would have weathered yet another storm.

For the moment, that was enough.

Seven

"How come we don't have sex anymore?"

Wilma knew she had shocked her husband even before he swung around and confronted her, his eyes narrowed behind his glasses.

"I don't—" His voice failed, as if he didn't know how to respond.

She couldn't disregard his face, either; it was flushed, clearly reflecting his revulsion at being put on the spot with such a question.

"Oh for pity's sake, James, stop acting like you're as pure as the day you were born."

The veins in his neck stood out. "That doesn't deserve an answer."

Wilma shrugged innocently. "I don't know why not."

"You do know," he said in an irritated tone.

Before they married, she had known he was on the reserved and prudish side. Surprisingly though, he'd turned out to be a better than average lover. But after Cassie had been born and he'd been called to the ministry, his studies and preparation toward that goal had taken precedence over everything else, except Cassie.

She herself had gotten a fair amount of his attention. When he became a full-fledged pastor, however, and his church began to grow in attendance, along with his stature in the community, it seemed as if he had suddenly become saintly.

Sex had been the first thing to go.

But that no longer mattered to her. Some perverse side of her had just wanted to shake him up, shake him out of that pious shell he'd erected between them.

Maybe her illness had dried her up inside as well as out, making her cruel. Or maybe it was because her life had ceased to mean anything since her heart had decided to go haywire.

"You knew how I was when you married me. I haven't changed."

"Wrong," Wilma corrected from the bed, where she was propped against a pile of pillows. "You *have* changed. When we married, you contributed your share to this marriage."

"Wilma, this is not a conversation I'm interested in having."

"Oh, really? I never would have guessed." Her voice was filled with unvarnished sarcasm.

"Sex is the last thing that should be on your mind," he added red-faced. "You're ill and shouldn't exert yourself unnecessarily."

She ignored that and added more fuel to the already simmering fire. "When did I lose you to the cause? When did you become so dedicated to your work that you forgot how to be human?"

"That's not humorous in the least."

"I didn't mean it to be."

"So where is this conversation going?"

"I'm not sure. After all, you still haven't answered my question," Wilma pressed, unsure why. She had no desire to make love to her husband. The truth was that he no longer turned her on. Apparently she no longer turned him on, either.

But to the outside world peeping in, they were the ideal couple. If her friends and his congregation only knew, they would have a gossiping field day.

"I know what's wrong with you," James said.

He remained standing in front of the chest of drawers in their massive bedroom, which was filled with some of the most priceless antiques money could buy. A lot of good that did her, she thought. She rarely got to show her treasures off. As a preacher's wife, her standards were expected to be on a higher plane, which didn't include boasting about money or things.

Wilma frowned at James's back when he turned and opened a drawer. He didn't have anything on but an undershirt and boxer shorts. Her gaze dropped to his legs, which were as white as snow and as thin as toothpicks.

She almost laughed out loud, wondering how they could hold him up, even though he certainly wasn't overweight. He was much too vain to eat anything that might make him gain a pound. Why had she ever married a preacher?

She hadn't enjoyed one day of that life-style. What she wished more than anything right now was for a fried pie and a cigarette.

Would James have a conniption fit if he knew that? For a second, she was tempted to tell him. But what good would it do? None. She couldn't put her money where her mouth was, so to speak. If she did, she would be signing her death warrant for sure. While she might be gravely ill, she wasn't ready to be put underground just yet.

There was still fire in her belly, and as long she was breathing, she had hope.

"Wilma, did you hear what I said?"

"No."

"I said, I know what's wrong with you. Having Cassie appear on our doorstep was a shock."

This time Wilma didn't have a comeback. Perhaps that *was* what was behind her sudden agitation, making her want to strike out at something or someone. In so many ways, Cassie had been a disappointment.

But disappointment or not, Cassie had returned, a fact they both had to deal with. Wilma masked a sigh, wishing she and her daughter had been closer. That had been her fault, not Cassie's.

Her own mother, Elizabeth, had been cold and had kept her at arm's length, fearful of showing any emotion. More than that, her mother had been conscious of family money and the responsibility she felt it carried. The Hillcrests were to set an example, and if that meant keeping their emotions buried, then so be it.

Early on, Wilma had rebelled, had become her parents' wild child. Behind their back she had drunk, danced and smoked—all forbidden in their household. Once she had married and become a woman, she'd been trapped by the image of what she was expected to be, not what she actually was.

Somewhere over the years, the former had won, and she had become as stuffy and standoffish as her husband, who had also come from a strict religious background.

Because of those flaws, it had been difficult for her to show real affection to Cassie, something she regretted. And she feared it was too late to rectify that now, considering how Cassie's life had taken such a dramatic and traumatic turn.

"Wilma, I'm talking to you!"

He had turned back around and was looking at her through irritated eyes. "Okay, you're right," she said at last. "I was shocked."

"Then finding out our son-in-law is behind bars was a double shock."

"Ex-son-in-law," Wilma pointed out.

James didn't respond verbally, but he didn't have to for her to know what he was thinking. His shoulders tensed again, and his face reflected more frustration.

"You might as well accept the fact that their marriage is over," she said.

"I won't ever accept that. I don't believe in divorce."

"No matter. That one's a done deal."

"Well, done deals have been known to undo."

"Don't start trying to play God with Cassie."

"And don't you tell me how to treat my daughter." James's tone was hostile.

Wilma ignored that hostility. He hadn't ever been able to intimidate her and, sick or not, she wasn't about to let him start now. "Someone needs to tell you."

"If only she had tried harder, seen a counselor like I begged her to, she and Lester and Tyler would still be a family."

Wilma blew out a breath. "Give it a rest, James. We've hashed this over too many times as it is." She paused. "Besides, it's really your own pride you're worried about. Now that she's back, questions you can't answer will start all over again."

"That's right," he said tersely. "And for a minister, that's an unacceptable position to be in."

"If you press her, she'll leave, and we might never see her again."

He ground his lips together.

"Is that what you want?" she demanded into the silence. "Remember, if she goes, Tyler goes with her."

"I know," he said, a slight quaver in his voice now.

"So I'd advise you to bite your tongue when it comes to Lester."

James balled his hands into fists. "I just wish I knew exactly what sent her over the edge, what made her take their child and stay gone for five years. Perhaps, if I knew that, I could let it go."

"Maybe in time she'll give us all the details."

"And maybe she won't."

They were both silent for a long moment, lost in their own tormented thoughts.

James was the first to break that silence. "Do you think she'll stay and take your place at the hotel?"

"Only if you listen to me and don't harp on her and Lester getting back together."

James's shoulders bowed. "I don't need you to tell me how to conduct myself."

"See, there you are, back on that high horse. Well, get your ass down."

"Wilma, I won't tolerate your talking—"

"Oh, shut up, James."

He didn't say another word, but Wilma knew he'd had to bite his tongue to keep from lashing back at her. Another bout of color flooded his face before he stomped into the closet.

She didn't see him again until he was fully dressed in a suit and tie. Instantly, Wilma felt his eyes tour her body, though his thoughts were once again hidden behind a calm demeanor. "I'm going to the church."

"Are you taking Tyler with you again today?" Wilma asked, suddenly feeling too tired to move. She'd already had far too much upheaval for one day.

"If he wants to go." James's features were back to normal. "I want so much to get to know my grandson again."

"Me too. And my daughter."

James tilted his head to one side, then stared at her for a long moment, a muscle ticking in his cleanly shaven jaw. "Do you think she can work with Austin?"

"Of course. Why not?"

"They're both headstrong."

"I'm headstrong," Wilma said, "and he works with me just fine."

James paused. "If Cassie refuses to take you up on your offer, are you prepared to tell her the truth concerning your heart?"

Eight

Cassie surveyed her surroundings. She had opted to have her coffee on the veranda, seated at a table accented by two bistro chairs refinished to match the whitewashed chandelier above.

Lifting her bangs, she wiped the perspiration off her forehead. Already it was too sultry to breathe. Perhaps she should have let Joy fix her some iced coffee instead of her strong, hot variety. Oh well, the climate was the least of her worries. In time she would adjust to that.

Suddenly Cassie's heart lurched. Unfortunately, she wouldn't have the luxury of waiting on time. Hers had run out. Again.

Cassie thought she heard footsteps, thankful for the intrusion into her morbid thoughts. Twisting around, she could see the sweeping turn of the stairway that gave a simple but elegant flair to the dining room.

Her daddy was on the last step. She watched as he paused and seemed to glance her way. If he saw her, however, he chose to ignore her, which further bruised her heart. She was the once perfect daughter who had fallen from grace and was now tainted.

Cassie fought back the tears as she turned and forced herself to take another sip of coffee. Moments later, she heard more noise, followed by a voice. She smiled.

"Hiya, Mom."

She faced her son and gave him a hug, all her problems seeming to dissolve. "Good morning, darling. I figured you'd sleep in."

"Papa woke me up."

Cassie raised her eyebrows. "Oh?"

"He wants me to go to work with him again."

"How 'bout something to eat?"

Tyler patted his knapsack. "Joy packed me some stuff."

"Figures," Cassie said ruefully.

"Why don't you come with us this time?"

"Nah, you need to be alone with your papa."

Tyler's eyes glowed. "Papa said we might go to the zoo."

"That gets my vote. Meanwhile, I hope his flock doesn't get short shrifted."

"What does that mean?" Tyler asked, shoving his baseball cap back on his head.

Cassie flicked him on the chin. "Papa's not supposed to cater to you. He has his weekly sermon to work on, in addition to visiting the sick and afflicted."

When Tyler gave her another one of "those" looks, Cassie righted his baseball cap, then gave him a soft tap on the rear. "Never mind, kiddo. Just go and have a good time. I'll see you later."

"Okay."

"You've done a fine job with that boy, Ms. Cassie."

"Thank you, Joy," Cassie said, watching as Joy refilled her cup. Her eyes misted. "He's the joy of my life."

"Are you ready for some breakfast?" Joy asked. "You look like you could use some of my cooking, for sure."

"Don't start, please. I'll stick to coffee."

"If you ask me, you need something to stick to those scrawny ribs," Joy mumbled to herself as she turned and shuffled back to the kitchen.

"I heard that," Cassie said, a hint of laughter in her voice.

Once she was alone again, that laughter ceased, and a sadness took its place. Everything inside her rebelled at the thought of leaving. She wasn't referring just to this house, either. She hated to leave Jasmine, period.

But what choice did she have? None. Although she hadn't seen Austin again, she knew she would. It was only a matter of time until he arrived unexpectedly, catching her unaware. Just the thought gave her the trembles. And the thought of working with him in the hotel on a day-to-day basis—well, that was not even an option.

A fresh sense of bitterness filled her. If it hadn't been for him, she and Tyler could find a house or an apartment and begin their new life here, giving Tyler the opportunity to enjoy his grandparents. More important, he would have a sense of roots, something he hadn't had and something she desperately wanted for him. And for herself. She was tired of running.

Damn Austin.

"My, but you look almost green."

Cassie swung around at the sound of Wilma's voice and forcibly blanketed her features. Her mother didn't have bragging rights. She didn't look well herself. Instead of green, her skin was yellow.

"Morning, Mamma."

She hadn't called Wilma that in a long time, not since she'd married Lester. Wilma didn't seem to take offense. Maybe that was because Joy chose that moment to appear once again, this time with her mother's breakfast, which Wilma proceeded to shove aside, opting for coffee.

"You should eat," Cassie said with a frown.

"So should you."

Cassie shrugged. "Okay, I'll be quiet."

Wilma didn't say anything for a long moment, then she asked, "Are you enjoying being home?"

"Of course, Mamma. You shouldn't have to ask."

"I was hoping you'd say that."

Another moment of silence ensued, this time an awkward one. Something was wrong with Wilma other than not feeling up to par. Cassie couldn't pinpoint what it was, nor would her mother be likely to enlighten her. But she had seen Wilma in this pensive mood before. Only after she'd married herself did it dawn on her that her mother didn't seem happy, that maybe she regretted her life. Regretted marrying James, to be more specific.

Still, her parents had remained together, through the good and the bad. That was something she couldn't say for herself.

"So, have you given any more thought to my proposition?"

"Of course I have, Mamma." Cassie felt awful, and for the first time experienced real regret at having to disappoint her mother.

It seemed she'd spent most of her life trying to get back at Wilma for keeping her only child at arm's length. Now that seemed like such wasted effort.

"I can't tell you how much I'm looking forward to having you do this for me."

"Mamma—"

"I love the Jasmine Hillcrest," Wilma continued. "If it hadn't been for my work, I don't think I could've—"

"Stayed with Daddy?" Cassie added, her voice soft and pain-filled.

Wilma's pale face suddenly flushed. "Yes. I wasn't aware my feelings were so obvious."

"They're not. It's just, since I've been through my own ordeal, I'm much more sensitive."

"Don't get me wrong, Cassie, I love your father, but let's face it, I was never cut out to be a minister's wife."

"A minute ago I was thinking along those same lines."

"However, in defense of myself, I stuck it out." Wilma's strong chin jutted slightly. "Besides, divorce was never an option."

Cassie didn't so much as flinch. She looked her mother directly in the eyes. "I'm grateful *I* had that option."

Wilma's sigh was visible. "From what you've told us, it appears you did the right thing."

Cassie's laugh had a hollow ring. "Appears. That's a poor choice of words. How much plainer can it be? The slimeball's in prison. Shouldn't that tell you I *absolutely* did the right thing?"

"Despite what you think, I'm on your side." Wilma paused. "But your father..."

"Will never be," Cassie finished for her.

"Right. He clings to the idea that you, Lester and Tyler will become a family again one day."

"Not in this lifetime," Cassie retorted, her eyes sparking. "If I had my way, Lester would be dead."

"Cassie, that's a horrible thing to say about your child's father."

Cassie turned her face toward the grounds and noticed how the earth seemed to literally burst open with color. That sight could always tame the wildest beast in her. But not today. Any time she thought about Lester or heard his name spoken, it enraged her.

"Cassie, I'm sorry, I didn't mean to open up old wounds."

"Lester won't see the light of day for a very long time." Cassie's tone was brutal. "Daddy might as well join the real world and face facts."

"Look, let's change the subject, shall we? My intention was not to upset you but rather to discuss your duties at the hotel."

"Mother, I can't."

"Can't what?"

"Stay and assume your place at the Hillcrest."

Wilma gave her an incredulous stare. "But why not? You don't have another job lined up, do you?"

"No."

"If it's a place to live, that's not a problem, either."

Cassie heard the desperate note in her mother's voice, which made her feel more like a dirty rat than ever.

"Of course we don't expect you to live here, although that would be fine, too."

"Mother, stop, please."

Wilma opened her mouth, only to snap it shut.

"First, I'm not sure I could ever fill your shoes there."

Wilma flapped her hand. "That's nonsense. You're a highly intelligent woman."

"I know that," Cassie responded with patience. "And I've done some hotel work while I was away, but not to the extent you're talking about."

"You can learn."

"Too, I don't think Austin would like it."

"Oh, for heaven's sake, child, that should be the least of your worries. Why, he adores you. You've always been like a sister to him."

Sister! Oh God, Cassie thought, her stomach revolting.

"In fact, he'll be thrilled. Since I've been ill, he's had to carry the full load of all the hotels. And with his horse farm to tend to, he's going in too many directions."

"Even so—"

"I refuse to take no for an answer."

Cassie swallowed with difficulty, then spoke with the bluntness she hoped would kill the topic once and for all. "Well, you're going to have to."

Anger pinched Wilma's features.

Oh dear, Cassie thought. Her mother wasn't used to having anyone tell her no. That aside, Cassie hated what she was doing, because she wanted to stay. Operating the hotel for her mother would be a godsend, something she would have loved to do.

But the risk factor was too great, for both her and Tyler.

"There isn't anything I can say that will make you change your mind?"

"No."

Wilma didn't respond for the longest time. Cassie was as much at a loss for words as her mother. What now? she wondered. Would Wilma send her packing today out of spite? Probably, but then, she had plans to go anyway, so she might as well hit the road, something that was all too familiar.

"Cassie?"

She shook her head. "Ma'am?"

"I'm dying."

Nine

"Shit, man, you look like you just found a bug in your food."

Lester Sullivan hissed an expletive into the prison phone, hopefully stinging the ear of Spider Hayes, a fellow militiaman with whom he'd been talking for several minutes.

"You would, too, if you were the one on this side of the glass," Lester said, looking around to make sure no guard was within hearing distance.

It wouldn't look good for them to see him upset. He had to walk the walk and talk the talk if he wanted to have a chance of getting out of this hellhole. Since he'd been incarcerated, he had been a model prisoner, though it had nearly killed him to keep his rage boxed in.

Even now, he wanted to explode, rip the table and chairs around him into bits and pieces with his bare hands.

"Hey, man, take it easy," Spider said, as if he could read Lester's thought. "Things are gonna be all right. You'll see."

"That's easy for you to say," Lester lashed back. "Your ass is free to walk the streets."

"Yours will be, too, in no time at all," Spider assured him in a cold tone, while fingering a long scar on his left cheekbone.

Lester gripped the receiver, swallowing another expletive. "So how *are* things on the outside?"

"We're making progress every day, gaining new members."

"That's good, real good," Lester said, feeling his hate festering that much more for what he was missing.

"We sure as hell miss you, though. Things just don't run as smoothly without you." Spider paused, then lowered his voice as if he, too, were paranoid. "How you planning on gittin' out of here?"

"My parents and my attorney are handling that."

"I know you've appealed."

"Ah, that shit takes too long. We're working another angle, one that damn well better pan out."

"If it's money you need, Mike said we'll do our part."

"Thanks," Lester said. "At this point, I'm not sure what it's going to take to spring me."

"Is there anything at all we can do for you?"

Lester's eyes turned into cold slits. "Yep, there sure as hell is."

"Anything. You just name it."

Lester's features turned stonelike. "Okay, listen up, then don't fuck up."

Cassie loved to visit with Jo Nell Benson. There was something special about her impulsive but loyal friend. Her small home had its own special charm, too. It was warm and inviting.

Since Cassie had last seen Jo Nell, neither she nor her house had changed. For that, Cassie was most grateful and relieved. She needed Jo Nell and her stability now as much as she'd ever needed her. But then, she had always been there for Jo Nell, so their friendship had never been one-sided.

Jo Nell, who owned and operated a successful beauty salon, had gone through an abusive and nasty divorce during the time of Cassie's marriage to Lester. Though they had lived apart in distance, they had spent countless hours on the phone sharing their pain and heartache. Cassie had been the one who had loaned Jo Nell the money to leave her husband and start her business. Jo Nell had long ago paid back the money, but she had never taken Cassie's favor for granted.

Now, as Cassie watched her friend finish preparing dinner in her bright, cheerful kitchen, she couldn't help but feel a stab of envy. Maybe one day she and Tyler would have a place of their own, just the two of them.

"Care to share?"

Cassie blinked, then smiled at Jo Nell, who had stopped what she was doing and was staring at her. For a moment Cassie stared back, thinking how little her friend had changed during the intervening years.

Jo Nell was still as pretty and slender as ever, which seemed to add to her height of five foot ten. Cassie had encouraged her to become a model, thinking she would be perfect, with her dark brown hair, sparkling brown eyes and beautiful teeth.

Unfortunately, that had never come about, because Jo Nell had gotten married and barely managed to survive, much less pursue a high-profile career. Besides, Jo Nell wasn't bent that way. She had declared she was too outspoken and opinionated to work with a bunch of weirdos.

"Something's sure cooking inside your head, girl," Jo Nell said at length. "You haven't said ten words since you got here."

Cassie smiled. "For one thing, I haven't been here very long, and for another, we've been too busy hugging each other to talk."

"I can't argue that, and it felt damn good, too, even though I felt like I was squeezing a bag of bones."

Cassie laughed outright. "How did I ever make it without your big, sassy mouth?"

"Since you mentioned it, how did you?"

Cassie quirked one eyebrow.

"Just kidding," Jo said, chuckling.

"I missed you terribly," Cassie admitted. "Talking by phone only made me more homesick for you."

"Me too. And speaking of sassy mouths, you used to have one yourself."

"I used to have a lot that I don't have anymore," Cassie said in a forlorn tone.

"Mmm, I bet that sharp edge is there somewhere. It's probably buried underneath all that baggage you're still lugging."

They were both quiet while Jo Nell filled two plates with chicken and spaghetti. A basket of bread and a bowl of mixed green salad were already on the table.

"I hope you made peach cobbler," Cassie said, as Jo Nell joined her at the table. Joy's cobbler was excellent, but Jo Nell's was outstanding.

"You got it. It's in the oven, just waiting for us."

"Good girl."

During the meal, they kept their chatter meaningless and in high spirits. Cassie was thoroughly entertained with incidents that had taken place at the beauty salon, a hotbed of gossip in any town, large or small.

By the time Cassie had cleaned her plate and eaten her dessert, her stomach ached from laughing so hard. Jo Nell had insisted they leave the kitchen for her to deal with later. Knowing it wouldn't do any good to argue with her stubborn friend, Cassie had given in.

Now they were in the living room, on the sofa with their feet curled under them, coffee in hand. But the laughter they had shared was no longer in evidence. The room seemed suddenly haunted by burdens almost too heavy to share.

"So spill your guts," Jo Nell demanded, staring at Cassie from over the rim of her cup.

"I'm not sure I have any left to spill," Cassie responded, uncurling her legs and hugging her knees to her chest, then resting her chin on them.

"First off, what are your plans?"

"Believe it or not, I didn't have any. I'd just hoped to kick back for a while and enjoy being home and being free."

"Only Austin changed that, right?"

Cassie nodded, her throat constricting.

"I'm sorry."

"Me too, especially as Mother asked me to stay and take her place at the hotel."

"You mean run it?"

"Yep, with no strings attached, or so she said."

"Only we both know better. There's a long string— Austin."

"That's why I told her I couldn't do it."

"Surely you didn't mention that *he* was the reason?"

"In a roundabout way. I told Mother that he might not want to work with me."

Jo Nell rustled a hand through her long hair, mussing it even more. "Bet she just pooh-poohed that off."

"Actually, she said he'd be delighted to work with me, that he'd always thought of me as a sister."

Jo Nell coughed suddenly, spewing coffee over the entire front of her T-shirt.

"Jeez!" Cassie cried, watching as Jo Nell grabbed a tissue off the table beside her and mopped at the stains.

"Couldn't help it." Jo Nell laughed. "*Sister!* Good Lord!"

"It's not funny, damn you."

"You're right, it's not. But you have to laugh or you'd cry." Jo Nell angled her head. "So what did you say?"

"I told her no, of course."

"Smart girl. Oh, don't get me wrong. I'd love to have you stay in Jasmine. Man, would we ever have fun now that lowlife Lester is behind bars, hopefully until he's too old to pick up a gun."

"So do I, but I'm afraid that will never happen. I'm just praying for enough time for Tyler to get over the trauma he's suffered and for me to get my life back on track."

"I'd say you have that and much more."

"I think so, too."

"So where are you going?" Jo asked.

"Nowhere."

Jo Nell blinked. "Excuse me?"

Cassie lurched off the couch and began pacing the floor.

"Cass, what the hell's going on?"

Cassie stopped, feeling her chin quiver. "When I told Mother I couldn't stay, she dropped a bombshell in my lap."

"And that was?"

"She's dying, Jo."

"That can't be."

Cassie paused and looked into her friend's pale face.

"The arteries leading to Mother's heart are in such bad shape she can't have surgery, which means she could go anytime."

Jo Nell got up and hugged Cassie again, then pushed her away to arm's length. "It also means that she could outlive you. My grandmother had practically the same thing, and she lived to be eighty-five."

"Somehow, I don't think Mother will be so lucky. She's so thin and frail, and now that she can't work, I'm afraid she'll go downhill that much quicker."

"I doubt that, though I do agree it's probably best for her to stay away from the hotel and its day-to-day pressures. But for heaven's sake, you should, too."

"I know, I know." Cassie's tone was bleak. "But how can I just walk out and leave her?"

"Austin's already doing most of the work. He'll just have to suck it up and continue."

Cassie trudged back to the sofa and plopped down on it. "I just wish Austin had moved on when Alicia died, or else stayed in the real estate business."

"Yeah, that would've been nice."

"I'm still reeling from the fact that he seems to breeze in and out of Mother and Daddy's house like he lives there."

"So what about Austin, *really?* I'm dying to know what happened when you saw him."

"Nothing."

Jo Nell snorted. "I don't buy that for a minute."

"Okay, so seeing him again knocked the props out from under me. Honest to Pete, Jo, I didn't know what to do." Cassie's mouth flattened. "For a second, I couldn't get my breath."

"I don't doubt it," Jo Nell responded. "So how did you feel?"

Cassie gave her a puzzled look. "I just told you."

"You know what I mean."

"No, I don't," Cassie said tartly, hoping Jo would get the message that she was treading on forbidden territory.

She didn't.

"I'll spell it out, then," Jo hammered on. "Was the sizzle still there?"

Cassie's eyes flared. "There was never any sizzle to start with."

"That's another crock, and you know it. There must have been something between you for y'all to get it on and make a baby."

Cassie turned scalding red. "As I look back on that evening and relive what I did, I still can't believe it happened. I must've been out of my mind."

"Since I had the pukes and wasn't there, I wouldn't know. Maybe if I had been, you wouldn't have gone off the deep end."

Cassie's eyes were glazed. "I still shudder when I think of how long afterward I lived in dread of Daddy finding out what I'd done. Even though I was mostly to blame, he would've killed Austin."

"You have to admit, what Austin did was the ultimate betrayal of a friendship. Why, that's fodder for a novel. Your daddy's thirty-two-year-old best friend has a quickie with his eighteen-year-old daughter and knocks her up. Yeah, I'd say that's pretty ball-busting stuff."

"You have such a way with words," Cassie bit out.

Jo Nell spread her hands. "Hey, I'm just rehashing the facts, though maybe in a more colorful way."

Cassie released a deep sigh. "You're exactly right. It was horrible then, and it's horrible now."

"Since it's a done deal, what you have to decide is if you can be around Austin and handle it, for your sake and Tyler's."

"Austin means nothing to me."

Jo Nell cut her a sharp glance. "You sure about that?"

"Yes, dammit, I'm sure."

"Okay, okay, but methinks you protest too much."

"Well, me, meaning you, can go to hell."

Jo Nell laughed, shaking her head.

"Don't you see, Jo? I have to try to make it work." Cassie heard the plea for understanding in her voice— or maybe it was vindication—whichever, she couldn't control it. "I just couldn't say no to Mother, not after all I've put them through, though I blame them for part of it, too."

"What a freakin' mess."

"Which could get worse," Cassie added, a tremor in her voice.

"What it could do is let the wildcat out of the sack, and that wildcat who can scratch a lot of people."

"Dammit, Jo, I don't need more gloom and doom from you."

"But it's the truth, Cass, and you have to face what you're up against, what bloody well may happen if you stay here."

"I swear that Austin will never know the truth."

"What if he does? What if he finds out that Tyler's his son?"

Cassie felt her stomach turn a somersault, and she couldn't say anything.

Jo Nell had no such problem. She was on a roll. "If the truth ever came out, it could ruin a lifelong friendship—James's and Austin's. And what about Tyler?

That poor little boy has been through the wringer, what with having to live with that creep Lester, the only daddy he's ever known, then being stigmatized by his going to the pen.''

"That's only half of it," Cassie added in a low, agonized tone.

"I can imagine, having been put through hell by a man myself. But the more serious danger is one I don't have to spell out." Jo Nell's voice was terse. "If Austin were to learn the truth, what would he do? Have you thought about that?''

"He'll never get Tyler away from me," Cassie said in a fierce tone.

"He sure as hell might try, and then where would you be? Up shit creek without the proverbial paddle, that's where. A custody battle would be something Tyler might never recover from.''

"Don't, Jo!" Cassie stopped up her ears. "Don't beat up on me anymore, please. Everything you're saying is true, but I still have to do this. And in staying, I have to have faith that no one else will ever know the truth.''

"Rest assured, my lips are sealed forever. And Tyler looks nothing like Austin. That's certainly in your favor.''

Cassie almost smiled. "Oh, but he has a lot of his ways. He's as stubborn as a mule.''

Jo Nell answered her smile. "That description fits you, too, my friend.''

"Look, I've got to go," Cassie said, glancing at the clock. "It's way late, and Tyler'll be wondering where I am.''

"Ah, he'll be all right. Stay a while longer. I'll get us some more coffee.''

"Thanks, but no thanks. I really do have to run. I'm going to the hotel tomorrow to try to get my sea legs." Cassie grabbed her purse, kissed Jo Nell on the cheek and headed for the door.

"Oh, by the way, Austin's seeing someone."

Cassie pulled up short and swung around, her eyes wide. "How do you know?"

"Heard it in the shop." Jo Nell angled her head and stared directly at Cassie. "That's good news, right?"

"Of course," Cassie said in a breathless tone. "That's the best news I've had all day."

"I'm glad you feel that way."

Shivering, Cassie walked out the door.

Ten

"Good morning, Paul."

The doorman tipped his hat. "Top of the mornin' to you, sir."

"How's the family?" Austin asked just before stepping into the hotel's revolving door.

Paul's plain features beamed. "They're good, sir. Thank you for asking."

"You give them my best," Austin said, just before the door swallowed him, then turned him loose on the other side, where he almost ran into one of the Jasmine's most frequent and contented guests. "Ah, Mrs. Gerald, you're looking great today."

She also beamed. "Why, thank you, Austin. Henry and I are about to browse the antique shops one more time." She rolled her eyes.

"Sounds like a winner. Hope you don't melt, though."

She flapped a fat hand, whose fingers were jammed with diamond rings. "Lordy, so do I. Have you ever seen it so hot?"

"No, can't say that I have."

She fanned herself with one of the old-timey fans that were provided in the rooms. "I guess we'll all survive."

"We have no choice," Austin responded with a

smile, making his way toward the elevators, his eyes missing nothing of the goings on in the lobby of this small but upscale hotel.

Great food. Great service. Great smiles. That was the Hillcrest motto, and it had paid off. Instead of talking about Wall Street, as so many of the other hotel chains were doing, he and Wilma talked customer service. Pleasing the customers started at the top, with management, and filtered down to the lowest staff member. Each had a reason for being there and a specific job to do. Austin made sure no one shirked that duty, including himself.

He had spent the night in his condo, something he rarely did since he'd become responsible for this hotel. He had a suite here, as well as a makeshift office, opting not to use Wilma's, as he expected her back soon.

Now, as he made his way into his cubbyhole and sat down, his gaze landed on the open folder on his desk. He sighed, thinking that the pending land deal in New Orleans hadn't gotten nearly the time and attention it deserved.

But then, it wasn't his responsibility to sweat the details. His friend and attorney, Randall Lunsbury, was in charge. If it hadn't been for Randall, there wouldn't be a deal.

Austin thumped his pen idly on the papers before shutting the folder. He wanted to get excited about the venture, but he wouldn't allow himself to do that yet. It was still in the raw, so to speak, and until he had a chance to visit with Randall again, he'd best contain his excitement.

At least Wilma had given her consent, which had been the first big hurdle.

Thinking of Wilma brought a frown to his face. He

was concerned about her health. She didn't look well, hadn't looked well in a long time. The fact that she hadn't been supervising the day-to-day running of the Jasmine spoke volumes.

He didn't mind the added responsibility, but coupled with the other two hotels, he was spread a bit thin. Because the Jasmine was the top-grossing hotel in the small chain, it required more attention, especially as it was beginning to show signs of physical wear that would soon have to be attended to.

With that thought in mind, Austin got up and walked to the window that overlooked a portion of the parking lot and the grounds. His gaze homed in on the latter which were green and luscious this time of the year. *Perfect* was the word that came to mind.

However, if he were to walk throughout the facility, the word *imperfect* would come to mind. Austin rubbed his chin. Clearly, he faced a dilemma. If the land deal in New Orleans materialized, then renovations on this facility would have to take a back burner.

Thank goodness he didn't have to make that decision today or anytime soon. He twisted around and eyed the folder, hoping it would lure him back to his desk. No such luck. Where he wanted to be about now was at the farm, breaking in a horse, feeling the sweat oozing from his pores, cleansing his mind and body.

Unfortunately, that was not to be, at least not until the day was over. He had other pressing business that couldn't be ignored. The manager was out ill, and the chef had resigned, which meant he had to find another one ASAP, because a huge wedding ceremony and reception were imminent.

With that in mind, Austin was about to turn away from the window when he saw her.

"Cassie."

When he realized her name had come out sounding like a sigh of longing, colorful expletives filled his mind. He didn't move, though, nor did he take his eyes off her.

She had on a pair of purple pants and a matching vest. Even from where he stood, the vibrant color of her outfit enhanced her understated beauty. Then, when she began to walk toward the back entrance, he watched as her silky, layered hair moved in rhythm with her body. She oozed a natural sexuality, more potent because she seemed totally unaware of it.

Too bad *he* wasn't.

Something happened inside him in that moment, something so powerful that he couldn't ignore it. His gut tightened, and he got hard, so hard that he felt the pressure from his zipper. That was when he jerked his eyes off her and stalked back to his desk.

Shit fire and save the matches!

What was he thinking? He wasn't. That was the problem, just like it had been the problem that evening nine years ago on the beach when he'd...

No! He'd promised himself he wouldn't travel down that path again, especially since he had finally met someone who stirred his interest. Her name was Sherry Young. She was an interior designer who was his age. Though he hadn't been seeing her long, he sensed she was interested, which made him feel good.

After Alicia's death, he had felt so empty, so depressed, the way he'd felt after his tryst with Cassie, that he couldn't imagine becoming involved with anyone ever again.

But time had healed, as promised, except for *that* evening.

"Can it, McGuire," he said aloud. Even if he wanted another taste of that forbidden apple—which he didn't, of course—it wasn't going to happen.

He just wondered how much longer Cassie would hang around town. Her presence was great for James and Wilma. For him, it was a pain in the royal ass.

He didn't like having the past dredged up and rubbed in his face. *Guilt.* Every time he looked at Cassie, that was what he felt. Ah, to hell with her, he told himself. She would be gone again soon, and he could go on with his life.

Cassie stepped into her mother's office, feeling suddenly and totally overwhelmed. Maybe part of that feeling stemmed from having noticed Austin watching her.

To hell with him. Surely he had something better to do than spy on her. Her heart thumped wildly in her chest. She had lied to Jo Nell. In spite of everything that had happened, he *did* disturb her—physically, at least—making her long for a magic she would never know or feel again. That brief time in his arms...

Tension suddenly bunched Cassie's shoulders as she switched her mind's gears. But her alternative thoughts weren't much better. She felt trapped, first by her marriage to Lester, now by the commitment to her mother. But she would thrust aside her selfish fears and insecurities and make the latter work, for Tyler, if for no other reason.

But there was another reason; *she* wanted to stay. While no doubt frightened by such a bold move, she was willing to gamble on her secret remaining just that.

When she had told Tyler they were going to stay in Jasmine, he'd let out a whoopee.

"Really, Mom?" he'd asked, his eyes sparkling and his face animated.

"I take it you like that idea?"

"That's cool. Papa said he'd take me camping and fishing."

Cassie almost choked. Fishing? Her daddy? No way. That image just didn't work for her, but what did she know? Having his grandson around might loosen James up a bit. And being around her daddy would be good for Tyler. He needed a man in his life.

No more thoughts about the family, she told herself, determined to concentrate on the task in front of her. Wilma had given her notes galore concerning her daily duties at the hotel. First thing, Cassie intended to go through those. She still had doubts that she could fill her mother's shoes, but she had made the commitment, and it was too late to renege, despite Austin's unsettling presence.

In order not to think about him, she quickly picked up a folder labeled Important, opened it and began perusing its contents.

"Good morning."

The sound of his gravelly voice, along with his unexpected presence, caused her to jump visibly. April, her mother's secretary, wasn't at her desk, which had apparently given Austin carte blanche just to walk in. Maybe he had it anyway. After all, this was as much his hotel as her mother's.

Cassie heart sank, for more reasons than one.

"Morning," she responded, hearing the breathlessness in her voice. Damn, she would have to do better than this or she would be a basket case. But how could she? He looked so in control, leaning against the doorjamb, using it as a prop for his sexy body.

For a second she was tempted to tell him to leave her alone. Not a good idea, she thought. She didn't dare let him know he bothered her.

"Sorry if I frightened you."

"You didn't," she lied.

The tension between them suddenly seemed palpable. "What's going on?" he asked.

She studied him, realizing that he wasn't as "in charge" as she had first thought. He seemed as uncomfortable around her as she was around him, which was in her favor. That meant they would avoid each other, another thing in her favor.

Yet she couldn't stop her eyes from soaking up everything about him, from his dark hair and heavy-lidded blue eyes down to his silk shirt and casual slacks. Three buttons at the neck of that shirt were unbuttoned, allowing her to see the black hair nestled at his throat.

She swallowed, stopping her gaze from traveling lower, to the zipper of his jeans and the power she knew was hidden there.

Feeling her face burn, Cassie turned away to collect herself. After clearing her throat, she looked back at him and said, "I'm working."

He pushed himself away from the door and walked closer to the desk. She smelled his cologne, which further tantalized her senses, making her angry at herself.

"That's not necessary, you know," he said, easing down on the edge of the desk.

"I wish you wouldn't do that."

"What?"

"Sit there," she said tersely.

He shrugged, then moved to a nearby tapestry chair. "So how's Wilma feeling?"

"Why don't you stop beating around the bush and ask what *I'm* doing here in Mother's office?"

"I thought I already had when I asked 'What's going on?'"

"Mother's dying, Austin, or at least that's what the doctors have told her. Did you know that?"

Austin vaulted to his feet. "Hell no."

"I thought Daddy would've told you."

"Well, he damn sure didn't." Austin turned away and rubbed the back of his neck. "It's her heart, right?"

Cassie nodded, her throat too full to speak. She hadn't as yet come to grips with the ramifications of her mother's bombshell. It was difficult to talk about, especially with Austin. But because of the hotel situation, she had no choice.

"I'm sorry," he finally said, an awkwardness in his tone. "For all of us."

"Well, she's not dead yet. And I'm holding out hope that the doctors are wrong."

"I'm with you on that."

Cassie took a deep breath. "So, to get back to your earlier question, I'm taking her place here at the hotel." There, she'd said it; she'd dropped her own grenade.

From the stunned look he gave her, it had definitely exploded. He'd had no idea, but then, how could he?

"You mean you're staying in town?"

"For now, yes."

His gaze pinned her, centered more on her breasts than on her eyes. He did that on purpose, she knew, trying to disconcert her.

A telltale flush invaded her cheeks, but she still didn't give an inch, even when he continued to challenge her.

"Do you think that's a good idea?"

"Whether it is or not isn't your call."

"I can handle this hotel. Hell, I've been doing it since Wilma got sick."

"I know, but she doesn't think that's fair."

"Fair?" He laughed an ugly laugh. "When the hell has anything in this life been fair?"

Before she could answer, he pressed his hands on her desk and leaned toward her, so quickly and so closely that the bottom dropped out of her stomach while her eyes widened. She could see every line, every angle, of his face.

For a moment their eyes locked, and she held her breath.

"Dammit," he muttered harshly before rising and turning his back on her.

Cassie finally breathed into the tense silence. "Look, I know how you feel about me."

He swung around. "You don't know the first thing about me."

"I know you blame yourself for what happened that evening," she lashed back, then wanted to cut her tongue out.

He sucked in his breath. "I see you haven't lost your razor-sharp mouth."

"Sorry, Austin," she responded in a weary voice. "I didn't mean for that to slip out."

If only she had known how hard it would be to carry on a civil conversation with him, she would have had second thoughts about confronting him.

"This isn't going to work, you know."

"I say it is."

"Maybe it would be best if you left town again."

Cassie gasped, but she still didn't flinch. "That's not going to happen. Look, what happened between us on that beach has remained our dirty little secret all these years. There's no reason why that has to change now.''

A smirk touched his lips.

"Besides," she added, "we're both grown adults now who should be able to control our emotions.''

His smirk deepened. "You really believe that shit?"

"Damn you! I don't like this situation any better than you do. But I *can* and *will* handle it.''

Austin's eyes ran up and down her body while his brows arched mockingly. "I hope the hell you know what you're doing.''

"Get out of here.''

"My pleasure.''

He turned then and stomped out the door.

Eleven

"Hey, boss, those two colts are due to be delivered tomorrow."

"'Bout damn time," Austin said to his trainer.

Robb grinned, and when he did, Austin could see a piece of tobacco lodged between his two front teeth. He averted his gaze. If there was anything about Robb that irritated him, it was his penchant for chewing tobacco, especially when he didn't keep his teeth clean. That dark, wet string looked worse than a piece of spinach.

"You want me to do anything else before I hightail it outta here?" Robb asked.

Austin shook his head. "You've earned a Saturday afternoon off. Get going."

Robb gave a careless wave. "See ya Monday."

"No, you won't. I'll be tied up all day. Call on the cell if it's an emergency."

"Will do."

Once Robb had sauntered off, Austin nudged Bluebonnet into action. He'd been at the farm all morning, mending fences along with sundry other things. Even with Robb and another part-time hand, all the work never seemed to get done.

But that was all right. Austin enjoyed doing as much of it himself as he could. It continued to be his panacea for forcing the kinks out of his body and mind. Lord knows, if he'd ever needed the latter, it was now.

He hadn't bothered to stop by the hotel this morning. Hell, if Cassie was going to take over the Jasmine, then let her run with it, sink or swim.

Of course, nothing terrible was going to happen. First, he wouldn't let anything or anyone endanger the hotel. Second, she was just a figurehead. She didn't know diddly-squat about overseeing a major hotel.

To his way of thinking, Wilma had used the hotel as a ploy to keep her daughter in town, which he could understand, her being so gravely ill. Austin flinched, thinking about Wilma and her condition. Poor James.

Ill though she might be, Wilma remained very much in charge of her faculties. He would miss her sharp mind, her ability to come up with new and innovative ideas that would keep their small, independent chain from being gobbled up by the superhotels.

Maybe Cassie had that same knack. Austin snorted. No such luck. She would just be a nuisance. Still, he understood and didn't fault Wilma.

He had a solution in mind for side-stepping the explosive situation. He would spend more time at the other hotels and at the farm. Cassie didn't want to be around him any more than he did her. She had made that quite plain yesterday.

On the surface, she had appeared as if all her emotions were intact, that she could handle anything, especially him.

Bullshit.

She wasn't as immune to him as she would like him to think. He had seen the way she reacted when his eyes dropped to her breasts, despite her display of icy hostility.

Maybe that was what had gotten into him. Maybe he'd wanted to shatter that ice around her. He couldn't deny that he was attracted to her, which was his own sexual hang-up, pure and simple.

Simple, hell! When it came to Cassie, nothing was simple. He was getting blamed for that forbidden romp in the sand when it had been her fault. Suddenly his conscience kicked him.

It hadn't been *all* her fault, not by a long shot. He had been the grown-up, the supposedly responsible party, who should have been able to call a halt instead of giving in to her sexual advances.

She had a right to despise him. But it rankled, nonetheless, when she looked at him as if he were contaminated, all the more reason why it dumbfounded him that she had agreed to stay in Jasmine.

He figured her motive was the kid. Austin felt a sudden pinch in his gut. Tyler. Nice name for a kid. He hadn't seen him yet, but he knew that was bound to change, because James had bragged that his grandson had become his shadow.

Ah, to hell with further thoughts about *her.* Too many mind games could drive a sane man nuts.

Austin kicked his horse into a canter, then felt the animal ease into a smooth gallop. Ah, this was the life, he told himself, raising his head.

Soon the sun would be swallowed by the clouds already gathering around it. He almost smiled as he watched the scene play out above. By nightfall it would more than likely be raining.

When that happened, he would go inside, take a cool shower, then weed through the chef applications he'd brought with him. Afterward, surely he would be so tired he would sleep like the dead.

He grimaced, thinking that hadn't been the case since Cassie hit town, which was why he had to get a grip on himself.

Later, long after those clouds had indeed gobbled up the sun, Austin headed back to the barn, where he fed, watered and brushed down his horse.

It was when he rounded the corner headed toward the house that he saw the car. Groaning, he stopped in his tracks. What was Sherry doing here? He hadn't invited her. Perhaps she felt she didn't need an invitation, that a surprise visit was in order.

That wasn't how he felt. Right now, she was the last person he wanted to see. Still, he trudged up the hill toward the house that at one time had been so run-down and filthy inside it had gagged him.

He'd hired a cleaning crew to come and haul off all the garbage. Following on their heels, he'd hired a carpenter to redo the kitchen and the one bathroom.

Then, out of the blue, he had met Sherry. When he learned she was an interior designer, he'd hired her on the spot to make the inside livable, keeping it simple, uncluttered and masculine.

However, it wasn't until six months later that he'd begun seeing her. To date, nothing serious had developed between them, despite her pluses. She had a well-paying job and was voluptuously attractive, not that that mattered. What did matter was that she was quiet, dependable and easy to be with. And though she had two children, they were grown and gone.

He knew that if he popped the question, she would marry him in a minute. A few days ago that thought might have appealed to him.

Thanks to Cassie, that had changed.

Frowning, he walked into the brightly lighted

kitchen, where something delicious simmered on the stove. However, his uninvited guest was nowhere in sight.

"Sherry?" he called, heading for the living room. It was as empty as the kitchen. Yet he didn't move, his gaze wandering over the beamed high ceilings back down to the stone fireplace that covered one wall.

Bookcases bordered the fireplace and were filled with books and other mementos that he'd collected over the years. The furniture also matched his taste. A burgundy leather sofa and matching chairs were the other dominant items. They were as soft, lush and inviting as they appeared.

Austin cast a longing eye in the direction of a chair, only to sigh and head for the bedroom, the only other place his guest could be, a thought that didn't set well with him.

"Sherry," he called again.

Still no answer.

What the hell was that woman up to? Austin clamped his jaws together when he strode down the hall and saw that the bedroom door was closed. Without knocking, he pushed it open.

"I'd about given you up," Sherry said in a purring voice as she stood by the bed dressed only in a thin, black negligee.

Austin stood transfixed in the doorway.

She smiled. "I thought it was past time the two of us got better acquainted." She paused, cocked her head, then smiled. "Don't you?"

Randall Lunsbury wished he could stop sweating. He couldn't; the sticky moisture trickled down his face and saturated his silk shirt. But then he had enough worries to make him sweat like a stuck pig.

"How the hell did you get this number?" he whispered into the receiver, all the while keeping an eagle eye out for his wife.

He was in the foyer of their opulent home, having been on his way into the family room when the phone rang. His mind elsewhere, he'd answered it. Thank God he had.

"I told you not to call me at home."

"I know," his latest bimbo whined, "but I haven't seen you in over a week, and you won't return my calls."

"That's because I've been busy." He wanted to add the word *bitch* to the end of the sentence, but he refrained. It wouldn't be smart to further antagonize her. The important thing was getting rid of her before Mary Jane, his wife, got wind of something foul in the air.

"Well, get unbusy. Tonight."

"Listen, you little two-bit whore—"

"Who gives you the things you want most."

"Dammit!"

"Call me."

God, did he ever need what she had to offer. She had dangled the right carrots in front of him. It was all he could do not to tear out of the house, straight to her.

If he did that now, his marriage, his career, his *life* would be in jeopardy.

He had barely replaced the receiver and was mopping his face with a handkerchief when his wife appeared in the adjacent doorway, her pretty features marred by a frown.

"What on earth was that all about?"

"It's nothing."

"Nothing? That's absurd, when you're flushed and perspiring like you have the flu. Your eyes are glazed, too."

"Maybe that's what's wrong with me," Randall lied. "Maybe I'm coming down with something."

Mary Jane's frown deepened, and her eyes went from sympathetic to suspicious. "You're not sick, Randall. You're lying."

Ignoring her last statement, he demanded, "Is dinner ready?"

"Yes."

They ate in silence in the dining room that the best designers in Lafayette had decorated. The remainder of the mansion was outfitted in the same grand manner. The bad part about it was that he was still paying for it, along with tuition for twin girls in one of the most expensive universities that money could buy.

"What's going on, Randall?" Mary Jane asked at last, laying her fork down and staring at him. "I've never seen you like this. You're wearing your nerves on the outside of your skin and have been for months now."

"I don't want to talk about it." His tone was as sullen and withdrawn as he could make it. Hopefully she would get the hint and leave him be.

She glared at him. "Is it work?" she pressed. "Has one of the other attornies pulled a boner?"

"No, dammit."

"Okay, is it the pending land deal with Austin? I know it's not going well."

Randall gave a start. "How the hell would you know that?"

"I heard you talking on the phone in your study."

He glared back at her. "Have you taken up eavesdropping between bridge games?"

"Why, you bastard," she said between clenched teeth. "What's happened to you? To us?"

Randall blew out a breath. "Look, I'm sorry. You're right, I've been under a lot of pressure lately, especially at work."

Mary Jane's features lightened. "I'm relieved your foul mood doesn't have anything to do with Austin. He's such a good friend to both of us."

"Don't you worry your pretty head about that. Everything's fine on that front."

"And our finances are still in good working order, I take it."

Randall's heart jolted. "Why do you ask?"

"Because I want to have some more work done on the house. I'm not as pleased with our bedroom as I should be."

Before he realized his intentions, Randall lunged to his feet, then threw his empty wineglass against the mirror on the back wall, shattering the Waterford into a million pieces.

The silence that followed was equally shattering.

"Have you lost your mind?" Mary Jane cried, her eyes wide and frightened as she looked at him as if he had turned into some kind of monster.

"Don't you dare spend another fucking dime on this house, you hear?"

Mary Jane's chin quivered, and tears filled her eyes. "You need help, Randall, desperately."

He knew he'd frightened her, but he didn't care. At the moment, he was barely holding body and soul together.

"You're the one who'll need help," he warned, his tone uglier than ever, "if you don't do like you're told."

Twelve

Cassie rounded the corner and came face-to-face with her daddy.

"Good morning, daughter, dear," James said in his usual uplifting manner.

"Hi, Daddy." She leaned over and brushed his cheek with her lips, then wiped a finger across that same cheek. "Oops, gotcha."

"Don't worry. It'll give the women at the church office something to gossip about."

"Why, Daddy, shame on you."

He smiled absently, as if his mind had shifted to bigger and better things. "Are you off to work?"

"Well, I'm headed in that direction," Cassie responded ruefully.

"Ah, you'll do just fine. You have your mother's talent." James paused, then added, "By the way, having you here seems to have made a marked difference in her. She's feeling much better."

"I just hope it works out, Daddy."

"It will. It's already working out."

"Are you sure you and Joy can handle Tyler while I'm at the hotel?"

He seemed taken aback. "Of course. Why, we're already a team."

"He can be a handful."

"That's what energetic boys are supposed to be. Another session of day camp will be starting soon. He'll enjoy that."

"That he will." Cassie broke into a smile "But meanwhile, don't say I didn't warn you."

"Speaking of warning," James said in a sobering tone, "I'm trying to see Lester."

Her face and lips went colorless. "No."

"Now, Cassie, don't be like that. He's still Tyler's father."

"Don't, Daddy. I don't want to hear that again. And I don't want you anywhere near that prison."

"I'm a minister, a man of God, in case you've forgotten." His tone was firm but gentle. "I'm concerned about Lester's soul."

Cassie wanted to scream, to stomp her feet. She wanted to curse, but most of all, she wanted to laugh. Soul? If Lester had ever had a soul, he had long since sold it to the devil. It wouldn't do any good to point that out to James, though. He was oblivious to what went on in the real world.

And if it made him feel better to live in his make-believe one, then so be it. However, there were limits to her patience.

"Do what you have to do, but I won't allow you to involve Tyler."

He looked as if he wanted to argue but didn't, obviously having picked up on the steel edge in her voice.

"I can live with that," James said after a moment.

Cassie released her pent-up sigh. "Just so we understand one another. Now, I'm out of here. I'll see you later."

"I'm not far behind you." James paused. "Oh, I want to thank you, too, for staying here with us."

Cassie had dickered over her living conditions once she'd conceded to remain and work in the hotel. She had considered renting an apartment or a house. But when she'd talked it over with Tyler, he had wanted to stay here, on the estate. In fact, he'd begged. She had given in, though only because the entire upstairs would be theirs.

"I don't plan to stay indefinitely, but for now, Tyler has my arm twisted behind me."

James chuckled. "Smart boy."

The heavyset but impeccably dressed manager held out his hand and smiled. "Welcome to the Jasmine Hillcrest, Mrs. Sullivan."

Cassie returned David Smithhart's smile and hand-shake. "It's Cassie."

"All right, Cassie."

"And thank you for the tour. It was an eye-opener."

And it was. She had reacquainted herself with every nook and cranny of this grand place, and it had been a real treat.

"You're right about it needing a face-lift." David angled his head, and, for a moment, his gray eyes were piercing. "Any chance of that happening?"

"If I have my way, you betcha."

David pushed his hands through his light hair. "I'm not sure how Austin feels."

"You leave him to me."

David smiled, then winked. "That'll be a pleasure."

"By the way, I'm glad you're back and feeling better," Cassie said, switching the subject.

"Lordy, me too," David drawled. "I don't know what kind of virus I had, but it knocked me to my knees."

"Well, it's good to see you upright."

He nodded, just as his pager went off.

"Go ahead, take care of business," Cassie said. "That's where I'm headed."

A few minutes later she was sitting behind her desk, trying to concentrate on business. But for some reason her mind kept wandering. She felt restless, suspecting the earlier conversation with her daddy was partly to blame.

Dammit, she didn't want to think about her sicko ex-husband. More to the point, she didn't ever want to see him again. Lester was where he deserved to be. That alone gave her the confidence to get out of bed each morning and do what she had to do. Whatever James did was on his conscience, just as long as he didn't involve her or her son.

Her gaze drifted to the window. Instead of spring fever, she had summer fever. The gorgeous day, heat and humidity aside, demanded one be outdoors, literally inhaling the scent of jasmine.

While she had lived in one place after another, the memories of her childhood home with its lovely trees and gardens had been her lifeline. At times she had even found herself longing for the beach house, envisioning herself strolling along the shoreline, listening to the pounding surf and nestling her toes in the hot sand.

But now that she had returned to Jasmine, she hadn't wanted to go back there. She knew why. She had seen Austin, and he had brought back the reality of what had taken place on that deserted stretch of sand.

Suddenly Cassie shook her head, determined not to think about *him*, not today, anyway. Her agenda was clear. She would delve into the contents of the folder that had been on her mind since she had first seen it.

Ignoring the sound of birds chirping outside the window, she opened the file and began reading. By the time she finished, the fury coursing through her made her temples pound.

"In your dreams," she muttered, slamming the file shut, then standing.

"Whoa, take it easy, okay?"

Austin tried to keep his voice as low and calm as he could. However, that was difficult, especially when a hysterical woman was on the other end of the receiver.

He had stopped by his cubbyhole at the hotel before heading out of town to check on the other two facilities. He had remained in Jasmine longer than he intended. He hated leaving his farm, but since his new colts had finally been delivered in good health, he had no excuse for staying.

Even at that, he only planned to be gone overnight. He still hadn't hired a chef for this hotel, but now that David had returned, they would put their heads together and make the decision.

At the moment, however, he had to deal with Mary Jane Lunsbury, who had just told him what had taken place between her and Randall.

"You wouldn't tell me to take it easy if you'd been on the receiving end of that fit he had." Much of the hysteria remained in her voice. "I'm lucky that glass hit the mirror instead of me."

"Sounds like more than luck was with you."

Austin sat down. The phone had rung the second he'd walked in the door, briefcase still in hand. His entire body tensed. He didn't need this shit, not now, not with Cassie's presence already taking chunks out of his gut.

On the other hand, he had no choice but to listen. Not only was this his friend's wife who had just told him some extremely disturbing news, but Randall was handling the land deal.

"I've...never seen him like that, Austin."

"From what you've told me, I haven't, either."

"Something is wrong. I feel it in my bones, but I don't know what it is or what to do about it."

"I'll talk to him. He might have had a bad day at the office, but don't get me wrong, that's no excuse for his behavior." Austin hoped to hell that was all it was. When Mary Jane had told him that it had been the mention of money that had set Randall off, Austin had flinched.

"If that's the case, then it must've been a dilly of a bad day."

"Are you going to be all right?"

"I guess so," she responded with a shudder. "Oh, did I tell you he never came back home, that he stayed out all night?"

Hysteria was rebuilding in her voice. Austin cursed silently. It wouldn't do for him to get his hands on his friend about now. He would shake the living daylights out of him.

"That's not good, either," Austin said.

"Do...do you think he's involved with another woman?"

"I hope not, Mary Jane. But I can't say for sure."

"Oh, Austin," she wailed, "what on earth am I going to do?"

"Get through this, that's what. Go talk to your pastor. Why not talk to James? He's a wonderful counselor."

"I might later, but right now, I'm too upset and confused to tell anyone else. I only told you because I think if anyone can do anything with him, it's you."

"I hope you're right. I'll be back in touch."

"Thanks, Austin."

He wanted to tell her not to thank him yet. He didn't have any idea what had set Randall off like a rocket. If it was personal with him and Mary Jane, then Austin didn't feel he had the right to interfere. However, if it was financial, then maybe he did have a right.

Then again, maybe he didn't. Randall's financial problems could be purely personal, nothing to do with their deal. And he knew for a fact that Mary Jane could spend more money faster than anyone he knew.

So much for marital bliss.

That thought made him grimace; it brought to mind the stunt Sherry had pulled the other evening. Seeing her standing in his bedroom in that flimsy negligee that showed off her large, rosy nipples and the dark hair at the apex of her thighs had sent his piss factor off the charts.

He shouldn't have been surprised or taken aback by her actions, but he was. He had known she was attracted to him, had wanted him from the get-go. The attraction had been reciprocated. Having sex with her had definitely been on his short list. So why the hell hadn't he taken what had been so generously and sincerely offered?

He hadn't known then, and he didn't know now. All he'd been able to think of was getting her dressed and out of his house. Though he had masked his coldness and used as much diplomacy as he could muster, the situation had been awkward at best.

"This wasn't a good idea, was it?" she'd asked, pulling her lower lip between her teeth to keep it from trembling, he suspected.

He had made his way deeper into the room, though not close enough to touch her. "No, it wasn't." He had kept his tone as gentle as possible.

"Do you mind telling me why?"

Her voice shook, which made him feel lower than something stuck on his boots that came from the barnyard. "I don't know."

"I see."

"I wish the hell I did," he muttered, more to himself than to her.

Sherry turned toward the bathroom, where she had apparently left her clothes.

"Uh, wait," he said.

She halted, then faced him once again, hope gleaming from her eyes and her lips parted, neither of which had a bearing on him physically. His dick remained passive.

"Look, this is not your fault."

Her shoulders sagged. "Really? Somehow, I don't find that comforting."

"I'm sorry," he said lamely.

"What's going on, Austin?"

"I told you, I don't know."

"I thought we were getting along fine."

"We were. We *are*."

Sherry's eyes were troubled. "Then what's the problem, unless you just don't want me?"

"It's not that simple, Sherry." Austin shoved a hand through his already disheveled hair.

"Is it Alicia?"

He knew exactly what she was getting at. To pretend

otherwise would be insulting. "I'm not still in love with my wife, if that's what you're asking."

She shrugged. "I guess I was. Is there anyone else? I mean…"

Suddenly and without warning, Cassie's face filled his vision. Bile filled the back of his throat, and his knees almost buckled.

"There is someone else," Sherry said in a dull tone.

"No, dammit, there's not. I'm only seeing you. All I can say is that the timing's just not right."

"Well, suppose you let me know when it is." Sherry's tone was a mixture of pain and sarcasm.

"Please, I don't want this to end our relationship."

"Jeez, Austin, you're something else. You knock a hole in my ego the size of the Grand Canyon, then you tell me you want a relationship. What kind of crazy idea is that?"

"I can't answer that."

"All right. I'll give you the benefit of the doubt." Sherry's tone hardened. "But if you ever insult me like this again, you can go straight to hell."

"I wouldn't want it any other way."

Now, after the fact, he still refused to give Cassie's presence the credit for his limp-dick syndrome. So why was he relieved that he was going out of town and wouldn't be seeing her?

Suddenly Austin felt the urge to pull a Randall and throw something. But indulging in temper tantrums was not his style. Besides, he had things to do—get on the road, then call Randall from his car phone and set up an appointment.

A few minutes later he stepped into the hall. That was when he heard the sharp voice. "Perfect. You're just the person I wanted to see."

Austin choked on every graphic swear word he knew.

Thirteen

"Aren't you afraid you'll catch my virus?"

"Virus?"

"Yeah. The way you've been avoiding me, I figured I must have something catching."

"That's not funny," Cassie responded, her mouth pinched.

"Okay, let's have it." Austin scrutinized her. "What's on your mind?"

Cassie squirmed under that scrutiny, fighting the urge to to lean across her desk and slap him clear into tomorrow. Since that was not an option, she had to pull herself together and take charge of a situation that was already teetering on the brink of exploding.

He thought this get-together was a joke, that *she* was a joke. That was the way it was when they were together, which was unfortunate. So how was she going to pull off her earlier declaration of bravado?

That feat appeared doubtful when he seemed able to look at her and through her at the same time.

Why did she sense he was thinking about their tryst on the beach? Maybe it was because that was what she was thinking about. When Austin came near her, that moment of passion, humiliation and mortification jumped to the forefront of her mind as if their coupling had just happened.

Guilt and betrayal also played a major part in her inability to look directly at him for any length of time. Unfortunately, he seemed to have no such reservations. His unrelenting gaze had not budged, except maybe to drop to her chest where her breasts moved in concert with her erratic breathing. Did he notice?

Red-faced at her own thoughts, Cassie leaned forward on the desk and propped her elbows on the high-glossed wood. "I—"

"It's not going to happen," he interrupted.

She stiffened. "I don't know what you're talking about."

"Oh, I think you do," he drawled, his slight Cajun accent emerging as it did on occasion.

She ignored what that sound did to her system and immediately jumped on the defensive. "All I know is that I called you in here to talk business."

"Could've fooled me."

"Stop it, Austin."

"You're the one who's so damn uptight, not me."

Her eyes flashed. "I'm just fine."

"Sure you are."

"Look, we have to call a truce."

"Then stop behaving like I'm going to leap across that desk and jump your goddamn bones."

Cassie gasped. "You bastard. That was a low blow."

"Maybe, but it's the truth."

"It's not the truth. Nowhere near it." Her temper flared even more.

Austin shrugged, his gaze traveling over her. "Whatever you say."

She wanted to lash back at him again, but she thought better of it. They were already too close to overstepping that line in the sand that she had drawn. She could not handle rehashing that evening in detail—not now, not ever.

Too much was at stake, beginning and ending with the well-being of her son.

"So what did you want to talk about?" he asked, sounding bored.

"This hotel."

"I'm listening."

"Make fun if you want, but I'm taking my job seriously, as Mother expects me to."

Austin sat up, and his jaw tensed. Mentioning Wilma had apparently gotten his attention, which she considered a bonus for her.

"I have no problem with that," he said.

"As long as I don't get too serious, right?" she countered, a smirk altering the line of her lips.

"I didn't say that."

"You didn't have to."

"So, you're into reading minds now, huh?"

Cassie bit back another sharp retort, determined to bring this verbal slinging match to an end. "Look, I thought we'd agreed to call a truce."

"Okay, so maybe I am underestimating you."

"That's a mistake. I can do this job."

"Suit yourself."

"You won't fight me?"

"That depends."

"On what? My stepping on your toes?"

"I didn't say that, either."

Cassie was quiet for a moment, trying to keep herself on track, to remain businesslike and professional, and not let him and his cocky attitude get the best of her. She wanted to show him that she could do everything he could do, and just as well. Only actions and time would prove her right.

"How's Wilma?"

Cassie blinked, trying to figure his angle in abruptly switching the subject. "Weak."

"Dammit, I just wish there was something more that could be done."

"Me too," Cassie said in a fragile tone.

Another silence fell between them. Austin broke it. "If there's nothing urgent, then I'm off to check on the other hotels."

"Not just yet. Actually, what I have in mind *is* urgent."

"Then let's get to it."

She heard the impatience in his voice but chose to ignore it. "I'd like to know more about the proposed land deal in New Orleans." Cassie lifted the folder and held it out to him. "This information's rather sketchy."

"That's because it's my deal."

"I disagree, especially since you made a down payment on the land with company money."

Austin lunged to his feet, seeming suddenly to tower over her, his features drawn. "It's all aboveboard. Wilma will vouch for that."

"I didn't say it wasn't."

"Then what are you getting at?"

Cassie forced herself to remain calm. "I want to be brought up to speed on what's going on, where we are with the deal."

"Now's not a good time."

His eyes were cool.

"It is for me."

"All right, Cassie." He sat back down. "We'll play it your way for now."

''Thank you.''

His lips twitched suddenly, and his eyes turned sultry.

For her own peace of mind, she ignored both. But dammit, what kind of game was he playing? ''So where's the property?''

''In New Orleans, on supposedly prime land.''

Her eyebrows rose. ''Supposedly? You mean you don't know?''

''I haven't actually seen it.''

''Why, that's the craziest thing I've ever heard. You paid out this kind of money, and you don't know what it looks like?''

''Nope, but I'm not worried. My friend and attorney, Randall Lunsbury, who lives and works in Lafayette, is spearheading the deal. But then, you know that. It's all in the folder.''

''Do you trust him?''

''Implicitly.''

''That's who you gave the money to?''

''Yes.''

Austin's tone was clipped. Cassie sensed his patience had run its course. She didn't know how much longer he was going to sit there. But she wasn't giving in or up. She wanted answers to some very important *unanswered* questions.

''Actually, a new hotel was Alicia's idea and her dream,'' he said. ''She talked about it incessantly, intending to keep the same homey atmosphere, the same values and traditions that the Hillcrest properties are known for.'' Austin paused and cleared his throat. ''Her dream became contagious.''

Austin's mention of his deceased wife threw Cassie

an unexpected curve, but she couldn't let emotions keep her from doing what she thought best.

"I want you to ask for it back."

"'It' meaning the money?"

"Yes. I'm not in favor of building."

"That's too bad."

Cassie's anger was palpable. "How dare you blow off my opinion as if it's not important? I've already told you, I'm going to do what I think is best for the company."

"Fine, but why are you so against the venture? You're a risk-taker yourself."

"Have you looked around here lately?"

"What the hell kind of question is that?"

"A good one. This hotel is falling down around our ears, Austin."

"That's an exaggeration, though I'll admit it could use a little cosmetic surgery."

Cassie laughed a mirthless laugh. "What it needs is a full-blown face-lift." She paused and eased back in her chair. "Maybe later we could build."

"Well, now," he drawled in a mocking tone, "that's mighty agreeable of you."

"Knock off the sarcasm, okay?"

"How 'bout you knocking off that superior attitude?"

Cassie's mouth thinned.

"As for the deal, it's too late to back out now. So any time you're ready to look at the land, we'll go. Meanwhile, I'll keep you posted on what's happening."

"I'm going to fight you on this."

He laughed, then stretched his legs out in front of him, looking totally in control and relaxed. "You know, I think you've finally grown up."

That unexpected comment caught her completely off guard. "Don't push it." The warning was clear in her tone.

Austin held up his hand. "I know. I know. You don't want to get personal."

"That goes without saying."

"There's something else that goes without saying. You've turned out to be a beautiful woman."

There was a husky note in his voice that made every nerve in her body tingle. He stared at her for a long moment, and without thinking, she stared back. Despite the air-conditioning being on, sweat pooled under her bra as something vital seemed to leap between them.

"Did he ever hurt you?" That husky note again.

Sudden tears burned Cassie's eyes, from anger and another emotion she didn't want to identify.

"Lester's off-limits," she snapped.

"Okay. What about Tyler? Is he off-limits, too?"

Her heart dropped somewhere around her ankles. Watch it, Cassie. Play it cool. "I guess not."

"You guess not, huh?" he muttered. "Well, that's real charitable of you."

Cassie shifted her gaze, feeling the muscles in her body grow taut.

"So tell me about him," Austin pressed.

"What do you want to know?" The stiff caution remained in her tone, but she couldn't temper it.

"When am I going to meet him, for starters?"

"As much as you're at the house, I'm sure it'll be soon."

"Ah, so you're going to stay there?"

"For now."

"I think that's wise, considering what you've been through."

"And just how do you know what I've been through?"

"Hell, Cassie, your daddy's my best friend, and I'm family, remember? Although he didn't tell me much, I know you had a nutcase for a husband who forced you into hiding all those years."

"I won't talk about that, Austin."

"I'm not asking you to."

Cassie remained silent, sucking her lower lip between her teeth. Thinking she heard his sharp intake of breath, she whipped her gaze back on him. His face told her nothing, although his next words did.

"Dammit, Cassie, you're right. We can't go on like this. Somehow we have to get over our past."

She went rigid. "I already have."

He didn't say anything for a moment. When he did, it certainly wasn't what she expected. "So take your best shot."

She frowned in confusion. "Excuse me?"

"You aren't the least bit curious about me, are you?"

Bitterness edged his words, and something else, too, perhaps a hint of pain. Whatever it was, it made her uncomfortable.

"Of course I'm interested," she finally said.

"Liar," he whispered.

Cassie's face flushed a deeper red, and she clenched her fingers into fists. "Why are you doing this?"

"What?"

"You know very well what!"

"I wish the hell I knew." His eyes were on her, generating heat.

"I know you're...seeing some—" Mortified at her carelessly spoken words, Cassie stopped short of finishing her sentence and turned away.

"Does that bother you?"

That loaded question sent her into orbit. "Of course not," she snapped. "Why should it?"

"No reason."

Unwittingly their eyes met, and a torturous tension sprang between them.

"Look," Cassie said at last, blowing out a shaky breath, "when we're together, I'd prefer we concentrate only on business."

"No problem."

Austin stood, but not before dragging his gaze over her body in what she saw as a deliberate attempt to further unnerve her.

He got what he wanted. That provocative look hit its target—her stomach and below—forcing her to feel a sensation she had hoped was long dead.

"I'm outta here," he said roughly.

And none too soon, Cassie thought, her mouth drier than powder and her head spinning.

Fourteen

He didn't know how much longer he could stand this hellhole. But he had no say-so in the matter, Lester reminded himself while standing in a corner of the exercise yard.

He had been jogging in place for thirty minutes, and though he felt slightly winded, he was in top-notch condition. If he had to, he could whip a bear with a switch. A smile almost pushed through his tight lips, but smiles weren't his forte, never had been, never would be.

What was his forte were weapons—guns of all makes and models. God, he wished he had one in his hands right now, aiming at anything moving.

Guns were the answer to this country's problems. Trust guns and not God or government. Why couldn't the millions of unconcerned idiots walking the streets see that? If America had a chance to survive as the country it was meant to be, then those who cared, such as his militia group, had to take charge.

Taking charge meant owning and—if need be—using a gun.

"Hey, Sullivan, whatcha doing, playin' with yourself?"

Bawdy, harsh laughter followed the tall, burly man's outburst. He and several others were gathered across the yard, watching Lester. Gut instinct told him they were up to no good.

Shit. He didn't want any trouble from those no-brainers. He wanted to be left alone until the day he could walk out of here, which he hoped would be soon. He didn't know how much longer he could survive, caged up for the better part of the day like the village crazy.

And while *he* wasn't crazy, those men watching him were.

"Piss off," Lester called back.

The burly guy with the big mouth and tatoos to match started toward him, only to stop midstride as if rethinking what he was about to do.

Ah, hell. Lester would love a good fight, having no doubts in his mind that he would win. Because he'd lost most of his body fat, he might appear weak and defenseless, but he was a long way from that. With nothing to do, pumping iron had become his obsession. He knew, too, that it would benefit him when he got out.

He also knew that if he got into a fight with Tiger, as the man was called by his gang, he would end up in solitary confinement for whipping Tiger's ass.

Since he'd been behind these walls, Lester had prided himself on taking the high road, becoming the model prisoner. This bastard wasn't going to goad him into doing anything stupid that might jeopardize an early release for good behavior.

Besides, Tiger, like a lot of others, was all talk and no action. The first night in Lester's cell, another prisoner blessed with the same physical attributes as Tiger had cornered him in the john and proceeded to describe what he was going to do to him.

"Yeah, Lester boy, I'm staking my claim, and you're it." He licked his fat lips. "Starting right now, you and me are going to get to know each other real well." His eyes shifted downward. "That meat on your ass belongs to me, you hear?"

Lester hadn't so much as blinked, though his heart had been racing like an engine out of control. "You might have your way with me, you bastard. But afterward, I'd advise you never to close your eyes again."

Apparently he had made an impression on that creep, and others, as well. No one had bothered him, except for now. But he wasn't afraid. The only thing that frightened him was the thought of not getting out of this place.

The thought of remaining behind these walls for his full term almost caused him to soil his underwear.

"Hey, Sullivan!"

Lester twisted around and watched as a guard came toward him. Out of the corner of his eye, he saw Tiger and his group slink off into the distance. Again, Lester almost smiled.

"Yeah?" Lester said, focusing his attention back on the husky guard called Red, who was now in front of him.

"You got some visitors."

Lester didn't say anything. He simply followed Red into the visitation area, where he found his parents, Dewitt and Charlotte, sitting on the other side of the glass partition, looking like two frightened deer staring into the headlights of a moving vehicle.

He nodded as he sat down and lifted the phone, all the while thinking how much he hated them. It was critical that they didn't know his true feelings, though, at least not until he was a free man.

"Hello, son."

His daddy's tone was so rigid that Lester thought he heard it crack.

The owner of a small but successful insurance company, Dewitt was a born talker, a take-charge kind of guy who had never quite understood his only son. Not only were they opposite in personalities, they had nothing in common.

Lester had never liked to talk. His thing was studying politics and learning about weapons. He had no desire to follow in his father's footsteps. His goal was to take back America from the gangs and the idiots in Washington, something his parents would never understand. Yet they seemed to love him and believe in him, which was certainly in his favor.

Stupid people. But necessary.

"So how are you, Dad?" Lester finally asked, trying to put Dewitt at ease. If he was going to get sprung from this joint, he needed them. At the moment it was imperative that he play the doting son game, especially with his mother present.

"As long as you're in here, I'm not so good," Dewitt said. "Neither is your mother."

Lester faced Charlotte and watched as her chin quivered; he noticed that her face seemed to have acquired more winkles.

"That's right, son," she said. "I can't bear much more of this." A shiver followed that declaration.

"Me, either," Lester exclaimed, not bothering to mask the bitterness festering inside. "Any progress on getting me out?"

"Yes, as a matter of fact, there is," Dewitt said.

"How?" Lester couldn't control his impatience.

Dewitt's eyes circled the area. Lester's impatience

grew. He gripped the receiver so hard he thought his fingers might snap.

"Your lawyer's onto something, but he'll have to tell you himself. We just had to see you and make sure you were all right."

"I'm fine," Lester lied, anger boiling inside him. "So how's my kid? Have you seen him?"

Dewitt and Charlotte looked at each other, obviously taken aback by what he'd said.

Lester's jaw clenched. "So she hasn't gotten in touch?"

"Are you talking about Cassie?" Dewitt asked.

"Yes, dammit. She's back in Jasmine."

His parents' mouths fell open. It was Dewitt who spoke. "How do you know that?"

"I have my ways. For now, let's just leave it at that."

"Maybe we'll see Tyler soon." Charlotte's voice had taken on new life. "I'm sure Cassie will call."

"She damn sure better." This time Lester forced himself to smile. "When you see my boy, give him a big hug and tell 'im his daddy loves him."

Where the hell was Randall?

Austin placed the receiver on the hook one more time, having called his friend repeatedly, but without success. Not only did he need to speak to Randall on Mary Jane's behalf, as promised, but on his own, as well. After that round with Cassie, he needed to know the status of the deal.

Even without it, he planned to go forward with the project, whether she liked it or not. However, Cassie did have a vote, Austin reminded himself, and that was what galled him.

With Wilma's support, he'd had a green light to proceed. Now Cassie was threatening to throw a monkey wrench in his plans. If only Wilma hadn't put her in charge. If only Cassie hadn't returned.

But she *had*, and he had to deal with her in more ways than one. His stomach knotted. Was she deliberately opposing him in order to get back at him? Did she somehow blame him for her rotten marriage?

As preposterous as it sounded, he couldn't rule that out. But blaming him didn't make any sense. It wasn't as if he had done the unpardonable and taken her virginity that evening. He hadn't. As for marrying Lester, no one had forced her. Hell, it had been her idea, having boasted that Lester had already proposed to her.

Besides, no one told Cassie what to do. As long as he had known her, she'd been stubborn and headstrong and had done what she damned well pleased, somehow managing to get around her parents.

Well, she wouldn't get around him. He was determined to work with her and not let her bother him. Sure, McGuire. He was lying through his perfect white teeth, and he knew it.

While Cassie had been verbally shredding his ass, she had never looked more desirable. Just thinking about her flashing eyes and jutting breasts made him want her, something that wasn't going to happen.

Why couldn't he let her and that one summer evening go?

What was done was done. He couldn't change that. What he *could* change was his out-of-control libido.

Unable to bear his thoughts or his office a minute longer, Austin charged out the door, not stopping until he was in his car. He didn't know where he was heading until he pulled into the Worthams' circular drive.

He knew for a fact that Cassie was still at the hotel,

meeting with several women's groups who wanted to use the facility for their monthly meetings.

Whether she was at home or not wouldn't have made a difference. He wanted to check on Wilma, as well as James, whom he hadn't seen in several days. Cassie's presence had altered his routine. He no longer felt comfortable just popping in when the notion hit him. Cursing, Austin braked the car and got out.

Joy answered the door and greeted him with a smile and a hug. "We've been missing you."

"I've been missing your buttermilk biscuits."

"It's your own fault."

"Who's fault is what?" James asked, suddenly rounding the corner. When he saw Austin, his face lit up, and he smiled. "It's about time you showed your mug around here."

Austin shook James's outstretched hand. "It's past time."

"Come on in. I'm in the library with Tyler. You've never had the pleasure of meeting my grandson, right?"

"Right," Austin responded in a low, uncertain tone.

James grinned. "He's a super kid."

Austin duplicated his grin. "Man, it didn't take you long to turn into the doting grandparent."

"Once you meet him, you'll see why."

"So how's Wilma?" Austin asked as they headed toward the library.

"Not good today, I'm afraid," James replied.

"Tell her I asked about her, and that I'll see her another time."

James nodded, remaining sober until they reached the room where Tyler sat on the sofa, a computer on his lap. "Tyler, I'd like you to meet a special friend of mine, Austin McGuire."

Austin watched as Tyler looked up, giving him a quick once-over before returning his attention to the computer. "Hi, Mr. McGuire."

"Call me Austin, okay?"

"Okay," Tyler said in a haphazard tone, his attention back on the screen.

James did indeed have reason to be proud of his grandson, Austin thought as he looked at the child. Tyler certainly favored Cassie, with his thin face and brown hair. His green eyes were hers, as well. As Austin watched them track the cursor, they were sparking with the same curious energy he'd seen countless times in Cassie's.

Though he looked for something of his father's genes in the boy, he found none. But then, it had been years since he'd seen Lester Sullivan. And for all he knew, Tyler might have Lester's personality. Heaven forbid if that were the case.

"You wanna play a game with me?" Tyler asked, forcing Austin's mind back on track.

"Yeah, don't mind if I do." Austin gave James a knowing look before crossing the room and sitting beside the boy.

James gave them both an indulgent smile, then said, "I'll be back shortly. I'd rather do most anything than sit at a computer."

"Aw, Papa," Tyler said with a mischievous grin.

Austin nudged Tyler's arm. "He's just afraid we'll beat him."

James chuckled. "You're right about that. Oh, before I get lost, how 'bout you two going with me to the church's annual youth campout?"

Campout? Austin couldn't imagine James participating in such a thing. But what the hell, it might be fun.

He looked at Tyler with his eyebrows raised in question. "How 'bout it, you game?"

"Can we fish, Papa?" Tyler asked, switching his gaze from Austin back to James.

"You betcha."

"Do you know how to fish, Austin?" Tyler asked.

Austin drew back and stared at him. "Are you kidding? I'm a champ at it."

Tyler giggled. "When can we go?"

"And just where are you going, young man?"

Austin whipped his head up. His vision was instantly filled with Cassie, whose loveliness robbed him of his breath for a moment. She, too, seemed to have the same problem, or else she was holding hers, looking like she'd seen a ghost. Then almost as quickly, her features changed, and she smiled at her son.

"Oh, hi, Mom," Tyler said, then added with flashing eyes, "Me and Austin are going with Papa on a campout."

Fifteen

Austin tried to get comfortable on the plush leather sofa in Randall's office. But he couldn't; he was too agitated.

He glanced at his watch and noticed that Randall was already running thirty minutes late. His secretary had let Austin into the office, assuring him that Randall had called and was on his way.

Like hell, Austin thought, his impatience mounting by the second. He didn't have time to waste like this. His desk was overloaded, and if he intended to take a few days off for that church shindig, he had to get his butt in gear.

Thinking of that outing brought a smile to Austin's lips. He couldn't believe he'd committed himself. But now that he had, he found himself looking forward to it.

Tyler was a neat kid. If his own had lived, he would someday have been doing the very same thing. Suddenly that thought was so painful, it hit like a blow to the chest.

When Austin recovered and could breathe again, his thoughts turned to Cassie, who was almost as disturbing. His features turned grimmer. While she hadn't said Tyler couldn't go, she hadn't said he could, either. She hadn't been overjoyed at the idea; that was obvious. He'd picked up on that right off.

James, on the other hand, had been oblivious to the tension in the room, assuming that the campout was a given. Austin wasn't that sure. If he hadn't been going, Tyler's participation would have been assured, but since *he* was going...

His face was bleak but set when the door suddenly opened and Randall walked in. Austin stood, and stuck out his hand, only to wish he'd remained seated as another jolt of shock hit him.

"My God, Randall, you look like shit—shit warmed over, to be exact."

Randall's dark, thick hair was mussed, and the wrinkles in his face were so deeply grooved that he appeared much older than his years. But it was the look in his gray eyes that concerned Austin. They were streaked worse than any road map he'd ever seen. A chill shot through him.

"Thanks, buddy." Randall's tone was sarcastic, but he still took Austin's hand and shook it.

"Hell, did you sleep in your clothes?" Austin pressed, wanting answers.

"What if I did?"

Randall was clearly on the defensive, which added to Austin's uneasiness. Usually his friend was impeccably dressed, smooth-tongued and aggressively charming. Today none of those adjectives applied.

"How you choose to sleep is no sweat off my balls," Austin said in a frigid tone, "unless it interferes with your ability to take care of business—my business, in particular."

Color surged into Randall's pale features, making him look feverish. Something was definitely rotten in

Denmark, and Austin decided he wasn't leaving until he knew what it was.

If Randall had fallen apart, and the land deal with him, he would have his friend's head on a platter. In turn, he suspected Cassie would have his. But right now wasn't the time to think about *her*.

"I'm okay, even if I don't look it," Randall said tersely.

"Now why don't I find that comforting?"

Without responding to Austin's caustic question, Randall made his way to the bar and helped himself to a large mug of coffee.

Austin was thankful he hadn't reached for the bottle of bourbon he kept under the counter. At least that was in Randall's favor.

"I'm glad you're here, actually," Randall said, after doctoring his coffee with cream and sugar, then returning to his desk and sitting down.

Austin poured himself a cup of coffee. "I find that hard to believe, since you've ignored my calls and messages."

Randall's color deepened, and he dropped his nose down in his cup. Austin guessed he was buying time while the wheels of his brain worked to come up with an answer. Lack of sleep had a tendency to slow everything down. He knew that from experience.

"I've been busy."

"I know, screwing around on Mary Jane."

Randall stood so quickly that coffee sloshed all over the desk. He cursed, his face going from red to purple. "That's not true."

"Liar," Austin said in a low, cold drawl.

Randall remained standing and held on to one corner

of the desk with his free hand. "Did Mary Jane call you?"

"That she did."

"Damn her. She had no right."

Austin leaned forward and placed his cup on the corner of the desk. "She had every right, especially after that stunt you pulled at dinner the other night."

"I lost control, but it won't happen again."

"It had better not."

Randall's lips thinned. "What goes on behind the closed doors of my house is none of your business."

"That's where you're wrong, friend. Not when it affects your ability to do business."

When Randall didn't respond, Austin went on. "I care about you and Mary Jane, and I'd hate to see you throw her and your marriage away." He paused, hoping his words had an impact. "And pulling stunts like breaking mirrors, then disappearing for an entire night, is tantamount to doing just that."

"You're right."

"So what's going on?"

"I *am* seeing someone else."

"Shit, Randall. I thought you were made of better stuff."

Randall glared at him. "Okay, so life's not perfect. *I'm* not perfect, but sometimes things just happen."

"That's a cop-out, and you know it."

"If Mary Jane finds out, she'll kill me."

"She'd be within her rights."

"Dammit, Austin, you're making too big a deal out of it. Men screw around on their wives every day."

"You're not just any man, and she's not just any wife. You're like family."

"I don't think I can get out of the relationship."

Austin cursed. "That doesn't make sense. Just end it. Walk off and don't go back."

"It's not that easy."

"Well, then, tell Mary Jane. At least give her the option of kicking your sorry ass out the door or putting up with your mistress."

"You can be a real bastard when you want to."

"I won't deny that," Austin replied. "And since this is personal between you and Mary Jane, I'm bowing out. I don't want to be in the middle. So I suggest you take care of it."

"In other words, you don't want my wife bending your ear."

"Like I said, I refuse to be a go-between," Austin said in a frigid tone.

"I'll take care of it." Randall rubbed his scratchy chin. "So, can we get down to our business now?"

"Gladly, since that's the main reason I'm here. What's the status of the deal? When do I sign on the dotted line?"

"Actually, I need more money."

Austin almost choked on the anger that rose up the back of his throat, which gave Randall time to add, "Things haven't gone quite as smoothly as I'd hoped."

"What the fuck does that mean?"

"I know you're upset—"

"That's putting it mildly. Why the hell would you need more money after the chunk I've already given you? I agreed to pay a certain amount up front, which is what I did. Unless the deal's done, why come back for more now?"

Randall was sweating profusely which increased Austin's fury and worry.

"Look, forget I said anything."

"Randall, don't play games with me. It's not smart."

"What are you going to do, beat the shit out of me?"

"That has occurred to me." Austin's voice and eyes were as hard as iron. "For more reasons than one."

Randall visibly blanched. "Look, just forget I said anything, okay?"

"Unless you're asking for money on a personal level?"

Randall seemed to wilt with relief. "That's what I was about to do, only you jumped the gun and didn't let me finish. So how 'bout it? Will you throw a few more dollars in the pot for personal use?"

"Sorry, no can do."

Randall let go of an expletive.

"Hell, man," Austin said, "you knock down a ton right here in this office. How could you possibly be broke?"

Randall pitched back his head and laughed a bitter laugh.

Austin frowned. "Mary Jane mentioned you exploded when she asked you about doing some more work on the house. Is that what your money woes stem from?"

"Partly. And there's not a goddamn thing wrong with the house the way it is. Mary Jane just can't stop spending. There's not enough money on this earth to keep that woman happy, or our girls. Like mother, like daughters."

"And now you've added a mistress, which takes more and bigger bucks."

"Who said she was my mistress?"

Austin snorted. "Give me a break."

Randall tensed and turned his back.

"So, is the deal still intact? That's my main concern."

"Of course it is," Randall said quickly, facing Austin once again.

"Well, it had better be. I won't take kindly to losing company money because your mind's on your dick instead of your business."

Another flush stained Randall's face. "Everything's going according to schedule, I promise."

"Good, then we'll let it go at that and end this chat on a positive note."

Randall swallowed. "Fine."

"Oh, just so you'll know where I'm coming from, Cassie's working in Wilma's place at the hotel, and she's not in favor of buying the land. In fact, she's demanding I kill the deal."

Randall's eyes took on a terrified look, which raised another red flag. Still, Austin felt he had to trust Randall until he had a concrete reason not to. Randall was having an affair, which didn't bode well for his personal integrity, but Austin certainly had no right to pass judgment or cast stones. He had his own skeletons, his affair with Cassie being the biggest of them.

"Can she stop it?" Randall asked, his eyes darting nervously around the room.

"Nope, not if there're no screwups on your part."

"Not to worry."

"I won't, then, and you don't worry about Cassie. I can handle her."

"Why is she against building a new hotel? You'd think she'd be overjoyed at the prospect."

"She wants to refurbish the Jasmine Hillcrest and hold off on building. But don't worry. Wilma's on my side." Austin paused and trapped Randall's gaze. "You didn't ask for this advice, but I'm going to give it anyway. I suggest you clean yourself up and start looking like the attorney you're supposed to be, instead of someone who slept in a garbage dump all night.''

Randall winced. ''That's a low blow.''

Austin smiled, though it never reached his eyes. ''Looks like that's your problem—too many low blow *jobs.''*

The veins stood out on Randall's neck, and Austin knew his needle had hit its mark. He didn't care. He had to do what was necessary to protect the company's interests. If that meant insulting his friend, then so be it.

''When the final papers are ready, call me.''

''That won't be for a while yet,'' Randall said to his back.

At the door Austin stopped and turned around. ''Just a reminder, counselor, it had better be your mistress who gets screwed and not me.''

Sixteen

"Have you lost your ever-loving mind?"

"Shush, Jo. Everyone's staring at us."

Following Cassie's hissed command, Jo Nell clamped her jaws shut and glanced around. Seconds later, she faced Cassie again, a telltale flush staining her cheeks.

"See, I told you so." Cassie felt her own face flame, feeling several pairs of curious eyes boring into them.

"So what?" Jo Nell said. "They don't know what we're talking about."

"Still, keep your voice down, okay?"

"Okay," Jo Nell responded, looking as if she were legitimately chastised, then she grinned.

Cassie groaned inwardly, then said, "You love getting these old biddies' dander up."

"Sure do. It's high time they had something new to gossip about. They've been chewing on and spitting out the same old garbage for months now. Hell, for years."

Cassie smiled, then shook her head for lack of anything better to do. When Jo Nell was in one of her wild moods, there wasn't much one could do except let her run.

After Jo Nell had styled her hair, they had decided to grab a bite of lunch. Because of Jo Nell's tight schedule at the salon, they had chosen a nearby coffee shop.

They had wanted to eat outside, but it was simply too hot. Too, the varmints of summer were alive and hungry. The meal had been light but just right, and, as always, Jo Nell made her smile, which was good.

"You should do that more often," Jo Nell said.

"What?" Cassie asked, purposely keeping her tone low, still noticing eyes on them.

"Smile."

"Oh," Cassie said, taken aback that Jo had read her thoughts.

"Yeah, smile. You see, it's real easy. You just flex your lips and—"

"Stop it, you nut. I know how to smile."

"Coulda fooled me." Jo Nell's features changed. "But then, you haven't had much to smile about in a long time."

"Only Tyler. If it hadn't been for him, I don't think—I know—I could not have made it through those terrible days, months and years."

"All I can say is that you're made of better stuff than me. I would've just killed the bastard and been done with it."

"May God forgive me, but I thought about that myself," Cassie admitted, her eyes darkening with remembered pain. Then she forced those dreary thoughts aside. "But at least I don't have to worry about Lester anymore."

"I hope he rots in that cell."

"That makes two of us, and I think he will."

Jo gave her an odd look. "I know there's a lot you can't tell me, but now that you're back, I'm dying to know how you pulled off your disappearance."

"The women's shelters were my biggest ally, which

you already know. Then, when we arrived in Saint Louis—''

"Ah, so that was your first stop," Jo interrupted.

"Yep. Anyhow, I learned right off about another organization called Displaced Homemakers. They offer counseling for women in crisis."

"What a windfall."

"That's an understatement. Without them, I couldn't have made it. They came up with my fake name and a fake baptismal certificate."

"You're kidding?"

"You know I'm not. And believe it or not, that document was a lifesaver more than once."

"Even so, I still don't see how you did it. What about your Social Security number? Hell, you can't do anything without that."

"I was able to get a new number under my new name. In addition, I still had some ready cash and was able to buy a new car, which made me feel more secure, especially traveling with a baby."

"And you obviously had no trouble getting jobs."

"That's right, thanks to both organizations and the fact that I was willing to gamble and tell some people along the way the truth."

"Man, what a story."

"Trust me, I wouldn't ever want to do it again. When I arrived in Saint Louis, I was a basket case—devastated and crumbling on the inside."

"I can imagine. Still, Cass, I don't know how you did it."

"It wasn't easy, but I had no choice. I couldn't let Lester get his hands on Tyler." She shuddered, then smiled. "Luckily for Tyler and me, it worked out."

Jo Nell reached over and squeezed her hand. "What an incredible story. What incredible *grit*."

"I don't know about that. I just did what I had to for my child."

"Well, you have no idea how nice it is to have you around again. I missed you terribly."

"Likewise." Cassie's eyes turned misty.

"Ah, don't go all maudlin on me."

Another wobbly smile burst through Cassie's tears. "Eat your food, it's getting cold."

For a few minutes both were quiet as they munched on chunky chicken salad and sipped hot soup. Only after they were both finished and had coffee laced with thick cream in front of them did they resume conversation.

"Boy, I sure steered us off track," Jo Nell said. "So back to my original question. Have you lost your everlovin' mind?"

"You'll notice I didn't answer."

"Well, if you want my opinion..."

"I don't," Cassie said with a deadpan expression.

Jo Nell seemed momentarily disconcerted; then she flapped her hand dramatically. "I'm going to give it anyway."

"Surprise, surprise." A smile played over Cassie's lips before disappearing. "But I want you to, actually, because I don't know what to do."

"Simple. Don't let Tyler go off with Austin."

"Are you forgetting about Daddy? He'll be there."

"In body only. I love James, you know that. But let's face it, he lives on another planet."

Cassie chuckled. "I couldn't agree more, but Tyler will be with the other kids. I'm not sure he'll even give Austin the time of day."

"Still, it's risky."

"I know," Cassie wailed. "That's why my nerves are shot. But if I protest too much, that will raise a red flag in front of my parents and Austin, which might raise questions." Cassie paused. "So you see, I don't have any choice but to let Tyler go."

"What if Tyler has a birthmark?" Jo Nell asked abruptly.

"He doesn't."

"What if he has an expression or some special gesture like Austin's mother had? Something, sweet pea, that *you* wouldn't know about. Only Austin."

For a second Cassie's confidence bottomed out. "Jo, don't do this to me."

Jo Nell lifted her shoulders in a careless shrug. "Maybe you want Austin to find out."

Cassie's mouth fell open. "Have you lost *your* ever-lovin' mind?"

"Just making sure."

"Sometimes, Jo, I'd like to box your ears."

Jo grinned. "Goes with the territory. What can I say?"

"How 'bout nothing?"

"Then who'd keep you on the straight and narrow?"

Cassie had to smile. "Okay, you've made your point."

"Do you think Austin has an inkling?"

"No, and I don't think he will." Cassie paused again. "Although, I have to say, when I saw them side by side on the sofa, heads together, playing that computer game, I almost dropped dead."

"I bet you did."

"But then I got control of myself and scrutinized Austin closely for some kind of sign that he might be suspicious. There was nothing." She was the one with something to hide. The thought of a boy and his father, who would never get to know one another, filled her with a deep sadness.

"Then it looks like you might be home free."

"I wish I could be that sure."

Jo Nell rolled her eyes. "Then we're back to square one. Girl, I'd rather untangle a barbed wire fence than your thoughts."

Cassie leaned forward with a frown. "I'm just scared and confused down to the bone."

"Ah, I get it now. You're worried about yourself."

"That's not true." Cassie heard the defensive tone in her voice and knew that Jo had, too.

"Tut-tut. You're telling a big white lie, as sure as I'm sitting here."

Cassie's mouth tightened, then relaxed as she sipped her coffee. "Okay," she said after a moment. "I'll admit this whole thing makes me crazy."

"Then just say he can't go." Jo Nell's tone clearly showed her exasperation.

"Oh, Jo, he's a little boy who's already had more upheaval and heartache than most kids will have in a lifetime. He really wants to go. And Daddy wants him to go just as badly."

"Then let him go and stop worrying."

"I'm a royal pain in the ass, aren't I?"

"Yep."

"Don't be so smug. Your time's coming. When you're in the middle of one of your flings, you'll expect my undivided attention and advice."

"You got it."

Cassie giggled, and it felt damn good.

"One more quick question," Jo Nell said. "Then I

gotta run. Old lady Bullock's getting the works this afternoon. Talk about a pain in the ass, now she's one.''

"You can handle her."

"Right, but can you handle Austin? That's my question."

Cassie hesitated. "On a personal or business level?"

"Both."

"Businesswise, we've already locked horns. He wants to buy land and build a new hotel."

"Oops, from the look on your face, you're against that."

"Absolutely. I want to renovate the one in Jasmine."

"And personally?"

Cassie kept her face blank. "He's my daddy's friend."

"You're sure that's all? No sexual embers still smoldering?"

"Don't you think I've learned my lesson?" Cassie demanded tersely.

"I sure hope you have, but it seems to me by staying here, you've lighted a match that's liable to set your butt on fire."

Cassie shoved back her chair, then snapped, "Go beat up on Mrs. Bullock."

Jo Nell's chuckle followed her all the way outside.

"He's a fine young boy, don't you think?"

"No question about that." Austin adjusted his sunglasses on the bridge of his nose. "Cassie's done a bang-up job."

Austin tracked James's eyes as they followed Tyler, who was playing with a group of youngsters nearby. The day of the outing was magnificent, and Austin was glad that he had come. He'd been able to spend quality time with both Tyler and James. More with James, of course, which had been his intent.

Yet, surprisingly, Tyler had intrigued him to the point that he wanted to get to know the boy better. Austin couldn't pinpoint the reason. Maybe it was because he would never have a child of his own. Or maybe it was because Tyler was part of Cassie.

Hell, there he went again, playing those psycho mind games.

"How are things going with you and Cassie?" James asked in a seemingly casual tone.

Austin had been waiting for that question, but when it hadn't come earlier, he hadn't forced it. He would rather not discuss Cassie with James.

"Okay, I guess," he said with equal casualness.

"Which, translated, means not good at all."

Austin cut the reverend a look. "How'd you know?"

"It's bound to happen with two headstrong people."

"She's against buying land and building a new hotel."

"You'll just have to convince her otherwise."

"Then you're behind me?"

James held up his hands. "I don't have an opinion one way or the other. You'll have to duke that out with her. I do know Wilma's in your corner, which says a lot."

"Cassie's got a mind to match her mouth."

James chuckled again. "I have faith that y'all will reach an understanding. I'm just praising the Lord she's here and plans to stay."

Austin wished he felt that certain. His gut burned when he thought about seeing her and not touching her. The past that separated them was as solid as a concrete wall.

"Another thing I'm praying for, and I hope you will, too, is Lester."

Austin stopped in his tracks and gave his friend an incredulous look. "Excuse me?"

"All right, maybe I'm being too optimistic. I realize you would have difficulty in praying for him."

"It's not going to happen."

"That's unfortunate. I want so much for the three of them to become a family again."

"Surely you aren't serious?"

"They are still married in the eyes of the Lord."

"What about in Cassie's eyes?"

"She'll come around." The set of James's chin was obstinate. "I know she will."

For the first time ever, Austin had to quell the urge to shake his friend. No way would Cassie ever live with that sorry piece of shit again. What had happened to James? When it came to marriage and family, he had either gone around the bend or else he was turning into a religious fanatic.

"You know what your problem is, my friend?" Austin said, trying to temper his words. "You see only good in everyone. Maybe you ought to consider whether Lester's really the man you think he is."

"I know in my heart that he is. I just have to convince Cassie. And I will. That's my mission."

"What if he doesn't ever get out of prison?"

"That won't change my mind."

Austin once again quelled the urge to manhandle his friend. "Does Cassie know how you feel?"

"No, not completely, and I don't want you to say anything to her. When the time's right, I'll do the talking."

Austin didn't know how to respond to such mind-boggling garbage. Anyway, what more could he say? He was on the outside looking in, he reminded himself bitterly. What went on in that family, especially when it pertained to Cassie and Tyler, was none of his business.

A sudden and irrational sense of anger made him sick to his stomach.

Seventeen

"Hey, Mom, look who's coming."

Cassie put her buttered biscuit back on her plate and swung around, surprised by her son's sudden exuberance. When she saw Austin threading his way through the tables in the restaurant toward them, the breath rushed out of her lungs. He was the last person she wanted to see this morning, especially in light of the difficult task she had facing her.

"Can he sit with us?" Tyler asked, his face still beaming.

Oh, brother, she thought, her stomach flip-flopping, making the eggs in front of her totally unappetizing. She pushed the plate away. "I imagine he'd rather eat alone," she said in quiet desperation.

"No, he wouldn't," Tyler countered with unabashed certainty.

Cassie hid her sigh as her gaze unwittingly tracked Austin, whose dark hair glistened as if he'd just gotten out of the shower. His face was cleanly shaven. He was dressed in an off-white sport shirt and a pair of slacks that showed off the strong muscles in his legs as he moved.

He appeared so calm, so cool, so in control. It must be nice, she thought with a bitterness that shocked her. Even though the air-conditioning was blasting, she felt clammy all over, and a choking feeling assailed her. She didn't want to react to Austin in this way. But, dammit, his sex appeal was undeniable.

He smacked of it, the room suddenly filling with an erotic energy.

It was Saturday and, on the spur of the moment, she had decided to stop by the hotel and eat breakfast before heading out of town. She had thought Tyler would enjoy the novelty of eating the lavish brunch, plus she had wanted to check out the food and the service. So far, both had been superb. Austin was on target with the new chef; she would have to give him that, only not in person.

"Hiya," Tyler said, his mouth stretched into a full grin when Austin reached their table. "Mom said you wouldn't want to sit with us, but I bet you do."

Cassie cringed inwardly and wanted to shake her son. Instead, she forced herself to meet Austin's direct stare. Humor lurked around the edges of his eyes and mouth, which heightened the pull he exerted on her.

"You bet right," he said. "If it's okay with your mom, that is."

Cassie didn't dare look at Austin. Anyway, she was too busy trying to control her emotions.

"Aw, she doesn't care," Tyler quipped.

Cassie forced herself to rally and gestured toward the empty chair. "Of course I don't."

"So how are the Sullivans this bright Saturday morning?" Austin asked in that Cajun drawl that never failed to send tingles up her spine. His cologne didn't help any, either. It was subtle, yet seductive.

And those eyes.

They were delving into—and through—her with shameless hunger. She had thought she was immune to their effect. She wasn't. Their intensity seemed to strip her bare as they concentrated on her coral-stained lips.

Suddenly Cassie had the urge to cross her legs, to offset the heat building there. Dear Lord, she had to stop letting him get by with this attack on her senses. But how? If not for Tyler... No. She couldn't afford to indulge herself like that. She might want him, but she could never have him.

"We're fine," Cassie said, finally regaining her composure.

Austin's eyes changed, but the lurking humor teasing his lips burgeoned into a smile as he tousled Tyler's hair. "How's the grub?"

Tyler giggled. "It's the best, especially the hotcakes."

"Glad you like 'em. That's one of our specialties." Austin's gaze, hot again, sought hers. "What do you think?"

Cassie swallowed. "Actually, I haven't tried them."

"Mmm, too bad." Austin took a bite out of Tyler's oozing pile of hotcakes and winked at the boy.

While he was blatantly toying with her senses, he was also making an all-out effort to be pleasant. Why couldn't she? Well, she was still peeved about the land deal, for one thing, and if he thought buttering up her son was going to make her change her mind, he couldn't be more wrong.

When Tyler had returned from the campout, all he had talked about was Austin this and Austin that. That kind of hero worship had made her a nutcase. But she had once again refrained from saying too much, for fear of tipping her hand.

But the main reason for her uptightness was his potent sensual effect on her. There was only one way to combat that. She had to get a grip on herself and relax, stop flinching every time he came near.

The church outing had not done any real harm. Her secret remained safe. Tyler was safe. And as long as she kept her relationship with Austin strictly business, *she* would be safe.

With that in mind, Cassie turned the tables on him and flashed him a real smile, which took him aback. His sharp intake of breath bore that out. "Mother wouldn't be able to find fault with the way you've run things in her absence."

"What about you?"

Cassie's eyes swept the premises, taking in the huge urns of flowers, the beautifully set tables and the happy-faced customers. "I'm impressed."

"At least I've done something right."

"As far as I know, you've only made one mistake."

He shrugged, then said in a low, easy tone, "We'll see."

Before she could make a stinging rejoinder, Tyler cut in, as if he resented being left out of the conversation. "Hey, Austin?"

"What, buddy?"

"Do you know my daddy?"

Cassie froze, too flabbergasted to do anything else. She didn't know what she had expected from Tyler, but it wasn't that. She had never made it taboo to discuss Lester, but she didn't encourage it, either.

"I've met him," Austin was saying.

"Did you know he's in prison?"

This time Cassie reeled. Two back-to-back missiles dropped by her son was hard on her heart. What on earth had possessed Tyler to blurt that out? She turned away for a moment and tried to pull herself back together.

At last she faced her son and said, "Honey, I don't think Austin's interested in that subject."

Austin shook his head, then gave Tyler a sweet smile, a smile that stole what little breath Cassie had left. That was how he had looked at her years ago, when he'd called her brat, before she'd forced him into making wild, hot love to her, changing things forever.

"It's okay, buddy. I'm interested in anything you have to say."

Tyler's face was serious. "He did something he wasn't supposed to. He—"

"That's enough, Tyler." Cassie's tone was firm but gentle. "Finish your breakfast."

"If he wants to talk," Austin said, disapproval strong in his voice, "I'm willing to listen."

"Well, I'm not." Cassie's voice shook with suppressed anger, but not at Tyler. He was innocent, and her heart wrenched for him. At this moment her anger was directed at Austin. He had no right to interfere, to usurp her authority.

"We're about to get on the road," Cassie said into the uncomfortable silence, feeling Austin's eyes sweep over her, knowing that if she met his gaze, she would see her own anger reciprocated.

Tyler perked up, smiling at Austin. "We're going to see my other grandparents. They have some presents for me."

Austin smiled back at Tyler. "Sounds like fun."

"You could come with us, if you want to."

"Tyler!"

Austin tousled Tyler's head once again, then shoved

his chair back and stood. "Thanks, kid, but I'd best stay here and mind the store."

Once again that drawling voice pulled Cassie's eyes up to him. For a long second they stared at one another, the heat flaring again.

"Y'all be careful now, you hear?"

Cassie could only nod. Her throat was too tight to do otherwise.

"When will we see him again?" Charlotte asked Cassie.

"I'll try to make it soon."

Tyler was already in the car, playing with some of the many gifts the Sullivans had given him. Cassie hadn't approved of such extravagance, but she hadn't said anything. After all, they hadn't seen Tyler in years. They had just been making up for lost time, or so they'd said.

"It doesn't seem like you've been here long at all." Charlotte stopped short of whining as she patted her bubble-style hairdo. "Time simply flew."

"It did for Tyler, too, I'm sure." Cassie made herself smile. "But we've been here for hours."

"Hours hardly make up for years," Dewitt put in, a hard edge to his deep voice.

Cassie didn't let their disapproval get to her. At one time they had been able to both intimidate and bully her. No longer. However, they were having difficulty in accepting this new, strong-willed Cassie.

No one was ever going to run roughshod over her again. She had their son to thank for that.

Even so, Cassie stared at her ex-in-laws with mixed emotions. On the one hand, she had trouble even tolerating them, while on the other, she felt sorry for them.

Dewitt and Charlotte Sullivan still believed their son was innocent of all charges against him. They had told her that while Lester was in jail, awaiting trial on the weapons charge. Consequently, they had done everything in their power to see that their son was released and his record cleared.

When their efforts failed, they simply started all over again. Cassie had to give them A plus for effort and perseverance. But that was all she intended to give them, except limited access to Tyler.

"I'll bring him back," Cassie said at last, feeling the heat get to her. She knew Tyler would soon be calling her to come on. The heat combined with the humidity was unbearable.

"Next time we'd like him to stay," Charlotte said, her eyes darting to Dewitt's, as if asking for support, before returning to Cassie. "At least for a weekend."

Cassie purposely pretended to misunderstand. "It's impossible for me to get away right now, with Mother's condition and all." She smiled her sweetest smile. "I'm sure you understand."

"Well, actually I...we thought he could stay with us alone." Charlotte paused and pursed her lips. "We would take good care of him, but then, you know that."

That was the problem, Cassie thought bitterly, she didn't know that. Their idea of taking care of Tyler was talking nonstop about Lester and what a fine man and father he was, and how much he loved his son.

Blind, doting parents. Thanks but no thanks. As far as Cassie was concerned, these two people had created a monster and were continuing to feed it.

She wasn't about to expose her son to that. He had already been down that road. Besides, her conviction that she was right had been borne out by Tyler's conversation with Austin. It had demonstrated just how confused and vulnerable her son was when it came to Lester.

"I'll give that some thought." Cassie's lie broke into the silence at the same time that her head began pounding from the heat.

Dewitt stiffened, registering his displeasure. "Is that all you can say?"

He wasn't used to being crossed, and he didn't like it one iota. Cassie, however, was deriving great satisfaction from doing just that. "At the moment, yes."

"I want some time alone with my grandson." Unveiled hostility now filled his voice.

Ah, so the velvet gloves had finally come off. She had been wondering when that would happen. They had sat in their cluttered living room where they ate, drank and tried to be merry. Only Tyler had been the merry one, oblivious to the underlying tension.

"Now, Dewitt," Charlotte cautioned, "please don't get something started."

"Be quiet, Charlotte. Let me handle this."

Charlotte turned red, but she didn't say another word.

"This can all be handled in a civil manner, Dewitt," Cassie said in an even tone, though she longed to raise her voice. She was hot and tired and longed for a bath. Besides, her emotions had been taxed enough for one day, after that encounter with Austin.

"As long as we play by your rules." Dewitt's eyes iced over. "Hell, we couldn't even mention Lester's name in our grandson's presence."

Cassie stood her ground. "That's right."

Dewitt let go of an expletive, and Charlotte's mouth pinched in displeasure.

"Mom, I'm burning up!"

Cassie turned and saw Tyler's red face framed by the open window. "Coming, darling."

"Oh, one more thing," Dewitt said.

Cassie paused on the bottom step and twisted around. "Yes?" Her tone was terse, and she didn't care.

"There's a good chance that Lester might be getting out soon."

Eighteen

At least that was settled, and her panic had subsided. Lester would *not* be getting out of prison before his time was up.

Once she had left her in-laws, Cassie had dropped Tyler off at her parents and gone to the office, where she could be alone. Immediately, she had picked up the phone and called her attorney, Marty Mitchum.

"Ah, hell, that's just wishful thinking on the Sullivans' part," Marty had said, his tone free of doubt.

"When Dewitt blurted that out, Marty, I got so dizzy and sick to my stomach I was afraid I couldn't drive."

"Hell, you're made of stronger stuff than that."

"You're right, I am. I just thought of Tyler, turned and walked away."

"You did the right thing."

"Oh, Marty, what if—"

"Stop worrying and trust me."

"All right," she said on a ragged breath.

"Look, where are you?" Marty asked.

"At the hotel."

"Go home, hug your kid and forget about that creep. He's locked up, and he's going to stay there for a very long time."

"Thanks, Marty. I don't know what I'd do without you."

Once she'd ended that conversation, something had prodded her into making another call, this one to her contact at the women's shelter. Again she had received reassurance that Lester would remain behind bars.

Feeling suddenly like she could use a cup of cappuccino and a good laugh, she had called Jo Nell, only she hadn't been home.

Suppressing her disappointment and suddenly feeling claustrophobic, Cassie moved from behind the desk. Scares like that one were hard on the blood pressure. Maybe she should take Marty's advice and go home. It was late, long after the clerical staff had called it quits.

Even Austin, who worked a lot at night, was nowhere in sight. He was probably at his farm, playing with his horses, or, better yet, playing with his latest squeeze, which was just fine with her.

No, it wasn't.

She was green with jealousy, an admission that made her heart constrict. But there wasn't one thing she could do about it, so why punish herself needlessly?

Cassie was making preparations to leave when the house phone rang. It was Fred Dykes, head of security.

"Ms. Sullivan, you best come quick to the lobby," he said. "I can't find Mr. McGuire."

Without hesitating, Cassie made her way to the door. Security would never have called if trouble hadn't been brewing. Where the hell was Austin?

She heard the high-pitched, screeching voices just as she walked off the elevator. Upping her pace, Cassie rounded the corner into the lobby, only to instantly pull up short. Surely her eyes were playing tricks on her? What she was seeing couldn't be happening, not at the Hillcrest, for crying out loud.

Two women were engaged in hand-to-hand combat.

"How dare you try and steal my idea?" a bleached blonde yelled, at the same time grabbing a handful of the other woman's red hair.

"How could I steal something that was mine to begin with?" The redhead kicked the blonde in the shin.

"Bitch!" the blonde screamed.

Although the women had an audience, everyone kept their distance, even hotel security, Cassie noticed as she marched toward the women, determined to stop this madness. She wasn't about to allow such antics on her watch.

"Break it up, right now," she said in a hard but controlled tone.

They paid no attention to her, probably because they didn't even hear her. They were too busy screeching, kicking and grabbing at each other.

Damn! These women were here for a conference. They were both executives in the cosmetics business, women whom Cassie would have thought were above public brawling.

"I tried to make 'em listen to me, too," the thin security guard told her, "but as you can see, I was just wasting my time."

"Well, I'm not going to waste mine." Cassie's own temper had gone past the boiling point. "This nonsense has to stop, now, before someone gets seriously hurt."

"What do you aim to do?" the guard asked, his voice troubled.

"Whatever it takes," Cassie snapped, edging closer to the woman, whose fists and legs were still flying.

"Ma'am, uh, wait up," Fred said. "Here comes Mr. McGuire."

Cassie paid no heed to what he said. She was already beside the blonde and had a hand on her shoulder.

"No more, ladies!" In order to be heard, Cassie had to shout herself.

"Not until this bitch admits she stole from me!" the redhead hissed, drawing back her hand.

Later, Cassie had no idea what possessed her to do what she did. At the time, though, it seemed the only alternative. She stepped between them.

"Cassie, no!"

She heard Austin's shout, but it came too late. Something hard, something that felt like a flying brick, slammed into her right cheekbone.

The pain was all she could remember before a black void sucked her under.

"Hey, lie still."

"Where am I?" Cassie moaned, forcing her eyes open, despite her throbbing head.

"In my room."

Her eyes widened as she recognized the voice, then saw Austin sitting on the sofa next to her. Another kind of panic cut off her breath.

As if he sensed that, Austin whispered, "It's okay. Everything's all right. *You're* all right."

By whose definition? Cassie wanted to ask, but the effort was too much.

"Did I pass out?" she asked instead, licking her dry lips.

His eyes darkened. "No. You were knocked out."

"Oh my."

"You came to on the way here." Austin frowned. "Don't you remember?"

"Vaguely."

"Dr. Miles checked you over, then gave you a couple of pain pills."

"Maybe that's why I feel so disoriented."

"You don't remember taking the pills?"

In some distant part of her brain, Cassie thought she heard a note of panic in Austin's voice. She didn't want him to feel that or anything else for her. His concern only made matters worse, keeping her on that emotional roller coaster that would eventually crash with her on it.

"How…how long have I been out?" she asked, trying to avoid his eyes.

"Not long." He let go of a harsh breath, then pressed, "You do remember what happened, don't you?"

"It's slowly but surely coming back. One of those so-called ladies had an iron fist and I ran into it."

A smile tickled the corners of Austin's mouth. "That you did. I warned you, but it was too late."

Cassie winced.

Austin frowned again. "You need something else for the pain? It might be too soon, though."

"Good Lord, no. My head's reeling already."

Austin chuckled. "Strong stuff, huh?"

She nodded, and when she did, a lightning bolt of pain shot up her cheek. Grimacing, she raised her hand, determined to feel the lump that must be the size of a goose egg, only to run into something cold instead.

"Here, let me have the ice pack," Austin said.

Once the ice was gone, Cassie placed a couple of fingers on the welt, only to quickly remove them.

"Hurts, doesn't it?"

"Yes."

"I could kiss it and make it well, like I used to."

Those thickly spoken words packed such a wallop

that Cassie couldn't respond. She held her breath while he held her gaze.

It was in that moment that the mood changed. It was as if they suddenly realized what a compromising position they were in due only to their sheer proximity.

Cassie's heartbeat did a dance, and the room seemed too warm. It sizzled. Or was that her insides?

"Cassie."

Her name came out sounding like an ache as Austin's face came closer, stopping only scant inches from hers. She felt his breath against her cheek, saw on his chest, through the thin material of his shirt, the hair that she knew tapered to his navel—and lower.

She must have groaned or made some kind of sound. His eyes darkened, and he answered with a strange sound of his own. If she were to move a millimeter, he would touch her, touch her mouth.

She moved that millimeter, and his lips met hers, only to freeze as if shock had them wedged in its powerful jaws. Then his mouth moved again, his lips and tongue licking and tasting.

Sweet. Oh, so sweet.

Cassie's fingers danced on his back as their wet, devouring mouths turned to hot adhesive—sticking together. Cassie wanted to pull away, wanted to stop the insanity, but she didn't have the strength or the will.

It was the stab to the lower stomach, and the gathering moistness at the apex of her thighs, that set off the alarm. However, before she could push him away, Austin jerked his mouth from hers and lunged to his feet.

He didn't say anything, but he didn't have to. His erratic breathing and the bulge behind his zipper gave his thoughts away. If he hadn't pulled back...

"Dammit, Cassie!"

Mortified, she sucked her bruised lower lip between her teeth to stop it from quivering while hoping the pain would offset her swimming head.

"Cassie," he said again, sounding like he was choking.

"Don't say anything, please," she managed to whisper before sinking into another blessed void.

"Why don't you have the money?"

Sweat was thick on his skin, but Randall felt chilled, chilled to the bone marrow. In fact, he was shaking inside like some defenseless, hungry dog fighting for a bone.

"I will have it, I promise," Randall wheedled, facing his accusers, two men who could pass for ordinary businessmen, dressed in nice suits, from nice neighborhoods, with nice wives and two-point-three nice children.

Too bad for him that was a smoke screen. They were evil, heartless bastards hired to beat up guys like him who didn't pay their debts to the boss.

If they punched him in the stomach one more time, he would puke all over their Gucci shoes. What did he have to lose? Just his life, he reminded himself painfully.

But what the fuck, maybe that was the answer.

His life wasn't worth a red cent anyway, and he sure didn't have any dignity left. When he had driven to this out-of-the-way place and found them waiting for him, with those looks of steel on their faces, he'd soiled his pants on the spot.

The thinnest of the two had noticed that immediately. Snickering, he'd nudged his playmate from hell and said, "The boss didn't send a diaper. That's a shame, too, 'cause it looks like we need one."

The other man had thrown back his head and laughed out loud. "From now on, we'll have to put some in the trunk for leaky asses like this one."

Randall had never been as humiliated in his life as he'd been at that moment. However, fifteen minutes later, his humiliation, now mixed with fear, skyrocketed.

"I'll ask again, Lunsbury, just in case some of that shit went in your ears. Why don't you have the money?"

"Because I'm strapped for that kind of cash right now."

The tall one with the loud laugh slapped him across the face, bursting his lower lip. Randall yelped. The man hit him again. He yelped again.

"Please, don't hurt me," he begged. "I promise I'll get the money. I've never let your boss down before."

The two men looked at each other while Randall shivered in the hundred-plus temperature. He'd had no option but to tell the truth. He didn't have the money, but if he hadn't shown up, they would have come after him.

That would have been worse. Instead of looking into their baby blues, he would be lying in some ditch bleeding. But maybe that would be preferable?

Hell no, it wouldn't. He was tougher than that. Besides, he had an out. Two outs, actually. His problem was, he hadn't figured out the best one to use. He would, if he lived through the day.

The thin goon reached out and suddenly patted Randall's cheek, then straightened his tie. "Tell you what," he said, a brittle smile on his lips, ''we're gonna give you another chance to make things right.''

Randall's stomach rebelled against the foul taste in his mouth. He swallowed hard. ''I...you won't regret it.''

''Oh, we know that.'' It wasn't what he said but the way he said it that made Randall long for a bona fide toilet.

''You bet,'' Randall said, squeezing the cheeks of his buttocks together. ''I'll be in touch.''

Both men grinned, then one nudged the other and said in a mocking tone, ''He just cracked a funny.''

''Yeah, so he did.''

The thin guy's eyes turned mean. ''You be in touch, all right. But we'll *stay* in touch.''

After they left, Randall didn't know how long he stood there before he was able to get in his car and drive off.

Nineteen

"So how's business?"

"Okay, I guess," Cassie said.

She was sitting at the foot of her mother's bed after having had her coffee downstairs. Wilma, whose day hadn't started off well, had opted to have breakfast in bed.

"What do you mean, you guess? You don't know?"

Cassie heard the teasing note in Wilma's voice, but she found it difficult to respond in the same vein, not when her heart and mind were heavily burdened. If only she hadn't let Austin kiss her, but she had. Now she had to try to make sense out of something that made no sense at all.

Her best explanation was that she had gotten caught up in the moment. It wasn't every day that she walked into someone's flying fist, she reminded herself with dark humor.

Still, that didn't right a wrong. She had dropped her guard, something she had sworn she wouldn't do. Tyler's happy and contented face flashed to mind, and her stomach knotted. Because of her stupidity, they might have to leave town after all.

"Are you with me?" Her mother snapped her fingers.

Cassie jerked, then smiled sheepishly. "Sorry, my mind was wandering."

"So back to my question."

"On a day-to-day basis, things are going pretty smoothly."

Wilma chuckled. "Smoothly? In the light of what happened to your lovely face, that's a strange choice of words."

Cassie's lips twitched. "What can I say? I should've known better than to jump between two women in a catfight."

"I can't believe that actually happened in our hotel."

"These days, Mamma, it could happen anywhere. People have no respect for anything or anyone."

"You're right, and that's too bad."

"But there is some good news. Austin hired a new chef, who's working out great. In fact, the food's absolutely delicious."

"Speaking of Austin, I sense all is not well there."

"What do you mean?" Cassie asked, careful to keep her voice neutral.

Wilma frowned, making the lines in her face more pronounced. "Oh, I don't know, or maybe I just can't put my finger on it. But it seems that you stiffen when he's mentioned. I'd hate for the hotel to come between you two. You were always so close."

Close. Cassie almost laughed hysterically. If her mother only knew the half of it. But she didn't. "Well, I'm still against buying land and building on it. I'd much rather see us renovate the Jasmine Hillcrest, but then, you already know how I feel about that."

Her mother turned toward the open French doors. For a moment they were both quiet, listening to the birds chirp outside.

"I'll agree, it's in a sad state," Wilma said. "But can't we manage to do both?"

"No way, not with the amount of money Austin's already plunked down on that land."

"Surely we could make some of the repairs," Wilma pressed in a weakening voice. "I'm sure Austin would go along. Besides, you have as much say-so as he does. Remember that."

Now there was distress in her mother's voice, and Cassie knew she'd overstayed.

"Look, we'll talk about this later. You need to rest, and I need to get to work."

Wilma's hand on her arm stalled her. "I think you and Austin should take a trip to New Orleans."

Cassie shook her head. "Oh, I don't think that's a good idea."

"Why not?" Wilma asked bluntly, giving her a strange look.

Cassie did some fast dancing. "Maybe the word I should've used is *unnecessary.*"

"I disagree. You don't approve of the venture, and I respect that. But before you two come to blows over it, you should at least see the land. Who knows, maybe you'll change your mind. It might be a gold mine of opportunity."

"I doubt that. I think our gold mine's right here in Jasmine."

"Go, Cassie, for me. After all, I gave Austin permission to spend company money."

Suddenly Cassie felt trapped, with nowhere to go. Under the circumstances, how on earth could she make that trip? But if she didn't, her mother might really become suspicious, and then where would she be? In deeper trouble.

"All right, Mamma, you win. I'll go, but only for you."

And for herself, too, Cassie admitted later, after calling Austin and leaving a message on his voice mail. She had to know that she could be around him and control her emotions.

Also, she had to prove that that kiss had been a fluke—a knee-jerk reaction, nothing more, nothing less, despite her heart telling her differently. While his lips on hers had been heady stuff, it was his obvious arousal that had shot her emotions into the danger zone.

Nonetheless, there would be no repeat performance.

Judging from Austin's reaction, he hadn't been that overjoyed about the encounter, either, which would make ignoring it easier. A good thing for both of them.

Bottom line, life went on.

"You didn't know, did you?"

Austin threw Cassie a glance before turning away. "I damn sure didn't. But you can bet I'm going to have Randall's narrow ass for this."

When Austin had gotten Cassie's message, he hadn't believed she was serious. He believed it now, after having driven all the way to New Orleans with her sitting beside him stiff as a board and quiet as a church mouse.

Sexual tension.

He had felt it the instant she'd gotten into the car. Now, as they stood side by side staring at the huge tract of land, it sizzled between them, hotter than the enervating heat.

Austin didn't know how much more he could stand when all he could think about was his burning need to taste those lips again and bury himself between those sweet thighs.

"How could you have condoned this?" Cassie asked, forcing him back to the moment at hand.

"Randall was never all that candid. He never came right out and said there was a dilapidated hotel on the premises."

"Much less the fact that homeless people probably live in it." Sarcasm, blended with anger, deepened her voice.

"Dammit, do you think I'm happy about this?"

Cassie faced him, and even though she wore sunglasses, she still raised a hand and shielded her eyes, which drew his attention to her full breasts, tantalizingly visible under the damp, clinging material of her blouse.

He cleared his throat and shifted his gaze, but not before he saw how quickly air was rushing in and out of her lungs. His own breathing constricted as he turned back and their eyes met again.

Hell, nothing was working out like he'd planned. But then, nothing had since the day he'd walked into the Wortham mansion and seen her there.

"So are you going to nix the deal?" she asked at last.

"No."

"No?"

She had removed her sunglasses and was wiping the perspiration from under her eyes. He noticed only a slight discoloration remained where she'd been hit.

He ached to touch that spot. Instead, he shoved a hand through his sweat-drenched hair and said, "Surely you can see the potential here, what with it being practically on the water's edge."

"Of course I can."

"Well, we agree on something, at least."

"But that doesn't mean I want to build on it."

Austin muttered an expletive. "So much for the power of positive thinking."

"Nor do I want to buy it. I'm convinced we should take care of what we have, then spread our wings, so to speak, at a later time."

"You've made up your mind, then, to fight me to the death on this." It wasn't a question but a bitter statement of fact.

"Yes."

"And every other damn thing, right?"

Though Cassie didn't respond, their eyes met for another brief second. Cassie was the first to look away, her face pale.

"Let's get the hell out of here," Austin said hoarsely. "Even with the breeze, it's too damn humid to breathe."

When he pulled up in front of the Wortham mansion and brought the car to a halt, Cassie immediately reached for the doorknob.

"Whoa, hold your horses," he said, putting down the window on both sides. Though the air remained hot and humid, it had a sweet, sensual fragrance that permeated the interior of the car.

And the moon. It was an incredible sight, hanging huge and bright in the sky.

Cassie swung back around and gave him an impatient look that the moonlight allowed him to see. In fact, the glow landed softly on her face, a lovely face, drawn, yet remarkably clear of the anguish from a past filled with horrors he would never fully understand.

"I think we've had enough of each other's company

for one day, don't you?'' she asked, a slight tremor in her voice.

"No."

His bluntness seemed to give her pause, which bought him the time he needed. Something had to give. The drive home had been as uncomfortable as the drive there, making him long for a six-pack of beer.

Being penned up with her again, inhaling her sweat mixed with her perfume, had played havoc with his mind and his body. Now that they had reached Jasmine, he would have his say. If they were to continue working together, then the air had to be cleared, one way or the other.

"Why don't you just admit it?"

"Admit what?" Cassie asked with such innocence that, for a moment, he thought he might have been mistaken about this sexual "thing" between them.

Then he saw the sudden rise and fall of her chest, along with her hardening nipples, and he knew he was on target.

"You liked the hell out of it, same as I did."

"It?" That innocent look again.

"Don't be coy with me, Cassie. That kiss in my suite. You gave back as good as you got."

Cassie's delicate chin jutted. "That's a lie."

"Oh, come on, what do you take me for? I know when someone kisses me back."

Her body tensed. "In my case, you're wrong."

"Oh, yeah? We'll see about that!"

Austin reached out and jerked her against him. The suddenness of his action winded her, parting her lips. Groaning, he took advantage of that unintended but ripe invitation and crushed his mouth against hers.

He wanted to make her hurt as much as he was hurting. He wanted her to admit that she wanted him, and to hell with the consequences.

As she had in his suite, Cassie remained icy in his arms. Then he cupped a breast and gently squeezed it. She whimpered then, and locked her arms around his neck, matching his fierce hunger.

Later, he had no idea when he lost total control. Before he knew it, he had his hand under her bra, surrounding a bare, full breast.

Cassie moaned against his lips, adding more fuel to the raging fire inside him, making him bolder. That same hand left her breast and slid under her skirt, then inside her panties.

"Oh, Austin!" she cried, arching herself against the fingers now circling gently inside her.

It was only after she had climaxed that he felt her hot tears on his face. The bottom dropped out of his stomach, but it was too late to undo what he'd just done. Swearing graphically, he let her go and moved back behind the wheel.

"What can I say, Cassie?" he asked when he could talk again.

"Please," she said, her breathing coming in shallow pants. "Don't say anything."

He didn't. Instead, they both sat unmoving in the smothering silence.

"Why are we punishing ourselves this way?" Austin asked, wiping the sweat off his brow.

"Please, I don't want to talk about it." Her voice sounded bleak.

He faced her, and his breath caught. She looked so fragile, as if she could easily break. Still, he couldn't give in to her; he had to bring what happened to closure. "We have to."

"We're no good for each other, Austin."

"That may be, but I still want you, and you still want me."

He stared at her rigid profile as he waited for an answer.

"So what are you saying?" she whispered, clasping her hands tightly in her lap.

"That I'm not sure I can keep my hands off you."

She took a deep breath. "You have to."

"Why?"

"You know why," she said, facing him, her eyes still misted with tears.

It was all he could do not to grab her again. "You're right, I do know," he admitted in a harsh tone. "I'm almost old enough to be your father." He paused. "And I'm your father's best friend and brother-in-law." When she didn't respond, he went on, "And he would kill me and disown you if he knew we'd ever touched."

Cassie still didn't say anything. It appeared as though she had gone into shock. "Talk to me, dammit."

"What more is there to say?" she asked in a faint tone.

"Where we go from here would be a good start," he said recklessly.

"Nowhere."

He cursed.

"And you know why, for the reasons you just named plus some you didn't."

Something seemed to wither and die inside him, but he would be damned if he let her know that. "I won't apologize."

"Fine, just don't ever touch me again." A measure of strength had returned to her voice.

"If that's the way you feel."

"That's the way I feel." Cassie pushed a strand of hair out of her eyes, as if to see him better. "Go back to your lady friend. She's much more suited to you than I am."

"Don't tell me how to run my love life!"

"If you touch me again, I swear I'll leave town."

Austin looked her up and down, heat from watching her orgasm still flooding his body. "I won't touch you again. Not until you ask me, that is."

Cassie's shoulders hunched. "You just don't know when to let it go, do you?"

"I gave you my word, so I suggest you get out while I'm still willing to keep it."

She scrambled out of the car and slammed the door. He waited until she was inside the house, then drove off, burning rubber.

He knew he was behaving like a horny adolescent, but he couldn't help it. He was scared shitless by the emotional turmoil that raged inside him.

Hell, maybe *he* should be the one who left town.

Twenty

"**W**hat do you mean, he hasn't been there in days?"

Austin was trying to control both his voice and his frustration, but he was having one helluva time.

"Trust me, Mr. McGuire, we're as puzzled and concerned by Randall's behavior as you are."

Then why the hell aren't you doing something about it? Austin was tempted to lash back. But he refrained. He was talking to one of the senior partners in Randall's firm, a man to whom he owed some respect. Besides, his temper was on a short leash, thanks to Cassie.

Since that trip to New Orleans, he'd been meaner than a junkyard dog in heat and hornier than a sailor six weeks out of port.

"He's been absent more than he's been here," Mr. Ashton was saying. "The latest excuse was that he had the flu."

"Mary Jane hasn't been any help?" Austin asked, forcing his mind off Cassie and back on track.

"No, and I've spoken to her several times. She's extremely distraught."

That was probably a gross understatement, Austin thought, envisioning Mary Jane having a hissy fit "Look, sir, if you hear from Randall, tell him it's urgent that he get in touch with me."

"Is there anything I or the firm can do, meanwhile?"

"No, thanks. This is a personal matter."

"I understand."

Austin placed the phone back on the receiver just as a knock sounded on his door. He turned just as Mary Jane Lunsbury walked across the threshold, her face swollen from crying.

His blood chilled, but for her sake he remained calm. "Before you say anything, sit down," Austin said, closing the distance between them and helping her to a nearby chair. "Would you like something to drink?"

When she was seated, Mary Jane shook her head. "Thanks, but not right now."

She appeared almost in shock. "What happened?" Austin demanded, leaning against his desk and facing her.

Mary Jane blinked hard then raised her eyes, "He…he's cleaned out our savings and our checking account." She began sobbing.

Another chill shot through him. "Do you know where he is?"

"No," she whispered. "I just know he didn't come home again last night."

"You mean he doesn't have the flu?" Austin didn't bother to mask the sarcasm in his tone.

Mary Jane gave him a bewildered look. "I don't know what you're talking about."

Austin told her about his conversation with the partner.

"That doesn't surprise me. Since he took our money, I'm worried about your deal with him."

This time a nasty expletive polluted the air.

Mary Jane wiped her nose with a tissue. "I didn't…don't know what to do."

"Well, I sure as hell do." Austin's features were grim. "I'm going to find the son of a bitch."

The front desk clerk was clearly frazzled.

Cassie rubbed her temple, feeling a headache coming on. "What's wrong, Luke?"

"It's Mrs. Fortenberry again, in 1219. She's raising Cain about her room, says housekeeping left a hair in the tub." He paused and pulled one end of his black mustache. "She's not happy, of course, and insists on talking to you."

Cassie wanted to tell him that she didn't give a damn if Mrs. Fortenberry was happy or not. And furthermore, the hair was probably the woman's own.

Instead, Cassie smiled at Luke, who had been unlucky enough to get caught in the cross fire. "Get the head of housekeeping. Let him handle her."

Luke gave her a polite smile. "I understand."

"I don't know what this hotel would do without you."

Luke turned red from his neck to his ears, but Cassie could tell her compliment had pleased him. Suddenly she wondered if Austin ever spoke personally to the employees.

Feeling her own face turn red, Cassie banished such thoughts from her mind. After that disastrous trip to New Orleans, a week ago today, she hadn't seen him.

Apparently he'd spent his time seeing to the other hotels. His absence had given her the opportunity to regroup. She had promised herself that she would sort through her emotions, dig deeply to see if anything salvageable lay hidden underneath a heap of pain, guilt and anguish.

However, she had reneged. She couldn't bear to think

about how he'd manipulated her mind and her body with his kisses, his hands, his fingers. God, his *fingers*, inside her. More than that, she couldn't bear to think about the fact that she'd let it happen, knowing what was at stake.

And she hadn't wanted him to stop. That was the awful part. If he had jerked her panties off and taken her there, she wouldn't have stopped him.

What did that say about her?

"Ms. Sullivan?"

"Huh, sorry, Luke, I was wool-gathering. Anything else?"

"No, ma'am. I was just wondering how Ms. Wortham's doing. We sure miss her, not that we don't like having you around."

"Mother has her good days and bad." Cassie gave him a sad smile. "I'll tell her you asked about her, and thank you."

Fifteen minutes later, Cassie was out of the hotel, sitting on a shaded park bench. She was due to meet Jo Nell here for lunch, an outing they both needed.

Cassie looked up at the moving clouds, thinking they had picked a good day, since the sunless sky made it cooler. Hopefully it would rain, which was the norm on these long summer days.

"Hey, what's up? You look like you're on another planet."

Cassie peered at Jo Nell, who plopped down on the other end of the bench, dropped her purse, then stretched her legs out in front of her. "Jeez, I'm tired."

"Lots of blue-haired ladies already, huh?"

Jo Nell mouth curved down. "Actually, it's been a mixture of pains in the butt. Nothing I've done so far has pleased anyone."

"I can identify with that. The natives are restless at the hotel, too."

"At least your face is back to normal." Jo squinted her eyes on Cassie.

"Thank goodness for that."

"So, where's the grub?" Jo Nell asked, changing the subject. "I'm starving."

Cassie reached into her carryall and pulled out two sacks. She had stopped at her favorite deli and picked up sandwiches and chips. They munched in silence for a while.

"Whatcha smiling about?" Though Jo Nell's mouth was full of turkey, she talked around it.

"You."

"Me?"

"Yep. I was just thinking how much I needed a Jo Nell fix."

Jo Nell stopped chewing and quirked one eyebrow. "Is that a compliment?"

"Of course," Cassie said, chuckling.

"Works for me, then."

Another silence followed while they finished eating, slapping at flies along the way.

"So, you went to New Orleans," Jo Nell finally said, wadding up her sack and pitching it into the nearby garbage can. "And with Austin, no less."

Cassie's stomach tightened. "How'd you know?"

"Wilma told me."

"Oh."

"When were you going to share that tidbit with me?"

"Today."

"So what happened? Did you like what you saw?"

Cassie told her about the site, opting to leave out the

personal aspects of the trip, too embarrassed and confused to share them, even with her best friend. But she would have to be careful. Jo Nell could read her like a book.

"You mean there were actually people living in that rat-infested building?" Disgust rearranged Jo Nell's features.

"At one time. Maybe now. Who knows? Hell, Austin wasn't even aware there was a building on the property."

"You believe that?"

"Yes, I do. Austin may be a lot of things, but dishonest he's not. The situation upset him, too."

"What about his friend? You know, that attorney who engineered the deal?"

"Right now, I'd hate to be in Randall's shoes."

"Reckon that's a deal breaker?" Jo Nell asked, sucking the last of her drink from the straw.

Cassie pursued her lips. "As far as I'm concerned, it is. While it's a great location, on the water and all that, I still want to improve what we already have, not spend money tearing something else down. Period."

"So I can expect the sparks to fly?" Jo Nell paused and gave her an odd look. "Or are they already flying?"

"They're flying, all right, but not the kind *you're* talking about," Cassie said, lying through her teeth.

"Whatever you say."

"Dammit, Jo Nell! You're a born troublemaker."

Jo Nell looked incredulous. "Me? You're the one on the defensive."

"I don't want to talk about it," Cassie said, squirming in her seat.

"Why not, unless you have something to hide?"

"Give it a rest, okay?"

"I'll say this, then I'll hush. Be careful." Jo Nell's tone lacked humor. "Austin's not for you now any more than he was nine years ago."

"Don't you think I know that?" Cassie snapped, only to follow that with an apology and a smile. "Sorry."

Jo Nell flapped her hand. "No apology necessary. You're just suffering from PMS."

"You think so?" Cassie asked on a forlorn note.

Jo Nell's eyes twinkled. "Yep. But it's okay. You're entitled."

After more chuckles and polishing off a peach tart apiece, Cassie bid Jo goodbye and headed back to the hotel. By the time she reached the entrance, rain was falling. Hopefully it would be a fast-moving front, as she'd promised to go swimming with Tyler later that afternoon.

Since returning to Jasmine, she hadn't seen as much of her son as she would have liked, though she was thrilled he had made friends through the church, friends who invited him places and kept him occupied.

However, Cassie missed their time together more than she cared to admit. Her baby boy was growing up, and that depressed her. Thinking about Tyler brought a smile to her lips that remained after she'd walked into her office.

A few minutes later, she was behind her desk jotting down ideas for renovating. She was so deep in thought that she didn't realize she was no longer alone.

"Hello, Cassie."

She jerked her head up, and at the same time her

heart jumped into her throat, almost gagging her. She blinked, then blinked again, but the image in front of didn't change.

   "You!"

Twenty-One

She couldn't pass out, Cassie told herself. But her head spun and the room seemed to tilt. She gasped deeply for air just to breathe, when all she wanted to do was scream.

Lester? It couldn't be. God wouldn't play that kind of trick on her. But he had. Her ex-husband, in the flesh, was standing in front of her.

"I'm no ghost who's going to disappear." His chuckle was cynical and vicious.

Cassie's skin crawled at the veiled warning, and a loathing as deadly as poison shot through her system. She had sworn that she would kill Lester if he ever came near her or Tyler again. She hadn't meant that, not literally, of course. But now, she wasn't so sure. When it came to protecting her son against this man, she would do whatever it took, God help her.

How had the unthinkable happened? How had he gotten out of prison? She had been assured that wouldn't happen, only it had. She bit down on her lower lip so hard she tasted her own blood.

"Yo, Cassie, darlin'."

Cringing at that sarcastic endearment, she glared at him. "Get out of here." Her voice was as cold and sharp as an icicle.

But her jabs didn't seem to faze him. His rigid stance

didn't change, nor did his reaction. "Just be patient, wife dear."

Her eyes flashed. "I'm not your wife any longer, you bastard."

He shut the door and leaned against it, his expression still unchanged. "You'll always be my wife," he countered in a chilling tone.

Gut-wrenching fear replaced Cassie's fury. Her stomach rebelled even as her eyes raked over him. Five years had made little difference in his appearance, except that he seemed bigger. Not taller, but stouter, like he'd spent time lifting weights.

He'd grown a mustache, which gave his unlined face an added degree of maturity. But the buzz-style haircut hadn't changed, nor had his blue eyes; they remained as remote and dead as ever.

This couldn't be happening, Cassie thought again wildly. This had to be another version of the nightmare she'd had during the years in hiding in which Lester and his cronies hovered over her in bed, laughing, holding Tyler out to her, then snatching him back.

Cassie shivered visibly.

"Taking a chill, darlin'? You know I'll be glad to warm you up."

"Stay the hell away from me!"

He looked her up and down, a sardonic twist to his lips. "I have the right to go anywhere I please and that includes near you. I'm a free man."

"How?" Somehow Cassie managed to squeeze that word through her stiff lips.

He grinned with unvarnished confidence. "Let's just say I got lucky, darlin', and leave it at that. I'm out, and that's what counts."

Cassie wanted to die.

"And unless I screw up, I won't be going back." Lester winked. "But we both know that's not going to happen. I've learned my lesson."

"And I can walk on water, too."

"Mmm, I see you still have that sharp tongue." He smiled an empty smile as he sauntered deeper into the room and sat down, easing his legs out in front of him.

"I want you to leave. Now!" Cassie's jaw was clenched so tightly that the words were barely audible.

"No."

"I swear to God, I'll call security."

"No, you won't." Lester gave her another empty smile. "Not until you know what I want."

"I don't give a damn."

He merely shrugged. "Actually, I'm a changed man. I got some of that religion your daddy preaches from behind his almighty pulpit."

"You don't even know what the word *religion* means," she declared.

He smirked, then said in a jeering tone, "We'll let that be our little secret. Among others."

Ignoring that barb, Cassie demanded, "Say what you came to say. This is your last chance."

"It's simple. I want you back."

She gasped. "What?"

"You heard me. I want my wife and kid back."

Kid! Oh, dear Lord, Tyler. This time her fear was like a stake in the heart.

As if he could read her mind, Lester went on, "I want us to be a family again."

"If you think for one minute I'd let you touch me or my child again, you're crazier than I thought."

Lester jumped up, his features turning fierce. "Don't cross me, bitch."

Cassie held her ground, though she could hear her heart pounding in her ears. "I'd advise *you* not to cross *me!*"

She didn't know how long she could hold on to her composure and bravado. His presence had clobbered her mentally and physically. Still, she had to find a way to get him out of there.

If she chose to call security, there was no telling what kind of ruckus he'd create. However, if the situation worsened, she wouldn't hesitate to act on that option. Somewhere on Lester, there was a weapon; she would bet her life on that.

"I'd watch that smart mouth if I were you."

"If it's more money you want—"

"Now, that's awfully tempting, I'll admit. But like I told you, I want you in my bed and my boy in my lap. Those are my rights."

"Dammit, you have no rights."

"We'll see about that."

Lester's eyes hardened. "I want to see Tyler."

"No!"

"You can't keep me from him."

"Get the hell out of here—*now*—before I make good on my threat and call security."

Lester shrugged, then leaned over the desk, as if moving in for the kill. Cassie tasted her fear in the form of bile, but she refused to move herself.

"He's my son."

"Stay away from Tyler." Her voice shook. "I'm warning you."

"Whatcha gonna do, shoot me?"

"I just might."

Lester pitched back his head and laughed. "That'll be the day."

"Why don't you just crawl back into that hole you crawled out of?"

Suddenly he grabbed her by the shoulders and pulled her out of her chair, his fingers digging into her arms.

"Get your hands off me."

"Not until you understand this, bitch. Don't try to keep me from my son. And if you push me too far, you'll both be sorry."

He let her go with such force that she almost fell.

"First rattle out of the box, I'll tell Daddy the truth, that his perfect daughter got fucked and knocked up." He chuckled. "Hey, that kind of rhymes, doesn't it?"

Before Cassie could find her voice, he spun on his booted heel and stormed out the door. Clutching her stomach, she sank into the chair and nursed the crippling terror that threatened to consume her.

What was she going to do?

"Cassie, are you all right?"

Austin.

Her heart sank even lower. Where had he come from? More to the point, why had he come? Hotel business, she thought, answering her own question.

She rose to her feet and crossed her arms over her body to try to stop herself from trembling.

"Cassie, answer me."

She gazed at him through stricken eyes. His face was lined with concern and something else—rage.

"No." She began to shake all over. "I don't think I'll ever be all right again."

"So that was *him*?"

"Yes," she said in a tiny whisper.

"I'll be a son of a bitch!" Austin rubbed the back of his neck and began pacing the floor. "What the hell is he doing out of the pen?"

Cassie drew several deep breaths far down into her lungs, then let them out. "He said he just got lucky, which could mean anything." Hysteria bubbled beneath the surface of her composure. She knew that if she ever let go, she would go down for the count.

Words that she'd never heard spewed from Austin's lips.

"I had no idea this was coming," Cassie said. "In fact, I'd been assured he wouldn't get out, not for years, anyway."

"That's our sorry justice system for you. The victims don't have any rights."

Tears burned her eyes, and her shaking worsened.

"Sorry. Sit back down, okay?"

He moved toward her. She panicked and held up her hands. "Don't. I'm...fine."

"I was only trying to help," Austin said hoarsely.

If he touched her now, she wasn't sure she could remain intact. As it was, seeing him had further loosened something inside her. Despite the incident in the car, she didn't trust herself not to seek the haven of his strong arms and body, begging him to hold her and make the fear go away.

But that wasn't the solution. *Austin* wasn't the solution. In fact, he was another complication, one she had to deal with just like she did Lester.

Another frisson of fear surged through her.

"You're far from fine," Austin said, his gaze piercing.

"Austin, don't push, please. I...I can't take any more."

His features darkened, then twisted. "I'm not the one you need to fear."

Oh, but you are, she cried silently. My heart fears you.

"I just want to make the hurt go away," he said in a husky voice. "No strings attached, I swear."

"If you mean that, then you'll leave me alone."

"I can't." His voice sounded broken now.

"Don't you understand that you and Lester are on the same level in my book?" she said with cruel intent.

Her blow struck. His face drained of color, and he winced.

She hated that, but she hadn't known what else to do. Her world was crumbling in front of her. Even though Austin had backed off a bit, he was still too close, making her long for the freedom and the magic of a long-ago time, a time she would never know again.

"If it makes you feel better to kick a dog while he's down, then go ahead. I can take it."

"Go away, Austin," she said in a dull, faraway tone. "I want to be alone."

"Suit yourself." His mouth worked. "At least for now."

The unscented water was so hot it scalded her toes. Though Cassie felt the tingling pain, she didn't care. It was nothing compared to the horrific pain raging inside her.

So many questions and no answers circled through and around her brain, taunting and teasing. When she had left the office, she had gone straight home to her room. The big house had been empty, except for Joy. James, with Tyler in tow, had taken Wilma for a drive.

Now, as she sat in the tub, Cassie blamed herself for not having stayed on top of the situation concerning Lester. Because of her lax attitude and her attorney and the network's failure to notify her, she had been caught raw and exposed.

Damn! Damn! Damn!

What to do? That was the most pressing question. Should she take Tyler and leave again? Or would snatching her son from his newfound and secure environment harm him psychologically forever?

Her mind said run. Her heart said stay.

When she put the situation in perspective, Lester truly had no legal rights, which meant she could get a restraining order against him. But she would just be wasting her time. To Lester and his militia group, a piece of paper didn't mean squat. They operated under their own rules, made them up as they went along. For the most part, they got by with that tactic, too.

Lester's arrest had been the result of a slipup, one that she bet wouldn't be repeated.

Cassie closed her eyes, sinking further into despair. If only she had never married him. If only she had been honest with her parents. If only she had told Austin the truth.

She could "if only" herself crazy, and it wouldn't change one thing. When she had learned she was pregnant by a man fourteen years her senior, a man who was her daddy's best friend and who was engaged to marry her mother's sister, she had done the only thing she knew how to do.

Survive.

In the process of doing that, she had tried to make her farce of a marriage work. After learning Lester was affiliated with a militia group, she had continued to try, thinking she could change him, make him into the father and husband she longed for him to be.

It had been after Tyler turned three that Cassie realized nothing would ever change Lester, that he was indeed a monster in disguise. Even now, the terror of that moment was as strong as if it had happened yesterday.

It had been late, because she had gone to class, then to work. Tyler was supposed to have been at day care; she'd already made a point, though not an obvious one, never to leave Tyler alone with Lester.

That was why she had been so stunned when she'd walked into the house that evening and found her son home with Lester. She had dropped her things and hurried into the den. What she had seen had literally knocked her breathless.

Tyler had been perched on Lester's knee, holding a pistol in his tiny hand.

Fright so numbing, so gagging, had welled up inside of her that for a moment she couldn't talk, couldn't move. Somehow she got her bearing and remained calm.

"Tyler, honey," she said, "Mommy's home."

Both Tyler and Lester had faced her. Tyler smiled. Lester frowned.

"Give that gun to Daddy and come here."

"He's fine just where he is," Lester said, clamping a hand around Tyler's waist.

Tyler grinned as he held the weapon out to her. "Looky, Mommy, gun."

"Is that loaded?" she asked, her voice quavering.

"You betcha. I'm teaching my son how to be a good soldier." Lester mussed up Tyler's hair and smiled at him.

Cassie almost choked on the mounting terror. "Lester, you should be committed!"

"Back off, Cassie," he warned. "This is my party, and you're not invited."

"I swear if something happens to—"

Suddenly Tyler started wiggling, still holding the gun. Before she thought, Cassie dashed across the room, took the weapon out of the child's hand, laid it down carefully, then snatched him up.

Only after she reached the door did she turn back around. Lester was sprawled against the sofa, a grin on his face. "So, you won a battle? Just remember, the war's far from over."

"You bastard!"

Taking Tyler, she left and spent the night in a motel, fearful of going to any friend's home and endangering them. After a sleepless night she reached a decision. The following day she made Lester an offer she prayed he would take.

She marched into his office and, after shutting the door said, "I want a divorce, and I want you to give up all rights to Tyler."

He laughed. "And just why would I do something crazy like that?"

"Money, to further your group's cause."

"What if I don't want your money?"

Cassie didn't blink. "Oh, but I think you do." "But even if you say no, I'll get a divorce."

"I could fight you in court."

"You could, and you might win, but then again, you might not, especially if I tell some of the things I know about you and your group."

Lester's face turned ugly. "You'd best watch what you say. You're in way over your head."

"So are you. Now, are we dealing or not?"

"How much money are we talking about?"

"Fifty thousand."

He scoffed. "You don't have that kind of money, and your parents won't give it to you. They think I'm a great guy and won't believe a word you tell them."

Cassie ignored that last taunt. "I do have the money, left to me by my maternal grandmother. It's in a savings account. I had planned to use it for Tyler's education."

Lester straightened. "You can get your hands on it?"

"Tomorrow."

"I'll let you know tomorrow, then."

"No, you'll let me know right now or the deal's off."

"Okay, I'll take it."

"Good. When I get home this evening, you be gone, bags and all. Our only communication will be through my lawyer."

She sensed he'd wanted to argue, but he hadn't. And he had kept his word, having signed the appropriate papers at the appointed time.

Several months later, she'd had her life back on track, having graduated from the university and landed a great job, when the unthinkable had happened....

"Mom, we're home!"

Cassie wilted with relief, her torturous stroll down memory lane brought to an end by the arrival of her family. She lunged out of the now-cold water, dried off, slipped into her robe and strode into the bedroom just as Tyler walked in.

"Hiya, Mom."

Without saying anything, Cassie grabbed him and squeezed him close to her heart.

Twenty-Two

"Do you have to go?"

Austin smiled at Sherry as he pecked her on the cheek. "'Fraid so. The lunch was delicious."

"Thanks."

Sherry was in the habit of inviting him to lunch when she took a vacation day from work. She loved to cook, and he loved to eat. In the past, Austin had looked forward to those occasions. Today had been different. He had enjoyed her company, but it wasn't the same. He knew why.

That episode at the farm hung between them, though they both had tried to ignore it. He had worked extra hard not to make Sherry feel any worse than she already did, especially as he felt responsible. He was surprised she had called after putting the burden on him.

"If you didn't have such a good job," he said, switching his mind off that unsettling thought, "I'd hire you at the hotel. That peach cobbler you whipped up is the best I've ever put in my mouth."

"If you don't watch out, I'm going to get a big head."

Although Sherry smiled, Austin noticed that the smile never reached her eyes. They were sad, and he knew he was to blame for that. She wanted more from him than he could give her. Yet he didn't have the guts to tell her.

"Nah, you're too nice a person," he said in a light tone.

"I'm beginning to think you're right. Maybe I should develop a mean streak."

Austin walked to the door, not about to touch that subject. Although her tone had been coated in silk, she'd taken a shot at him and his neglect of her.

"I'll call you, okay?"

She cocked her head. "Are you sure?"

"I'm sure."

"So what's going on at the hotel today?"

"I'm after someone."

"Mmm, from the tone of your voice and the look on your face, that someone's in big trouble."

"That's a real possibility."

"Uh-oh."

Austin cleared the scowl, caused by thoughts of Randall, off his face. "It's no big deal, or at least I hope it isn't."

"When are you coming for dinner?"

Austin didn't like being pressured, and that was what Sherry was doing. Apparently she wasn't giving up on him.

"Soon, I promise."

"I'm going to hold you to that."

Austin suppressed a sigh, then made himself smile. "See ya."

Although he would call her, he had to make a firm decision regarding their relationship. After getting into his car, he knew he couldn't continue to see Sherry when his thoughts were filled with Cassie.

Groaning, he tightened his knuckles on the wheel

while he let the air-conditioning blast, desperately willing Cassie's face to disappear. Like the stifling, wet heat, his mind showed no mercy. Her lovely, fragile features stayed with him all the way to the hotel.

Once he arrived, he deliberately passed by her office, only to notice that her secretary was absent and her door was closed.

God, he had it bad. Cassie reached him on a primal sexual level that no other woman ever had or ever would. But his fixation with her was more than that.

She had touched something deep inside him right off, something more than lust, though she certainly aroused that, too. Possibly it was that womanly fragility hidden under a show of outward toughness and courage that stirred him, that made him ache for her every second of every day.

It had been that ache that had driven him to her office yesterday, as well. To her face he had lied like a dog, telling her that he had come about business. What a joke, especially following that hot incident in the car.

He had been thinking about that when he'd passed her scumball ex-husband, whom he hadn't recognized. If he had, no telling what he would have done—probably confronted him, which wouldn't have been a smart move.

Learning that her visitor had indeed been Sullivan, icy anger and shock had almost consumed Austin. Cassie had obviously felt the same. He had thought she was going to faint, and that had scared the hell out of him. The fact that she had kicked him out, too, hadn't stopped him from worrying about her or the situation.

Now, as he entered his office, Austin wondered what was going on behind Cassie's closed door. With Lester back in the picture, instinct told him she was wildly trying to figure out what to do. Since she wouldn't let him help her, his only recourse was to take care of business—land business.

That bought him time to locate Randall and find out what the hell was going on. Lifting the phone, Austin punched out Randall's office number for the second time that day. He spoke to his secretary again.

"Ah, so Mr. Lunsbury's back."

"Finally, sir. But he's behind closed doors with the other partners."

"Tell him I'll call back."

Once he hung up, Austin expelled a breath of relief, thanking his lucky stars that Randall was at least present and accounted for. He leaned back in his chair and smiled a lop-sided smile, wishing he was a fly on the wall in that meeting. He would bet Randall's ass was getting chewed to shreds.

Austin planned to take over where the partners left off. His friend had a lot to answer for, especially his failure to mention the fact that a tenement was on the site. Too, he wanted formal verification that the upfront money he'd given him to secure the deal was still in escrow. If not, then Randall was in over his head in more ways than one.

Suddenly Austin wondered if the pending deal was even important to Cassie anymore. Now that Lester had been let out of the pen, it wouldn't surprise him if she left again. That thought almost stopped his heart. Even though she had been a pain in the butt from the moment he'd seen her, he didn't want her to leave, which made no sense.

Shit!

With her gone, his problems would be over, especially when it came to the hotel business. Once he jerked Randall back in line, his plans could go forward without a hitch.

More important, he wouldn't feel that pang of guilt when he was around her for the sin he'd committed in the past and the sin he *wanted* to commit in the future.

Also, it would make it a helluva lot easier to look her father in the face again without feeling like pond scum. He couldn't forget about Tyler, either. That gem of a child reminded him of the son he would never have.

So why didn't he just stay the fuck away from her and let her sink or swim on her own? After all, she had made it plain she didn't want him around.

Too bad. After what had happened between them in the car, after he'd touched her, made her climax with his fingers, he couldn't leave her alone.

It was the building fire in his loins that sent him striding back down the hall to her office. No one was there. Smothering a curse, Austin left the hotel, got in his car and drove to the Worthams', Cassie's stricken face continuing to haunt him.

He had to know that she was all right, either firsthand or from her family. But when he pulled into the drive, he balked. What if James and Wilma didn't know? What if she hadn't told them Lester was back?

Perhaps he should forget this impulsive visit, especially when he noticed Cassie's car in the garage and another one on the street, parked slightly beyond the drive. Was someone from the church there?

The slamming of a car door behind him jarred Austin out of his thoughts and out of the car. From beside his vehicle, he watched as Tyler headed up the sidewalk. It looked like he'd been swimming; his hair was wet and a towel was draped around his middle.

"Hey, buddy," Austin called out. "Wait up."

Tyler stopped, his face lighting up, which made Austin glad.

"Hiya," Tyler said, shifting his backpack. "Wanna come in and play a computer game with me?"

"Thought you'd never ask."

Tyler giggled as Austin placed an arm around the boy's shoulders, and they walked inside the house.

Was it midafternoon?

Cassie glanced at her watch and sighed. She hadn't accomplished a thing, except think about Lester.

Damn him and his soul to hell.

Her daddy would have a heart attack if he knew she was thinking such thoughts. But she couldn't worry about her daddy or her mother. At the moment her only concern was for her son and his well-being.

Was Tyler in danger? Was *she* in danger? Those questions had been on her mind since her encounter with her ex. And she still didn't know the answers, which made her the victim once again. But only if she allowed it, a small voice whispered.

Lester had jerked her chain long enough. Maybe it was past time she jerked his. If she crossed him, would she be gambling with Tyler's life? She had to keep in mind that it wouldn't just be Lester she was crossing, either. It would be his entire militia group, who thought putting a gun to someone's head was the way to solve a problem.

Cassie's stomach revolted. Yet enough was enough. And she'd had enough. She refused to take Tyler and sneak into the night once more, never to see her parents again or Jo Nell or... Her mind stumbled on Austin's name. Yet she couldn't ignore him or pretend he meant nothing to her.

Last night had been miserable, so miserable she had gotten up early and sought the sanctuary of her office, where she immediately called Jo Nell.

"You mean that bastard's out?" she had practically screamed into the phone.

"Shh, Jo, someone will hear you."

"No one's here right now."

"Good."

"So what happened?"

Cassie told her what had transpired with Lester, opting to leave out Austin's part in the horror show.

"I'm so sorry, Cass. It's just not fair. I hate to see that creep ruin your life again."

"It's not me I'm worried about. It's Tyler."

"What are you going to do?"

"I'm not sure yet."

"Look, I gotta go." Jo's voice turned to a whisper. "One of the girls just came in. We'll talk later. Meanwhile, you keep your chin up and don't do anything rash, you hear?"

So far, Cassie hadn't done anything at all. She hadn't even told her parents that Lester was back. As for Tyler—well, she had no idea what to do about him, how to explain that the only father he knew was back, dragging danger with him.

Thinking about *that* danger, Cassie had decided to go home. Maybe if she sat in the swing on the veranda, she could make some sensible plans; more to the point, maybe she could make sense out of what had happened.

Workwise, the day had been a wash, anyway. She'd planned on meeting with the architect and his contractor concerning renovations, but she had canceled. She had been too upset to concentrate.

All that mattered now was reassuring herself that Tyler was all right. He had gone with the church group on a picnic at a nearby lake. While she didn't think Lester would pull any crazy stunts at this juncture, it wouldn't hurt to cover all bases. Besides, she had to tell her parents about Lester.

A few minutes later, Cassie walked in the side door into the kitchen. Joy was making a pie.

"Mmm, that smells good."

Joy grinned. "I hope it will be."

"Is Tyler home?"

"Not yet, but your Daddy is. He has company in his study."

"I'll run up and see Mamma."

Joy nodded, then asked, "Are you all right, child?"

Suddenly Cassie longed to throw her arms around the housekeeper and cry her eyes out. But she couldn't indulge herself that way. Besides, she had to remain strong for Tyler.

She made herself smile. "I'm okay, and thanks for asking."

Cassie had decided to tell both her parents at the same time about Lester's return, but since her daddy was occupied, the bad news would have to wait.

She had just passed the closed door and had one foot on the bottom stair when she pulled up with a jolt. Had she heard right?

"Actually, Reverend, I was never part of a militia group. Cassie just imagined that."

Everything in Cassie's body shut down. She couldn't move. She couldn't think. She couldn't even breathe.

Lester was *here!* And Tyler was due any moment.

Twenty-Three

Cassie couldn't stand to hear another word come out of that lying viper's mouth. Unlocking her legs, she thrust open the door and stormed into the room.

Both men swung around and stared at her, a dumbfounded expression on their faces, obviously taken aback by her unexpected intrusion.

James recovered and gave her a pasty smile. "Cassie, my dear, look who's here."

"I'm well aware of who's here." Her voice shook with rage as her gaze landed on Lester. "And that's the problem."

Lester didn't say a word, yet there was a smug turn to his lips that further infuriated her. She clenched her hands to keep from striking her ex-husband, who was standing in the middle of this room as though he belonged there.

"Hello, Cassie," he finally said, that smirk still in place. "So we meet again."

"How dare you come here?" Her voice was still wrapped in rage.

"Now, Cassie," James said, a pleading note in his voice. "Let's try to keep things civil."

Lester focused his attention on her father with a nod. "I couldn't agree more."

Cassie's rage was now off the charts, and it was all

she could do not to lay into both of them. But she had to keep a cool head or she would play into their hands. Time, though, was of the essence. She had to get Lester out of the house before Tyler got home from the picnic. When and *if* Tyler saw Lester, it would be her call, not his.

"What do you want?" she demanded, forcing herself to look at her ex-husband, although it sickened her to do so.

Again, her frigid attitude didn't seem to phase him. Lester crossed to the polished cherry desk, leaned against it, then folded his arms across his chest, as if he hadn't a worry in the world. "Oh, I think you know the answer to that."

"I told you to stay away from my son." Rage flooded her face with color.

James straightened, his eyes settling on her. "Cassie, please, control yourself. I want to hear what Lester has to say even if you don't."

"Daddy, this is none of your business."

"I beg your pardon." James's eyes darted from one to the other. "Of course it's my business. We're talking about a family here—you, Lester and Tyler."

"No! We're not a family."

"In the eyes of the Lord you are," James added in a quiet but firm tone.

"Daddy, you don't know what you're saying. You don't know this man like I do."

"It's you who doesn't know me," Lester said, his tone low, smooth and condescending. "Even though I went to prison, I was innocent."

"Oh, puhlease." Cassie rolled her eyes while her panic rose.

Lester went on as though she hadn't said a word, his

gaze centered on James. "But I hold no grudges, sir. You have to believe me."

"I'm the one who doesn't believe you," Cassie countered. "And I'm the one who counts."

"I beg to differ with that, young lady," James said. "The Lord is the one who counts."

Lester smiled at him. "Speaking of the Lord, while I was in prison, I was saved. I took Jesus into my heart."

Cassie forced herself not to laugh. Instead she prayed she wouldn't upchuck on her shoes as she watched her daddy's face change from dark to light.

Lester was feeding James exactly what he wanted to hear, and her daddy was lapping it up like a starving vagrant who'd found food. Not only was Cassie repulsed by the entire charade, she wanted to scream at the injustice of it all.

Instead she thought of Tyler.

"Enough!" she shouted. "I know what you're up to, Lester. I can see through you, even if Daddy can't."

Lester held out his arms. "Hey, what you see, baby, is what you're getting."

"Like hell," Cassie choked.

"Cassie, for heaven's sake," James said in a rebuking tone, "you must try to work things out with your husband."

"He's not my husband."

"I'll always be your husband," Lester said in a cajoling tone. "In the eyes of the Lord, that is."

"Mom! Where are you?"

Oh no! Cassie's worst fear had materialized. What should she do? For a moment she was paralyzed and couldn't do anything. It was that state of paralysis that cost her.

"In here, Tyler," James said, walking to the door and opening it.

"Don't!" Cassie said in a frantic but broken voice.

No one paid her any heed. Not only did Tyler hurl himself into the room and toward her, but Austin was right behind him.

If it hadn't been for her son's bright face, Cassie would have wished for death to claim her. The two men she feared most were together in this room, and she didn't know what to do.

She wasn't alone. No one else seemed to know quite what to do, either, except Tyler who was unaffected by the hostility that tainted the air.

"Boy, Mom, we had a great time."

"I'm...I'm glad you did, darling. Why don't you go see what Joy has for you?" Cassie tried to keep the desperation out of her tone as her eyes collided with Austin. His face looked like a brewing thunder cloud, his eyes stuck on Lester.

"Not so fast, Tyler," James said.

"Daddy, don't," Cassie warned again, this time in a louder, harsher tone.

Lester stepped forward. "Tyler, do you know who I am?"

"Damn you, Lester!" Cassie spat just short of clawing his eyes out.

"Cassie!" James said. "Mind your manners and your mouth."

"Mom?" Tyler inched closer to her, his confusion evident.

"It's all right, son."

"You bet it's all right," Lester said with a smiling cockiness. "I'm your Dad, Tyler. Don't you remember me?"

Tyler stared up at Cassie, disbelief registering on his features. "Is he my dad, Mom?"

"Hey, Tyler," Austin said, stepping forward, then placing an arm across the boy's shoulders. "I thought we were going to play a computer game? Why don't you go fire it up?"

Before Tyler could respond, Cassie said, "That's a good idea. We'll be there in a second."

Cassie pursed her lips and glared at both Lester and her daddy, daring them to dispute her order. Lester merely shrugged. James pinched his brows into a frown.

Once Tyler was out of hearing distance, Cassie turned to James and said, "If Lester doesn't leave, Daddy, I will. And if I do, I won't come back. Ever."

"All right, Cassie," James said in a tired voice. "We'll play it your way."

Cassie jerked her gaze back to Lester, her expression fierce. "Get out! Now!"

"Come on, Lester," James said in a clearly irritated voice, "I'll walk you to the door."

Although Cassie braced herself for a parting shot from Lester, none was forthcoming. Instead, he simply stared at her, then at Austin, with those cold eyes and self-righteous smirk.

Without warning, Austin moved toward Lester, his fists doubled. For a second Cassie's breath went into overdrive as the two men tried to stare each other down. Cassie sensed Lester wanted to see if Austin was bluffing, but he didn't. Most likely the menacing look on Austin's face was the deterrent that made Lester rethink his plan and follow her daddy out the door.

Once she and Austin were alone, a silence fell over the room while Cassie took deep gulping breaths. Without looking at him, she eased into the nearest chair, her legs unwilling to carry her weight any longer.

"You're right," Austin said into the silence. "He's a sorry sack of shit."

"Why can't Daddy see that?" she wailed, beginning to feel sorry for herself and hating it.

"Simple. He doesn't want to."

"But why would he take Lester's side against mine? I just don't understand. You'd think Daddy could see the evil that lurks behind Lester's eyes."

"It's the divorce. That sticks in James's craw for more reasons than one."

"One reason is that he's a preacher whose daughter has fallen from grace."

"I'll buy that, and another is that he truly believes divorce is wrong."

"Well, he'll have to get over that or disown me." Cassie gritted her teeth. "I'll never go back to that bastard."

"I could put a stop to all this, you know."

"How?"

"There are ways."

"Beat Lester up, for instance?" She almost laughed.

"That's occurred to me, among others."

Cassie shuddered. "Even though he backed down a moment ago, it wouldn't happen again. Besides, he's got his militia buddies to back him up. You'd end up getting hurt."

"Don't count on that."

"It's not your fight, Austin."

"What if I want to make it mine?"

"I don't want your help."

"Cassie—"

"I mean it," she interrupted, her voice and resolve

strengthening. "I'm capable of handling my own affairs."

"Sure you are."

His sarcasm wasn't lost on her. "Don't try to be my knight in shining armor. I told you, I don't want you in my life any more than I do Lester."

"You're lying again," he said. "And we both know it."

Her face went white. "I don't lie."

"You might not want me in your life, you damn sure want me in your *bed*."

"Damn you," she whispered, her eyes filling with tears. "You're playing dirty, and we both know that, too."

He leaned close to her, and she could smell his cologne; it made her light-headed.

"Fair or not," he said in a low, husky tone, "that's the way it is."

"Please leave," she said, swallowing.

"This is the second time you've kicked me out."

Then, totally without warning, he clutched her chin and gave her a quick but solid kiss on the lips, which took her breath away.

"There won't be a third," he said on another husky note. "I'm leaving you now only because your son's waiting."

With that, Austin walked out, leaving her alone with her tormented thoughts.

"I've left him, Austin, for good."

"I can't say I blame you."

"I meant to call and let you know that before now," Mary Jane said, "but to put it mildly, my life's been turned upside down. Having to go back to work hasn't been easy."

"So where are you living?"

"In an apartment."

"Is he still in the house?" Austin asked.

"As far as I know."

She paused, and Austin heard her heavy sigh through the phone line. "I'm assuming you haven't tracked him down."

"I tracked him down, all right, but he refuses to return my calls. That's why I'm glad to hear from you."

Austin had been about to leave his suite at the hotel when the phone rang. He had considered not answering it, but thinking it might be Cassie, he'd picked up.

Cassie. Thinking about her was driving him nuts, especially with that sicko ex of hers on the loose. If only she would let him help. Dammit, she was too hardheaded for her own good.

Shutting down those thoughts, Austin willed his mind back to the conversation. His patience with Randall had run out.

"Watch yourself with him, Austin," Mary Jane was saying. "He's an explosion waiting to happen."

"I'll be fine. You just take care of yourself."

Once he was off the phone, Austin immediately left the hotel and headed toward Alpine Road. When he pulled into the drive, he peered at his watch. Eight a.m. Randall usually didn't go to the office until around nine.

Maybe he would get lucky and find the bastard home.

Instead of going to the front door, Austin went to the back, where luck was indeed with him. The door was open, and he walked in. An eerie quiet greeted him as his eyes took in the mess in the kitchen.

Frowning, he moved down the hall, toward the bedroom that Randall and Mary Jane had shared. Surprise was his best offense, he told himself. With as little noise as possible, he eased the door open.

Austin had no idea what to expect. His mind had conjured up Randall in bed humping his latest bimbette or simply alone, sleeping.

The bed was unmade, but empty. Grim-faced, Austin made his way toward the bathroom, where the door was open.

What he saw there grabbed Austin by the short and curlies, making it impossible for him to move. "Why, you crazy son of a bitch!"

Randall was standing in front of his vanity, leaning over, snorting white powder up his nose. Cocaine. Randall was a cokehead. Good godamighty, Austin thought, sick to his stomach.

Randall's eyes bulged, and his mouth gaped when he saw Austin's reflection in the mirror. "Well, if it isn't my old friend."

Hot, white rage sent Austin flying across the room, where he jerked Randall up by his tie and slammed him against the wall.

"Let go of me!" Randall squealed, his Adam's apple bobbing.

"Not until you level with me or I beat the living shit out of you." Austin's nostrils flared. "It's your choice."

"I'll...I'll level with you," Randall said in a choked tone.

Austin let him go and stepped back, but not too far. If anyone deserved to have a fat lip, it was Randall. Cocaine! Austin was both repulsed and furious. No wonder Randall was broke.

The land money? Austin's blood chilled. Was it in jeopardy?

"Start talking," Austin said. "Before you have to be fitted for a new set of front teeth."

"I said I'd talk, so back off."

"Now's not the time to get a smart mouth."

Randall swallowed, then nodded.

Austin patted his cheek a bit harder than necessary, then smiled. "I'm glad you agree." His smile disappeared. "And once we've had our little talk, I want a promise that you'll get help."

"That...that takes money."

"Money I'm guessing you don't have?"

Randall smacked his lips. "You're right."

"So what about the land money?"

Randall went white, and Austin noticed he was shaking as if he were having a seizure. Not a good sign.

"Suppose I listen, friend, while you sing me a song, like a bird." Austin patted his cheek again. "And while in concert, you'd best not tell me the money I gave you has gone up your nose."

The ominous ring in Austin's voice was more than obvious, Randall's eyes glazed over and his body shook even more. "Of course it's not. I'd...never do anything like that. I...I promise the deal and the money are still intact."

"Mmm, now that's just the song I wanted to hear. How 'bout singing another verse, which should say you *will* get all the paperwork and let me take a look-see?"

"I...I can do that," Randall said, continuing to shake and sweat.

Austin patted the other man's cheek, then stepped back. "Good. And don't keep me waiting."

Twenty-Four

"Is something the matter?"

Austin didn't answer his trainer right off. Instead he continued with his task, which was rubbing salve on one of his prize mare's front legs.

"Okay, so I'll mind my own business."

Austin stood, then patted the horse on her back before facing Robb. "There's a lot going on."

"Anything I can do?"

"Just don't feed my paranoia."

Robb gave him a weird look. "Whatever you say."

Austin half smiled. "When I left the hotel, I had the feeling that someone was watching me."

"Huh?"

"I know it sounds crazy, but it was so real that I kept looking over my shoulder even after I was in the car. Today's not the first time I've had that feeling, either."

"Any idea who would do such a thing?"

"Maybe," Austin hedged, thinking of Randall and Lester and the hatred that had shone from their eyes following his encounter with each of them.

If that feeling wasn't a figment of his imagination, he doubted the culprit was Randall. He had his friend pegged as a gutless wonder. Still, Austin wasn't counting him out, since Randall had yet to come through with the papers concerning the money.

Lester and his cohorts, however, remained the most likely suspects. That ex-con was up to no good; Austin was convinced of that, despite Lester's boasting to the contrary. Those words had been bullshit sacked in silk.

Austin didn't believe for a second that Lester wanted Cassie and Tyler back because he cared about them. No siree. That bastard had an ulterior motive, and he wouldn't rest until he found out what it was.

"Are you in any danger?" Robb asked after he finished straightening a row of bridles.

Austin scoffed. "Hell, no."

"I hope you're right. But you gotta know, people are nutzo these days."

Austin's face hardened. "Tell me about it."

"Anything I can do?"

"Just keep on taking care of the farm and horses."

Robb removed his hat and wiped the sweat off his forehead. "You can count on that, providing I don't drop dead from heatstroke, that is."

Austin mopped his own brow. "You and me both. This is one hot-ass summer."

"And it ain't over yet."

Austin looked out of the barn into the distance, where he spotted several of his mares running in the pasture. What a pleasurable sight, he thought. One of these days he hoped to make some big bucks with them. But more than the idea of making money with his stock, he was simply thankful he had this place to come to when he needed to unwind and to think.

"How're the two colts we got from Mannard?" Austin asked, forcing his attention back to Robb, who was watching him closely. He hadn't fooled his friend. Robb knew he was distracted and out of sorts. Austin wished he could confide in him, but he couldn't.

"Doing just great," Robb said. "In fact, I've almost come around to your way of thinking. One of 'em just might win you some big money."

"And old man Mannard let him go? That's hard to believe."

"Well, the verdict's still out on whether we have a winner or not," Robb cautioned, "but we'll see." He paused. "If we're through here, I'm off to the south pasture. There's another break in the fence."

"Man, you don't have to fool with stuff like that. Hell, hire someone."

Robb replaced his hat. "Nah, no need. I'm hoping a little manual labor will take some of this gut off."

"Just be sure to drink plenty of water. You could very easily have that heatstroke."

Robb shook his head. "Don't worry about me. I'm outta here."

Austin watched as Robb mounted his horse and rode toward the pasture. Deciding to take a shower before he returned to town, Austin made his way toward the house.

Once in the shower, his thoughts turned to Cassie and the scene that had taken place at the Wortham house yesterday. It had been all he could do to keep his mouth shut. But his brain hadn't stopped boiling.

Poor kid.

Tyler didn't deserve having a jailbird for a dad. Worse, that jailbird was now an ex-jailbird, one who didn't give a damn about anyone or anything but himself and his evil cause.

When that deadbeat had blurted out his identity to Tyler, Austin had wanted to smash his fist into Lester's self-righteous face. But then, he'd wanted to flatten James, as well. God was going to get him for harboring such ill feelings toward his best friend, but he couldn't help it. James was too naive for his own good, and certainly for Cassie's.

The idea that Lester and Cassie should get back together was ludicrous. Although he didn't know the sordid details of their relationship, he knew something god-awful must have happened for Cassie to take her son and disappear. It was obvious Lester frightened her, and that was what had him upset.

Austin had tried not to let her continuing hands-off policy get to him. That was why he had left the room in search of Tyler, not only to keep his promise to play a game but to check on his frame of mind. After all, the kid had been mentally manhandled by that creep of a father.

But despite their plan to play a game, Tyler hadn't been around, having gone to his room and shut the door. Austin hurt for the boy and for Cassie, when all he wanted was for her to be happy.

More to the point and totally selfishly, he wanted Cassie to be happy with *him*. He wished she were with him right now, under this steamy water, their naked bodies rubbing together, creating that erotic friction...

Don't!

He had to stop torturing himself. She had reinforced her claim that she didn't want him to touch her anymore or to interfere in her life. Maybe he wouldn't have to worry about the constant ache in his groin much longer. With Lester back in the picture, he felt certain that nothing short of a miracle would keep Cassie here.

Cold goose bumps covered Austin's skin despite the hot water pounding it. He didn't want her to leave; that hadn't changed. And he aimed to do everything in his power to see that she didn't.

Lester and his cronies might think they were in control. He had news for them. If anyone messed with Cassie, Lester would live to regret it. With that thought uppermost in his mind, he dried off, dressed and headed into town.

Foolish or not, he had to make sure Cassie was all right.

Cassie had been expecting the question, though it had come later than she thought. Moments after Austin and Lester had left yesterday, she had gone to Tyler's room.

He had been on the floor, playing with his train. He'd looked up at her with rounded, sad eyes, and her heart had twisted. She had knelt and touched him on the cheek. But he'd pulled his head back and stuck out his lip.

"We should talk," she said in a low, calm tone, though her heart was breaking.

He shook his head. "No."

She had waited a minute to see if he would change his mind. He hadn't. Fighting off her own depression and tears, she had left him and gone to her own room, where she'd taken a sleeping pill and crawled into bed.

Decisions had to be made, hard ones, but she'd been too bone weary to think. She had told herself instead that tomorrow things would look brighter.

They hadn't.

She had gotten up early this morning, with a hangover from the pill. Still, she intended to confront her daddy about Lester. When she had gone downstairs, however, James had already left for the church, as if he'd sensed a showdown was imminent.

Cassie had drunk her coffee alone, checked on her mother and Tyler, then headed for work herself.

Now, as she sat behind her desk in the late afternoon, the door opened and a subdued Tyler walked in.

"Hi, sweetheart," she said, getting up. "What a nice surprise."

He didn't answer. Instead, he sat on the edge of a chair and slid his backpack off his shoulders. She ached to hold him and kiss him, but she dared not. She had to let him make the moves.

"How was your day?" she asked.

He shrugged. "Okay."

He was now enrolled in the second session of day camp sponsored by the city and had been having a ball until yesterday, when Lester showed up. Damn Lester, she thought again, her insides crawling with hate and fear.

"Mom?"

"What, sweetie?"

"Is...is that man really my dad?"

Blind panic rendered her speechless for a moment while she groped to find the right words to answer him.

Before they came to mind, Tyler went on. "I don't care if he is, I don't like him."

"Why is that?" she asked carefully, feeling as though she were holding a lighted stick of dynamite in her hand.

Tyler shrugged. "I don't know."

"Well, it's okay. You don't have to like him. And you don't have to see him, either, if you don't want to."

"You won't be mad at me?"

"Of course not, darling. Look, Lester doesn't think like we do. He has nothing in common with us."

"What about Papa? I think he likes him."

A spurt of anger shot through Cassie, but again she

had to tread lightly. "You know how Papa is, being a preacher and all. He always thinks the best of everyone, regardless." She paused. "But you let me worry about Papa, okay?"

"Okay." Tyler was quiet for a moment, then added, "I wish I had a daddy like Austin."

Oh, dear Lord, Cassie thought, what next? How many blows to the heart could one take and survive? She didn't know, but she was close to her limit. "He can be your friend," she said in a shaky voice.

"Mom?"

"Huh?"

"We don't have to go away, do we?" Suddenly his chin began to quiver.

"I don't know," she said honestly.

He didn't say anything, just lowered his head and dug the toe of his shoe into the carpet.

"Come here," she whispered. "I need a hug."

He ran into her arms, and for a few precious seconds, she held him tightly. Then he scrambled out of her arms and looked at her.

"It's going to be all right, I promise."

As if that was all the reassurance he needed, Tyler threw his arms around her one more time. After pulling back, he said, "I gotta go. Papa's in the lobby waiting for me."

"Since you have a ride home, I'm going to stay and work a while longer."

"Okay, bye."

Like a small whirlwind, he was out the door and gone.

Cassie made it to the nearest chair, sat down, leaned her head back against the cushion and let the tears flow. She had earned them, she told herself, giving in to the intense pain, the doubling-over kind, the kind she'd experienced so many times when it came to Lester and his relationship with Tyler.

Unwittingly, another incident jumped to mind, even more traumatic than yesterday's episode. It had happened after the divorce had become final. She had just put Tyler down for bed and walked back into the living room, only to halt abruptly. Lester had been leaning against the mantel.

"You have no right to be here," she had managed to say through stiff, white lips.

"It doesn't matter," he'd responded with an easy grin.

"Get out now, or I'll call the police."

His eyes darkened with hatred. "I wouldn't do that, if I were you."

"You can't tell me what to do. In case you've forgotten, we're divorced."

"That was a mistake. When you offered me money in exchange for your freedom and Tyler's, you caught me at a weak moment."

"Well, that's too bad. The divorce and its terms are a done deal, so get out."

"I want my son, Cassie."

"Dammit, he's not your son!" She darted to the phone, picked it up and shook it at him. "If you don't leave right now, I'm calling the law. Count on it."

Two long strides put Lester within touching distance of her, his nostrils flared. She backed up, but there was nowhere to go. The wall stopped her.

"I'll leave," he said in her face, "but I'll come back. And when I do, I'll take Tyler with me." He paused and ran one finger down a cheek. "And there won't be anything you can do about it."

He had been wrong. She had done something. She had taken her child and fled. But now her nemesis was back, as dangerous as before.

Cassie stood and wiped the tears from her eyes. Too bad she couldn't wipe away her soul-pain as easily. There were no words in the dictionary to describe that feeling.

This evening the terror associated with it was stomach-churning and produced the urge to bolt, to run away again, to try somehow to squirm out from under the agony. But there was no escape.

The key was survival.

But how? And at what cost? The choices she had to make sapped her energy, making her wish she was a screamer. Instead, more silent tears trickled unchecked down her face.

Fear.

That was the worst component of the pain—the fear that her child would be harmed. That fear was so overwhelming, so like an incurable disease, that her mind couldn't take it in.

But to seize Tyler and run again was not an option, not after her session with him. She couldn't do that to him. She wouldn't.

What she would do was stay and fight Lester. Suddenly Austin's face popped into her mind. If only... No, she wouldn't think about him, about how much she ached to lean on his strength.

A tap on the door gave her a start. She dabbed at her eyes with a tissue, then said, "Yes?"

The door opened, and Austin walked in. Her eyes rounded. "How did you—"

"How did I what?" he asked in a soft voice, his eyes narrowing on her face.

"Uh, nothing," she said, a warm feeling seeping through her.

Their eyes met and held for a moment, then she looked away.

"Cassie, I know you've been crying." His voice sounded raspy. "You don't have to hide from me."

She faced him again, licking her bottom lip with her tongue. She saw his eyes follow the small movement before she asked, "What brings you here?"

"You. I wanted to make sure you were all right. Are you?"

She looked at him and felt that current pulling her to him. This time she didn't fight it. "No, I'm not," she whispered.

Twenty-Five

A taut expectancy hovered between them as he continued to hold her gaze. She saw the concern in his eyes, along with something else—raw hunger.

Heat radiated through her, from the top of her head to the tips of her toes, while he made his way deeper into the room, stopping within touching distance, only he didn't touch her. But she wanted him to. Every nerve in her body cried out to have his mouth and hands on her.

Such intoxicating indulgence on her part was reckless. It had been reckless years ago, and it was reckless now. Yet she stood there, weak and defenseless, his for the taking.

"Cassie, Cassie," Austin whispered, his voice low and hoarse.

She knew he ached to hold her, to kiss her. She wouldn't stop him from doing either, feeling herself drift slowly toward him, like someone making her way through a fog.

In that moment, the phone rang. They both jumped.

"Ignore it," he rasped.

"I can't." Cassie's voice trembled. "It could have something to do with Tyler. Or Mother."

He cursed a blue streak, but stepped back when she reached behind her and lifted the receiver.

It was her father-in-law, Dewitt Sullivan. Of all people to call, she thought, disgust settling over her face. She watched Austin watching her. A questioning frown knitted his brows.

"This is not a good time, Dewitt," she said.

Damn! Austin mouthed.

She averted her gaze. As disturbed as she was at who was calling, the timing had been perfect. She had been about to do something she would most certainly regret.

"What did you say?" she asked, forcing herself to concentrate on the conversation.

She listened, then responded, "I refuse to even think about that right now."

Dewitt's next words made her see red. "I refuse to argue about it, as well. So before we both say something we'll regret, I'm ending this conversation."

And she did.

"Lester's old man?"

Cassie nodded.

"Was he threatening you?"

She gave him a startled look. "How did you know?"

"Why else would you get your back up like that?"

"I wouldn't," she said in a terse voice.

"What does he want that you don't want him to have?"

"He wants me to let Lester have Tyler so they can spend the weekend with them, meaning Dewitt and Charlotte."

"You mean they actually believe that hogwash Lester's feeding them, that he's a changed man?"

"Of course they believe it. Like my daddy, they think he was wrongly accused and falsely imprisoned."

"What a crock. I took one look at that sonofabitch

and knew he was lying through his pearly whites. More than that, he's a walking time bomb, ready to explode."

"That's exactly what I think, which is why I'm crazy with worry." Cassie rubbed her arms as if to restore life to her cold limbs. "I feel like Lester's closing in on me, along with these walls."

"All the more reason to get out of here."

"You're right. I'm going home."

"First, you're coming with me."

Her chest constricted. "I don't think that's a good idea."

"I do." Austin's tone left no room for argument.

Cassie argued anyway. "It's late, and I'm tired."

"And upset," he added. "Which is why my suggestion—"

"Suggestion? Don't you mean your order?"

"Whatever you say, brat."

That last statement brought an unexpected smile to her lips. "Somehow your logic escapes me."

Austin returned her smile, with one whose potency completely obliterated her defenses, leaving her suddenly at his mercy.

As if he sensed that, he cleared his throat, then said, "Let's get out of here. Time's wasting."

Cassie sat up with a start when she felt the car come to a stop. Had she fallen asleep?

Blinking, she turned toward the driver's seat. "Where are we?"

Even though she couldn't see Austin looking at her in the dark, she knew he was. She could feel the intensity of those eyes, as if they were caressing her.

"My farm."

Cassie blinked, while her pulse jumped.

"Don't start fretting." Austin's voice was as caressing as his eyes. "We won't stay long. Besides, I make a mean cup of cappuccino, which is guaranteed to perk up tired bodies."

"How can I resist that?" she asked, her mouth softening into a smile.

"You can't," he muttered, jerking open the door to the sound of chirping crickets that couldn't outdo her hammering heart.

They remained quiet as they walked toward the porch, the moon their only guide.

Cassie felt sweat settle into every bend in her body. The sun had lost its power, but not its steam. And the humidity was cloying. She tried to suck the thick air in and out of her lungs, but it was almost impossible.

Letting her eyes drift, she peered up at the huge oak trees draped with moss that surrounded the frame house. In the distance, she heard a horse snort, then whinny.

"Do you actually own this place?" she asked, stepping onto the porch and watching as he unlocked the door.

"Yep," he said, indicating that she should go in.

Cassie walked into a small living room that was suffocatingly hot, hotter than outdoors. Or maybe it was her body temperature that was elevated, because Austin was standing next to her, close enough for her to smell the sweat on his body along with his cologne.

The mixture was heady, and she found herself unable to move, standing like a mute, staring up at him.

He reciprocated her stare with those hungry eyes. The moment was highly charged even before he reached for her and pulled her against his chest.

"Austin, please," she whimpered, her arms wedged between them.

"Please what? Kiss you until you can't breathe?"

"I—"

His lips ground into hers, shoving further words down her throat. Moaning, she wrapped her arms around his neck and revelled in the feel and taste of him.

His moist, searing lips seemed to cling forever, sucking every last ounce of resistance from her body as he backed her down the hall into the bedroom. But before they fell onto the bed, clothes were discarded, thrown down at will.

Together, they fell naked onto the bed, where he took control, turning her to face him, his lips burning across hers again, then down her neck, to her breasts.

"Oh, Austin." Her breathless words came out sounding like a prayer of thanksgiving, instead of a prayer for forgiveness.

His tongue, as wet and hot as his lips, frantically circled her nipples, leaving them hard and aching.

"Touch me," he urged, reaching for her hand and placing it on him.

She moaned when his erection became thick under the clammy pressure she exerted. She massaged the flesh around and under until she felt a drop of moisture on one finger. Her hand stilled, and for a moment she was tempted to bring that finger to her lips and taste him.

Austin uttered a guttural groan, as though he could read her thoughts. "You have no idea what you're doing to me."

"Please, I want you inside me. Now." Her words came out sounding broken and desperate.

As if giving in to his own desperation, he nudged her lips apart again with his. While kissing her, he cupped one cheek of her buttocks and swung that leg over his thighs, giving him easy access to her.

And as he'd done before, in the car, he eased two fingers inside her. Cassie bucked, then begged, "I want you!"

Without taking his eyes off her damp face, he thrust inside her, and instantaneously flesh pounded against flesh until their cries filled the air, leaving them both wet with sweat and too spent to move.

"Did he ever make you feel like this?"

Cassie stiffened in his arms. For a moment Austin didn't think she was going to answer him. They had finally fallen asleep after endless hours of making soundless love. He had lost count of the times he'd taken her on top, on the bottom, from behind. Yet he could take her again right now. Just the thought made his penis rise to the task.

"No, never," she said in response to his question.

Austin pulled back so that he could see her face, the moonlight allowing him that privilege. "You mean he never made you come?"

Her sharp intake of breath sounded like a cannon shot in the quiet. "Only one...man has accomplished that."

"Are you saying what I think you are?"

"Yes," she whispered with vulnerable sincerity.

"Dammit, Cassie, what kind of man were you married to?"

"A monster, though he never physically abused me or Tyler."

Austin held her close for a long moment, while their hearts beat as one. How could he ever let her go now that he'd been with her again? Hell, he hadn't wanted to let her go after that first time. He had known that then, only he wouldn't, *couldn't,* admit it.

"Will you level with me? Will you tell me what that sorry sack of shit did that sent you into hiding for five years?"

"It's an ugly tale."

"I expect it is."

She told him in a halting voice about the evening she had come home and found Tyler sitting on Lester's leg, holding a gun. She also told him about Lester's threat to take Tyler from her.

"That sorry bastard," Austin said. "I'd like to get my hands around his neck."

"It's not your fight, Austin. I thought I made that clear."

He didn't respond, because he knew it would piss her off and part them, something he didn't want to happen.

"Are you leaving again, Cass?"

She peered at him, her eyes wide and haunted, which made him want to grab her again and kiss her until that look went away.

"I don't know. I don't trust Lester, and I'm definitely afraid of him and his cronies. But on the other side of that coin is Tyler. My concern for his well-being is equal to my distrust and loathing of Lester."

"You feel another transition will damage Tyler psychologically?"

"Exactly."

"So stay and fight. You're older, wiser and stronger. And you have your family, who don't want to lose you again." You have me, too, he wanted to add, but didn't, feeling such a bold claim would shatter the delicate truce between them.

"How can you say that about Mother and Daddy, especially Daddy? He's made it plain whose side he's on."

"Not if it means losing you."

"I don't know. Daddy's so steeped in his religious beliefs that it colors his sound judgment."

"I know that. Still, I have to think that, if push comes to shove, he'll back you. Besides, Lester's walking a thin line. If he so much as breathes wrong, they'll have his ass back in the pen."

"Then he'll just have someone else break the law for him."

"That's why you need me. And that's why I'm willing and able. Doesn't that count for something?" Dammit, he hadn't meant to say that. The words had just slipped past his lips like they'd been greased.

"Tonight must never happen again, Austin." Cassie paused, and he heard her sigh. "You know that, don't you?"

He didn't know any such thing, but he wasn't going to say that, either, and have her bolt like the frightened, fragile creature she was.

Wrong, he corrected himself silently. She wasn't fragile. She might look it and feel it, but she had a will of iron and more grit than any woman he'd ever known. In fact, he didn't think he knew another woman who would have had the courage to take her child, leave everything and everyone she loved behind, and start a new life with strangers.

"Austin?"

"I heard what you said, Cassie."

"Do you agree?"

"Do you want me to lie?"

"No."

"If I tell you how I feel, you won't be happy."

"I'm not happy now," she said in a small voice.

Austin sighed, his guts twisting. "I don't want us to stop seeing each other."

"It's not your call." Her tone was cold as she pulled away, got out of bed and, bending over, reached for her clothes.

Austin's gaze froze on her backside and the delectable crease in her buttocks, feeling himself hardening again. Shit!

"Why are you fighting what's between us?" he asked.

She turned and faced him, her face devoid of expression. "I don't owe you any explanation other than the one I've already given. Please, just take me home."

Angrily, Austin got out of the bed that still smelled of their loving. "Gladly," he said though gritted teeth.

Twenty-Six

"So how's it going?"

Lester made a face, then turned his back on the group's leader, Grant Hoople, and walked into the kitchen, where he opened the refrigerator and helped himself to a beer. After unscrewing the top, he took a long draw on the cold suds.

"Feel better now?"

Several other members of the group chuckled at the sarcasm in Hoople's voice as his eyes tracked Lester. Lester couldn't have cared less. Hell, it was damn hot, and he was thirsty. He'd been taking target practice at the militia's camp in the woods in this stifling heat. There wasn't a dry stitch on him.

"Yep, sure do," Lester said, grabbing another beer before sauntering back into the small living room of Hoople's unpretentious frame house, located in a quiet neighborhood in Lafayette.

Over the years, little had changed here, except the members could no longer gather as a group in these cramped quarters. The decision makers, including himself, were the only ones allowed.

"So how are you faring with your assignment?" Hoople asked.

Lester shrugged. "Fair to middlin'."

Hoople's large lips thinned. "Which translates into not worth a shit."

"You pretty much nailed it," Lester mumbled in a dark tone, sitting and chugging down half of the second beer.

"So your ex isn't cooperating, huh?" Hoople scoffed. "If you're going to convince her of your born-again status, your acting skills are going to have to improve."

"I know, and I'm working on them," Lester said, having added a cutting edge to his tone, feeling all eyes on him. He changed positions as though on the hot seat, feeling damned uncomfortable.

Following his incarceration, where he'd been told what to do every waking moment, Lester had sworn he wouldn't take orders again. But he had no choice, since it had been the group's money that had bribed the judge to bring him back from prison and place him on parole.

His dumb parents and their stupid lawyer didn't have a clue as to what had gone on behind closed doors. But Lester did, and that was why he had to tread lightly. Grant Hoople was one mean son of a bitch. Anyhow, Lester wanted to do what was right, wanted to contribute to the cause he believed in and would die defending if he had to.

"How are you working on it?" Hoople pressed. "Details, man. I want details."

"For starters, I'm using my old man and hers to put the screws to her."

"But it's not working, or you wouldn't look like you're headed back to the cell block."

"I admit it's slow going. She's a much tougher nut to crack than before."

"Oh, I think that little lady's always had balls, which

means you gotta find another way of yanking 'em. Your son would be my suggestion.''

Suddenly sweat gushed out of every pore on Lester. Granted, he wanted to yank Cassie back in line, teach her that a woman's place was beside her man. But that had to be done with finesse. He hadn't told Hoople or anyone else that he'd given up his rights to the child. To do so now would severely hamper his power and perhaps put him in danger. Thinking that he still had legal rights to the brat was their ace in the hole.

"You're right about Tyler," Lester finally said in a cautious voice, "but that's going to be tough. She poisoned him against me."

"Well, you'll just have to find an antidote for that poison. That boy needs to see you as a hero."

"What if she takes him and hauls ass again?" Lester asked. He wasn't about to admit that the possibility kept him awake at night, though certain members had been taking turns watching her to make sure that didn't happen.

Still, Lester didn't trust Cassie to stay or his cronies to watch her carefully enough. He would like nothing better than to knock her across the room and just take the boy. Of course, he couldn't do anything that radical, the first reason being that he would end up back in the pen.

Other reasons were money and Austin McGuire. The group needed more ready cash to buy additional weapons, and Lester knew Cassie's family still had plenty of the green stuff.

McGuire, however, was another matter altogether. He was getting too close to Cassie and Tyler to suit him, besides sticking his nose where it didn't belong.

But dammit, that was another puddle of quicksand

that could suck him under. The Reverend thought McGuire could walk on water. And Lester couldn't afford to offend James, who was his biggest ally.

"Stop stalling, Sullivan," Hoople demanded. "We need a solid plan. Now."

"Damn, cut me some slack, okay? I told you, I don't have one yet."

"Come up with one," Hoople barked. "And that's an order."

She never got her cappuccino.

Cassie almost laughed out loud hysterically, at such an absurd thought, only she didn't. Nothing about that evening was the least bit humorous. Whenever the details came to mind, in vibrant color, no less, she felt sick and confused.

It had been two weeks since she and Austin had made hot, passionate love like two people who had the freedom and the right to indulge themselves.

Hotel business in Baton Rouge and Shreveport had taken Austin out of town, a blessing in disguise. But all blessings come to an end. He was back.

According to her son, Austin had stopped by the church, and when his papa couldn't get away to take him home, Austin had volunteered. On the way, they had stopped for a sundae. Once they had gotten to the house, Austin had played several computer games with Tyler.

"Austin's cool, Mom," Tyler had told her over and over last evening. "He whipped my butt—"

"Tyler, you know better than to use that word," she had responded in a sharper tone than she'd intended. However, her life was splintering in too many different directions. She had to regain control.

"Sorry, Mom," Tyler said, giving her a strange look. "Why don't you like Austin?"

His blunt question caught her so by surprise that she'd had to scramble for a suitable response. She'd finally answered with a question. "What makes you think that?"

Tyler shrugged. "You always holler at me when I mention him."

"Why, Tyler Sullivan, that's not true, and you know it. I've never hollered at you."

He gave her a sheepish grin. "Well, you know what I mean."

He was right. She did know what he meant, but she wasn't going to address it. Besides, this conversation had gone far enough. "Look, I like Austin just fine. He's a nice man, but I don't want you to be a nuisance to him or become too attached."

"Why?" Tyler asked with childlike sincerity. "He likes me a lot."

"I'm glad," she said lightly.

"He told me he'd like to have a son just like me one day."

Swell.

While that conversation had set her teeth on edge, Cassie had refrained from saying another word. Despite the fears pounding her from all sides, she remained determined to stay in Jasmine. Given that, she had come to terms with her fragile emotions and vulnerability where Austin was concerned.

Had she fallen in love with him? Yes. She had always loved him. That love was what had driven her to pursue him that long-ago evening, making it impossible for him *not* to make love to her.

Yet she couldn't act on her heart's desire. Even if

her parents could get beyond Austin's betrayal and accept them as a couple, she couldn't. She simply couldn't risk Austin finding out that he was Tyler's father. He would feel betrayed and angry, no telling what he would do.

Besides, this mental torture she was putting herself through regarding Austin was futile. He wanted her in his bed; he made no secret of that. But that was all. He had never spoken the word *love*.

If he had, it wouldn't change anything, not when there was such a fine line between love and hate. She couldn't ignore *her* guilt, either. She had denied Austin one of life's most precious gifts—a son. *His son.*

Stop it, Cassie! Stop torturing yourself. Instead, she should savor the memories of that night in Austin's arms, when she'd felt so secure, so loved, and make those memories last a lifetime.

While they might have slept together, they could never live together. Because of that, her secret was safe. Rational thinking told her that.

What she had to worry about was Lester and how to handle him. His presence had her back in limbo. She was damned if she left and damned if she didn't. For now, she had only what Austin had told her to cling to, that if Lester stepped out of line, he would be back behind bars.

Hopefully her ex would think long and hard before he did anything stupid. Too, he had to know that he wasn't dealing with a scared young girl anymore, one who was willing to go through hell to make her marriage work and to provide a father for her child.

That young girl was no more.

When it came to James, she had no qualms, although it saddened her that he had sided with Lester. While

she hadn't taken her daddy to task for his betrayal, there
was, nonetheless, a definite change in the air when they
were together.

It was only a matter of time before she would confront him, but for now, she kept her mouth shut. She
had considered taking her mother into her confidence,
but Wilma's failing health had nixed that.

Besides, her mother was only interested in her taking
care of the hotel, which was another problem. Hopefully Austin had gotten out of the land deal and put the
money back into the company.

Thoughts of the hotel forced Cassie back to the ren-
ovation plans on her desk. She was anticipating and
preparing for the rescheduled meeting with the architect
and contractor the day after tomorrow.

She had yet to inform Austin about it. A sudden
smile flexed her lips. It would be interesting to see what
happened. Unconsciously, she glanced at her watch,
then moaned. It was too late to do any serious work;
she might as well go home.

Her daddy was the first person she saw when she let
herself into the Wortham mansion.

"Hi, Daddy," she said, half smiling.

He didn't return the smile.

"Are you alone?" he asked.

"Yes, why?"

His eyes narrowed. "Tyler's not with you?"

Panic, sharp and hot, jabbed her in the stomach. "No.
You mean he's not here?"

"No." Something akin to fear changed the color of
his eyes.

"But you...you were supposed to pick him up, like
always."

"Someone called my secretary and said you were getting him today."

Cassie slammed a hand against her heart. "Oh no!"

"Now, now, calm down. It's probably nothing, just a misunderstanding."

"A misunderstanding!" she yelled. "How can you say that, when we don't know where he is?"

"We'll find him," James said in his still-unflappable tone.

"What about Austin?"

"I just called him. He hasn't seen him, either."

"Oh no," Cassie said again, sinking onto the bottom step of the stairs, feeling like all the blood had just drained from her body.

"It's Lester," she said in a broken voice. "He's...he's taken my son."

"I'll call the police," James said.

The tall, lanky man sat down in a chair in Austin's office, and blew out his breath. "This is the hottest fuckin' summer I've ever lived through."

"You and everyone else," Austin said, scrutinizing his longtime friend, Hank Medford, who had once been a cop. Now he was a private detective, in business for himself.

"Mind if I take my tie off?" Hank asked.

"Why the hell do you have one on?"

Hank grinned, his weather-beaten features crinkling like old paper. "Respect, man, respect."

"Horse manure," Austin replied, rolling his eyes.

"It's true, man. You oughta know that. You wear these son of a bitches yourself," Hank added, jerking the tie from around his neck and stuffing it in his pocket.

"Not on days like this," Austin declared. "Respect or no respect. So, you got something for me?"

"Do I ever."

Austin's eyes turned steely. "Shoot."

"Funny you should use that word. Your boy's back playing with his guns."

"You dead sure about that?"

"Is sweat tickling my underarms?"

"Cute."

Hank grinned.

Austin had hoped the information Hank brought him would be to the contrary. He wasn't surprised, of course, knowing that Lester certainly hadn't been born again, as he'd professed. Still, Austin had hoped Lester wasn't up to his old tricks. Now that he knew he was, Austin felt genuine fear.

Lester was nuts, and no one could predict which way he would jump. Austin was convinced Lester was tailing him. Consequently, he had decided to return the favor in the form of Hank.

Austin wasn't worried about himself. He could take care of Lester. Not so Cassie and Tyler. He feared for their safety, yet he wanted her to stay and fight the bastard.

"I followed the scumbag to a house in Lafayette," Hank said. "A place in low-class suburbia, where I got the license plates off the owner's pickup. When I ran the plates, I couldn't believe the guy is still walking the streets."

"A renegade, huh?"

"That's putting it mildly. Grant Hoople's rap sheet is longer than the government's budget. What gets me is that no one's made the charges stick, even the weapons violations."

"Lester took that fall."

"But I suspect they got him out."

"No doubt."

"So where do we go from here?" Hank asked.

Austin wrote out a check, then stood. "Don't let Sullivan out of your sight."

Once he was alone, Austin sat back down, his mind in turmoil. Dammit, he felt helpless, though he was doing as much as he dared. If Cassie knew he had hired a private detective, she would be furious. And James—well, he would have a fit, too.

Thinking about James made him see red. How could he be so gullible, so naive? But he was, and that wasn't going to change, especially when he still had illusions of Cassie and Lester getting back together.

Over my dead body.

Dammit, he loved her. While that truth was what this gut-churning was all about, it came as a bitter pill to swallow. Even though he hadn't faced it, he had known it shortly after he'd married Alicia. Something besides good sex had been missing from his marriage. Now he knew what that something was—deep and abiding love.

Austin dropped his head in his heads, giving in to the sadness washing through him. God, he loved Cassie so much and yearned to make the world a safe place for her and her son.

Not only did he want to protect her and cherish her as she deserved, he wanted to see that sparkle back in her eyes instead of the pain.

Most of all, he wanted her to love him back.

He wanted Tyler to love him, as well. Thinking of her son and the fun they'd had yesterday increased Austin's ache twofold.

Suddenly Austin struggled just to get a breath. Even

if Cassie were to reciprocate his feelings, it wouldn't work, not as long as James was in the picture. For Tyler, Cassie would cross her daddy, break his heart, if necessary, which she had. But for him, no way.

But Lester wouldn't have her again, either. No matter what it took, he would see to that.

"Mr. McGuire?"

Austin almost jumped out of his skin, he was so deep in thought. It was his secretary. "Yes."

"You have an urgent call on line one."

Twenty-Seven

"Ma'am, we're doing our best to find him."

The overweight detective with the baby face had been telling Cassie that from the moment the police had arrived.

Now it was the following afternoon, and there was still no sign of Tyler or his whereabouts. Cassie wanted to believe Detective Mike Conn, *had* to believe him, yet she was inconsolable with fear and doubt.

She stared up at him and nodded, her eyes, already bloodshot from having cried so much, filling with unshed tears.

"He's right, ma'am," his partner, Dave Winslow, added. "We're not about to leave any stone unturned."

"Then why hasn't he been found?" Austin demanded, his eyes darting from one officer to the other.

Cassie heard the accusing note in Austin's voice and for once didn't try to challenge his interference. In fact, she was glad he was there with the family, having more or less taken charge.

"It's not that easy, sir," Detective Conn responded in a calm tone. "We have an all points bulletin out on Mr. Sullivan's car. But if the boy got in the car with a stranger, then..." His voice trailed off when Cassie whimpered out loud.

"It's all my fault," James muttered, taking a cup off

the tray Joy held out to him, only to grip it with both hands to keep coffee from sloshing onto the floor.

Like her, James was in a state of shock at the brutal turn of events. While members and staff from the church had been by to offer their support and comfort, nothing had helped.

Her mother was feeling ill and was in bed, sedated. Because of that, Wilma hadn't even been told that her grandson was missing, for fear the bad news would trigger a fatal heart attack.

Cassie couldn't have dealt with one more tragedy. She would have toppled over the edge she was now teetering on. Yet she didn't blame her daddy.

She blamed that bastard Lester.

"It's not your fault, James," Austin said. "We all know who's responsible."

Cassie watched Austin's jaws bunch before he peered over at her. She wanted him to hold her, to assure her that Tyler was going to come home, that nothing terrible had happened to him. But Austin couldn't hold her, nor could he promise her that her son was okay.

Her insides were scraped raw, and whenever she thought about the horrors that might have befallen her precious child, she nearly lost her mind.

"It's going to be all right, I promise," Austin said, as if he knew what she'd been thinking. "We'll find him."

"What if we don't?" she asked through chattering teeth, fear making her cold. "He's been missing since yesterday evening."

"As soon as they find Lester, they'll find Tyler."

Cassie wanted to scream, but she had to remain strong. She couldn't fall apart now. After Tyler was home safe in her arms, then she would allow herself that luxury.

So when she spoke again, it was in a low, controlled voice. "What's taking them so long?"

"I haven't a clue," Austin said harshly. "If something doesn't break real soon, I aim to find out."

"If he's hurt Tyler," Cassie said, "I'll kill him myself."

James closed the distance between them and sat beside her. "Now, honey, please don't talk like that."

She glared at him. "Don't placate me, Daddy. I meant every word I said."

"Leave her be, James," Austin told him in a gentle but firm way. "Don't worry, she won't have to take him on. That will be my pleasure."

"Austin, I—"

"Don't say it, Cassie. This might not be my fight, as you've reminded me, but I'm making it mine now. Tyler's my buddy, and he doesn't deserve to be the pawn in this game."

"You're right about that," Cassie whispered.

They exchanged intense glances for a long moment before Cassie looked away. She was too tired, too frantic, to argue with Austin. All she wanted was her child back.

While it was unthinkable for Tyler to be in Lester's hands or those of the men he hung around with, the rational part of Cassie's mind told her that her ex wouldn't harm Tyler. At least, not until Lester got what he wanted, which would hopefully buy them the time they needed to find her son.

If she hadn't had that to hold on to, she couldn't have stood the awesome terror that had her crippled in mind and body when she thought about Lester having fled with Tyler.

"As soon as they find your ex-husband, then we'll be off and running, Ms. Sullivan," Detective Conn said, helping himself to a glass of iced tea and some finger sandwiches that Joy had prepared.

Cassie turned away from the food, the sight and smell of it making her ill.

"When a noncustodial parent entices a child away from the custodial parent, it's a state matter," Conn added. "If it's someone else, then we call in the FBI."

"Is it possible you know something you're not telling us?" Austin asked in a harsh, frustrated tone.

Detective Conn answered, "Unfortunately, no. Sullivan's our main concentration, along with Grant Hoople. Neither one is home or any other place we've checked."

"Then why doesn't Lester call?" Cassie cried, balling her fists so tightly that her fingernails pierced her skin. The self-inflicted pain proved that at least she was still alive. "I know he wants something. He always does." Her tone was a mixture of anger and bitterness.

"Why is it that you can't locate his parents?" Austin hammered, rubbing the growth of beard on his face, which Cassie thought gave him a demonic look, making him seem tougher than either of the detectives.

She shivered for more reasons than one.

"They're apparently out of town," Detective Winslow said, moving toward Cassie. "We have a man staked out there. The second they return, we'll talk to them."

"If need be, are you up to going on television?" Conn asked.

"Do you think it'll come to that?" Cassie whispered, her heart sinking.

"If it's not your ex-husband who has the boy, then it just might. I have to be brutally honest, ma'am."

"Shit," Austin muttered under his breath, but Cassie heard him, and so did James, whose lips tensed with displeasure.

Cassie had to turn away, thinking that she didn't like her daddy at this moment, not because she blamed him, but because of his inability to let his guard down, to turn off the automatic preacher pilot and be human.

She needed James to climb down from his pedestal and comfort her. Maybe if she had remained the perfect daughter, then his arms might be around her. But since she'd fallen from grace, that wasn't going to happen.

"There's no doubt who has my son," Cassie said tersely. "We just have to find Lester."

"I couldn't agree more," Austin added, peering at her.

She tried to read what was behind those incredible eyes, but she couldn't, or maybe she didn't want to. Involving Austin in this mess was also lethal. But for the moment, and under the circumstances, her will to fight him was nonexistent.

"Since they can't find the Sullivans, do you think Lester and Tyler could be with them?"

"You should know the answer to that better than me," Austin said. "I've never laid eyes on those people."

"Well, they're good people. Even though they still believe in Lester's innocence, I can't believe they wouldn't take part in the kidnapping of their grandson."

"Then we're back to Lester and his schizo group."

Austin paused, then said, "I'm going to make a call. I know how much you resent my help, but—"

"Right now, I'd take help from the devil himself."

Cassie saw Austin flinch at the comparison, but she couldn't worry about that now. Feelings, including her own, weren't important. Tyler's safe return was all that mattered.

"I'll be right back," Austin said, striding off.

Cassie closed her arms around her body and rocked back and forth, whispering a prayer. "My baby, Lord, take care of my baby."

That broken prayer got to him. Austin had to turn away or jerk her into his arms, which would only add to her suffering. Anyway, his top priority at the moment was to use his cell phone away from listening ears.

"Are you leaving?" James asked.

Austin halted and turned around, his gaze quickly perusing the room. James stood adjacent to him; the two detectives remained across the room. One was on his walkie-talkie, and the other was staring out the window at the drive.

Waiting.

That was what they were all doing, and not accomplishing one damn thing. He was tired of waiting. More than that, he was tired of watching Cassie's pinched face and frantic eyes.

He wouldn't pretend he knew what she was going through, the depth of her suffering, never having held his own child. But he could imagine the horrors that were playing out in her mind. If it were his child who was missing under these circumstances and he got his hands on the creep responsible, he would be hard-pressed to turn him over to the law.

Cassie felt the same way, he knew. Any parent worth his salt would feel the same way.

After James had called him and asked if he had by chance picked up Tyler from day camp, Austin had come straight over, but not before calling his private detective friend. If anyone could find the kid, it would be Hank, especially as he'd already been tracking Lester. Austin had left the Worthams' number, but so far, he hadn't heard from Hank. He prayed the detective's voice mail hadn't screwed up.

"I'll be back," Austin said.

"I don't know what to do," James whispered in an urgent tone. "Cassie looks like she could break at any minute. Do you think I should call our doctor?"

"I'd wait a little longer and see what happens."

"I still find it hard to believe that Lester would do something like this."

"Dammit, James, join the real world."

The reverend flushed under Austin's unvarnished criticism.

"As badly as I hate to say this," Austin said for James' ears alone, "I hope he does have him, instead of some sexual pervert."

The red in James's face faded to a sickly gray. "Oh, dear God, I hadn't thought about that."

"I'll be right back. I need some fresh air."

A few moments later Austin sat in his car and punched out Hank Medford's number. This time the detective answered.

"Dammit, why haven't you returned my calls?" Austin demanded without preamble.

"I just walked in the door. Haven't even checked my messages. What's up?"

Austin told him.

"Well, you can forget about Lester himself."

Austin went stiff as a board. "How do you know that?"

"'Cause I'm on the job, that's how, like you told me. One of my men was staking out Lester's house and saw him get in a car with two elderly people."

"His parents," Austin said, his nerves starting to tingle.

"Right. I ran a check on their plates. Lester had luggage. I'm guessing they were headed out of town."

"Damn! What about his militia friends? Think they did his dirty work?"

"Yep. Don't you?"

"Sure do, but how do we prove it?"

"What about the cops?"

"Two detectives are here."

"Standing around with their fingers up their butts, right?" Hank chuckled at his own choice of words.

"I'd say that's a pretty accurate description."

"Want me to see what I can find out?"

"ASAP."

"I'm on it."

Austin sat in the car a moment longer, wondering how in hell he was going to tell Cassie what he'd just learned. But he had no choice.

With heavy steps, he trudged back into the house. Cassie was still in the same position. Although he didn't touch her, he eased down beside her and said, "I have some news."

It seemed as though everyone's ears in the room perked up. Before he was bombarded with questions, he added, "Lester doesn't have Tyler."

Wide-eyed, Cassie stared at him. "You know that for sure?"

"Yes, but I don't know any such thing about those gun-toting radicals he hangs out with."

"I told you Lester wouldn't do anything like that," James said.

"Shut up," Austin told him, stopping him in his tracks.

"Ma'am," Detective Conn interrupted, "I think you'd best come here."

Austin stood abruptly, picking up on the strange sound in the detective's tone. Cassie followed suit, immediately making her way to the detective's side.

"Ohmygodohmygod!" she cried, struggling to get to the door.

Austin stood behind her and watched as Tyler ran up the long drive toward the house.

"Mom! I'm home!"

Cassie lunged out the door and ran to meet him.

"James," Austin said in a low, gravelly voice, "it's your grandson. He's home."

James darted past him, making his way outside.

Austin felt tears prick his eyes as Cassie knelt in front of her son, grabbed him and hugged him as if she would never let him go. Suddenly he turned away, wishing he never had to let either of them go.

But then, he couldn't hold what wasn't his.

Twenty-Eight

Cassie couldn't take her eyes off her son, though he now lay sleeping peacefully in his bed. When he had first crawled under the sheet, he had been pale and drawn and frightened, but unharmed.

Although Tyler hadn't come right out and asked her to sit with him, wild horses couldn't have dragged her away, at least not this night. Lying there, he seemed so small, so vulnerable, such a child, that tears once again stung her eyes.

Cassie willed those tears back and rubbed her forehead, feeling a headache coming on. If that was the only ill effect she would have from the ordeal, then she should count her blessings.

The precious child now curled up in fetal position was her only concern. Leaning over, Cassie brushed her lips against Tyler's cheek one more time, then got up and walked to the window, where darkness, relieved by only a few stars, greeted her.

She lifted her shoulders up and down, then rolled her head from side to side, trying to get rid of the kinks in her body, which she thought would have been completely numb by now.

Following her exercise routine, Cassie slid her eyes back to the bed, to her son. She still could not believe what had happened. Even though she was looking at

Tyler, in the flesh, she still couldn't believe that he was here, with her, in his bed, sleeping like a newborn.

Bizarre.

There was no other word to describe the entire incident. Bizarre or not, she knew everything that Tyler had told them had been the truth. Besides, the phone call to the church had substantiated his story.

When she had managed to let go of him long enough and lead him back inside, she had been so overcome with emotion that, for a minute, she couldn't speak. But then, everyone else had the same problem, even the detectives. Both men's faces were pictures of bewilderment.

The room had been as quiet as an empty funeral parlor.

Austin had been the first to speak, once again seeming to take charge. "Man, are we glad to see you." His voice had been gruff, but gentle.

Cassie's gaze had rested briefly on Austin, and when she saw the concern etched in his features, another emotion, one she hadn't wanted to acknowledge, stabbed her.

"Are you hungry, darling?" Cassie asked, suddenly at a loss for words.

"No, ma'am," Tyler replied, looking up at his mother. "That man fed me."

Cassie kept her arm around his shoulders and nudged him forward. "Let's go sit down, and then suppose you tell us what happened. We've all been worried out of our minds."

Once Tyler sat on the edge of the sofa, his big eyes, underscored by dark circles, eased toward the two detectives, whose badges were obvious, since neither was wearing a jacket.

"It's okay, darling. They're the nice policemen who've been trying to find you." Cassie introduced them, then turned back to her son.

James had moved to sit in a chair close to the couch. He didn't say anything; he just reached over and squeezed one of his grandson's hands.

Cassie saw James's chin quiver and knew that he, too, was overcome with relief and thanksgiving.

Dismissing everyone else from her mind, Cassie concentrated on Tyler. "You said a man fed you. What man?"

Tyler shrugged, then peered down at the floor, as if suddenly shy from all the attention focused on him. Wisely, the detectives remained in the background, as if they sensed Tyler might clam up if pressed by anyone other than her.

"I don't know his name," Tyler admitted in a muffled voice.

Cassie brushed some hair off his forehead, aching to squeeze him close again. But she refrained; it was imperative that she and the detectives learn who had kidnapped Tyler, though she was convinced it was one of Lester's militia buddies. She would bet her life on that. Whether that could be proved was another matter altogether.

"Tell Mom how you got together with that man." Cassie kept her prodding gentle and low-key, terrified of spooking him. She knew without asking that he was exhausted and needed sleep more than anything else. But she couldn't allow him that luxury, not now, anyway.

Tyler's eyes shifted to his granddaddy briefly before going back to the floor. "When no one picked me up,

I started walking toward the church to ride home with Papa.'' He paused, his chin quivering.

"It's all right, darling," Cassie said, wanting to kill the bastard who had traumatized her son. "Someone called Papa's office and told him I was going to pick you up, which wasn't true."

"He was mean."

Cassie inhaled sharply at the same time that she heard Austin mutter a curse. Both detectives also inched closer, though they didn't say anything. Detective Winslow, however, was busy writing down everything Tyler was saying.

"Did he hurt you?" Cassie could barely get those ugly words through her lips.

Tyler's chin jutted. "No, but he locked me in a room."

"Can you describe what he looked like?"

Tyler nodded.

"We'll get him down to the station," Detective Conn put in, "and put him with an artist."

"Then find the bastard and nail him," Austin said, which garnered a disapproving look from James.

Cassie secretly cheered Austin's succinct outburst, although *bastard* was a nice word compared to what she was thinking. As for her daddy—well it was a fact that she could forget him ever facing reality about anything.

"Go on, honey," Cassie said, into the building silence. "Finish your story."

Tyler didn't respond. He merely scraped the floor with his shoe.

"Hey," Cassie prodded in a sweet tone, "why did you get in the car with someone you didn't know? I've told you never to do that."

"But, Mom, he told me Grandmother was in the hospital and he was supposed to take me there to meet you and Papa."

"How could someone do a thing like that to a child?" James blurted out, getting up and grabbing a mint julep off the tray that Joy had replenished.

"It's easy, sir," Detective Winslow said, "when you're up to no good."

"When we first got there, he—"

"Where's there?" Cassie interrupted.

"Somewhere in the woods, I think," Tyler said, "but I don't know, 'cause he put a blindfold over my eyes."

Horrified at that thought, Cassie almost cried out, only she didn't. She didn't want anything to stop him from talking, knowing he couldn't hold up much longer. His eyes were drooping and his body sagging.

"Oh, honey, I'm so sorry you had to endure that," Cassie said instead.

"When he put me in that room, he took the blindfold off, but it was dark, and I couldn't see."

"Did you hear anything?" Detective Conn asked.

"Birds and crickets," Tyler said, gazing up at him for a second before looking back at Cassie. "Can I go now, Mom?"

"In a minute. Don't you want to find the man who did that to you?"

"I tried to get away, even kicked him in the leg when he tried to shove me in a closet."

Cassie blew out a breath of fury, thinking how she would like to have Lester in front of her about now. "Tried. You mean he didn't put you there?"

"No. He said if I'd be good, he wouldn't make me go in there. I sat in a corner all night."

Cassie was dying little by little on the inside, but she couldn't let it show. "So how did you get away?"

"He just came in and told me that he was taking me home."

"Just like that?" Austin said in an incredulous tone, then clamped his lips together as if he feared he'd spoken out of turn.

Cassie looked at him, and their eyes met for a millisecond. She turned away, fighting off the urge to once again seek comfort in Austin's arms, taking Tyler with her. She shivered inwardly, knowing thoughts like that would merely add to her troubles.

"He didn't say another word to me," Tyler was explaining, "except to tell me to get out of the car." His gaze found Austin. "I think he was mad about something."

"It's okay," Austin said with a smile. "You're home now, and that's what counts."

Cassie felt Tyler's eyes return to her. She smiled at him, too, though hers was a bit wobbly. "You're a brave boy, and I'm so proud of you."

"We all are," James said, finally coming over and hugging the child.

When James had stepped back, Tyler said, "Can I go to my room now, Mom, and maybe take some of Joy's tea cakes with me?"

"You sure can." Cassie stood on weak legs. "How 'bout some milk to go with those cookies?"

Once upstairs, she had supervised his bath, then watched as he ate his cookies and drank his milk. By the time he'd emptied the glass, he could no longer hold his eyes open.

He'd been sleeping ever since.

Now, as Cassie continued to hover over him, she

tried to make some sense of his bizarre tale. She couldn't. Why would one of Lester's cohorts kidnap Tyler, keep him locked in a room overnight, then let him go?

It made no sense.

Had Tyler's kidnapping been solely for her benefit? Had Lester been trying to terrorize her into capitulating to his demands concerning Tyler? Probably. But it wouldn't work.

She wouldn't run, nor would she allow Lester to bully her. She had made her stand to remain in Jasmine, and she wouldn't budge, though she was aware that Tyler couldn't be left alone anymore.

Cassie could count on Austin, but he was a threat on his own, one she didn't know how to deal with, either. Unwilling to think about *him* now, Cassie switched her thoughts back to her ex-husband.

Hopefully Lester wouldn't be as big a problem as she feared, not when the man who took Tyler was picked up and fingered her ex-husband as the mastermind behind the kidnapping.

Voilà! He would go right back to the pen.

Come morning, she would take Tyler to the police station. If the police were unsuccessful in tracking down the culprit, then she would do something, though she didn't yet know what.

Lester Sullivan was not going to get away with this latest escapade. "I'll see you in hell first," she whispered to the four walls.

Austin had pulled some dumb stunts in his life, but this one was perhaps the dumbest, if not the most dangerous. But he'd had to do something. He simply couldn't sit back and wait on the police. They weren't moving fast enough to suit him, even though Tyler had given a description of the man to the police artist a couple days ago.

He hadn't seen Cassie, purposely keeping out of her way, knowing she didn't need any further distractions or problems. He figured himself to be both.

Dammit, he thought, as he tromped through the woods, hoping that the hot, sticky thicket would provide him adequate cover. Lester, whom he was following, had probably already reached his destination; at least, that was what Austin was counting on.

After he had left the Wortham household, following Tyler's return, he'd been a man at war with himself and everyone around him. Like Cassie, he was convinced that lowlife Sullivan had been behind the kidnapping. But why, since nothing seemed to have come of it? That was the question that nagged at Austin, kept his guts churning.

He couldn't talk to Cassie. She had looked so frightened and delicate, as if she couldn't hold up another second, which had ripped his heart to shreds. But she'd hung tough, much like a scarred warrior who had been through many battles and won.

He had attempted to talk to James, but right off he'd found that to be a mistake. That conversation had only sharpened the knife already jabbing him.

"I'm convinced Lester's innocent," James had said the following day from behind his office desk.

"That's a crock of crap," Austin lashed back.

James expelled a sigh. "I knew you'd say that."

Austin gave his friend a hard look. "Then how do you explain what happened to your grandson?"

"I don't know. Maybe someone's out to get Lester. After all, he's been in the pen."

That explanation had been so naive, so sickening, that Austin hadn't said another word. Instead, he had walked out before he puked all over the brand-new carpet in James's study.

Still seething over James's turning a blind eye and his own fear that the police would botch the investigation, Austin had called Hank. Unfortunately, the private detective had been out of town on another case.

That was when Austin had decided to take matters into his own hands. He'd driven to Lafayette, chancing that Lester might be at home or would eventually end up there.

He had struck instant paydirt.

Just as Austin pulled his car up alongside the curb across the street from Lester's nondescript house, the ex-con was climbing into his truck.

Austin had followed him out of town, where he'd eventually turned onto what looked to be a private road. Austin had left his car off the highway and followed on foot, over and around mosquito-infested bayous.

Now, as he paused behind a huge oak tree, heavy with moss, he wiped the sweat out of his eyes and stared ahead.

In front of him was a campsite, crawling with men, women and children.

He crouched on his belly and watched.

"Damn!" he mouthed a short time later, feeling his blood turn to ice.

Twenty-Nine

"What's bothering you?"

James Wortham turned and stared at his wife, who was still in bed, where she remained most of the time these days. He curbed a sigh, realizing that Wilma would never again be the strong, vibrant woman he had married.

"You know me too well," he said, trying to dodge the question. He doubted he would have much success. Wilma's body was impaired, but not her mind. It was as sharp as ever.

"So stop hedging."

He smiled a fleeting smile.

"A few minutes ago you were scowling. Now you're smiling. What's going on?"

"I was just thinking that nothing gets by you, my dear."

"Especially when it comes to your moods. Is it Tyler and the kidnapping?"

Although James had been reluctant to confide in Wilma concerning the incident, he'd had no choice. Sooner or later someone would have slipped, most likely Tyler himself, and Wilma would have resented being excluded and made life hell for him.

As expected, the news had upset her terribly, but the

fact that Tyler had come through the crisis safely tempered her anxiety.

"No one's been arrested yet," James said at last, standing at the mirror, knotting his tie.

"And you're still convinced Lester's innocent?"

James swung around. "Absolutely."

"What about the group he's associated with?"

"I don't believe any of that garbage, either."

"Well, you have to admit that something he did landed him in jail, James."

"Not necessarily. Lots of innocent people go to jail. Besides, I refuse to hold the past against him. I believe he's a changed man, that he's found the Lord."

He watched Wilma frown as her fingers plucked at the top sheet. "I hope you're right."

"I take it you don't trust my judgment in this." James made a flat statement, fighting off a feeling of irritation. He knew he was right in his assessment. Why couldn't everyone else see that?

"It's not that I don't trust you," Wilma said. "It's just that I haven't talked to Lester myself to form my own opinion."

"I didn't think you were up to that."

"Oh, I'm up to it, all right, only I didn't want to alienate Cassie."

"Ah, Cassie. She's so bitter and hostile toward Lester. Her attitude breaks my heart, especially for Tyler's sake."

"Maybe you should give up trying to make them a family again. Maybe it's not meant to be."

James's eyes narrowed, and his voice turned huffy. "I refuse to accept that. As soon as Cassie realizes that Lester's totally without blame in this incident with Tyler, I'm positive she'll listen to reason and give him another chance.''

Wilma's frown increased. "I don't know about that, James. I think you're meddling in something that's not any of your business. After all—''

"She's my daughter," James interrupted. "And I only have her best interest at heart.''

"Are you sure it's not *your* best interests?''

"What's that supposed to mean?" James demanded in a tight voice.

"You're a brilliant man. You figure it out.''

"Sarcasm doesn't become you.''

Wilma pushed an errant strand of hair behind her ear with an unsteady hand. "Look, I'll admit I'm crushed at the mess Cassie's made of her life thus far. And I take responsibility for part of that.'' Wilma paused. "We weren't the most attentive, loving parents, you know.''

"Nonsense. We were perfect parents and still are.''

"I'm not going to argue with you," Wilma said in a tired voice.

"Good," James responded, hearing the snap in his tone and not liking it, but deeming it necessary. He couldn't allow Wilma to side against him. On family matters, they had to band together.

"What I *am* going to do, however," Wilma was saying, "is pray that whoever took our grandchild is caught.''

James slipped into his suit coat. "Me too.''

"You're not convinced he was even kidnapped, are you?''

James stopped midaction and gave her a startled look. "What makes you ask that?''

"I don't know." Wilma lifted her bony shoulders in a shrug. "Just a feeling I have."

"Well, it's almost too bizarre to believe, but considering some of the circumstances, such as the phone call, I have to give Tyler the benefit of the doubt."

"But...?" Wilma's smile lacked intensity.

"But I *am* having trouble digesting it."

"Poor Cassie. I'm almost sorry now that I pushed her into staying here."

"I won't have you talking like that." Again James heard the harsh note in his voice. But a man in his position had to take charge and look after his own. He was merely doing the Lord's will.

"You're right. Besides, I'm selfish enough to want her to carry on the business in my place. I think she's doing a wonderful job, don't you?"

"Of course. What did you expect? She's our daughter."

Wilma rolled her eyes. "How are things between her and Austin?"

"Fine, as far as I can tell." James shrugged. "But then, you know those two. They're like brother and sister, which means they tend to disagree."

Wilma smiled. "They'll work it out, even if a few sparks do fly."

James walked over to the bed and placed a kiss on Wilma's cheek. "You have a good day, you hear?"

"You too."

"I will, but only if our family situation straightens out. You know the elders don't like their minister to have problems that everyone's talking about."

"Oh, James, stop being so stodgy."

"Stodgy? How can you say that, when you feel the

same way? You've always abhorred anyone knowing our business and discussing it.''

"I still feel that way, except I'm worried about Cassie and Tyler. Right now, I'm more concerned about them."

"They're going to be fine. You just concentrate on yourself and feeling better. You know, the church body is really talking seriously about starting our new sanctuary. I need you by my side when that comes about."

"Go to work, James. We'll talk later."

He walked out and shut the door behind him, thinking how wonderful it would be if he could remarry Cassie and Lester in that new house of the Lord. The thought buoyed his spirits.

Cassie couldn't believe she had let Tyler talk her into this excursion. But she had no excuse for this indulgent behavior, and she offered none.

They were at Austin's farm, and it was a lovely Saturday afternoon, if one liked heat and humidity. And bugs. She liked none of them. However, those nuisances were hazards of summers in the South and weren't likely to change to suit her fancy.

After what Tyler had been through, she had rewarded him with this trip to Austin's farm, a trip the two of them had instigated behind her back.

When they arrived, Austin had given them the tour of the house, then a portion of the land, having been met by his trainer and friend, Robb.

Cassie had to admit that Austin had a nice setup, with the potential for making money from his stock. She wondered if he had ever brought his girlfriend here. More to the point, she wondered if he was still sleeping with her.

Wincing again at the sharp jab that thought brought on, she pulled her T-shirt away from her damp body, wishing she didn't have on a bra. In fact, she wished she were naked. Color suddenly invaded her face, especially as her gaze fell on Austin, who was with her son in a distant corral.

Before taking Tyler and mounting him on a horse, then leading him by the reins, Austin had made sure she was out of the sun's direct line of fire, having spread a quilt under a huge oak whose limbs were dripping with leaves and moss.

Nearby was a bayou that wound through this part of the property, which made the stickiness worse. In addition to her thin T-shirt, she had on shorts and was barefooted, so she would survive. She hoped Tyler fared as well, although she had lathered him in sunblock, and Austin had put a hat on his head.

Watching them together now was almost more than she could bear. Yet she couldn't take her eyes off them. Austin had halted the horse and was talking to Tyler, apparently giving him instructions.

Cassie's pulse upped its beat as she once again thought how rough, how mature, but oh, how appealing Austin looked, and how much she wanted him again. Her gaze concentrated on the long legs and strong thighs that had clasped her lower body while he'd pounded inside her. Heat of a different kind pooled between her legs, and she crossed them.

Damn, she had to stop thinking such thoughts. She hated herself for her weakness, but when she was alone, her mind betrayed her.

Even Jo Nell had picked up on her obsession with Austin and hadn't minced words about it.

"You're miserable, and I'm willing to bet he's the reason."

"I don't know what you're talking about." Cassie heard that prim edge in her voice and didn't blame Jo for snorting. "Okay, so I'm attracted to him. I won't deny that, but that's as far as it can go."

"I'm not sure I agree."

"It's not up for discussion."

"It damn well should be." Jo Nell stared at her over the rim of her tangy orange drink, her eyebrows raised. "Get my drift?"

Cassie had invited her friend to have lunch with her in the hotel's atrium dining area. They had both taken their lunch hours for this quick visit.

"I get your drift, all right, but you know better than anyone that Austin and I have no future. To keep talking about it is tantamount to beating that same old dead horse."

"Correct me if I'm wrong, but that old dead horse smells to high heaven with love."

Cassie flushed. "You should've been a stand-up comedienne."

Jo Nell grinned, then her lips flattened. "Looks like you've got yourself in a hell of a mess, my friend."

"I'll admit that, but nothing's going to come of it, so we might as well change the subject."

"Okay, I give up." Jo glanced at her watch. "In the short time I have left, tell me about the kidnapping. That's the wildest story yet."

"And the scariest."

The day after Tyler showed up in the drive, Cassie had called Jo Nell and told her what had happened. Today was the first time they had talked about the incident in person.

"You're still positive your ex was behind it?" Jo Nell asked.

"I know he was, despite his ironclad alibi."

"Good old Mom and Dad."

"Right."

"So are you going to stick around?"

"Yes." Cassie clenched her jaw. "I've decided that bastard's not going to dictate my life any longer, though I can't turn my back on Tyler, not for a second, not until Lester's back behind bars."

"Which we pray will only be a matter of time."

"Hey, Mom, watch!"

Tyler's proud voice jerked her mind off that disturbing conversation with Jo and back to the present, which was equally disturbing, especially with both Austin and Tyler grinning at her. She rose and watched as Austin released the reins into Tyler's hands and he began walking the horse on his own.

"Way to go, son," she called back, though she wanted to throttle Austin for turning Tyler loose on that huge animal.

Then, as if Austin could read her thoughts, he motioned for Robb, who suddenly appeared and began walking alongside Tyler. Cassie breathed a sigh of relief, only to find the feeling short-lived.

Austin sauntered toward her. From where she stood, she could see the sweat glistening on his body. She knew she should turn away and stop soaking up every detail about him. She couldn't, so she steeled herself not to react when he stopped in front of her.

"We're not having fun yet, are we?"

Cassie cut her eyes up to him. "Cute."

"Relax," he said in a low, sexy voice as he leaned toward her, a devilish glint in his eyes. "I'm not going to ravish your body."

Thirty

Cassie felt her face turn as red as the wildflowers in front of her. "Damn you, Austin," she said in a thin voice.

"Unless you want me to, that is," he added, as if she hadn't spoken.

Cassie's breath caught, and she stared up at him. "That's not fair."

His eyes darkened. "I'm tired of playing fair."

"You're just making things worse," she whispered, her tongue unwittingly wetting her bottom lip.

This time *his* breath caught. He moved closer, his back blocking them from the view of Tyler and Robb, who weren't looking in their direction anyway. Then, in a husky voice, he said, "If I don't kiss you, I won't make it another second."

"You're—"

His lips melted into hers, hotter and more moist than the air around them. Cassie ached to push him away, but she couldn't, not when his teeth were nibbling on her lower lip and a hand was reaching under her shirt and bra.

"Mmm, I love your breasts. They're perfect."

"Austin, please," she murmured weakly against his lips as his hand closed around one of those breasts.

"I dream about waking up every morning with a nipple in my mouth, sucking it."

"No," she pleaded, pulling her mouth away from his.

"Yes," he countered thickly, forcing her to look at him despite her efforts to the contrary. "What's more, I'd give anything to watch a child we made suck those nipples."

"No!"

This time she pushed with such force that he was caught off guard. When his hands and arms automatically relaxed, she lunged back, out of harm's way. Still, she was dizzy, and the air seemed to have compressed against her skin, making it tingle.

It was obvious he was struggling to regain his composure, as well. He was staring at her, and his breath was coming hard.

"Sorry, I was way out of line."

"That you were."

"But dammit, I meant every word I said."

She couldn't have answered even if she had wanted to. Her body was in shock, a different kind of shock than what she'd been through with Tyler, but shock, nonetheless.

A child we made. With those words screaming silently at her, Cassie turned and placed a hand over her throbbing lips to keep from crying out loud.

Tell him! Tell him the truth. What better time than now? But the words wouldn't come. Fear immobilized her, surrounded her like a suit of armor.

But if he loved her, he would forgive her. He'd never said that, she reminded herself. He had never spoken those words, which might have been the key that unlocked her heart and made her spill her secret.

He wanted her, and she wanted him. Did that translate into love? She didn't know. Right now, she was too confused and disoriented to think rationally.

"Cassie, talk to me, please."

She twisted around and faced him again. His features were pale, and sweat was visible on his skin. She fared no better. In fact, she felt his eyes settle on her chest, where she knew her nipples were visible under her damp shirt and bra.

She swallowed hard, and he averted his gaze, but not before she saw a nerve twitch in his jaw.

"If you want to talk about us, then forget it."

"You can't run from me forever."

"Oh, but I can."

"Yeah, I guess you can at that."

His words were bitter, and that galled her.

"We were never meant to be, Austin."

"How do you know? You won't give us a chance. If only…" His voice trailed off, and his mouth tensed.

"You were engaged to Alicia," Cassie said in a soft, defeated tone.

"And you were in love with that gun-lovin' son of a bitch."

"I was not!"

"Then why the hell did you marry him?"

"Why did you marry my aunt?" she returned.

He seemed stunned for a moment, then his eyes narrowed. "Are you saying that it would've made a difference? That you cared about me when you enticed me between your legs?"

"That's crude," she said, the high dots of color on her cheeks spreading over her entire face.

"No, it's the truth."

"Was that all it was to you?"

"No."

That simple word, spoken with such tormented honesty, stunned *her,* and she sank back onto the quilt, feeling what little energy she had left drain out of her.

Austin followed suit, then said, "When you touched me that evening, I had never felt that way before."

"Austin, don't tell me that. It's useless to rehash the sins of the past. Besides, I find that hard to believe."

"It's the truth. You set me on fire." He paused. "Unfortunately for me, that fire never burned out." His voice had grown low and harsh.

"That evening was a mistake, Austin."

"Okay, I'll concede that. You were eighteen, and I was thirty-two, which was not good, not to mention the other reasons. But it happened, and we can't pretend it didn't. Nor can we deny that we both enjoyed it."

"I've never denied that," she said without looking at him.

"And you can't deny we've enjoyed making love since then, either."

"No, I can't."

"So why are you fighting what we feel?"

"And just what is that?" she asked before she thought. "Lust?"

"Is that what you think?"

"I don't know what I think anymore."

"Well, I sure as hell know what *I* think. I feel a whole helluva lot more than lust for you, and I don't want to stop seeing you or sleeping with you."

"Even if there's no future?"

His face lost its color. "I won't accept that."

"I can't make commitments, Austin," she whispered, feeling a sadness that was like death stealing

over her. "In my heart, I think that's what you're asking for."

"I'm willing to give you all the time you need."

"I can't think about anything until Lester's out of
our life," she said, unable to meet his eyes for fear he
would see that she was lying.

"I can handle Lester," Austin said with cold and
calm assurance.

"That's part of the problem. If I became involved
with you, that could make the situation worse."

"That bastard shouldn't be allowed to ruin the rest
of your life and Tyler's. He's already done enough
damage as it is."

"And he's still doing it. Take Tyler's disappearance.
We both know he's the one who instigated it."

Austin didn't respond, but she saw him stiffen and a
fierce look come over his face. A warning bell went off
in her head.

"You know something you're not telling me."

"No, I don't."

"Yes, you do," she said flatly. "I can take it, whatever it is."

"I followed Lester to their campsite in the woods."

"That wasn't smart." If anything had happened to
him... She shuddered.

"I did it anyway."

"And?" She could barely get the tiny word out, so
afraid was she of what was coming.

"Toddlers were standing in a straight line, guns
clutched in their hands, aiming at a target."

"Dear Lord in heaven," Cassie wheezed. "Now you
know why he must never get his hands on Tyler again."

"I have to tell you, that sight turned my blood to ice,

and it was all I could do not to storm that camp and jerk Lester's heart out—that is, if he has one.''

"You stay away from him, you hear?"

"I can't promise that, Cassie."

"Yes, you can, dammit. I'll kill him myself if he comes near Tyler again."

"Despite the kidnapping incident, you've decided not to leave?"

Cassie lifted her head definitely. "That's right. But I can't let my guard down for a minute, especially with Daddy thinking Lester's a changed man."

"It's only a matter of time until James sees the light. If need be, it'll be my pleasure to expedite that happening."

"You leave Daddy to me, as well."

Austin let out an expletive.

"I've told you more than once that I don't want your help."

"Well, that's too damn bad."

For a long time neither spoke. In the distance, they could see Tyler and hear his laughter.

"You can't run roughshod over me, Austin, not when it comes to my family or the hotel."

"Ah, I was just wondering when we were going to get around to the other sore spot between us."

"I'm still against buying that land."

"Well, I'm not."

Cassie tightened her lips to keep from crying. She knew she shouldn't have come here. She had capitulated for Tyler's sake. But it had been a big mistake that was growing bigger by the second.

"It's time you took us home."

Austin got to his feet. Refusing to have him looming over her, she also scrambled up. They stood facing each other in an explosive silence brought on by the way his eyes roamed over her.

"Whatever lie you're feeding yourself, you just keep right on. Sooner or later, though, judgment day's coming. You're mine, Cassie. You always have been, and you always will be."

"Stop it!"

"All I have to do is pull you against me and you'd be begging me to take you."

"How dare you talk to me like that?" Her eyes filled with tears as she swung away, only to smother a groan. Tyler had left the corral and was headed toward them.

"Perfect timing, I'd say," Austin drawled.

She ignored him and waved at her son, who didn't stop running until he stood in front of Austin. "Did you see me?" he asked, his eyes sparkling.

"You bet, and you did super. Why, you'll be riding by yourself in no time."

"Can we come back, Mom?"

"I don't think—"

"Sure you can," Austin interrupted smoothly. "Any time you want to."

"I'll bring my good luck charm back with me," Tyler added.

"And what is that?" Cassie made herself ask for the sake of conversation. Her conversation with Austin had rattled her so she couldn't think at all, much less think straight.

"This." Tyler held out his hand, and in it was a small toy train car.

Cassie frowned, not recognizing it. "Where did you get that?"

Tyler's expression sobered. "I found it in that room where that man took me."

"May I see it?" Austin asked.

Cassie cut her eyes toward him. It wasn't what he said that drew her attention but the way he said it. His voice sounded choked, and his face was devoid of color. Suddenly she was afraid, only she didn't know why.

"Do you mind if I keep this for a few days?" Austin asked.

Tyler shrugged. "Okay."

"Austin, what's going on?" Cassie asked.

"Let's go," he said in an abrupt tone.

She had no choice but to grab Tyler's hand and follow.

Thirty-One

"So what's the pervert been up to lately?"

Cassie almost smiled at the way Jo Nell referred to Lester. But nothing pertaining to her ex held any real humor.

"All's quiet for the moment," Cassie responded. "Which makes me even more nervous."

She and Jo had been talking on the phone for a while, catching up on day-to-day happenings.

"I hope you're not letting Tyler out of your sight," Jo said.

"He's either under my eagle eye or someone else's. However, I'm trying to keep Tyler from picking up on that. He's been through too much already."

"Anything new on the kidnapping?"

"No, but I'm counting the days until Lester's arrested for his part in it."

"That goes without saying," Jo said, then asked, "So how are things at the hotel? Have you decided to go forward with the renovations?"

"Yep. I finally met with the architect and contractor, though I haven't given them the definite go-ahead. First, I have to pin Austin down. He has to get our money back."

"I'm sure you'll find a way to convince him."

Color swept into Cassie's cheeks. She was just glad

Jo Nell couldn't see through the phone line. "What's that snide little remark supposed to mean?"

"You know what it means, and you know what I think about it, too."

"You're right, of course," Cassie said in a dejected tone. She wished she could stay away from Austin. That would certainly solve the emotional and mental anguish she was going through.

Since she had admitted to herself that she'd fallen in love with him, she was in a mess, a mess she didn't know how to clean up.

"Enough lecturing for the time being," Jo said decisively. "I have to get back to work. My next appointment just came in."

"I'll talk to you soon," Cassie said absently, then hung up, her mind already back on Austin.

Suddenly the phone rang again. She jumped; then, ridiculing herself for lack of control, she reached for the receiver.

It was hotel security.

"We need you down in the lobby right now."

Cassie knew something was wrong. The urgency in Fred's voice was a dead giveaway. "What happened this time?"

"One of the guests took a tumble, tripping on Lord only knows what."

"Did you call 911?"

"Yes, ma'am."

"I'll be right down. Meanwhile, find Mr. McGuire."

"Will do. Right away."

Fuming, Cassie tore out of her office. Austin *would* get the company's money back on that land deal today, and the renovations *would* be done.

She wouldn't settle for anything less.

* * *

Randall never knew what hit him; Austin made sure of that.

"You broke my nose, you bastard!"

Randall's hoarse cry fell on deaf ears as Austin jerked him up again and looked into the attorney's face, which did indeed sport a bloody nose.

"If you don't stop whining, I'm going to throw a broken jaw into the pot."

"Please, let me go," Randall begged.

"My pleasure." Austin let him go so hard that if it hadn't been for the wall, Randall would have hit the floor. As it was, he sort of slid down, settling into a crouched position on the floor. "I hate dirtying my hands on the likes of you."

"You're crazy!"

"Shut up and get up," Austin demanded. "As much as I hate to, I want to look you in the eye when you spill your guts."

Randall struggled to regain his balance. Once upright, he yanked a handkerchief out of his suit pocket and held it over his nose, his terrorized gaze never leaving Austin.

"You're not going to hit me again, are you?" Randall's voice quavered.

"Depends."

"I'll...I'll tell you what you want to know."

"Then start talking."

"Please, can't I sit down?"

"No, dammit, you can't."

"Austin—"

Austin drew his hand back, prepared to punch him again.

Randall twisted his head, but not before raising both

hands in front of his face. "I'll...do anything you say," he stammered. "Just please don't hurt me again."

"Stop blubbering and tell me why *you* kidnapped Tyler."

"I...didn't. I...I had it done."

Austin's laugh was ugly. "That doesn't surprise me."

"I had to do it."

Austin put some space between them, afraid that if he didn't, he would end up literally beating the stuffing out of Randall, lifelong friends or not. The bad part about that was he didn't consider himself a violent man, able to name on one hand the times he'd hit another man with his fists.

Anger, underscored by love, was a strong motivator, one that had driven him to attack his once-trusted friend and attorney.

"I'm listening," Austin said in a voice that was as ugly as his laugh had been a moment ago.

"I hired someone to do the dirty work," Randall admitted, sniffling.

"For god's sake, why? Why do it at all?"

"I needed money."

"To feed your habit?"

Randall nodded in the affirmative, then held the handkerchief back over his nose. "Please, I need to see a doctor."

"You can forget that."

"Dammit, my nose is broken, and I'm in pain."

Austin leaned over Randall, who cringed back into the wall. "If you don't start talking, every bone in your sorry-ass body is going to be broken. *Then* you can talk about pain."

"When did you get to be such a mean son of a

bitch?'' Randall's tone rose until he sounded like he was singing soprano.

''When you fucked with someone I love.''

''I had no choice.''

''We all have choices. You just happen to have made the wrong ones.''

Randall removed the cloth and stared up at Austin. Randall's eyes were pleading, and his chest was heaving, as if he were having difficulty breathing.

Austin wasn't moved one bit. ''You're wasting your time trying to con me with all that emotional crap, counselor.''

''I knew you'd been seeing Cassie, that you two were an item.''

Austin stiffened. ''You've been following me?''

''Yes.''

''Damn you.''

''I didn't want to, but I had to.''

''Stop saying that,'' Austin ordered, his tone sharp. ''Or by God, I'll tear your throat out as my bonus.''

''I...I knew you were close to Cassie's family, as well, and would do anything for them.''

''Go on,'' Austin said through tight lips when Randall paused, his eyes skirting the room as if looking for a way out.

Austin voiced his thoughts. ''You can forget about going anywhere.''

Randall's now swollen face lost what little color it had left. ''You can't keep me here.''

''I don't intend to.''

Randall began to shake violently. ''What does that mean?''

''You'll find out soon enough. Right now, what happens to you is not top priority.''

"How...how did you find out I was involved?"

"Let's just say a blind hog found another acorn."

"Stop talking in riddles."

Austin's features turned fierce. "Hey, you're not calling the shots here. I'll talk however I please, and you'll think it's music to your ears." Austin patted one of Randall's cheeks. Hard.

Randall gulped as if he'd just swallowed a peach pit.

"But just so you'll know you were outsmarted by a kid, I'll tell you. Remember that train set you bought your girls and y'all played with when they were little tykes?"

Randall nodded.

"It just so happens that Tyler found one of the cars—the caboose, to be exact. He called it his good luck charm. Now isn't that a hoot? Or is it justice? Which do you think it is, counselor?"

"It's that whore's fault, the one I've been seeing. She's not only possessive, but she's hooked on the stuff worse than me."

"Even if your mistress is a worse junkie than you, the kidnapping wasn't her doing. It was *yours*, you lowlife." Austin's gaze roamed over the man he had once held in such high esteem.

"What a waste," Austin added. "Looking at you and what you've become makes me sick to my stomach—among other things."

"It's those other things that worry me," Randall mumbled under his breath.

"Which is smart on your part." Once again Austin's tone was dark and threatening.

"Look, can't we work something out?" Randall wheedled. "If I promise to get help—"

"What scumbag took Tyler?" Austin didn't so much

as raise his voice, but he didn't have to for Randall to get the message. His friend began shaking like a whipped dog. Good comparison, Austin thought, disgust and anger almost choking him. "I want a name and where to find him."

Randall gave him the name, though reluctantly, then asked, "What are you going to do?"

"Have the bastard arrested."

"But he let the kid go," Randall said in a shrill voice.

"And you think that makes what the two of you did all right?"

"But no real harm came to him," Randall said. "That ought to count for something. After I paid the guy to take the boy, I knew I'd screwed up. That's why I let him go without asking for any money."

"Oh, really? How perceptive of you."

"Please, Austin, cut me some slack. The dealers who supply me with cocaine are after my ass. They've already hurt me once."

"Tut-tut. My heart's bleeding."

"What do you want from me?" Randall asked in a frantic tone. "I'm a sick man. Can't you see that?"

What Austin saw was red. He reached down and grabbed Randall by the shirt, then jerked him halfway up, so they were practically nose to nose. Randall's teeth were banging together so hard that Austin thought they might break. He couldn't have cared less. Whatever happened to Randall was better than he deserved.

"You think that excuses what you did?"

"I told you, I was desperate and grasping at straws. I knew the Worthams would pay the money to get the kid back. Old lady Wortham's rolling in dough." Randall paused, then continued in a low, trembling voice.

"I was so scared of those goons, I guess I wasn't thinking straight."

Austin laughed another ugly laugh. "Straight? Hell,
you weren't thinking at all. Kidnapping that boy was
your lowest moment."

"I know that now."

"I don't think you do. What brains you had are obviously gone, fried from sniffing that crap up your nose.
But just for the record, when you kidnap a little boy, it
can't help but affect him." Austin paused, fighting for
control of his runaway emotions. "What if someone
had done that to one of your girls?"

Randall's face turned ashen, and for the longest time
he didn't say anything. "I...I thought about them, and
then I looked in the mirror and didn't like what I saw."

"Well, that makes two of us."

"What's going to happen now?" Fear once again
tainted Randall's tone.

Austin ignored that question, along with the smell of
fear that seemed to seep from Randall's pores. "What
about the money from the land deal? Did you lie about
that, too?"

Austin hated to ask that, for fear of what he'd hear,
but he had to know. Ball-busting time had finally come.

"You...you wouldn't, can't, understand." Randall's
chin quivered, and his gaze shifted.

"Try me."

"I'm sick, Austin." Randall was sobbing openly
now. "I can't seem to stop buying the stuff."

"The money, Randall! Did it go up your nose along
with your family's savings?"

"Yes," he whispered around the sobs. "I never even
gave it to the real estate company."

Even though Austin had suspected that was coming,

he still felt as if he'd been flattened by a bulldozer. "Not one red cent?"

"Not one cent."

For a moment silence filled the room. Austin's throat was paralyzed, making it impossible for him to say another word. Randall was frightened, too, he knew, once again leaning back into the wall as if to dodge the blows he feared his confession would bring.

"That wasn't my money, you sorry piece of shit," Austin said at last, bearing down on Randall again. "That was company money."

"I'm sorry, Austin. Honest I am."

"Save it, counselor, for the judge."

Randall's eyes widened. "You mean you're going to turn me in?"

"As sure as God made little green apples."

"You can't!" he squealed, sounding like a stuck pig. "What about Mary Jane and the girls?"

"What about them?"

"Think what it will do to them."

"I don't give a shit. And if you did, you should've thought about it before you kidnapped an innocent boy."

"Dammit, Austin, I'm like family. You can't have me arrested. I need to be in the hospital."

"That's up to the courts, not me."

"Please don't do this," Randall begged, his face wet with tears and sweat.

Austin threw him a disgusted look, his lips curling back. "Stop grovelling. I'm calling the cops, and there's nothing you can do to stop me."

Randall's sobs grew louder as Austin punched out

the number to the police station, wondering what the hell he was going to tell Cassie and her parents.

Thanks to him, they had been fucked without so much as a single kiss.

Thirty-Two

Where was Austin?

Of all times for him to be out of reach, Cassie fumed
after assessing the situation. In her estimation, it
couldn't have been worse. Yes, it could. The man who
had tripped on a broken piece of tile and hit the floor
face first was not dead, which was a miracle, considering he was seventy-five years old. And he *was* injured.

"Don't worry, my dear," Mrs. Stanfield, his wife,
was saying. "He's going to be all right."

Cassie watched the small, blue-haired woman as she
sat in the chair nearest her husband, who remained
sprawled on the floor, a pillow under his head and a
blanket over him. An ambulance was due any moment
to transport him to the hospital.

Although his wife spoke with assurance, Cassie saw
the concern mirrored in her eyes. Oh, dear Lord, why
did this have to happen when both the manager and
Austin were gone? The manager was attending a conference in New Orleans. And Austin—well, she had no
idea where he was.

"I'm so sorry about this, Mrs. Stanfield." Cassie
heard the anxious note in her own voice and knew now
was not the time to get emotional. For the hotel's sake,
she must be cool and calm. But she was angry, damn

it. If repairs on the hotel had been done, this accident would not have happened.

Where was the ambulance? Cassie peered at her watch. It should have been here already.

Her eyes took in the surroundings. Thank goodness there wasn't much activity in the lobby at this hour. What few people passed didn't linger, but their gazes registered their curiosity.

"Daddy, you're going to be just fine," Claire Stanfield said to her husband, who had reached out a hand to her. She leaned over and clasped it tightly.

"Are you all right?" he asked in a halting, stressed voice.

Mrs. Stanfield smiled, then placed a hand on his forehead, which was drenched in perspiration. "You don't worry about me now, you hear?"

Tears welled up in Cassie's eyes, watching them, their love for one another so obvious. She turned away as a pang of despair walloped her upside the head, the mental blow staggering her when she realized why. Austin. That was how she wanted him to look at her.

However, at this moment, she could actually and cheerfully have throttled him, which was a much more settling thought.

"Mrs. Stanfield, can I get you anything? Coffee? Water?" Cassie wanted to do something, anything, to occupy her hands and mind.

"No, thank you, dear. I'm fine."

"I'm so sorry about this." Cassie said, cutting her eyes toward the door. "Ah, here come the paramedics."

On the heels of the two uniformed men was Austin. She steeled herself to show no reaction.

"What happened?"

The briskness in his voice failed to mask his apprehension. She saw it in his eyes. Suppressed anger was there, as well. Cassie didn't know how she knew that, but she did. Something had set him off.

He seemed tense, on edge, as if he were itching to pick a fight. If that were the case, then he'd come to the right place. She would be glad to accommodate him.

"I think the situation speaks for itself." The sarcasm in her tone was thick, though she was careful to keep her words confined to his ears alone.

His look turned smoldering. "Is he okay?"

Cassie didn't answer him right off. She was too busy trying not to notice how his mussed-up appearance, along with the five o'clock shadow on his face, made him more appealing than ever.

"Let us pray," she said, averting her gaze to the paramedics, as they strapped the man on the gurney and wheeled him toward the door.

"I'll go to the hospital with them," Austin said.

Cassie shook her head. "If one of us has to go, it would be better if I went. Mrs. Stanfield might be more comfortable."

"I can handle her." Austin almost smiled. "Sweet old ladies are my thing."

"We'll see about that after she slaps a lawsuit on the hotel."

"She's not going to sue us," he responded with irritating confidence.

"I hope you're right."

"I'll be back as soon as I can."

Cassie stifled a sigh as she watched him join Mrs. Stanfield, who was walking alongside the stretcher to the doors.

Striding into the hotel at the same moment was Bill Spalding, the architect. Cassie slapped her forehead in frustration when she remembered she had an appointment with him, one that she'd forgotten about amidst the confusion.

"Hello, Bill," she said, holding out her hand and pasting a smile on her lips.

"Ready to go to work?" he asked without preamble.

He was lean and short and had a baby face, which somehow didn't go with a head that had lost more hair than it had retained. However, his looks weren't what she was interested in.

He was a master at his profession and had already put together some awesome plans for renovating the Jasmine Hillcrest. Hopefully the cost would be affordable.

"Let's go to my office," she said, staring around him just as the doors to the ambulance were slammed shut.

Cassie turned back around, and they headed toward the elevators.

"Someone have an accident?" Bill asked when they stepped inside the first one.

"Yes, unfortunately."

"I hope you have good insurance."

"We do." Her tone was clipped; she hoped he would get the message that she didn't want to discuss the matter with him.

"That's good. You know how people are these days. This country's in a suing frenzy."

"You're sure making my day, Bill."

He looked sheepish. "Sorry. But I promise I *will* make your day before it's over. I have a final cost for you, and it's damn fair."

"Then let's get down to work."

Two hours later, the meeting was over and Cassie was alone. While the session had indeed gone well, and she was ecstatic with the price he'd given her, she couldn't settle down. Her insides were one lump of nerves.

Austin hadn't returned from the hospital. Had Mr. Stanfield suffered serious injures? Could he have died? Her heart almost stopped at that thought. Something had to be keeping Austin. She could either call, or she could go there herself.

Deciding the latter was the best option, she grabbed her purse and was about to open the door when it opened in front of her.

"Oops," Cassie said, jumping back, her pulse rate escalating as she and Austin almost bumped heads.

"Close call." He grabbed her shoulders, steadying her. His hands on her, combined with his intense stare, set her face on fire. If only he wouldn't look at her as if he wanted to ravish her on the spot, she could handle him.

She stepped back, then turned and walked to her desk, standing behind it as if using it for a protective shield. She hadn't fooled him. His trademark smile told her that.

"Hey, rest easy," he said, his features suddenly sobering.

Cassie's eyes flashed. "Under the circumstances, that's not possible."

"Mr. Stanfield's not seriously injured."

"That's a relief."

"His daughter arrived before I left, so both of them are in good hands. Plus, the doctor on call is one of the best."

"You assured them the hotel would cover all expenses?"

"Despite what you think, I've been around the block a few times."

She pursed her lips. "I didn't mean to insinuate—"

"Yes, you did. But that's okay. I fully expected to be raked over the coals about the accident, but first, I have to tell you something."

"Can't it wait?"

"No, dammit, it can't."

"Then what?"

"I know who kidnapped Tyler, and it wasn't Lester or anyone associated with him."

Cassie gaped, and she fought to digest what he'd just told her. When she could find the breath to push the words through her quivering lips, she stammered, "Who...who was it?"

"Randall Lunsbury, my attorney."

She gave him a dumbfounded look.

"I know how you feel."

"You don't have a clue how I feel," she lashed back harshly.

"You're right. I don't have a child, so I can't know."

"But why?" Cassie's voice turned shrill. "I mean, I don't get it." Lester hadn't taken Tyler? Her mind reeled from shock. What was going on?

"It's a long story, so you'd better sit down."

Weakly, Cassie sat in her chair, while Austin continued to stand in front of the desk, his features contorted. She swallowed against the panic that constricted her throat and stared at him, her eyes wide and questioning.

"First off," she asked, "is this the man who's in charge of the land deal?"

"One and the same."

"Oh dear."

Austin rubbed the back of his neck. "Randall's big

302   *Mary Lynn Baxter*

into cocaine and women. Because of that, he was desperate for money.''

''Maybe I'm dense or just not thinking straight, but how could he possibly think taking Tyler would help his cause?''

''He was planning me to get to your family and their money—your mother's money, to be exact.''

''I can't even comprehend that.''

''It gets more bizarre.''

''Go on,'' she said, feeling her temples begin to throb.

When Austin finished telling her about the man Randall had hired and the toy train car he had recognized, Cassie's head was spinning and she was sick to her stomach.

''Are you okay?'' Austin asked.

''No.''

''I don't suppose you would be. I'd say I was sorry, but you wouldn't accept it.''

Her eyes blazed, and she stood. ''You're damn right, I won't.''

''Well, at least you should feel some relief it wasn't Lester.''

She couldn't dispute that point. Though, while he might not have been involved in that particular incident, she still didn't trust Lester, would never trust him. For the time being, however, he and his cronies seemed to be behaving themselves.

''Also, you have to be relieved that Randall's fidgeting in a jail cell even as we speak.''

''I don't buy that.'' Cassie's tone was as cutting as a whiplash. ''I imagine another sorry lawyer has already sprung him.''

''Maybe, but he won't stay sprung. He confessed to

the cops. I heard that confession with my own ears. You can bet he's a dead cert for some kind of prison time."

"I wish I had your confidence. My faith in the justice system is nil. If they'll let Lester out, then Randall's really sitting pretty."

"It'll be a cold day in hell before he walks."

"We'll see." Even if Randall did time, that wouldn't make what she and Tyler had gone though any less traumatic. The scars were deep and oozing.

"I take full responsibility for what happened."

Austin's blunt, out-of-the-blue statement took her by surprise.

"If I hadn't let him talk me into this land deal, then Randall wouldn't have gotten involved in our lives."

"No doubt you made a mistake about the land, but there's no way you could've known he'd stoop to kid-napping."

"What I should've known was that he was on dope."

"How?"

"I don't know. Maybe if I'd paid more attention to his erratic behavior. It was off the charts, yet I didn't figure it out."

"The money's gone, isn't it?" Cassie's voice was devoid of emotion.

"Yes, up his nose."

"Which means we can't renovate and prevent other accidents like the one that just happened?"

"I intend to pay back every cent."

Their gazes tangled for a long moment. "Do you have it?"

"Some. The rest I'll get."

"Damn you for trusting that bastard."

"I told you I'd make it right, Cassie, and I will."

"It doesn't matter anymore."

"Don't say that." Austin's eyes were tormented. "Don't do this to us."

Cassie laughed a mirthless laugh. "There is no us, Austin. When are you going to get that through your thick skull?"

"Never. I realize this is a setback, and you're pissed, but it can be fixed."

"No, it can't be fixed, just like *we* can't be fixed. Now, please, leave me alone."

He was tempted to argue, she knew, but he didn't. When he walked out and slammed the door, she put her head down and wept.

Thirty-Three

"Do you think the press will ever let the story go?"

"It doesn't look like it."

Wilma laid aside the newspaper and looked up as Cassie joined her on the veranda. Once Cassie was seated with her legs curled under her, Wilma turned her attention to the grounds, which were a riot of color.

"I'm sorry about all the publicity." Cassie's gaze tracked her mother's. Even though this summer was touted as being one of the hottest and most humid on record, it had its pluses, creating a lush beauty all its own. Like Wilma, she sat in awe and soaked up that beauty, praying that it would calm both their troubled spirits.

"At least the reporters are no longer swarming," Wilma replied. "If they hadn't gone away, I think your daddy would've had a stroke."

It had been two weeks since Randall Lunsbury had been arrested for kidnapping Tyler. But the newspaper hadn't let the story die. Since he was the Worthams' grandson, the press had continued to milk it for all it was worth.

"I really am sorry."

"Don't be silly. It's not your fault. You had no way of knowing about Randall Lunsbury and his crazy scheme to get money."

"I know, but—"

"I'm just grateful Tyler wasn't harmed," Wilma interrupted, "and that Lester wasn't involved."

"So you're siding with Daddy on Lester's behalf?"

"Would that be so terrible?" Wilma's tone was gentle yet held a hint of censure.

"Yes, it would."

Wilma reached for her glass of fresh lemonade and sipped it. After setting it back down, she said, "You're going to have to let the hate and bitterness you feel for Lester go or it's going to consume you."

"You tell me how I can do that when he's still hovering like something evil."

"Oh, Cassie, I hate to hear you talk like that."

"I'm sorry I'm such a disappointment to you."

"Stop apologizing, and you're not a disappointment."

Cassie didn't believe that for a second, but she didn't push the point.

"You were always rebellious, Cassie, and even though time and circumstances have matured you, you still haven't lost that rebellious streak."

"Is that bad?"

"You father thinks so."

"What about you?"

Wilma didn't say anything for a moment, but that hesitation was an answer in itself. Cassie felt like crying, something she had done often as a child when she'd disappointed her parents. It seemed as though she'd spent her entire life trying to please them, to live up to their expectations, especially her daddy's.

Would she ever get past that?

"I just want you and Tyler to be happy, and if that's

with Lester, then so be it. If not..." Wilma's voice trailed off into nothingness.

Cassie stiffened her spine and held her tongue, having learned long ago that she couldn't change her parents. What she *could* change was how she dealt with them.

"What's going to happen to that poor man?"

Relieved that the conversation had switched off her, Cassie said, "Prison, I hope." Feeling sweat gathering above her lips, she reached for a handheld fan on the table and began fanning her face and neck. "How can you call him poor?"

Wilma took another sip of her drink. "How can I not? Actually, he's to be pitied. All that talent gone to waste."

"I'd like to—" Cassie broke off, then added in a curt tone, "Never mind. What I'd like to do to him isn't repeatable."

Wilma sighed. "You have certainly hardened, Cassie. I'm not sure I like that."

Realizing the conversation had once again turned personal, Cassie asked, "Have you by chance talked to Austin?"

Once that question was out, she also realized she had walked into another potential land mine. Land mine or not, the money debacle was hotel business and had to be addressed.

"Yes," Wilma said simply and with little emotion.

"Then you know?" Cassie asked, her gaze locked on a bluebird, thinking it was the most beautiful creature she'd ever seen with its deep blue wings and orange breast.

"Austin told me almost immediately."

Cassie swung her eyes around and pinned Wilma's.

"I keep forgetting you've been working together for a long time and seem to have an understanding."

"One that the two of you don't have. Is that what you're getting at?" There was a humorous twist to Wilma's lips.

"Is it that obvious?"

Wilma chuckled. "It's more than that. In fact, he said you gave him tit for tat."

"He's exaggerating. What could I say, after the fact?"

"He's determined to pay it back."

"How?" She made a face. "Rob a bank?"

"That remark was uncalled for," Wilma said, her mouth pinched.

Cassie flushed. "You're right, it was."

"As you know, he had my permission to buy the land before you came back."

"I can't understand that, Mother. You knew what kind of shape the Jasmine was in. Why on earth did you agree to buy land before repairs were done?"

"I thought we would be able to do both."

"Now we can't do either," Cassie pointed out flatly.

"I disagree. If Austin says he'll make good, then I believe he will. He has some valuable horses, and if he sells them for the right price, then we'll be in fine shape."

"*If.* That's a mighty big word."

"It was an honest mistake, my dear. Why are you coming down so hard on him?"

Because I love him and can't have him, she wanted to shout. Instead, she said, "Look, we'll work it out, I promise. You don't worry about it. That's why you have me."

Wilma smiled. "You have no idea how comforting

that is. But I don't want you to worry about the hotel, either. If you have to worry about something, worry about Tyler.''

Cassie put down the fan and stood. ''That's why I'm heading to the office early.''

After kissing her mother on the cheek, she drove to the hotel, thinking that her life seemed to have settled into something of a pattern. She worked mornings and spent her afternoons with Tyler.

Lester seemed to have disappeared from the scene, which was both a relief and a concern. She wanted to think that he didn't care about them anymore, especially Tyler. Maybe his threats early on had been empty ones, and that once she hadn't shown her fear, he had backed down.

She hoped that was the case.

As for Austin, she hadn't seen him, either, which upset her more than she cared to admit. Tyler missed him. *She* missed him. That was the bottom line.

Her son kept asking where he was. Admittedly, her daddy hadn't seen him, either. Cassie's best guess was that Austin was busy trying to come up with the means to repay the company.

If she stayed in Jasmine, she was going to have to end her relationship with Austin, this time for good. Or maybe she already had, she reminded herself. After that last discussion, she might finally have convinced him they had no future.

A few minutes later she was behind her desk when her phone beeped.

''Yes, April,'' she said.

''It's Mr. McGuire on line one.''

Her mouth turned dry as cotton and her heart raced.

But when she spoke, she made it a point to sound polite but aloof. "Hello, Austin."

He didn't mince words. "Do you mind if Tyler goes to the farm with me this afternoon?"

His request caught her off guard, and Cassie didn't know what to say.

"I'm training a new horse, and I thought he might like to watch."

"I'm sure he would," she said in an almost breathless tone.

"Is that a yes?"

"Yes."

"Good. Is he at the house?"

"Yes, with Daddy."

"I'll be there within the hour."

"Austin?" she said quickly, refusing to think of the consequences.

"What?"

"Do you mind if I come, too?"

His sharp intake of breath rivalled her own. She clutched at her chest with her free hand. Dear Lord, what had she done?

"It's over between us, isn't it?"

Austin stared into Sherry Young's pale face and felt like someone who had just kicked an innocent dog. But Sherry wasn't a dog, nor was she innocent. Still, he didn't like what he was doing. But the die had been cast long ago.

"Yes, though I want us to be friends."

"But not kissing friends, right?"

"Right."

Even though she was baiting him in a teasing tone, he wasn't amused. He had intended to tell Sherry long before now, even before he'd kissed Cassie, but he'd been wrestling with what to say and how to say it. He hadn't wanted to hurt her. Too, he'd been buried in his own business problems and what to do about them.

He was determined to repay the money to the hotel ASAP. No way did he intend to have that debt on his conscience, even though Wilma had been more than understanding and had supported him all the way.

Of course, his determination hadn't won him any points with Cassie, but that didn't matter, either. For his own peace of mind, he had to do what was right.

The same went for Sherry. He couldn't see her when he loved Cassie, regardless of how Cassie felt about him.

"Does this sudden decision have anything to do with your attorney's arrest?"

"Yes and no. Needless to say, it's cost me big time."

"Knowing you, you intend to pay all that money back."

"Or die trying," he said in an offhand manner, but he was serious.

"How are you going to do that? I'm just curious."

"My horses. If I can find the right buyer, they'll bring in the needed cash."

"I hate to see you have to give up everything you've worked so hard for."

"Thanks, but that's the way it goes sometimes."

"I hope you find what you're looking for, Austin." Sherry paused and gave him a lackluster smile. "Maybe I should make that 'who.'"

"I have found the *who,* but so far it's not working out. However, I'm not giving up."

This time Sherry's smile was sad. "Well, if you ever need a shoulder—"

312   *Mary Lynn Baxter*

Austin raised his hand and halted her words. "You deserve better, Sherry. It's not ever going to happen with us."

"Well, at least you're honest, and I appreciate that."

He leaned over and kissed her on the cheek. "Be happy."

With that, he was gone. By the time he reached the truck and had the engine cranked, he could hardly contain himself.

Do you mind if I come with you? For a second after Cassie had blurted out that question, he couldn't answer. Her words had knocked the wind out of him.

But he'd recovered when she'd added, "Look, forget I said that. You...you didn't ask me. You asked Tyler."

"You know better than that," he said brusquely. "You don't need an invitation. I'm aching to see you."

And he was, had been ever since she'd turned him inside out about the kidnapping and the botched land deal. But dammit, he didn't know how to take her. One minute she was cold, keeping him at arm's length, then the next minute she was lava hot in his arms.

Just the thought of seeing her again made him hard. Whoa! he cautioned. She was joining him and Tyler. That didn't mean she had changed her mind about him. About *them.*

But he'd been thrown a crumb. At this point he was grateful for that. He pushed down on the accelerator and watched the speedometer climb. What if he got a ticket? Ah, hell, he didn't give a damn.

Getting to Cassie as soon as possible was worth the cost.

"Daddy, I'm home."

James came striding out of his study and smiled.

"Hello, sweetheart. You're early."

"I know, but after I personally took the garden club through the hotel grounds, I figured I'd earned an afternoon off."

"Maybe you and your mother can do something together."

"I was thinking more along the lines of spending it with Tyler," she said in an evasive tone. For some reason, she was hesitant to tell them that Austin was involved. Maybe it was because she felt so foolish. All the way home, she had kicked her backside for her spontaneous request to join them.

James's face was drawn, and he shifted from one foot to the other.

Cassie's heart upped its beat. Had something happened to her mother? "What's wrong?"

"Nothing's wrong."

"Yes, it is."

"No, it isn't," he countered strongly. "For once everything is just right."

"Whatever you say. Where's Tyler?"

"Tyler's the right I'm referring to."

"Daddy, you're not making sense."

"I will, if you'll give me a chance to explain," James said in a stern voice.

"Then by all means go ahead," Cassie said, barely holding on to her patience.

"I let Lester take Tyler to visit his parents."

"What!"

"Now calm down. You know how I hate it when you get all emotional."

Cassie darted past him, almost knocking him down.

"Cassie, where are you going?"

"To call the police!"

Thirty-Four

"Cassie, wait!"

Cassie didn't miss a step.

"Get a hold of yourself," James ordered as he followed her. "You can't call the police."

Cassie spun around. "I can do what I damn well please."

"I've asked you not to talk to me like that, young lady."

With fumbling fingers, Cassie ignored him and reached for the phone on a nearby table.

"What on earth is going on?"

Cassie, with a swimming head and dry mouth, stared at her mother, who stood in the door of the living room, clutching at the ties of her robe, as if trying to tie them.

"Ask Daddy," Cassie snapped in a near frantic tone.

Lester had Tyler.

Cassie bit down on her lower lip so hard she tasted her own blood. Before, when Lunsbury had kidnapped Tyler, she had suspected Lester. This time there was no suspecting to it. She *knew* Lester had her son. Just the thought of Tyler in the hands of that nutcase was so horrific that Cassie's mind couldn't deal with it.

Dear Lord, when would it all end?

If Lester... No! She wouldn't think about what could happen or she wouldn't be able to function. At the moment she could only count on herself and her ability to take action.

"I heard someone yelling," Wilma continued in a troubled voice. "I assumed you were carrying on, Cassie."

"You assumed right," James stated, beginning to pace the floor, though his gaze never strayed from his daughter.

"I'm calling the police, Mother," Cassie said, both her voice and hands unsteady.

"That's the most absurd thing I've ever heard," James countered in a hostile, pinched tone.

Wilma inched farther into the room and eased into the nearest chair, her eyes dark and troubled. "One of you, please, tell me what's going on."

Cassie didn't respond; she was concentrating on punching out 911.

"Call the Sullivans," James pleaded, his face pale.

"He's not there, Daddy," Cassie said.

"You don't know that. So for once, humor me and call them."

"Humor you?" Cassie laughed a hysterical laugh. "At a time like this? That's the last thing I intend to do." She was about to have a nervous breakdown, and he wanted her to humor him.

"What I'm trying to do is keep you from making a fool of yourself. If I'm wrong, then I'll take full responsibility, and we'll go from there."

Cassie pressed down on the disconnect button and held it, continuing to mangle her lower lip. The blood seeping from the wound tasted vile. Her stomach rebelled, but she kept gnawing. For some reason, she felt the need to punish herself for this latest debacle.

"Can anyone join the party?"

316 Mary Lynn Baxter

Austin!

Cassie had momentarily forgotten he was coming to take Tyler to the farm. Her, too. All eyes focused on him. He frowned as he made his way deeper into the room.

On his heels was Joy. Although she looked slightly disconcerted, she asked, "Can I get y'all anything to drink?"

"Uh, no, thank you, Joy," Wilma said, speaking for everyone.

"Yes, ma'am." Joy nodded, then quietly disappeared.

"Hello, Austin," James said with obvious relief, motioning with a hand. "Come on in." Then James turned to Cassie and asked, "It's all right if Austin stays, isn't it?"

"Whatever," Cassie said in a tight voice, hearing the censure in James's tone.

Austin's frown further grooved his forehead as his gaze swung to Cassie and remained there. "Something's wrong. What?"

She gulped back an onslaught of tears, warring with her own emotions. The irrational part of her was glad Austin was there; the rational part wanted to shove him out the door.

"Daddy let Tyler leave with Lester." Cassie's tone was hard and accusing as she rested her gaze on James, who didn't look in the least repentant.

"Good God, James, after that other fiasco? Surely you have better sense than that."

James seemed taken aback by Austin's unveiled accusation, yet he defended himself in a strong, brisk tone. "I thought it was the right thing to do."

Cassie didn't say a word. But if Tyler wasn't with his other grandparents, she would lambaste her daddy and have no regrets.

"What are you going to do?" Austin asked Cassie.

"Give Daddy the benefit of the doubt and call the Sullivans."

"Atta girl," James muttered under his breath.

Wilma patted the seat beside her. "Sit down, James, please. You're making me and everyone else nervous."

While Cassie dialed, she noticed Austin smiling at her mother and heard him say, "It's great to see you looking so good, Wilma."

"Thanks, Austin. It's a blessing to feel good for a change."

Answer, dammit! Cassie said silently as the ringing went on and on at the Sullivan home. Finally Charlotte picked up.

"It's Cassie."

"Well, hello," Charlotte responded in a surprised tone. "To what do we owe this pleasure?"

Charlotte's comeback was not encouraging, so Cassie didn't mince words. "Is Tyler with you?"

"Uh, no."

Profound terror washed through her.

"Why do you ask? Of course, we'd love to see him, but then, you know that." A petulant note lowered her tone.

"Lester picked Tyler up here and said he was going to your house."

"Why, that's wonderful," Charlotte cooed. "Thank you for letting us spend some time with that precious child. I'm sure Lester's thanking you, too."

"Charlotte, if he shows up within the next few minutes, call me. Meanwhile, I'm calling the police."

Apparently it took a while for Cassie's last statement to soak in, for a long moment of silence followed. "What?"

"You heard me, Charlotte."

"But why?"

"Because I didn't give Lester permission to take Tyler away from this house. My daddy did." Cassie forced her voice to remain calm when she wanted to yell, venting her fear and frustration.

"But—"

Cassie cut her off. "I have to go now. Call me if Tyler gets there."

"All right, Cassie, but you're being unfair and mean-spirited about all of this. James needs to do some serious praying for you. Actually, we all do."

"Goodbye, Charlotte."

"Cassie is he there?"

She faced Austin, who had asked the question, but she had trouble getting the words out. Fear had a lock on her throat. "No, he isn't."

"He will be," James declared, peering at his watch.

"Have they had time to get there?" Cassie asked.

James nodded in the affirmative.

"Call the cops," Austin said.

James jumped to his feet. "Now, see here, Austin, whose side are you on?"

"Tyler's."

Wilma shook her head at her husband. "Sit back down, James."

He scowled at his wife but did as he was told.

"You want me to call 'em?" Austin asked, his eyes delving into Cassie's.

She shook her head, then cleared her throat. "No. I'll take care of it."

Once she made the call, there was nothing to do but wait. She turned her back on everyone and walked to the window. If that bastard hurt her baby, hell would know no fury like her wrath.

Tyler, sweetheart, Mommy loves you.

"Ma'am, there's not a lot we can do."

The detective who had just arrived wasn't one of the two who had come when Tyler disappeared the first time. This was Detective Ray Malcom, a tall, stringbean of a man with a mustache that blanketed his upper lip.

"Sullivan's recently been released from the pen on a weapons charge," Austin said. "Doesn't that make a difference?"

The detective didn't so much as flinch. "No, sir."

"Then why did you come?" Cassie's tone was filled with hostility, and she didn't care.

"Out of respect for your family."

"And we appreciate that very much, officer," James said in an embarrassed tone.

Cassie threw her daddy a cutting look and was about to say something when Austin intervened.

"Exactly what *can* you do?"

"At this point, nothing."

"Dammit, my son's been kidnapped again," Cassie cried. She knew that if she told them that Lester had given up all rights to Tyler, they would have to act. But if Austin found that out, he might start putting two and two together. No, there had to be another way. She spoke again, all her fears coloring her tone. "Does he have to get murdered for you to take action?"

"Cassie, please," James pleaded, holding out his hands. "How can you say such a thing?" He shuddered visibly. "How can you even think it? You're blowing this all out of proportion."

"Stop saying that!" Cassie cried again. "You had no right to let Tyler go with Lester, especially without my permission. I can't imagine what you were thinking."

James bowed his shoulders. "I was waiting for that."

"Only because it's the truth. He's *my* son and *my* responsibility."

Wilma stood, her face pasty colored. "Both of you stop it. Now. I won't have you airing our differences in front of this nice gentleman."

"That's too bad, Mother," Cassie snapped. "It's my son's well-being we're talking about here, maybe even his life."

"I have to agree with your father," Wilma added, but in a much milder tone. "You're overreacting."

Cassie's eyes flashed. "Really? So have the Sullivans called?"

"No, dammit, they haven't," Austin said, focusing his attention on the officer. "The boy could be in grave danger."

"That's just not so," James muttered.

Austin went on as if James hadn't spoken. "Surely you can see why Ms. Sullivan's so concerned?"

"Yes, sir, I can, but even though they're divorced, Mr. Sullivan's still the boy's father, and since Reverend Wortham here gave the youngster permission to go, a crime wasn't committed, which pretty much ties our hands.''

Cassie wanted to give in to her mounting terror and frustration while yanking the detective's mustache out, one hair at a time.

''No crime's been committed,'' James said to Malcolm. ''That's the point we've been trying to get across to our daughter.''

Cassie almost choked on the words that threatened to pop out of her mouth. What was she going to do? With the exception of her and Austin, Lester had everyone snowed.

But Austin was not the answer she needed.

''All right,'' Cassie said, ''if the law won't help me, I'll find him on my own.''

''Whoa, Cass,'' Austin said, placing a hand on her shoulder.

She jerked away and glowered at him. ''Don't touch me.''

''Cassie, you have to get control of yourself.'' James crossed the room and stood in front of her. ''Lester is not going to hurt Tyler. You have to believe him when he says he's a changed man.''

''Well, I don't!''

''But you don't have anything to base that opinion on. He hasn't missed a church service, and I told you, he's accepted the Lord as his Savior.''

''Stop it, Daddy!''

''No, I won't stop it. You're going to hear me out. Lester is the boy's father. He just wants to spend time with Tyler, time that *you* won't give him.''

Cassie shook her head, her eyes wild. ''You don't understand.''

"I do understand." James turned his gaze on Austin. "Help me out here, will you? Maybe she'll listen to you."

Austin shook his head. "You know better than that."

"Stop talking about me as if I'm not here."

"Cassie, Cassie," James said in a cajoling tone, "how can you fault the man for wanting to be with his son?"

Goaded beyond her limit of endurance, Cassie screamed in her daddy's face, "Because Tyler is *not* Lester's son!"

Thirty-Five

For a moment the air seemed to crackle like dry leaves burning.

What had she done? *What had she said?* The truth. She had blurted out the naked truth for the world to hear. Suddenly she wanted to cringe, to hide from the eyes that were staring at her as though she had gone off the deep end.

Recoiling, Cassie lifted her hands to her flaming cheeks. Yet she was cold, chill bumps running rampant over her skin. Any moment, she feared her teeth would start chattering.

The policeman was the first to break the shocked silence by clearing his throat, then scraping one shoe across the floor. "Er...if you don't mind, I'll wait outside."

Cassie finally found her voice. "Thank you. But please, don't leave."

"No, ma'am, I won't," the detective responded.

Cassie knew Malcolm wished he could get the hell out of there and never return. And she didn't blame him, she thought, watching as he walked out the door.

She took a shuddering breath, then turned toward her family once again, feeling as if she were facing a firing squad. Her daddy's mouth was gaping. Her mother's hand was on her heart.

Austin!

What must he be thinking? She told herself not to look at him. But she couldn't stop herself; her eyes shifted to him. He was standing so rigid that it seemed as if his body were encased in a block of ice.

While his features had no color, it was his eyes that dealt the lethal blow to her heart. Dead. They looked dead.

He had figured out the truth: if Lester wasn't Tyler's father, then *he* was.

Cassie closed her own eyes for a moment, leaning forward, shoulders drawn together as if she expected to be physically struck. She wouldn't blame Austin if he chose to do just that. She would give anything if she could snatch those words out of the air and bury them back deep inside her.

She blamed her daddy. If he hadn't pushed her past her limit, then one of her most haunting nightmares wouldn't have turned into cold, stark reality.

"Cassie?"

She focused on James, who had spoken her name, but who appeared incapable of saying anything else as he leaned against the sofa. His eyes were narrowed to slits, and his Adam's apple bobbed like a cork in the water. If the situation hadn't been so fraught, she might have laughed.

As it was, there was nothing to laugh about. Instead, hysteria bubbled close to the surface. Her child was gone, and she might never see him again.

Dear Lord, she prayed in anguished silence, please don't let anything happened to my baby. Punish me for my sins, but not Tyler.

"Cassie," James repeated, only louder, his voice sounding like a croaking bull frog.

"Sir?" she whispered, trying to shake off the numbness that was threatening to suck her under.

"You didn't mean what you just said, did you?"

Cassie's heart began to race as she faced her daddy. Lie! Now was her chance to retract those words. But she couldn't. Besides, the damage had been done. No one would believe her, especially Austin.

She gave him another quick glance. He hadn't moved. He hadn't thawed out any. He hadn't stopped staring at her, either.

"Yes, Daddy, I meant every word," she said, shivering visibly.

James shook his head before making his way to the front of the sofa, which he fell onto beside Wilma, whose eyes were wide and troubled, but who didn't say anything.

Mercifully, Cassie felt as though she were having an out-of-body experience. She was in this room with those she loved most, with the exception of her son, yet she didn't feel connected to them or anything else.

Shock.

She was in shock, her downfall as well as her salvation.

"But how, I mean—" James stammered, falling short of finishing his sentence, his features now on the green side.

Cassie took pity on him. "If Tyler is not Lester's child, then whose is he? Was that what you were trying to ask?"

Although she was speaking to her daddy, her gaze was set on Austin, who had yet to utter a word, but who looked like he'd been clobbered with a baseball bat. *He knew.*

"Yes," James muttered.

Before Cassie could respond, Austin spoke up and said, "Mine."

That short, simple word had almost the same far-reaching effect as her earlier bombshell. It landed in the room with a thud, like a ton of bricks hitting the floor.

Mine. Mine. Mine.

Cassie wanted to plug her ears, but she knew the effort would be futile. The damage had been done. Pandora's box had been opened.

"Yours!" James clutched at his throat and struggled to his feet, his face no longer green but a vivid purple-red as he vented his rage on Austin. "How could you do such a thing? My God, she was a child. *My child!*"

Cassie watched Austin turn his gaze to his lifelong friend, open his mouth as if to defend himself, then snap it shut.

"No, that can't be," Wilma whispered in a tiny voice, seemingly more to herself than to the others.

Austin cut his eyes back to Cassie, stabbing her with their intensity. However, she couldn't read what lay behind them, which increased her torment.

"Yes, it can be, Mother," Cassie admitted in a fragile tone.

Wilma clutched at her husband's hand. "How?"

Cassie swallowed and looked at Austin.

The ice seemed to have suddenly melted. He bowed, then gestured with a sweeping hand. "It's showtime, Cass, and you're on center stage."

Terror seized her, and for a second Cassie was paralyzed, feeling as if she'd been tossed into shark in-fested waters. Austin wasn't about to come to her rescue. But why should he? He was the victim here, probably feeling like a shark had taken a bite out of his heart and soul. After all, he had just learned that he had a son, a son who might never know his real father.

Cassie forced back a scream and stood straight instead. She had kicked the dirt in their faces. Now it was up to her to try to clean it off, if she could. Only problem was, some stains lasted a lifetime.

"Austin *is* Tyler's father."

"Oh, Lord, please no," James moaned, lifting his head as if seeking heavenly guidance.

Wilma didn't say a word. She just sank back into the sofa and closed her eyes.

"James," Austin said in a tortured voice. "I—"

"Don't!" James glared at him. "I don't want to hear another word."

The phone rang.

Everyone flinched silently, except Austin. A litany of curses flew out of his mouth. For once James seemed oblivious to the foul language, staring at the phone.

"I'll get it," Cassie said thickly, the interruption a godsend. Racing across the room, she grabbed the cordless receiver.

She listened for a second, then cried, "Damn you, Lester!"

Her parents gasped, while Austin's head jerked up. Then, placing a finger across his lips, he moved to the extension and very gingerly lifted that receiver.

"You can damn me all you want to," Lester was saying in a calm but deadly tone. "Only it isn't going to do any good."

"If you've hurt Tyler—" Cassie couldn't go on; a sob choked off her words.

"What happens to the little creep depends on you, darlin'. If you cooperate, then he'll be just fine. If not..."

Cassie knew Lester had deliberately let his words trail off, knowing his unspoken threat would cripple her. He was right. For a moment she was incapable of a coherent response. That was when her eyes went to Austin.

He wasn't faring much better. His face was pale, and his lips were stretched into a taut line. His expression told her it was all he could do to keep silent, but he had no choice.

"What do you want?" Cassie finally managed to ask.

"Now, that's better," Lester said in a stroking tone.

"Lester!"

Austin shook his head and mouthed, *Don't antagonize him.*

"I'm listening," she said, covering the receiver with a hand and taking a deep breath. "Go on."

"I want money, of course. Lots of it."

"Let me talk to Tyler."

"Not so fast, darlin'. You're not calling the shots, remember."

"Lester, please, let me talk to him."

"I'll be in touch."

"Lester!" she cried. "Don't you dare hang up!"

He hung up.

"You bastard!" Cassie's curse rivaled the dial tone accosting her ear before she threw the phone onto the carpet.

"Cassie, what are we going to do?" James asked in a sick tone.

Cassie knew what she wanted to do—run into the nearest closet and curl up in the fetal position. But if she did, she would never get Tyler back. Now wasn't the time to turn into a weeping willow but rather to become a steel magnolia.

Her eyes immediately sought Austin.

His back was to her, and he was striding toward the front door. He opened it and stuck his head out and said, "Detective, Sullivan just called."

Cassie watched as Malcolm flicked his cigarette down, stepped on it, then strode back into the room.

"What did he have to say?" he asked, his eyes scanning the room.

Cassie could imagine what was going through the detective's mind, especially with their ghost-like faces staring at him.

"He...he has Tyler."

"Still, ma'am—" His impatience was obvious.

"Dammit, he's holding him for ransom," Austin raged, anger hardening the texture of his voice.

Cassie recoiled against that anger, knowing that half of it was directed at her.

"Well, now, that certainly adds another ingredient to the soup," he drawled.

"I thought you'd see it that way." There was nothing drawling about Austin's tone. It was sharp, clipped and concise.

"However," Detective Malcolm added, "by law he's still considered the boy's father."

"No, he isn't," Cassie said.

"How many more secrets are you hiding?" Austin demanded in a harsh, bitter tone.

Cassie tried not to let his attitude affect her, at least not now. She would deal with Austin's feelings and her parents later.

The detective cleared his throat again, then said, "Suppose you explain."

"When we divorced, I paid him a sizable amount to give up all rights to Tyler."

"Thank God, you did something right," Austin said into another polluted silence.

"In that case, we'll nail him," Malcolm said, all business now. "What's his next move? Did he spell it out?"

"He didn't tell me," Cassie replied. "He said he'd call back."

"We'll get on this right away."

"Oh, please, find my baby," Cassie pleaded. Before it's too late, she wanted to add, only she couldn't. The thought was too horrifying even to contemplate.

"What can I do, detective?" Austin's tone was as emotionless as hers had been hysterical. But she wasn't fooled. Austin was battling his own fears. Yet in a crisis, he had nerves of steel. He always had.

"You can tell me what you know, if anything, other than what Lester said."

"There is a possible hiding place, a campsite."

Cassie's gaze widened on Austin, but he had eyes only for the detective, who flipped open a notebook.

Moments later Malcolm said, "Now, exactly what did Lester say?"

Austin told him. When he finished, the detective crossed to the door. "We'll put a tap on the line."

He left, and when he did, the room fell silent again. Cassie looked at her parents, who remained on the sofa, looking as though they were in a semicoma.

Cassie opened her mouth to say something, though she had no idea what, when her parents stood. "We're going upstairs," James said in a cold tone. "We'll talk later."

Once they had left the room, Cassie stole a glance at Austin, who was moving toward the door himself.

"Austin?" Her huskily spoken question stopped him.

He swung around and faced her with empty eyes. "What?"

Her heart kicked at his unapproachable attitude. "I thought we could talk."

"Well, you thought wrong."

Her exhaustion and terror had come full circle. She didn't want him to leave. She didn't want to be alone. "Where are you going?"

The veins in his neck stood out as his gaze deliberately wandered over her. "To find that bastard myself and get *my* son."

Thirty-Six

He had a son.

Austin's emotions ran the gamut. He wanted to shout hip, hip, hooray, and he wanted to sit down and sob like a baby. He didn't do either. His come-to-Jesus meeting with those emotions would have to wait until after Tyler had been found and rescued.

Damn Lester to hell, Austin thought as he pulled alongside the curb of the ex-con's house. Since Lester had made that call yesterday, Austin had jockeyed his time between this dump and Grant Hoople's in Lafayette.

So far, nothing had gone his way. He had struck out twice. There had been no sign of life at either place. He had also been to that clearing in the woods, where he'd seen the group target shooting.

Nothing there, either. In addition, he had spent time at the police station, dogging Detective Ray Malcolm, demanding a continual update on the investigation.

But, as Malcolm had pointed out, until Sullivan called back and said how much money he wanted and where it was to be dropped off, they couldn't do much except issue an all points bulletin for Lester, which they had done, and watch his house.

As Austin suspected, "watching" meant sending a patrol car by every so often. That was why he'd taken matters into his own hands. He massaged the back of his neck, then rubbed his bleary eyes.

God, he was tired. He didn't know when he'd ever been this exhausted. However, he refused to give in to that exhaustion, not until that scumbag Sullivan was back behind bars.

He wouldn't be able to rest then, either, he reminded himself. He and Cassie were due to have *their* "come-to-Jesus meeting," too. Thank God for James and his stubbornness and inflexibility where Cassie was concerned. He had goaded her into dropping that lighted stick of dynamite into the already highly charged atmosphere.

Austin's stomach roiled when he thought of that moment when she'd cried out that Lester was not Tyler's father. The full truth had hit him instantly, with the force of a sledgehammer meeting concrete. His head had been that concrete.

Why hadn't he known? Why hadn't he at least *suspected?* Had it been simple stupidity that he hadn't put two and two together and come up with four? Or had his guilty conscience been the culprit?

After all, screwing his best friend's daughter when he was thirty-two and she was barely eighteen had not been one of his proudest moments. More than likely that was the reason he'd stuck his head in the sand and moved on.

Austin pounded the steering wheel, trying desperately to dam up the anger building inside him, fearing it would reach the explosive point. He wanted to throttle Cassie and hug his son.

Tyler.

It wouldn't do for him to find Sullivan before the

cops did. For the first time ever, Austin believed he could take another man's life and not blink an eye.

That thought scared the hell out of him.

If he were to do something crazy like that, he would never get near his son. So he had to play by the rules, fair or not.

"What the hell are you doing here, McGuire?"

Austin twisted his head around and encountered a fierce-looking Ray Malcolm staring down at him through the open window.

"What does it look like I'm doing?"

The detective toyed with his mustache, which glistened with sweat. "Meddling where you have no business meddling," Malcolm said.

"What would you do, detective, if you were in my place?"

The other man's cheeks turned a rough red, then he hemmed and hawed before saying, "Hell if I know."

"Yeah, you do. Your ass would be sitting exactly where mine is."

"Don't do anything foolish."

"Like blow the son of a bitch's brains out?"

Malcolm scowled. "That's not something to joke about, McGuire."

Austin wanted to ask who was joking, but he didn't. He wasn't about to get hauled off to jail himself on a trumped-up charge of obstructing justice. Nope, he intended to be around to see Sullivan's face when he was arrested.

"Not to worry, detective, I'm just helping the cause."

"Yeah, right," Malcolm muttered sarcastically. "Just make sure you don't *hinder* it."

"So what have y'all found out?" Austin asked.

"Zilch." Malcolm frowned. "We just left the Wortham place."

Austin wanted to ask how the mood was there, but he didn't have to. He knew. Cassie was all broken apart inside, and until Tyler was returned unharmed, no one could put the pieces back together, certainly not him.

Hell, *he* needed consoling.

"Why do you think Sullivan hasn't called back?"

Malcolm pulled on the brush that draped his lip. "He will. I figure he's just torturing his ex, hoping to milk more money out her."

"Damn him straight to hell," Austin muttered.

The detective coughed. "Under the circumstances, I can see where you're coming from. But this is a matter for us to take care of. Don't go thinking you're John Wayne."

"If I see the bastard or any of his cronies, you'll be the first to know. I don't want to do anything that would cause Sullivan to walk."

"Good, then we're together on this."

With that Malcolm strode back to his unmarked car and got in it. Austin immediately focused his attention back on the house. Still no activity. He would wait a while longer; then he would leave and go back to the hotel. Someone had to be in charge there. He couldn't count on Cassie for any help.

Cassie again. He had to stop thinking about her. Right now, his insides were too raw. And he was hurting.

Betrayal.

It was an ugly word with an ugly meaning. Unfortunately, Cassie and betrayal were synonymous. That was why he couldn't allow himself the luxury of confronting her, not until his son was all right.

Then...

For a second Austin's heart skipped several beats. *His son.* He didn't think he would ever tire of saying those words. Yet he had no idea what the future held for him as a father to that boy.

But in the blink of an eye, his life had changed again. He had thought he would never have a child, only to find that he'd had one for eight years.

Hitting the steering wheel again wouldn't help, but he did it anyway. If he inflicted enough physical pain on himself, surely it would relieve some of his mental anguish.

Deciding he was wasting his time here, Austin cranked the engine and drove off. His next destination was Grant Hoople's house in Lafayette. Maybe he would get lucky and find that son of a bitch at home.

If not, then he would keep on keeping on. The possibility that Tyler might have been taken out of the state didn't bear thinking about. He *would* find his son. And Sullivan *would* pay.

Austin gritted his teeth as the truck sped forward.

"I want my Mommy."

Lester glared at the boy, hatred churning inside him. "Stop whining."

"I hate you," Tyler muttered, his lower lip protruding.

Lester's eyes narrowed as he reached over, clasped a hand around Tyler's arm and jerked him up off the dirty pallet on the cement floor, not stopping until their noses were almost touching and their breath mingled.

"No more than I hate you, you little shit. I should've taught you to respect your elders a long time ago. Maybe it's not too late."

"Let me go!"

Lester grinned. "My pleasure."

He shoved the kid back down so hard that Tyler's head thudded against the wall. Lester watched as the boy's eyes closed, then reopened. But they were dazed. He knew Tyler had taken a dangerous lick.

Lester made a face as he kept his eye on the kid. Hoople would have his balls on a platter if something happened to the boy before they got the money. Knowing Cassie, she wouldn't part with a dime until she had seen the kid, which meant Tyler had to be in mint condition.

"I wanna go home," Tyler pleaded, rubbing eyes that were swimming with unshed tears.

"You'll go when I say you can and not before."

"I don't want you for my daddy."

"I don't want you for my kid, either."

Tyler straightened. "When I get home, I'm going to tell my friend Austin on you."

Lester's fury flared, since he'd always suspected that McGuire was the one who had humped his old lady and gotten her pregnant. But he'd never had proof of that, and Cassie had refused to tell him, regardless of how much he had harassed her.

"Ah, so you're going to tell on me, huh?"

Tyler jutted his chin. "Yeah, and he'll beat you up."

"Not if I kill him first."

The boy's face turned pale as sand, but he didn't flinch. Lester had to hand it to him. For eight years old, he already had balls. In fact, if this kid had truly been his son, he would be proud. As it was, he didn't give a rat's ass about Tyler.

If things didn't go as planned, and Cassie jerked them around and didn't come through with the money, he would kill the kid, wouldn't think twice about it. After all, he had nothing to lose. If he got arrested, he would never walk the streets again, so he might as well have a damn good reason for going back to the pen.

Anyway, putting a bullet though the kid's temple would make his day. Lester chuckled. Hell, he deserved a reward after *baby-sitting* this kid.

Thinking of "mamma" brought Cassie back to mind. He hated that bitch. She had made him out a fool when she took Tyler and ran. He'd had no idea she would do anything like that. It had taken guts.

Now he was the one with the guts who was getting even. And while he was at it, his group would get richer. Cash flow had been a problem for a long time.

"How's the kid?"

Lester swung around and watched as Grant Hoople strode through the open door. "Asking for a butt bruising."

"Why can't I go home?" Tyler demanded, his eyes on Hoople.

"Shut up," Hoople said without looking at him. Then, to Lester, "Come on. We've got work to do."

"Don't you think we should lay low for a while and let her stew?" Lester scratched his head. "Don't you think that'd be smart?"

"Are you questioning my judgment?" Hoople's voice turned mean.

"Huh? No, of course not," Lester said hurriedly, feeling himself flush. It wouldn't be smart to piss off his leader. Hoople and the others thought he could walk on water because he had the means and the power to get them over their present cash crunch.

Lester wanted his elevated position to remain secure.

"Let's just hope you're right about your ex and her willingness to play ball."

"You can trust me on that," Lester said in a scoffing tone. "She thinks this little bastard here makes the world go around."

"Let's just see to it that he makes *our* world go around."

Lester slapped Hoople on the back. "You just leave everything to me. She'll be a piece of cake." Lester mentally patted himself on the back. "This whole scheme will be a piece of cake."

Thirty-Seven

"**H**ow could you have done such a thing?"

Cassie swallowed a sharp retort and let out a harsh sigh instead. Her daddy was peering at her through eyes that were filled with hostility and disappointment.

She had expected as much. When she displeased him as a child, James wouldn't talk to her. That silence had hurt more than if he had taken a switch to her legs.

Her mother, on the other hand, vocalized her disappointment in a condescending way that frightened, then alienated, Cassie. Because of their demand for perfection, she had striven to be perfect, which meant she had lived under a microscope and under pressure.

With James continuing to stare at her, Cassie could feel that pressure more than ever. Suddenly she was a child again and had committed an unpardonable sin.

But she was *not* a child; she was an adult. They couldn't bully or intimidate her anymore. She had been through a hell that neither of them could imagine. She wasn't afraid of them or anyone else—except Lester, and him only because of what he could do to her son.

Cassie cringed. It had been two days since Lester had called. Since then, she hadn't budged from the house, fearing she would miss his next call. She hadn't slept or eaten, either. She didn't know how much longer she could hold herself together.

Now she was being put through a delayed inquisition by her daddy.

"Cassie, I asked you a question."

"I don't know why it happened, Daddy. It just did."

They were in the breakfast room, the three of them, having coffee and watching the phone. Cassie quelled the urge to scream at the damn thing to ring.

"It just did?" His usually low-key voice rose the way it did when he was behind the pulpit. "I won't accept that. Behavior like that doesn't just happen."

"It was my fault," Cassie admitted in a dull tone, knowing that she couldn't avoid this verbal skirmish. Besides, she owed them the truth.

"I refuse to believe that."

"Believe it because it's true."

After she had blabbed her secret, she had beaten up on herself unmercifully. Only when she realized she couldn't change the situation did she stop. Besides, Tyler's safety was all that mattered.

He had to be safe. She couldn't afford to think otherwise. If the cops didn't find Tyler, Austin would.

Austin. She couldn't think about him, either. Not now. When she did, her entire body felt as if she had stuck her finger into an electrical outlet.

"Oh, Cassie, how could you?" Wilma asked. "How could you do that to us?"

Cassie shook herself out of her reverie and said, "I can't answer that either, Mother."

"That's because I don't think you're telling us the truth."

"It *is* the truth, Daddy. You just don't want to accept it."

James's face was stroke-level red. "I refuse to believe that my daughter would initiate such a thing."

Cassie bit back another sharp retort. She didn't know how far down in the trenches she should take this conversation. She would love to spare her parents the gory details of how she had all but jumped Austin's bones that evening on the beach. But it looked as though they weren't going to accept a surface explanation.

"I'm prepared to give you the details, if you want them."

Wilma glared at her. James made a choking sound.

"Look, Austin and I made love on the beach the day of my eighteenth birthday party."

"Oh my stars," Wilma said, throwing her hands up, then dropping them over her heart.

"Are you all right, Mother?" Cassie asked anxiously.

"No, I'm not all right. I'll never be all right again, especially in light of the fact that soon everyone in town will know that you had a baby out of wedlock."

"I did not have Tyler out of wedlock. I married Lester in order to save you that humiliation."

"It's Austin's fault." James took a deep breath. "He did nothing to defend himself the other day, which is a sure sign of guilt to me."

"Stop it! Both of you." Cassie had never talked to her parents in such a manner, but she wasn't about to let Austin take all the blame.

James gave her a startled look. "I beg your pardon?"

"Would you for once just be my daddy," Cassie said, "and not a preacher?"

Her soft plea seemed to have hit its target. James looked at Wilma, his face flushed, before turning back to Cassie. "Go on."

"Making love to Austin and getting pregnant, then marrying Lester, was not what I had planned for my

life, that's for sure. But those things happened, and I
can't undo them.''

She paused to make sure she had their attention.
''Anyway, Austin was engaged to Alicia, and by the
time I knew I was pregnant, they were married.''

''This is a pastor's worst nightmare,'' James said in
a cold tone.

''That's why I never wanted you to know.''

''Then why did you tell us?'' Wilma asked.

''Because Daddy wouldn't let it go, wouldn't accept
that Lester hadn't turned over a new leaf, that he hadn't
stopped playing with guns. When he kept on about how
Lester had accepted the Lord and only wanted to see
his son, I couldn't help myself. That was the final
straw.''

Cassie broke off abruptly and stared at her father,
whose features still showed no remorse. ''I couldn't
take any more, because I knew that Lester didn't care
one thing about Tyler. He just wanted to use him for
his cause.''

''What you're saying is that I'm to blame for your
sin?''

''No, Daddy, I'm not. It's just that Lester knew how
to manipulate you and did. You're too good for your
own good.''

''That's not a compliment.'' James's tone was rebuking.

''No, but it's a fact,'' Wilma said, her eyes on her
husband.

James glared first at his wife, then at Cassie. ''Regardless, your behavior was inexcusable.''

''I'll have to agree with your father on that, Cassie,''
Wilma added. ''You know how much this family
guards our privacy. Now we'll be the talk of the town.''

Cassie felt such deep anger at this hypocrisy that for a moment she couldn't say a word. Finally she said, "It sickens me that you care what people think about something that happened a long time ago. It's also sickening to think you care more about the family name and reputation than you do your grandson."

"That's not true," James said in a huffy voice. "Of course we want our grandson returned safe and sound."

"Well, you sure could've fooled me."

James clenched his jaws. "I won't tolerate any more disrespect from you, young lady. This is all too disgusting."

"Don't you mean *I'm* disgusting?" Cassie asked quietly.

"That, too, if you must know. And Austin—I feel the same about him. He betrayed me and our friendship, two things I can forgive but can't forget."

"Oh, James, that's not the right attitude for a minister to have," Wilma said.

"I'm a man of God who preaches His word and who's expected to live His word," James said in his pulpit voice. "I expect both of you to remember that." He paused and stomped toward the door. "I'm going to the church. Let me know if Lester calls."

When he left, the room was silent. Cassie took a sip of her cold coffee and instantly regretted it. Her stomach rebelled. Getting up, she said to her mother, "I have to do something. I can't just sit here and wait for that damn phone to ring."

"I'm so sorry about all this, Cassie. And I certainly take my share of the responsibility. If only I'd been a better mother, more—"

Cassie gave her head a hard shake. "It's too late to

place blame. Besides, the blame is mine, and I fully
accept it.''

"What about Austin?"

Her heart sank. "What about him?"

"Have you two spoken about...Tyler?"

"No, not alone, that is."

"You have to talk, you know."

Cassie bit down on her lip. "I know, but right now
both of us need to focus our efforts on finding Tyler."

"I understand. So where are you going?"

"To see Lester's parents."

"If he calls again I'll ring your cell phone immediately."

Cassie nodded, grabbed her purse and practically ran
out the door.

"We don't know where he is."

Cassie wanted to call Dewitt Sullivan a liar, but she
refrained from doing so, the main reason being that she
didn't want to further antagonize him.

Neither Dewitt nor Charlotte was happy to see her.
But she didn't care. In the scheme of things, their feelings weren't important.

"He has Tyler, Dewitt," Cassie stressed. "An innocent little boy who's done nothing to deserve this."

"To hell with you, Cassie." Dewitt's face took on a
satanic glare. "You're not the only one who cares about
that boy, even though you think you are."

Cassie sighed. "I won't deny that since I've been
back I haven't let you see him much, but I was afraid
of this very thing happening."

"Maybe, if you'd been more understanding a long
time ago, Lester wouldn't have had to resort to such
tactics."

"That's right," Charlotte added in a tearful voice.

An alarm bell went off in Cassie's head. "Exactly what are you saying?"

"We know that Tyler's not Lester's child," Dewitt said.

"Which doesn't have anything to do with my not understanding your son. First of all, it was Lester who was willing to be bought off. I wanted a divorce and custody of Tyler. For money, he willingly gave me both."

"He took us into his confidence about that, too," Charlotte said. "At the time, that group he was mixed up with had him so brainwashed he couldn't think straight or he wouldn't have agreed to your terms."

How could they be so blind? It didn't take a rocket scientist to answer that question. Lester was their only child, and they loved the sorry bastard. Still, Cassie couldn't let that influence her. If she had to hurt them to get Tyler back, then so be it.

"You have to face facts here," Cassie stressed. "Whether you want to or not. Lester himself took the child and is asking for more money for his cause in return for my son."

Dewitt's body seemed suddenly to deflate, leaving him looking old and weak. Charlotte whimpered, which made Cassie want to slap her, only to follow that slap with a hug. They were both pitiful, but that was too bad, because the situation was critical.

"Look, I didn't come here to make you feel bad or to attack you. When this is all over and Tyler's home, we'll work something out. But right now, I have to know if Lester said or did anything that might have given you a clue as to where he was going or what he had planned."

"Like what?" Dewitt asked in a tired voice.

"I don't know!" Cassie's patience was gone, and it showed.

"Well, I did hear him talking on the phone," Charlotte said, frowning.

"To who?" Cassie asked.

"Some man, I think, who apparently asked Lester if the keys were still in the same place at the cabin. Lester told them they were."

"Cabin?" Cassie's tone was frantic. "What cabin and where is it?"

They told her. Minutes later, she was back in her car, punching out Detective Malcolm's number at the police station.

She was told he wasn't in but that they could get a message to him. Damn! She left her message, but she didn't want to wait.

Austin. She would call Austin.

Should he get out and walk around the house?

Austin was so damn hot, he was sure he would have a heatstroke in his vehicle. But the intense, breath-robbing heat wasn't going to stop him from doing the only thing he could think of to do—watch Grant Hoople's house.

Along with Detective Malcolm, Austin had put his private eye friend and his crew on Lester's house and the campsite in the woods. All bases were covered, and still no sign of any of the militiamen or Tyler.

Austin wanted to tear someone's head off. At the moment, he wouldn't be selective. If Lester or any of his cohorts harmed one harm a hair on that boy's head, Austin would be the one going to the pen for life.

He would kill the son of a bitch with his own hands.

That was at least something he could do for his child,
a child who he'd never had the pleasure of parenting,
thanks to Cassie.

Unable to sit there another second, Austin jerked
open the door and got out. After looking around the
deserted street, he crossed it. He didn't slow down until
he reached a clump of trees beside Hoople's home.

Knowing that he was taking a chance by going any
closer, he did it anyway. What if Tyler was in there,
alone? He didn't think that was the case, but one never
knew with those idiots on the loose.

Austin slunk down and ran toward the back window.
When he reached his destination, sweat ran into his
eyes. He blinked it back, plastering himself against the
wood, trying to control his erratic breathing. So far, so
good, he thought, easing his head around and peering
inside.

Nothing out of the ordinary greeted him.

The bedroom contained what looked like dilapidated
furniture and nothing else. No guns and no people were
in sight. Hoping he would fare better looking through
a side window into the main room, he crept around the
corner.

Once there, he was reaching in his pocket for a handkerchief to wipe the sweat off his face when he heard
a noise. Behind him.

He swung around and looked down the barrel of a
gun.

Grant Hoople was on the other side of that gun. "If
you so much as twitch, I'll blow your fuckin' brains
out." He laughed. "Is that clear, sonny?"

Austin cursed silently at the same time that his cell
phone rang.

Thirty-Eight

Cassie blanched.

Although Austin took his eyes off her, he didn't remove the gun from her sight.

"Whose is that?" Cassie asked, almost whispering.

"Mine."

"Where did you get it?"

"Bought it."

"Now's not the time to be sarcastic, Austin, no matter how you feel about me."

"Don't lecture me, Cassie."

Her cheek muscles contracted, but she didn't back down. "You know how I feel about guns."

"This is not about you or your feelings. Besides, I'm not going to be caught unprepared again."

"What does that mean?"

"You don't want to know."

"If it has anything to do with Tyler, I damn sure do."

For a minute, Austin held his silence in grim fashion. Then he said, "When you called my cell, I was at Grant Hoople's place."

"Isn't he that militia—"

"Yep, Lester's fearless leader."

Cassie felt a tightness in her chest. "What were you doing there?"

"Watching his dump for any sign of life, for any sign of Tyler."

"Where were the cops?"

"You'll have to take that up with Malcolm."

"Go on with your story," she said in a terse voice, a sinking feeling in the pit of her stomach.

"To make a long story short, I had managed to sneak up to the living room window when Hoople got the drop on me. I turned to find a loaded gun pointed in my face."

"How on earth did you get away?" Her scalp prickled.

"You called, and the unexpected noise caught Hoople off guard. That was all I needed. I knocked the gun aside, then knocked him out cold."

"You're crazy!" she cried. "You could've gotten yourself killed."

"That's right, but I didn't. And there was no sign of Tyler."

"Do you think Hoople is the brains behind all this?"

"Could be, but he didn't give up anything. When I called Malcolm and he sent someone to question Hoople, the son of a bitch was colder than ice."

"Damn him," Cassie said, fighting back the urge to give in to her emotions and squall like a baby, especially when her eyes drifted back to the gun, the loathsome thing that had set this nightmare in motion.

"I still don't understand why *you* have a gun," Cassie said in a bleak, unsteady tone.

"Actually, I've had it for a while." Austin tone was sharp but matter of fact. "With the hotels, one never knows."

Cassie didn't buy that explanation, but it didn't matter. Not now, anyway. Still, she was unable to bear the sight of that vile weapon. "I hope I never have to see another one of those as long as I live."

Austin didn't respond.

"Please, put it away."

"When the time's right."

Cassie faced him again, prepared to argue, only to change her mind. His entire body was rigid, indicating just how tightly wound he was. This was a side of Austin she had never seen, and it added to her anxiety.

But then, she was close to the breaking point herself, which made her understand the strain he was under.

When she had called Austin and told him about the cabin, he had told her that he would meet her there. It had taken them both about thirty minutes to arrive.

The Sullivans referred to it as a cabin; by her definition, that was a stretch. It looked more like a large shack than anything else. But Dewitt had told her that he camped there when he hunted on the surrounding land, land that belonged to them.

Now, as Cassie stole another glance at Austin, she didn't regret having called him. Reason number one, she might have saved his life, and reason number two, she had been afraid to come here alone.

Wisely, they hadn't parked too close to the shack, but they were close enough to see it. Austin had gotten out of his truck and climbed into the car beside her, a move that further unnerved her. She had no idea what he planned to do about Tyler now that he knew the truth.

However, he didn't say a word about that. She wanted to ask, yet she couldn't, for fear of what he might say. What if he decided to fight her for custody?

He suddenly looked dangerous and unapproachable. It was as if they were now strangers, which, under the circumstances, was probably best. Finding their son was the only thing that mattered. What came afterward— well, Cassie refused to think about that. Her mind could absorb just so much.

Where was the detective? She didn't know how much longer she could contain herself. She had to know if Tyler was in that creepy lean-to.

As if Austin could read her mind, he muttered, "Dammit, what's keeping Malcolm?"

"Do you think he got the message?"

"Hell, yes. I told him myself. But we might as well be chasing our tails as to sit here and wait."

Cassie squinted her eyes. "The place looks deserted, I know, but we have no choice but to get it checked out."

"Damn right. I'm not budging until I do just that."

"Malcolm has to be on his way. He just has to." If she didn't find Tyler soon, they would have to cart her off to the rubber room.

"Ah, to hell with him." Austin grabbed the door handle.

Cassie eyes widened. "You can't go up there alone."

"Who's going to stop me?"

"But, Austin, that's crazy!"

"I'm just going to take a quick look around."

"What if someone's inside and you're spotted, like you were at Hoople's house?"

"I'll cross that bridge when I come to it."

"If you do anything to endanger Tyler, I—"

"Hey," he cut in brutally, "I don't think you want to open that can of worms—not right now, anyway."

Cassie crushed her lips together.

"If you hadn't married that sick bastard, we wouldn't be here."

"Damn you, Austin," she lashed back, tears stinging her eyes.

"Aren't you damning the wrong person?"

With that, he jerked open the door, then looked over his shoulder. "Stay put and wait for Malcolm."

She didn't answer him. Instead, she stared straight ahead, furious that he thought he could give her orders. To hell with him. She would do as she pleased. And after waiting another five minutes, she pleased to follow him.

By the time Cassie wound her way through the woods, closer to the cabin, her heart was beating in her throat so loudly that it drowned out the birds chirping in the forest.

Where was Austin?

She didn't see him anywhere. But then, she couldn't see to the far side of the structure. Logic told her he was there or inside.

Her mouth dried up and her heart hammered louder as she moved from one big tree to another, suddenly feeling foolish, as it was obvious no one was around. The place had all the earmarks of long neglect.

Yet she crept to the back window, where she peeped inside. She didn't know what kept her from crying out at what she saw. Tyler was lying on a pallet. Unmoving. Fright stopped her heart. Was he dead? Oh, dear Lord, please let him be alive, she begged silently.

Not thinking or caring whether anyone else was on the premises, she tiptoed around the shack and up the back steps, then gently shoved open the door. A room littered with guns of all sizes, types and shapes filled her vision. Shuddering in horror, she dashed to her son's side. The instant she knelt beside him, it was obvious he was breathing.

With tears streaming down her face, she let go of her pent-up breath, then raised her head in thanksgiving. It was when she peered back down at Tyler that she heard the voice.

Lester's voice. And she knew who he was talking to. To scream was unthinkable, but that was what she wanted to do.

"Well, well, lookie who we have here," Lester said in an evil but mocking tone.

"Where's Tyler?" Austin countered in a sharp but calm voice.

Lester chuckled. "I always figured that brat was yours, though she never would say."

"Where is he, Sullivan?"

"Don't know."

"You're lying."

"I'd watch my mouth if I was you, lover boy."

Getting slowly to her feet, Cassie forced her jellylike legs to move toward the bedroom door. Luck was with her; it was open enough that she could see down the hall into the living room.

She gripped the door handle hard to hold herself upright. Lester had a gun, and it was pointed at Austin's heart.

Damn Austin for his John Wayne antics. She had been afraid something like this would happen. For a second Cassie's eyes darted back to Tyler. She wanted to snatch him off that bed, run like hell and never look back.

But she couldn't. She couldn't leave Austin at Lester's mercy.

"You won't get away with this, Sullivan," Austin said harshly. "Even if you kill me, the police are on the way."

"Won't matter," Lester said with cocky confidence. "You'll be dead by then, and I'll be long gone."

"Wrong."

Lester froze. "Cassie?"

"That's right, Lester," she whispered. "And it's the barrel of one of your own guns that's digging into your neck."

He chuckled again. "Who you trying to kid? Even if I shot lover boy right in front of you, you wouldn't pull the trigger."

"Cassie," Austin said in a soft, warning tone.

Ignoring the fear and concern in his face and voice, Cassie nosed the barrel deeper into Lester's flesh. "Are you sure about that? While I was hiding from you, you bastard, I learned to handle a gun like a pro."

"You're lying."

"Want to bet your life on it?"

For a moment the room was filled with silence, a silence that was suddenly broken by the wail of a siren.

"Give it up, Sullivan," Austin demanded. "You're in a no-win situation. You shoot me—" he broke off with a shrug "—she shoots you."

Cassie felt, rather than saw, Lester's hesitation. But that slight mistake was all Austin needed. Quick as lightning, he lifted his leg and kicked the gun out of Lester's hand. The pistol went flying across the floor.

"Why, you son of a bitch!" Lester cried, lunging for the weapon.

The second he bent over, Cassie hit him on the back of the neck with the butt of her gun. Lester groaned; then his body flattened on the floor, where it twitched for a moment before becoming still.

Cassie lifted horrified eyes to Austin, then, in a dazed fashion, dropped the gun.

"Dammit, Cassie, you could've been killed."

His words didn't register. Nothing registered except the horror of the moment. Lester was right. She had lied. She had never shot a gun in her life.

"Mommy, Mommy!"

A cry erupted from deep within Cassie's soul as she swung around and saw her son standing in the doorway, dried tears streaking his face. She ran to him and, regardless of his weight, scooped him up in her arms.

"It's all right, sweetheart. Mommy's here, and you're safe."

Thirty-Nine

"There, you're done."

An almost-smile altered Cassie's lips as she watched Jo Nell mist her hair with a final touch of light spray. "Thanks."

"Well, it helped a little."

Cassie gave Jo a look. "But not a lot. Is that what you're saying?"

"Mmm, now that you mention it, I guess so."

"Thanks for that vote of confidence." Cassie's voice was tinged with humorous sarcasm.

"I didn't mean it that way, and you know it." Jo Nell peered in the mirror and fiddled with her own hair, then turned her attention once again to Cassie. "It's just that you've been looking so drained and wrung out lately that it's affected your whole body, especially your hair."

Cassie got out of the chair. "Come on, walk out with me."

"I have ten minutes before my next appointment. Do you want to grab a quick cup of coffee?"

Cassie shook her head. "No, thanks, not today."

"I'll walk you out, then."

Only after they were on the sidewalk did Cassie speak.

"Jeez, it's hot." The saturating humidity almost took her breath.

"Look at those clouds," Jo said, raising her head. "It looks like the bloody bottom's about to fall out of the sky."

"If it does, it'll fit my mood to a tee."

"Now, you see here, Cassie Sullivan, your son's safe and that slimeball ex of yours is back in the pen for life, so you should be rolling in roses."

Cassie opened her car door and got inside, then stared up at Jo Nell. "Of course I'm grateful for the way things turned out. If they hadn't—well, I'd be in a rubber room bouncing off the walls."

"It's Austin, isn't it?"

"Yes," Cassie admitted grimly.

Jo Nell pulled her blouse away from her perspiring body and let out a sigh. "You have to talk to him, you know?"

"I know."

"And until you do, you're going to be in this mood and look like you've been through a war zone."

"I'm not arguing."

"Then why the hell are we having this conversation?"

"Because I'm scared, that's why."

"I can understand that, too. But dammit, Cassie, look what you've been through. I've told you this before, you've got more guts in one little finger than I have in my entire body."

"That's poppycock."

"No, it's the truth. I couldn't have taken my child and fled on a moment's notice and started a new life. No way."

"Yes, you could, Jo." Cassie tone was gentle. "If

you'd ever had a child and knew that he was in grave danger, you could do anything. Trust me."

Jo shrugged. "Maybe so, but I have to tell you, I'm selfish. Always have been and always will be."

"You're not selfish. You're a generous friend whom I love and couldn't do without."

Jo Nell slammed the car door and stepped back, grinning. "Thanks for saying that."

Cassie nodded, grinning back.

"By the way, how is Wilma? And James, too, for that matter?"

"Healthwise, Mother's still holding her own. Otherwise, they're having a tough time dealing with all this. Daddy especially."

"Ah, they'll come around. Still, I think you and Tyler should find a place of your own. You've lived with Mommy and Daddy long enough."

"As soon as I make up my mind what I'm going to do, then I will."

"Don't worry about Austin. If he was out to make trouble, he would've set things in motion already."

Cassie wiped the sweat off her brow. "I wish I was that confident. He might just be biding his time, weighing his options, so to speak."

"You and you only, Cass, can make this right. Or wrong. Whichever your heart dictates. No one else can—not me or your parents." Jo Nell frowned. "Besides, you've been trying all your life to please Wilma and James. Don't you think it's time you pleased Cassie?"

"I don't know what I think anymore, except—" Cassie broke off and stared ahead.

"Except what?"

"Nothing." Cassie reaching for her sunglasses, her

head splitting from tension and the sun's glare. "Anyway, I've taken up enough of your time. Your next customer's bound to be waiting for you."

Jo Nell stepped back. "No big deal."

"We'll talk soon."

"Promise?"

Cassie forced a real smile. "Promise."

A few minutes later she was back at the mansion, relieved to have the house to herself, something that was a rarity. Today the cards seemed to have fallen her way.

James was at the church, and Wilma had felt well enough to have lunch with some friends. Tyler was at day camp, and Joy had gone grocery shopping.

After fixing herself a glass of iced tea, Cassie kicked off her shoes at the foot of the stairs and padded barefoot onto the veranda, where she sat in a huge rocker, its soothing motion almost lulling her to sleep. Realizing that, she stopped and reached for her tea.

Then she lifted her eyes toward the sky and watched as thunder clouds continued to gather. The rain would come, but it would offer no relief from the heat. Instead, it would make it worse. But as she had told Jo Nell, the weather fitted her mood.

Tears pricked her eyes, but Cassie willed them back. She couldn't cry about Austin, not if she was going to make a rational decision concerning him. That was what this afternoon was all about.

It had been a week now since she had seen him. Once Tyler had been rescued, Detective Malcolm had driven her and Tyler home in his car. In all the confusion of the police's arrival and Lester's subsequent arrest, somehow Austin had managed to leave without her even knowing it.

However, the following day they had met at the police station to give their statements to Detective Malcolm. She had wanted to say something to him, but he hadn't given her the opportunity.

In fact, he had blatantly ignored her. Only once had their eyes met, and when that happened, the contact knocked her breathless. She had seen the pain reflected in his eyes along with something much more potent—betrayal.

"Austin," she had said, swallowing hard.

"Not now, Cassie."

His curt words had cut to the core, and she had shifted her gaze. Still, every detail associated with him seemed seared on her brain, from his mussed-up hair to the five o'clock shadow on his face, to his open-necked shirt with hair peeping through, hair she tugged on during the height of climax.

Cassie groaned, knowing that she loved him and would always love him. But mixed with that love was an acute fear that she had killed any feelings he might have for her and that he would only want Tyler.

What if he tried to take her son away from her?

She kept telling herself that Austin would never do that, especially after what Tyler had been through. Yet that niggling in the back of her mind remained, robbing her of the courage she needed to approach Austin and tell him she loved him and ask for forgiveness.

Somehow she had to find that courage. No matter what the end result, she had to talk to Austin. She owed it to him, to herself and to Tyler.

Their conversation just this morning had proved that. Over his protest, she had pulled Tyler onto her lap after he'd gotten dressed.

"Aw, Mom, I'm too big for this."

She hid her smile, thinking that he hadn't felt that way in that cabin or afterward in the car. He'd sat in her lap and snuggled against her and hadn't thought twice about it.

"Maybe so, but humor me anyway."

"Do I have to?"

Cassie tousled his hair. "Yep."

"Okay, but don't tell my friends."

She laughed outright. "Your secret's safe with me. Scout's honor."

Once he was against her, he asked in a muffled tone, "Do we have to go away again?"

"No, son, we don't."

"I don't like my dad. I told him I hated him."

At first Cassie didn't quite know how to respond to such an honest but bold statement. His grown-up words, however, had ripped her heart further apart.

"I don't like him, either."

"Do I have to see him again?"

"No, you don't. He'll never get out of jail." She paused, feeling him stiffen. "How do you feel about that, with your friends and all? Will they tease you?"

She had to ask those tough questions, since Tyler was sure to encounter the cruel tongues of his peers. She would give anything to shield him from that, but she couldn't.

So far, he seemed to have taken this latest crisis in stride with more wisdom than his years should have permitted. The fact that Lester hadn't physically harmed him had helped, and the fact that Lester had stayed with him, rather than one of his cohorts, had been another plus for Tyler's psyche.

At least Lester had shown Tyler that small touch of humanity, although Cassie wasn't sure why. Now that

Tyler was safe in her arms and Lester behind bars, her ex-husband's motives didn't matter. What mattered was that she and her son could start afresh, begin the healing process one more time.

"Sammy will probably say something smart," Tyler finally said in answer to her question.

"What will you do?"

"Punch him in the nose."

Cassie made a face, but she was careful how she responded, since she was on delicate ground. "Do you think that's the answer?"

Tyler cut his eyes up to her. "Will you spank me?"

"Do you think I should?"

"I guess so," he muttered.

"Then I guess you'd best keep your fists to yourself, young man."

Tyler's mouth turned down. "Okay."

Cassie kissed the top of his head. "Maybe your friends won't be ugly. If some are, try ignoring them. Soon they'll forget about you and your problems."

"I hope so." Tyler was quiet for a minute, then asked, "When can I go back to Austin's farm?"

Her stomach flip-flopped again. "Do you want to?"

Tyler sat up and looked at her with flashing eyes. "'Course I want to."

"Well, pardon me. Austin's still special to you, huh?" Cassie forced her voice to show none of the panic suddenly charging through her. While she was still willing to share her son, she wouldn't give him up. She would die first. But then, Austin would never demand that.

Or would he?

There was such a fine line between love and hate.

"Mom, I gotta go."

"You're right," she said, unclasping her arms from around his wiggling body. "Papa will be beating on the door."

He gave her a quick kiss, scrambled off her lap, then fled the room.

Now, as Cassie thought back on how her son had felt in her arms, she ached for Austin to experience that same feeling. So should she take the gamble that she could spill her soul and come out a winner—a winner in possession of both Austin and her son?

Cassie reached for a fan, closed her eyes and rocked.

Forty

Austin rubbed his scratchy jaw. He should shave. For that matter, he should do a lot of things he wasn't doing. He was too busy wallowing in self-pity.

Damn. *Damn Cassie.*

He stomped around his condo and for the umpteenth time noticed how bare and austere it looked. What it needed was a woman's touch. Baloney. What this pad needed was a new owner.

Austin glanced at the clock above the fireplace. He ought to be at the hotel in Baton Rouge. He had lost some staff members there, one of them his manager. But he didn't have the desire or the energy to take care of business.

Still, this pity party had to end. He was a grown man, with responsibilities that couldn't be shirked. Hell, he had already pulled a boner with the land deal, a boner that was costing *him* a bundle.

But there was light at the end of that dark tunnel, thank heavens. He'd found a buyer for one of his colts. That one horse alone would net him half the money he owed the company. Yet he wouldn't be satisfied until he had paid back all he owed. Then maybe the company could borrow the remaining amount required to do the renovations that Cassie wanted on the Jasmine Hillcrest.

Cassie. Cassie.

He couldn't stop thinking about her. He couldn't stop thinking about himself, either. His mind and guts had literally been blown to smithereens when she had dropped her bombshell. But with Tyler's kidnapping and dramatic rescue, he hadn't had a chance to put his true feelings under his mind's microscope until now.

Maybe if he went to the farm, he would fare better. Maybe an evening gallop through the woods would do the trick, would help him reach a decision concerning Cassie and Tyler.

Tyler.

His groan sounded more like a wail as he made his way into the kitchen, opened the refrigerator and grabbed a Coke. What he wanted was a beer, but he didn't have any here. When he got to the farm, he swore he would down an entire six-pack.

He loved her, dammit.

Austin slouched against the cabinet, unable to move. Cassie had ripped the lining out of his soul, and he wasn't sure it could ever be mended.

For eight years she had robbed him of his child.

How could she have done such a thing? Why hadn't she come to him? Why? Why? Why? Not knowing the answers to those questions was what had reduced him to this state.

He had never felt so empty, so betrayed, so helpless. How could he love Cassie and hate her at the same time?

His stomach clenched. He wanted to puke, and he wanted to cry. He couldn't allow himself the luxury of either. He was a strong man, with strong motivations and strong wants.

And he wanted his son in his life. Come hell or high

water, that was going to happen. How it happened would be up to Cassie, which meant he had to see her.

He was so deep in his own torment that it took him a minute to realize the doorbell was buzzing relentlessly. He set his Coke down on the counter and, with a stinging curse, strode to the door, not happy with the interruption.

When he jerked the door open, his happy factor dropped even more. Yet he stepped back and gestured with his hand. "Come on in, James."

His lifelong friend was the last person Austin had expected to see at his door, but then, the way his life had been going lately, nothing should have surprised him.

James Wortham crossed the threshold, pausing only after he reached the middle of the living room. "I hope you don't mind my intruding?"

"Now's not the time to pull that formality bull, James. Just say what you came to say."

James flushed, and his jaw tightened, but he didn't reprimand Austin, as if he knew better. "All right. I don't want you to blame Cassie for what she did."

"Oh, really." Austin crossed his arms, and a grim tilt altered his lips. "Why's that?"

"Because she was only eighteen, for one thing."

"She still could've told me."

"I know how you feel."

Austin snorted crudely. "I don't think so."

James's flush deepened. "Okay, maybe I don't. But Cassie's not to blame."

"Then just who is?"

"Me."

"Oh, come on, James, even for you, that's a stretch."

"Just listen, will you?"

Austin shrugged. "I'm all ears."

"First off, I'm not condoning what either of you did, especially you, Austin."

"You've already made that plain, so there's no need to beat that dead horse. I'm not exactly proud of myself, either."

"That aside for now," James went on, "Cassie didn't tell you because of us."

"Did she actually say that?"

"No, but I know my daughter."

Austin pressed his lips together and held his tongue. It wouldn't hurt him to hear what James had to say, although he doubted it would change his mind about Cassie's betrayal.

"She was afraid of telling us the truth. You see, we expected her to be perfect, constantly drilling it into her that she must never do anything to bring shame on us or the Wortham name."

"I'll buy that," Austin said harshly.

James's chin jutted at the obvious rebuke, but once again he didn't take umbrage at Austin's rudeness. "I deeply regret that she didn't feel that she could confide in us. Does what I just said help?"

"Help how?" Austin would be damned if he let his holier-than-thou friend off the hook. If James was willing to take the blame, then he needed to squirm a bit, though he didn't for one minute completely exonerate Cassie. When she had seduced him that evening, she had known exactly what she was doing.

"I just told you," James said in an irritated tone. "I don't want you to hold her responsible for not telling you about the...baby."

"Don't you mean *my* baby?"

"All right," James said tersely. "*Your* baby."

"Well, I appreciate your coming on her behalf, but it doesn't change anything."

James's head came up and his eyes turned belligerent. "What does that mean?"

"I still plan to have my day in court with Cassie."

"I wish you wouldn't."

Austin almost choked on his fury. "What do you suggest I do?"

"Let the past stay buried, for Cassie's and Tyler's sake. Don't you think they've been through enough?"

"I damn sure do, but then, so have I, James. Don't my feelings count at all?"

"Of course they count. You know how I feel about you and our friendship, but—"

"But what?"

"If you must know, I don't approve of a relationship between you and Cassie now any more than I would have then."

"Do you think I care?"

"I'm asking you to leave them alone," James snapped. "To stay at the hotel if you will, but that's all. Don't try to make an issue of this."

An issue. God, Austin wondered how he had ever become friends with this pompous airbag. He would like nothing better than to deflate James by blurting out how he and Cassie had made hot love since she had returned. He refrained, but not because he was a decent man. He didn't feel decent at all. What went on between him and Cassie was simply none of James's business.

Austin wanted his son in his life, and that was the only *issue*. He wouldn't settle for anything less.

When Austin kept his silence, James asked, "Do we have a deal, for old times' sake? Old friends' sake, if you will?"

"You know your way out, James."

Irritation flickered in James's eyes. "I won't ever forgive you if you don't comply with my wishes."

"Do you think I give a shit about *your* wishes? I don't. Nor do I give a shit if you forgive me. I'm the one who's been hung out to dry all these years. She denied me my son, dammit!"

"I knew it was a waste of time to come here." Bitterness colored James' tone.

"You're right about that. You're still my friend, James, and always will be—if you want to be. But you can't tell me what to do when it comes to my life." Repressed anger tightened Austin's mouth. "Now, I suggest you leave before this conversation deteriorates any further."

"Stay away from her, Austin."

"Goodbye, James."

James let out a long breath but didn't say anything. Instead, he wheeled around and stomped out the door.

Austin's curses filled the air as he grabbed his shoes and walked out the back door. An hour later, he let himself into the farmhouse, feeling as if he'd been beaten to a pulp with a bat.

What better time to get stinking drunk? he thought, headed for the kitchen, only to stop in his tracks.

To hell with it. By hightailing it to the farm, all he had done was trade the location of his misery. He was going to do what he should have done a week ago—confront Cassie, even though he had no clear plan or solution in mind.

The bottom line was that he wanted his son, but he wanted Cassie, too. He practically ran to the front door, then out it, only to stop in his tracks.

Cassie was standing on the porch. For a second he couldn't say a word.

"Where were you going?" Cassie asked in a halting tone.

"To see you."

She looked taken aback, but he couldn't read what lay behind her eyes. "Why?" she asked.

"Why did you come here?" he countered, stalling for time, trying to keep from jerking her into his arms.

She leaned her head to one side, but her gaze remained centered on him. "To see you."

"Why?" He finally got to say that word to her.

"To talk."

Austin rubbed the back of his neck. "This is a night for surprises. Before I came here, your daddy paid me a visit."

"I don't have to ask what he wanted."

"So, does his opinion count?"

"No."

Austin sucked in his breath, then let it out slowly. Dare he read more into this visit than was there? With her in front of him, in the flesh, looking at him with love—yes, that was love, he would swear to it—in her eyes, the answer was a resounding yes.

Then why was he standing there like an idiot, afraid to move or speak? Was he afraid he was dreaming, that she was a figment of his imagination?

"Cassie." He didn't recognize his own voice. The word sounded as if it came from someone's else's mouth.

"What?" Her voice sounded odd, too.

"Am I reading your eyes right?"

She smiled. "If you're reading love in them, then yes."

His heart leapt with untold joy. "Then get your sweet ass over here."

Whooping with joy, she ran straight in his arms. At the same time he kissed her long and hard, he swung her around until they were both dizzy.

At last he put her down, then looked into her eyes. "I will always love you."

"And I will always love you," she whispered in the same husky tone, tears shining in her eyes.

Without saying another word, Austin picked her up again and carried her inside, slamming the door shut behind him with his bare foot.

Epilogue

Six months later

"I don't think I'll ever get enough of you."

"Mmm, I hope not," Cassie murmured in a breathless tone, as Austin was suckling one breast, then the other.

Dawn was breaking at the farm, jump-starting what promised to be a colder than usual winter's day. They were snuggled together in bed, the covers thrown back as they had been making love off and on throughout the night. The smoldering embers from the fireplace in the bedroom had kept them warm.

In fact, Cassie was hot, but that feeling didn't have anything to do with the room temperature. Austin only had to come near her and she was in heat.

"How long have we been married now?" he asked, moving his tongue down her naked body, not stopping until he poked the tip in her navel.

She moaned, then dug her fingers into his thick hair. "Six months, but you know that." She moaned again as his lips moved lower and found its target.

"Ohhh, Austin," she cried, her climax coming hard and quick.

When it was over, he lifted his head and looked at

her, a satisfied expression on his face. "I love it when you make that certain little sound. It tells me you're about to come."

"Sometimes I think I'm going to come and you haven't even touched me."

"That's music to my ears, darlin'," he drawled.

"Turn over," she ordered, her voice still slightly dazed. "Turnabout's fair play."

Once he was on his back, Cassie leaned over and took him in her mouth. He reached around and cupped her buttocks, then squeezed as if the sweet agony she was bringing him was too much to endure.

"I want to be inside you," he said, panting. "It's time we made another baby."

Cassie's pulse went wild as he lifted her onto him. His full hardness rose like a spear high inside her. She bent slightly, enough for him to surround both her breasts with his big hands and hold on to them while she rode him hard and fast.

Once their cries rang out simultaneously, Cassie collapsed on top of him. Then he eased out of her and repositioned them so they were once again facing each other.

Austin smoothed her damp hair off her forehead and smiled at her. "I love you, Mrs. McGuire."

"No more than I love you, Mr. McGuire."

He chuckled. "Think we accomplished our goal?"

"It's the right time of the month, so that's entirely possible."

"Would you mind?"

"I'd love another baby."

He frowned. "You don't think it'd be too soon?"

"Are you thinking about Tyler?"

"Yes."

"He wouldn't mind. He's too happy and secure in our love for anything to matter."

Austin lay on his back, crossed his hands behind his head and stared at the ceiling, a contented look on his face. Besides their lovemaking, she knew what had put it there.

One week ago, Austin's adoption of Tyler had become final. But for them it had been real for a long time already. The day they got married, Tyler had looked up at Austin and said, "Does this mean now you're my daddy?"

Austin had dropped to his knees and, with tears in his eyes, said, "You bet, son. Now and forever."

Cassie had watched with tears streaming down her face as they had hugged each other. She had thought that was perhaps the happiest moment of her life, that nothing could ever outdo it.

But now she wasn't so sure. She hadn't come off that emotional or physical high since the night she had come here to the farm. During their fierce lovemaking, Austin had asked her to marry him, a deed they had done three days later.

Shortly thereafter, they had moved to the farm, where they planned to live until they could build a new home, having chosen a perfect place on the property.

"What are you thinking about?" Cassie finally asked after he remained quiet for a while.

"The day we got married."

"Me too." She propped herself on an elbow and peered into his eyes. "I haven't stopped being happy since."

"Even though your daddy didn't marry us? I hated that for you, thinking it must have dimmed your day."

"It made me sad, but that was Daddy's call, and he has to live with his decision."

"I think he regrets it now."

"Probably, although he's never said that to me."

"Me either," Austin said ruefully.

Cassie wasn't sure that James would ever relent. While he loved them both, he hadn't been able to justify their marriage in his mind or in God's eyes, and as a result, he had refused to marry them in his church.

Her mother, on the other hand, had given them her blessing. But because of James, she hadn't attended the wedding, either. Still, Tyler spent time with them, even if she and Austin did not.

"What if James never forgives us?"

"I'll deal with that then," Cassie responded. "Right now, I'm giving him all the space he wants. But his approval or disapproval is not going to change my life."

"What is?"

She smiled and said, "As if you didn't know."

He rose up and kissed her again, then said, "You're an amazing woman, Cassie."

"I don't see that."

"You're also the strongest woman I've ever known. I can't believe all you've been through since you've been back. Most women would have gone off the deep end."

"I'll admit it's been rough. But the bad times are behind us. Both Lester and Randall got their just deserts."

"And the hotel's getting a face-lift."

She grinned. "Something that still sticks in your craw. Right?"

''Watch it, woman. That smart mouth might get you in trouble.''

''Good.''

Austin chuckled, then his features sobered. ''We're talking about a lifetime here, you know?''

She opened her arms to him. ''I can't think of a better life sentence than that.''

From one of the world's most popular authors comes a novel that masterfully explores one man's attempt to climb beyond his station in life and the tragic consequences it will have on his family.

THE UPSTART

CATHERINE COOKSON

Businessman Samuel Fairbrother wants a home more in keeping with his recent wealth. The thirty-four-room mansion he purchases comes with a staff—a headstrong staff. In particular, butler Roger Maitland considers his new boss nothing more than an upstart. Soon Samuel and Roger are locked in a battle for supremacy of the household and for the loyalty of Samuel's own children. And Samuel is at a disadvantage.

As the years pass only Janet, the eldest daughter, remains. In her lies the only hope of reconciling the scattered family—even if she has to defy both her father and convention to do so.

MIRA

NOT FOR SALE IN CANADA

On sale mid-July 1999 wherever paperbacks are sold.

Wanting her became an obsession as powerful as his need to expose her...

She has no memory of her life before being captured by the Apache. Then suddenly she is given a name, a past—Anna Regent Wright, the long-lost Regent heiress, has come home at last.

But there is no doubt in Brit Caruth's mind that Anna is an impostor. And though this beautiful stranger has a hold on his body, he'll be damned if she'll get her hands on an inheritance that the Regents have long said was his....

Wanting You
NAN RYAN

New York Times bestselling author

JAYNE ANN KRENTZ

Having a baby was supposed to be the greatest event in her life, but for Pru Kenyon, it was bittersweet. Her relationship with her baby's father was exciting and satisfying…but Case McCord refused to commit.

She knew she could have this baby on her own and love her child enough for two. But Pru hadn't bargained on what Case would do for love.

THE FAMILY WAY

From *New York Times* bestselling author

Barbara Delinsky

Jenna McCue needs a favor—a very big favor—and Spencer Smith is her only hope. She's counting on his sense of adventure to give her something she wants more than anything: a baby.

But Spencer has a plan of his own. He just might give her that baby, but it will be the old-fashioned way! Since what Jenna doesn't realize is that he isn't willing to be *just*...

"One of this generation's most gifted writers of contemporary women's fiction."
—*Affaire de Coeur*

If you enjoyed what you just read,
then we've got an offer you can't resist!

Take 2 bestselling
love stories FREE!
Plus get a FREE surprise gift!

MARY LYNN
BAXTER

66440 HARD CANDY   ___ $5.99 U.S. ___ $6.99 CAN.
66417 TEARS OF YESTERDAY ___ $5.50 U.S. ___ $6.50 CAN.
66300 AUTUMN AWAKENING   ___ $5.50 U.S. ___ $6.50 CAN.
66289 LONE STAR HEAT   ___ $5.99 U.S. ___ $6.99 CAN.
66165 A DAY IN APRIL   ___ $5.99 U.S. ___ $6.99 CAN.

(limited quantities available)

TOTAL AMOUNT $_____
POSTAGE & HANDLING $_____
($1.00 for one book; 50¢ for each additional)
APPLICABLE TAXES* $_____
TOTAL PAYABLE $_____
(check or money order—please do not send cash)

To order, complete this form and send it, along with a check
or money order for the total above, payable to MIRA Books®,
to: **In the U.S.:** 3010 Walden Avenue, P.O. Box 9077, Buffalo,
NY 14269-9077; **In Canada:** P.O. Box 636, Fort Erie, Ontario,
L2A 5X3.

Name:_____
Address:_____ City:_____
State/Prov.:_____ Zip/Postal Code:_____
Account Number (if applicable):_____
075 CSAS

*New York residents remit applicable sales taxes.
  Canadian residents remit applicable GST and provincial taxes.

MIRA